Dead on Your Feet

Stephen Puleston

ABOUT THE AUTHOR

Stephen Puleston was born and educated in Anglesey, North Wales. He graduated in theology before training as a lawyer. Dead on Your Feet is his fourth novel in the Inspector Drake series

www.stephenpuleston.co.uk
Facebook:stephenpulestoncrimewriter

OTHER NOVELS

Inspector Drake Mysteries

Brass in Pocket
Worse than Dead
Against the Tide
Prequel Novella– Ebook only
Devil's Kitchen

Inspector Marco Novels

Speechless
Another Good Killing
Somebody Told Me
Prequel Novella– Ebook only
Dead Smart

ISBN-13:978-1546898801
ISBN-10:1546898808

In memory of my mother
Gwenno Puleston

Prologue

Moving a body proved more problematic than I had anticipated. Luckily, she had left her car in a poorly lit side street, so knocking her unconscious and bundling her inside my van, parked nearby, should have been straightforward. My heart raced as I fumbled with her arms, trying to keep her upright. I pressed her against the passenger door of the vehicle as I reached for the handle of its sliding door. It stuck and I cursed silently. Then I heard the sound of conversation and noticed a group of young people at the end of the street, laughing and joking. Three figures moved towards me so I turned, trying to conceal the body I was propping up against the van. Now I tugged harder at the handle and relief washed over me as it flew open. I bundled her inside and drew the door closed with a reassuring thud. Seconds later I sat in the driver's seat, thrust the key into the ignition and drove away.

It had taken me a week to draw up a shortlist of venues; places where I could exhibit successfully, that would do justice to my work and display my art to the widest audience. I had eliminated three of the possible premises. One had a complex alarm system, judging from the flashing lights on a box screwed to the outside wall, and far too many locks on the back door. A second had limited access from the rear. I had pondered the third location because it had a wonderful plate-glass window but it was right next to a pound shop and I couldn't bear the thought of exhibiting next to such a place. But a voice inside my head told me art must be for the masses and that I shouldn't be so bourgeois and elitist. There was a café across the road so I had sat there, drinking coffee, eating dried-up carrot cake, staring at the location and persuading myself I had to dismiss my petty prejudices. I visualised how things would look, how people might react, the comments, the public acclaim. A group of three men congregating outside the shop caught my attention because of their posturing and raised voices. When two girls walked past them they started jeering at them. It was a disgusting spectacle – just like football hooligans. I wanted to rush over to admonish them but common sense prevailed.

Did I really want my exhibition there?

I left my latte and enough change for the bill and strode away in disgust. And disappointment too, because I had to restart my search. But being dedicated to my artistic practice meant having to deal with setbacks, pick myself up and refocus. I did just that over the next few days and soon enough I was rewarded when I spotted a recently closed shoe shop. The location was perfect, adjacent to a boutique selling women's clothes and a delicatessen with expensive-looking cold meats and fancy cheeses from Europe on display. A brisk walk down the rear lane had established that the access was slightly smaller than I would have liked but practical nevertheless.

It meant I could plan, which was always the most exciting part of any new project.

That evening I passed the premises, checking carefully for any sign of activity from the nearby shops. Once I was satisfied nobody was around I parked some distance away from the lane at the back. I sat watching and waiting. Once it was quiet, I pulled out and drove down the deserted alleyway and reversed up to the rear entrance. I knew I had to work quickly.

Moving the body into the building had to take no more than a few seconds.

A makeshift timber platform enabled me to drag her from the van and in a few short steps I was inside. I closed the door behind me and struggled to move her into the storeroom behind the main shopping area.

I returned to the van, its sides covered with the design of a shop-fitting company. It complemented the entire project, added an authenticity. Once I had finished moving the rest of the installation from the van I locked the rear door and returned inside with various sheets of plywood, lengths of timber and the blackout blind I needed.

I had timed each section of work carefully. My chest tightened as I contemplated the prospect of being delayed. It pleased me when I finished setting up the electrical switches and circuit for the blind over the window bang on time. Now I focused on getting my installation completed. I had practised assembling the frame so many times it had become second nature, and in less than an hour I had everything constructed.

Ropes and wire and fasteners held her in place.

Perspiration prickled my forehead and I gulped down some water before turning to the rest of the work. Once I had everything set out, I carried out final adjustments to make the whole piece come together. Nobody could ever say it lacked detail.

I stood back and admired my handiwork.

Chapter 1

Despite having lived on his own for several months, Ian Drake was still unaccustomed to his new domestic routine. He sat by the kitchen table finishing a bowl of muesli, listening to the morning news on the radio. The new coffee machine that had pride of place on the worktop was one of the first purchases he had made alone, without input from Sian, his estranged wife. He finished his Americano and glanced at his watch. He missed his daughters, especially the hurly-burly of breakfast time. Briefly, he contemplated calling them but knew it would be a bad time.

He cleaned and dried the breakfast dishes before carefully stacking them away. Then he scanned the kitchen, checking that everything was neat and tidy. He walked through into the hallway and stopped by the mirror. A recent haircut had tidied his appearance, and he brushed away some imaginary dust from the lapels of his navy suit. That afternoon he was representing the Wales Police Service at a meeting of a police and community liaison forum. Superintendent Wyndham Price had made it quite clear officers of inspector rank needed to play their part in building relationships with local communities. Even so, Drake suspected it wasn't the most effective use of his time as a detective.

He peered more intently at his reflection. Was the suit looking a little shabby? Did it need to be dry-cleaned? He adjusted his tie a few millimetres to find the perfect position underneath the collar of his white shirt.

His mobile rang and, fishing it out of his jacket pocket, he was surprised to see Sian's number.

'Good morning,' Drake said.

'Look, I haven't got long. I need you to collect the girls from school this afternoon.'

Drake paused. Her tone was almost threatening, but he knew that mornings were often a stressful time for Sian.

'I'm representing Superintendent Price in a forum later ...' He heard her huff of exasperation down the telephone.

'I've got an important meeting about a dying patient with the palliative care team.'

Now it was a matter of life and death.

'I should be finished in good time.'

'Good.'

'Can I speak to the girls?'

'Not now, I've got to get them ready for school. I'll speak to you later.'

Drake heard the line go dead. How hard could it have been for Sian to let Helen and Megan speak to him?

After pulling the door to his flat closed behind him, he made his way down to the car, exchanging greetings with the elderly man from the apartment above him. It was a short drive to the newsagent's, where he bought a newspaper. Immediately he turned to the Sudoku puzzle. He solved four squares quickly, which lifted his spirits. He would find five minutes mid-morning and more at lunchtime to complete the rest of the numbers.

Indicating off the main road, he skirted round the wide-open parkland next to Northern Division headquarters and parked away from other vehicles. Before his meeting with Superintendent Price, he planned to read the background details of his new detective sergeant – Sara Morgan. With his previous partner, Caren Waits on maternity leave and awaiting the results of her inspector's exams – which Drake thought would be no more than a formality – there was every possibility Sara would be a permanent fixture.

Draping his suit jacket over a wooden hanger he smoothed out the shoulders before placing it on the coat stand in his office. Drake sat behind his desk, pleased the neatness he'd left the night before had been undisturbed.

Drake turned his attention to Sara Morgan's personnel file. He read the complimentary remarks from a detective inspector he knew. But working as a sergeant, making decisions, directing junior officers required a new set of skills. Drake recalled the words of wisdom he had received as a newly promoted young sergeant from the wizened inspector who retired to a flat in Spain soon afterwards – 'never forget who's the boss, lad'.

Then he started on the minutes of the previous meetings of the community forum. The document was laced heavily with references to involving various stakeholders to improve transparency and build public confidence. All the usual jargon, Drake thought.

By mid-morning Drake felt up to speed and walked over to the senior management suite.

'Good morning, Ian.' Hannah had worked for Price for years so her informality was nothing new.

'Morning Hannah. I've got a meeting with Superintendent Price.'

'I know, take a seat.' She nodded to one of the visitor chairs. Drake overheard her on the telephone telling Price he had arrived, and moments later he appeared at the door to his office and waved energetically at Drake. He wondered whether Sara Morgan was with him already.

'Come in, Ian.'

Drake's brogues sank into the soft carpet. Price jerked a hand at a chair and Drake sat down. Price did the same, pulling his chair to the desk, giving his shaved head a scratch. Drake was accustomed to the regular affectation. It occurred to him that if his hairline receded too far he might resort to shaving his head. He thought it might make him look like a thug, but a comb-over would make him look like an old man, a prospect Drake didn't relish.

'Have you seen the newspaper?' Price held up one of the broadsheets.

Drake felt guilty that he had gone straight to the Sudoku that morning and that the affairs of the world might have passed him by.

'We've had requests for details of how many foreigners were prosecuted in Northern Division last year, how many were convicted and how many were sent to prison. It's mad. What the hell do the press think? That we can spare time and resources to put this sort of data together?'

He slumped back in his chair. Price having a rant was commonplace and probably did the superintendent good. Drake made a mental note to check the headlines.

'Thanks for going in my place to the meeting this afternoon.'

Drake nodded.

'I almost throttled the chairman of that group after the last meeting. The man is a complete idiot.'

Now Drake realised he was merely a substitute for Price.

'I've read most of the minutes of the recent meetings.'

Price stared at Drake. 'Have you?' He sounded surprised.

'Do you want me to brief you when I get back, sir?'

For a moment Price looked worried. 'Whatever for?'

The telephone rang, sparing Drake the need to reply.

'Send her in.'

Sara Morgan walked into the room. Once the introductions were over and hands shaken, Price pointed to a chair next to Drake. Sara had thin auburn hair drawn into a plait that brushed her shoulders. She had fine delicate cheekbones, modest blusher, discreet lipstick and no earrings. She wore an expensive-looking navy suit, the sort Sian favoured for work at her GP surgery. The contrast to the disorganised and shabby appearance of Caren Waits could not have been more acute.

'Sergeant Morgan, as we've not met before I thought this would be a perfect opportunity to welcome you to Northern Division headquarters. In due course Detective Inspector Drake can deal with all the formalities.'

There were protocols for everything these days, Drake thought. Inducting an officer into his team meant forms to be filled and boxes ticked. Once completed, the paperwork would be returned to human resources to be double-checked. Price spent another twenty minutes explaining how he liked things to be dealt with and that he was 'an old-fashioned copper' who valued 'team work' more than anything.

Drake listened patiently, unimpressed by Price's pep talk – he had heard it before, many times. He expected Hannah to interrupt with coffee and biscuits but the door remained firmly closed. Once Price finished his speech, Drake left with Sara. They exchanged small talk on their way back to Drake's office and once there Sara sat down uninvited, the tension from their meeting with Price dissipating.

Drake fumbled for the right paperwork out of a drawer and deposited it all in the middle of his desk. 'Tell me about your work in Inspector Owen's team?'

Sara didn't have time to reply as the telephone rang. Drake stared at it for a moment, annoyed at the interruption – the induction had barely started.

He reached for the phone. 'DI Drake.'

He listened.

'When was the body found?'

He scribbled something on a notepad.

'Are there uniformed officers at the scene?'

He slammed down the handset and stood up abruptly. 'Let's go.'

Chapter 2

Drake crunched the car into first gear and tore off out of headquarters. He hurtled down to the A55, the main road that ran along the North Wales coast.

'The CSI team is on its way,' Drake said as he flashed his headlights at the vehicle in front of him. He sounded the horn and the traffic scattered to the nearside lane. 'A body has been found in a shop in Llandudno.'

'*Are* there uniformed officers at the scene?' Sara said.

'Three lads from the local station. Their names are on my note.' Drake found the scrap of paper in his pocket and thrust it at Sara.

Minutes later, they reached the junction for Llandudno and Drake indicated off the dual carriageway. In the distance, he heard an ambulance siren. He raced on towards the town and at the brow of a hill saw the Victorian resort bathed in the spring sunshine below him. A roundabout should have delayed his journey but the tyres screeched a complaint as he almost took it on two wheels.

He slowed when he saw officers ushering people away from a shop and cajoling others on the opposite side of the street to move away. He parked and jumped out. Sara followed. After showing their identity cards to two uniformed officers, they pointed to a man talking to another officer near the door of the premises.

'DI Drake and this is Detective Sergeant Morgan.'

'This is James Convery, sir.' The uniformed officer said. 'He's the property agent for this shop.' Convery stood with his back to the shop window and Drake could just spot the crumpled remains of a blind or curtain stretching along the base.

'It's disgusting. Foul. Who could do such a thing?'

At the sound of a slowing engine Drake saw the scientific support vehicle drawing up. He looked back at Convery. 'Who found the body?'

Convery gave him a puzzled expression. 'What do you mean?' he spluttered. 'She's ...' He raised his arm, pointing at the window. 'Anyone can see her.'

'What the hell ...?' Drake stepped around Convery towards the window, Sara by his side. He only took two steps before looking into the shop. Sara caught her breath. 'Christ almighty.'

The body stood upright somehow with one arm outstretched, dressed in what resembled a Roman toga. By her side was a single unmade bed with crumpled sheets and discarded papers. Crockery with half-eaten food lay on the floor with piles of clothes and newspapers. Now Drake understood what Convery meant when he'd described the crime scene. He turned and called over to the approaching crime scene manager.

'Mike, we'll need a tent built over this shop window immediately.'

Mike Foulds carried on walking.

Drake shouted. 'Do it now, Mike. The body is on display. Everyone can bloody see it.'

Foulds stopped and turned, barking orders to the CSIs, gathering their equipment. On the other side of the road, Drake glimpsed an onlooker pointing a mobile telephone in his direction. 'Stop that,' he yelled. 'This is a police investigation.' The individual ignored him so Drake barked at the nearest officer to stop him taking photographs. Drake could only guess at how many other sick individuals had already captured images. He dreaded to think what might appear on the internet.

He peered again into the shop. Sara held her hand to her mouth as she stared in at the murder scene. It was like nothing Drake had ever seen before. He spoke at Convery without making eye contact. 'So how did the killer get access?'

'The back door was forced, sir.'

Drake glared at Convery. 'Was the property alarmed?'

He shrugged.

'Find out now. And don't leave this scene until I tell you. Give all your details to this officer.' Convery gave a frightened nod.

Drake snapped on latex gloves; Sara did the same. He pushed open the door and entered. The sharp putrid smell of death was unmistakeable. Drake had experienced it before many times but his first reaction was always to choke back the nausea. They stood staring at the scene.

Glancing through the plate-glass window Drake saw the CSIs rushing to erect a barrier over the window. Across the road groups of people gawped, some gesticulating at the shop, others with hands over their mouths in shock. Drake looked at the crumpled curtain at the base of the window and at the far end noticed a laptop computer and some electronic equipment linked to a pulley system. It suggested a killer with some technical expertise.

'Shouldn't we leave the scene to the CSIs?' Sara said.

Drake shook his head in response. The first few hours of every murder inquiry were the most important, the most crucial; they demanded his complete attention. He stared at the body; he wanted to absorb everything about this abhorrent scene. Why had the killer posed a dead body like this? What could be the motive?

'We need to learn as much as we can here.'

Drake moved a few steps into the shop building. At a guess, the victim was mid-fifties, propped up at an angle with her left arm extended as though she was pointing at something. Moving to his left Drake made out the timber frame supporting her. The whole thing was like a macabre scene from some B movie.

Drake craned to see any blood, but there was nothing to suggest any violence.

'The killer has made a wooden frame to support the body.' Drake turned to a sickly-looking Sara.

'There must be something holding up her arm.'

Drake stared over the upright corpse. A flowing garment shrouded her left arm and cascaded over her body.

Sara continued. 'It's like a pose from an ancient Greek statue in a museum. What the hell was the killer doing?'

Drake scanned the rest of the room. Lying against the faux brown leather headboard were two pillowcases, one a deep turquoise, the other creamy yellow, but the sheets on the bed were white and blue. From the creases and stains, they looked well used. Drake turned up his nose. Draped over the bed in no apparent order was a pair of old jeans and shirts and various pieces of underwear.

A cheap reading lamp sat on the bedside cabinet with an alarm clock, a collection of old coins and a woman's purse. Instinctively he guessed the killer had left the victim's purse as part of the sick charade. He wanted to march over, pick it up and establish the woman's identity. But he would be breaking every protocol so he stood waiting for the crime scene manager to return.

'It's like that famous piece of art from years ago where one of those big galleries in London displayed an unmade bed,' Sara said.

'I know, I was thinking the same.' Drake knelt, surveying the floor, wondering what else was scattered under the bed. 'The whole thing is obviously staged … but why?'

On the floor by the cabinet lay an empty bottle of vodka and near it a large bottle of continental lager stood upright. Drake couldn't make out if it was empty.

Behind him, he sensed the bustle of activity from the CSI investigators erecting a tarpaulin over the plate-glass window ready to screen the inside against prying eyes.

'Let's have a look outside,' Drake said.

They made their way to the back of the shop where a doorway led to a storeroom. The door was ajar, its broken lock hanging limply. Outside a uniformed officer straightened when they emerged. A road led down the rear of the adjacent shops; a couple of delivery vans were parked a short distance away. Drake cast his gaze up at the various buildings. All the premises were shops or offices, making it unlikely anyone had witnessed the activity the night before. But it still meant house-to-house enquiries, owners of the premises being interviewed, in the hope that somebody had seen something.

Drake imagined the killer parking a vehicle, manhandling the body into the shop. It would have required careful planning – hauling a body around wouldn't be easy. He turned to the officer. 'Get the full details of anybody who passes. Whoever is responsible for this might still be around, watching this play out.'

'Yes, sir.'

Sara said very little. For Drake it made a pleasant change from the detailed commentary Caren would have started.

'Let's go back inside. Hopefully the CSIs will be ready to start work by now.'

They returned to the shop where Michael Foulds was dictating instructions to the investigators. A photographer stood to one side fiddling with his tripod. Drake stared at the scene; again, it had a hypnotic effect. Until they identified the victim and then spoke to her family there was little they could do.

'We need to find some ID.' Drake addressed Foulds as he tipped his head towards the cabinet. 'Can you check the purse?'

Foulds stepped towards the bed, waving the photographer to join him. Once they'd recorded the exact scene Foulds picked up the purse and flicked through the various debit and credit cards announcing the victim's name – Gloria Patton.

'Driving licence?' Drake said.

Foulds shook his head.

'The bank can give us her address details,' Sara added.

Foulds placed the purse into a plastic evidence pouch and fastened it securely.

Giving the scene one final look, Drake turned towards the door. As he did so a mobile telephone bleeped. It sounded muted and Foulds shared a glance with the officers in the room. Drake looked at Sara who shrugged her shoulders, telling him it wasn't her mobile.

Another message bleeped, this time harshly, as though the phone was sitting on a piece of timber. Foulds and Drake frowned and both glanced at the bed.

Foulds moved over to the bedside cabinet, yanking open the bottom drawer. He pulled out an old mobile telephone. It buzzed again in his hand. He stared at the screen and then over at Drake.

'There's a message. It's got a hashtag and then "I am the one".'

Chapter 3

A series of telephone calls established Gloria Patton's home address as being near a village in the Conwy Valley. Drake drove as Sara entered the postcode into the satnav. He followed the directions out of Llandudno, retracing his earlier journey until he reached the roundabout for the junction onto the A55. He skirted underneath the dual carriageway before heading south. He still missed the Alfa Romeo GT he had recently traded in for a more practical Ford Mondeo saloon. His mother had told him he needed something sensible when he had to ferry his daughters around. But it wasn't as much fun to drive as the Italian sports car.

Sara's mobile rang as they drove through Glan Conwy. He listened to her side of the conversation, trying to interpret what the caller was saying. 'Thanks,' she said before turning to Drake.

'I've got the name of Gloria Patton's husband – Hubert. Apparently they are both artists.'

'What do you mean? Like painters?'

Sara shrugged. 'That was all the information operational support had available.'

Spring sunshine glistened on the surface of the Conwy river. A cuddy took advantage of the high tide as the wide expanse of water stretched out to their right: eventually, it would narrow when the tidal effect dissipated as it neared Llanrwst and Betws y Coed. A few minutes after leaving Glan Conwy the satnav announced a left turn and Drake indicated. It took them through the country lanes above the valley until they found an old farmhouse, a chipped, slate sign – Tre Ifan – propped against a gatepost. He drew the car into the yard and they got out. In one corner, the sound of violins and crashing cymbals emerged from a wooden shed.

Drake didn't want to get his brogues any dirtier than he needed to so he avoided the larger stones and hollows as they walked over towards the sound of the orchestra. They stood on the wooden veranda in front of a door and Drake peered through the thin sheet of Perspex that covered the top half, but he could see nobody. He shouted, trying to make himself heard over the noise of the music, then he yanked the handle, which gave way after a brief tussle. The room they entered had a small table, a dusty leather sofa, its arms and sides scratched, presumably by the various cats roaming outside. Behind another door, the music continued unabated.

'Hello, Mr Patton,' Drake shouted.

The music stopped abruptly. Drake and Sara had their warrant cards ready when the door opened.

'Mr Patton?'

'And you are?'

'Detective Inspector Drake and this is Detective Sergeant Morgan. We need to speak to you. Is there somewhere we can talk in private?'

Breaking bad news was always something Drake dreaded, but inevitably it was a part of his job that had to be faced. He'd been on courses about victim support and empathy but it never improved his ability or made the task any easier. Patton led them back into the room he had just left. Light flooded in from a window in the ceiling. Enormous canvases were propped against easels, each a cacophony of abstract squares and circles and interconnecting lines. Paint splattered the walls, the floor, every square foot and every square inch of the tables laden with artists' materials.

Patton's grey sweatshirt was thin with age and Drake noticed his large hands that complemented his strong, powerful build. The painter was an inch or two taller than Drake at about six foot, with piercing dark green eyes. The table behind him sagged as he leant on it. He did not suggest that Drake or Sara sat down.

'I'm afraid I have bad news about your wife. She was found dead this morning.'

Patton didn't move or flinch for a few seconds, then he frowned. 'There must be some mistake.'

Drake reached for his smartphone and scrolled to find the image of Mrs Patton's purse. 'Do you recognise this?'

Patton nodded.

'Inside the purse were debit and credit cards.' Drake dictated the details of the bank account number and sort codes. 'They were all in your wife's name.'

'Where ...?'

Drake glanced at Sara who stared intently at Patton. At some point, he would be informed about the detailed circumstances. But for now it could wait. 'Her body was found in a shop in Llandudno.'

'A shop? What do you mean? Has she had some kind of accident?'

'When did you see your wife last?'

'Yesterday.'

'Were you expecting her home last night?'

Patton rolled his eyes. 'Normally I would have seen her at breakfast. We have breakfast together. I tell her about my plans for the day and she does the same. We sleep separately.'

'Didn't you think it odd that she wasn't at breakfast this morning?'

Patton shrugged then averted his gaze.

Drake continued. 'It didn't occur to you to report her missing?'

Patton made eye contact with Drake. 'She could stay out sometimes. I never asked where. I guessed she would stay with friends. You know, a glass or two of wine and she couldn't drive home.'

Drake continued. 'Do you know where she was going last night?'

Patton stood up. 'After working in the gallery she was going to that festival committee meeting. The whole damn thing has been taking over her life. Waste of bloody time if you ask me.'

'Gallery?'

'She has a gallery in town. It pays the bills and we all have to eat. Do you think I should call the staff there?'

Drake hesitated, trying to fathom out what exactly was going on in Patton's mind. 'We'll need the details. And what festival do you mean?'

'It's the Orme Arts Festival, of course. You must have heard about it. She was on the committee.'

Drake folded his arms as he continued to stare at Patton. 'I'll need some contact names and numbers before I leave.'

Patton nodded as Sara made her first contribution. 'How long have you been married, Mr Patton?'

'I'm not.'

Now Sara looked puzzled.

'Gloria and I weren't married. My name is Oswald.'

'Do you have any children? Or someone that we could call on your behalf?'

Oswald shook his head. 'Her mother died a couple of years ago and her father died when she was a child. We don't have any children. We are both dedicated to our art. Nothing else matters. We both decided long ago that having a family would prevent us from developing as artists.'

'Does Gloria have a studio she works from?' Drake said.

'We adapted two of the bedrooms in the house.'

'We'll need to see them.'

Oswald glanced at his easel, not attempting to leave the studio. Drake's patience finally ran out. 'Now, please.'

He glanced at Sara whose dark look matched his own feelings as they walked over to the farmhouse with Oswald. He showed them to the studio that Gloria used and then to her bedroom. He waved a hand lazily over a desk, a laptop and a dressing table. 'You'll find all of her stuff here.'

As Oswald made to leave, Sara used a kindly tone. 'Would you like us to inform anyone? We can arrange for a family liaison officer to call. They are specially trained to deal with circumstances like this.'

'Circumstances?'

'Gloria was murdered.' Even Drake could sense the chill in her voice.

'That is awfully kind of you, sergeant, but I can perfectly well manage on my own account.' The heavy emphasis on *awfully* resulted in a narrowing of Sara's eyes.

'Where were you last night Mr Oswald?' Oswald was by the door when Drake spoke.

Oswald stiffened, giving Drake a wintry glare. 'I hope you don't think—'

'Routine, I assure you.'

The glare hardened into contempt. 'I was here all night.' Then he paced away.

Once Oswald was out of earshot Sara turned to Drake. 'What an obnoxious man.'

'Maybe he's in shock.'

'*Perfectly well manage on my own account*,' mimicked Sara, not quite getting Oswald's Home Counties accent.

'Let's make him a person of interest in the inquiry. He's an artist after all. Did you see the size of his hands? He could easily have moved her body. We'll need to find out who benefits from Gloria's death.'

Sara nodded.

Drake folded the laptop into a case he found under the dressing table as Sara rummaged through a chest of drawers full of Gloria's clothes. He picked up an old-fashioned Filofax lying next to some face cream and flicked through it absently, his suspicions deepening about Oswald after his odd behaviour. 'We'll need to take most of the stuff back to headquarters. Gareth and the new DC can work through the laptop and her diary.'

Half an hour later Drake and Sara made their way downstairs, finding Oswald sitting in the kitchen by a battered table nursing a green bottle of continental lager. He gazed up at Drake, who caught a sense of sadness in the man's face now. Drake immediately recalled the scene in the shop earlier with the bottle of lager and vodka discarded by the bed and wondered if there was a connection.

'An officer will call to take a full statement from you in due course,' Drake said.

Oswald gave him a feeble smile before taking another long slug of beer. Then he held up a sheet of paper. 'These are the names you wanted.'

Drake scanned them; he had hours of work ahead of him. 'Does Gloria have a car?'

Oswald nodded. 'An orange Peugeot.'

'Registration number?'

He looked back blankly at Drake. 'No idea.'

'We'll need you to make the formal identification.'

Drake half-expected him to object, finding some clever justification for not doing so. But he just nodded. They left him sitting silently, a long-distance stare in his eyes.

A couple of the cats walked over the roof of Drake's car but jumped off as they saw him approach.

Back on the road, Sara turned to Drake. 'What did you make of him, boss?'

'One minute he's belligerent and then he's sad. He didn't seem to be affected by Gloria's death.'

'I thought artists were supposed to be an emotional bunch. But his eyes looked empty.'

'Once we've established a time of death, and established her movements last night we'll have another conversation with Hubert Oswald.'

Sara nodded enthusiastically.

'In the meantime we need to establish who saw her last. You need to speak to someone on that committee.'

Gareth Winder was directing two civilians erecting a board in the Incident Room when Drake and Sara returned to headquarters. A training course he'd been on that morning had been a complete waste of time and, more importantly, he had missed the opportunity of accompanying Drake and the new sergeant to a murder scene. Instead, he had to stay put in headquarters, fielding telephone calls from the public relations department and the pathologist's assistant, and meeting the team's new detective constable. Now that David Howick had been promoted to a custody sergeant's job in Wrexham, Gareth had been hoping the new constable on the team would be another man. Instead, Luned Thomas was a short, dowdy girl about his age.

'Do we call you Lyn?'

She'd given him a thin-lipped smile. 'This isn't England. I'm sure you can pronounce my name properly.'

Good start, he'd thought. At least she wouldn't call him Gar, which suited him as he didn't like it in any event.

When Drake and Sara came into the Incident Room Winder could barely contain his enthusiasm. He tried not to scan Sara but she was just as attractive as some of his friends had told him. She raised an eyebrow when he stared a second too long. 'What happened, boss?'

Drake ignored him and spoke directly to Luned. 'Detective Constable Thomas?'

She straightened and shook his hand. Drake walked over to the board and as he did so Winder passed him a photograph of Gloria Patton, which he pinned to the centre.

'Gloria Patton was found dead this morning in an empty shop in the middle of Llandudno. We should have photographs from the CSIs later this afternoon. The whole thing was macabre. She'd been propped up somehow on a board and dressed in a sheet that made her look like an ancient Roman statue.'

He paused and glanced at Winder and Luned before continuing. 'The killer sent a text to her mobile, which he had left in the shop.'

Sara continued. 'And there was an unmade bed in the room complete with a bedside cabinet.'

'Looks like we're searching for a right nutcase,' Winder said

Drake continued. 'The text message sent read hashtag iamtheone.'

'Any idea who it was from?' Winder said.

'That's what we need to find out. I want to know everything about the mobile telephone Gloria Patton owned: contacts, messages, etc. And a full trace on the mobile that sent the text.'

Drake hadn't finished but he stopped as the door crashed open and Superintendent Price walked in.

'Is it true?' He marched over to Drake's side as Winder and the others scrambled to their feet. 'It sounds like something from a horror film. Who the hell would want to build such a spectacle?'

Price scanned the officers, his fisted right hand tapping his left palm. 'The town council have already been on the telephone, as has the local member of the Welsh parliament. Is there any chance there could be photographs appearing on the internet?'

Winder registered the uncertainty on Drake and Sara's faces and their reluctance to answer.

'It looks like the killer set a timer to release the curtain that covered the window mid-morning when the most number of people would be passing,' Drake said.

'Christ almighty, what sort of person are we dealing with here?'

'And no, sir. I cannot guarantee there won't be images on the internet – in fact, it's very likely.'

Price raised his voice slightly. 'All of you realise this has top priority. Llandudno is a tourist resort and this sort of thing could hit the town badly. So we need to find the culprit quickly.'

And with that Price stormed out. A few seconds elapsed before anyone said anything. Luned was the first to break the silence. She had a clear, confident voice and a warm accent that suggested she was from a Welsh-speaking background. 'There was a famous artwork of an unmade bed several years ago. I think it won a prize. I'll look into it …'

Sara nodded. 'Gloria was connected to the Orme Arts Festival and her partner, Hubert Oswald, is an artist. We've just seen him.'

'How was he?' Luned asked.

'Not in the least surprised.' Sara settled into a chair by one of the empty desks.

'So he's our prime suspect?' Winder added.

Drake shared a glance with Winder and Luned. 'We've brought back a lot of personal stuff, laptop, Filofax. I want you both to start building a picture of this woman. Oswald mentioned she ran a gallery in Llandudno. You had better get over there. Talk to the staff, collect any personal stuff of interest.'

'There must be lots of forensics,' Winder said. 'The killer can't just leave a body like that without leaving some evidence.'

'I agree,' Drake said. 'And trace her car, it's an orange Peugeot. Sara and I are going to talk to the members of the festival committee.'

Drake glanced at his watch. 'I want progress by later tonight.'

Winder turned to Luned once Drake left. She gave him a studious and expectant look as though she wanted him to tell her exactly what to do. It was going to be another long day.

Chapter 4

Canolfan Tudno was a tall building set out on three floors. There were community centres like this in every village and town in Wales, built and paid for by the local population – probably like every other country, Sara thought. It was the sort of premises Sara remembered from her childhood when her parents dragged her to charity fundraising events.

Seeing the body of Gloria Patton today had sickened her more than she had first realised. She knew that being on Detective Inspector Drake's team meant dead bodies, but nothing had prepared her for the scene that morning. The superintendent had been right – it did look like something from a horror movie.

Drake and Sara reached the main door before finding the stairs and heading to the first floor where the inspector stopped abruptly before pulling his mobile telephone from his jacket pocket.

'I've got to make a call.'

Drake paced away from Sara and she heard snippets of his one-sided conversation.

'Put me through to Dr Drake.'

Sara stood, waiting, remembering that her last attempt to speak to her GP had met with an interrogation from the receptionist.

'I'm sorry, Sian, I can't collect the girls. There's been a murder in Llandudno.'

Drake paused and Sara tried not to listen.

'I know it's inconvenient …'

Drake shot her an embarrassed look before lowering his voice. 'Couldn't one of your friends …'

Sara gave an understanding nod. Detective work and successful family life was difficult, she knew, having seen the broken relationships among other officers.

Drake ended the call and barged his way into the room on the first floor where the committee were waiting for them. Sara followed him, struggling to keep up with his pace, and, as she entered the room, three people sitting around a table shot to their feet.

A man in his mid-fifties, about the same height as the inspector but with less hair, extended a hand towards Drake.

'Rhisiart Hopkin and this is Julie and Marjorie,' Hopkin nodded at the two women. 'Inspector Drake, can you tell us what happened? We are all so shocked. We can't believe it – we saw Gloria last night.'

Hopkin waved a hand over a couple of chairs. Drake didn't attempt to shake hands with Julie or Marjorie, although Sara sensed they expected such courtesy. She had noticed his rudeness with Oswald earlier but she had held her tongue. It was her first day after all. Sara sat alongside Drake and stared over at Hopkin. His Christian name was the seldom-used Welsh equivalent of Richard and she wondered whether he was the token Welsh speaker on the committee.

'We need full details of what happened last night,' Drake said.

Julie responded. Her strong Scouse accent confirmed her roots in Liverpool; her voice sounded harsh, grating. 'We were finalising everything for the festival. We had a long meeting. There's a shed-load of stuff to get through.'

Marjorie cut across. 'You won't believe the trouble we've had with the Welsh Arts Council about the modest funding they were providing. That's where Rhisiart has been such a dear.' Her cut glass accent sounded oddly out of place.

Hopkin blushed. 'Well I wouldn't say ...'

'Of course you have. Having a bank manager on

the committee is very helpful.'

'What was Gloria's involvement in the committee?'

Julie responded. 'She was the curator. She made the final decision about who would be exhibiting. She was responsible for assessing all the possible contributors.'

'So she must have disappointed some people,' Drake said.

'I suppose so ...' Julie stopped abruptly, staring over at Drake and then at Sara. 'Surely you don't suspect that somebody we've rejected might be responsible?'

'We have to consider all possibilities at this stage in our enquiry.'

Everything about the murder scene suggested to Sara that someone with an artistic interest had staged it or maybe somebody who was suggesting they had.

Marjorie cleared her throat noisily. 'There was this one person ...' She glanced at Julie and then at Rhisiart − both tilted their heads in encouragement for her to continue. 'Norma Buckland. She's a local artist who was rejected by Gloria and she took it badly. She wrote several extremely aggressive letters to all of us about the decision. She made some frankly outrageous comments.'

Sara reached for her pocketbook. 'Do you have the contact details for Norma Buckland?'

'Of course.'

'Do you still have the letters she sent?'

All three nodded. Hopkin used an undertaker's tone. 'We kept them all. Gloria kept them all in a file in her gallery.'

Drake looked at his notes. 'Was it just Gloria's decision to reject a submission?'

'Sometimes if she was in two minds she would ask us to make the final choice,' Marjorie added before realising what it implied. 'Surely you don't think we could be in any danger?'

'It's far too early to make any assumptions. Were there any others rejected by Gloria?'

'There were three artists rejected either by Gloria or by us.' Hopkin had obviously been prepared for Drake's question. 'I've noted down their names and contact details.' He pushed over a single sheet of A4 paper, which Drake scanned quickly.

'Let's get back to discussing last night – the last time you saw Gloria.'

Hopkin straightened his position in his chair. Sara assumed he had been delegated by Julie and Marjorie to provide the details. 'We started our meeting at about seven-thirty. We had a long agenda. After all, the arts festival is less than three weeks away and we still have a lot to do to get everything finalised. As it's the first time it's being held we want to make certain that it's a complete success.'

'How did Gloria seem?'

Hopkin shared a glance with the other two. 'No different than normal.'

'How long did the committee meeting take?'

'We had a break at nine and were finished by ten o'clock.'

'Did Gloria say where she was going afterwards?'

They looked puzzled. Julie was the first reply. 'I went home. I assumed Gloria was doing the same.'

Drake glanced at Hopkin and Marjorie for confirmation. Hopkin responded. 'She was the first to leave. I don't remember her saying anything about where she was going. Like Julie, I assumed she was heading home.'

Sara jotted down all the details in her pocketbook. 'Do you know where Gloria had parked her car?' Sara said.

'I'm sorry, sergeant,' Hopkin replied. 'I have no idea.'

'There's a car park at the rear of the property and sometimes she parked next to mine,' Marjorie said.

'And last night?' Sara said.

Marjorie shook her head. 'I didn't see her car.'

So they had at least ten or twelve hours unaccounted for. Perhaps the pathologist would be able to pinpoint an exact time of death, Sara thought.

Drake stood up and extracted business cards from his jacket pocket, which he handed over the table. 'Call me if you think of anything else.'

He nodded to Sara and they left.

Drake glanced at the paper before handing it to Sara as they walked back to the car. 'More suspects.'

Sara read the three names on the list with their addresses and contact details. Inside the car, Drake paused. 'We still need to find her car.'

'None of them seemed worried. I'd be really scared,' Sara said. 'Maybe the killer is a rejected artist, targeting the committee members.'

Drake gave her a worried frown. 'It's a possibility you're right.'

Drake started the engine. Sara wasn't certain whether he welcomed her contributions. 'Let's get back to headquarters,' he said. 'We need to find out if Gareth's been able to establish anything.'

Lights blazed in the Incident Room when Drake and Sara returned. Drake stood by the board, looking at Winder, his tie loosened a good two inches, and a tired, sweaty look on his face. Luned nursed a mug of coffee or tea, Drake couldn't tell. When Luned slurped noisily on her drink it reminded him of Caren's sloppy drinking habits, something he'd hoped was a thing of the past.

'How did you get on in Patton's gallery?'

'Patton's place is more of a trinket shop, boss. There's a gallery area on the first floor. Lots of paintings of landscapes … apparently.'

Drake nodded. 'Sounds like Oswald's stuff.'

'The gallery assistant was cut up. She'd just heard and she was closing early to go home.'

'We'll need to speak to her again.'

Drake turned to the board, behind him Winder continuing. 'The CSIs sent me these photos, sir. It looks like something from one of those CSI programmes in the US.'

The figure of Gloria Patton seemed artificial in the lights of the cameras with the bed oddly out of place. Drake stared at her face. It took him back to the shop and the smell of death returned to his senses.

'We've got three more persons of interest in the inquiry now.' Drake reached for the sheet Hopkin had given him and read the names.

'In the last month Gloria rejected various artists who wanted to exhibit at the Orme Arts Festival. One of them is Norma Buckland, who sent Gloria and the other members of the committee threatening letters. Another was a Jeremy Ellingham and the third is a man called Geraint Wood.'

'Are these all painters, boss? I didn't realise there were so many around.'

Drake looked over at Winder. 'That's what you and Luned are going to establish. I want background checks on all three of them.'

Drake noticed Luned nodding seriously.

Underneath the image of Gloria was an A4 sheet with the words #iamtheone printed on it in large letters.

'I've looked at the Twitter hashtag,' Winder said. 'There are dozens of people who use it to promote themselves.'

'Can we trace the mobile that sent the message?'

'Pay as you go and untraceable.'

'Did Gloria Patton use Twitter?'

'Occasionally, sir. But her mobile has got more links to her Facebook page.'

'We'll need a full analysis of both her accounts – people she's communicated with recently. Any groups she's joined or messages she's sent. Somebody wanted her dead, and they wanted to stage her body to prove a point ... why? Motive, there is always a motive, and we need to find out what it is – and fast.'

Drake returned to his office. He stopped for a second in the doorway. He had to reassure himself that the order and neatness was unchanged since he left the room hours earlier. Satisfied that nothing had been disturbed, he sank into his chair. The telephone rang and he reached for the handset.

'Inspector Drake? Are you in front of a computer?'

Chapter 5

Drake fumbled as he switched on his computer while Susan Howells from public relations dictated the web address for him to type into the browser. Tension clawed at his chest as the screen flickered into life. He had expected images from some sad individual unable to resist gawping and snapping with a smartphone but this was different. It looked like a proper professional website. Testimonials posted from various sources praised the anonymous artwork and its contribution to the development of 'the understanding of the interdependence of human conflict' and how 'lateral and bilateral thinking was essential for individual enlargement and temporal growth.'

Howells sounded desperate. 'The press are bound to be all over this like a rash in the morning. I need something I can tell them.'

Drake scrolled through the various photographs taken from inside the shop. There was no doubt this was the work of the killer. The sight of Gloria propped on the board waiting to be shown to the world like some cheap exhibit in a zoo sickened him.

His mobile rang. 'I'll call you back.' He said to Howells.

He ended the call with Howells and picked his mobile up, which immediately stopped ringing. Almost instantly the telephone on his desk rang again. Whoever wanted to speak to him had little patience. It was Price. 'What the fuck is happening, Ian?'

'I've only just been told about the website, sir. I'm looking in to it.'

'I need a progress report. Tonight.'

Drake slammed down the handset and bellowed. 'Sara, Gareth …' he couldn't immediately remember the new officer's name. Seconds later they appeared at the doorway.

'Take a look at this.' He adjusted the screen so they could all watch.

'Jesus. Is that inside the shop?' Winder said.

Drake nodded. Sara paled; Luned was rigid with surprise.

'Find out who is hosting this website and get them to take it down. I need everything they can tell us about where, who and how.' The three officers in his team stood, unmoving. 'Now. Tonight.'

Moments later, he heard the sound of a woman's voice. He rose, left his desk and found Susan Howells glaring at the Incident Room board. He walked towards her and thought he noticed Luned stifling a yawn. It would be another few hours before they'd be leaving for home, Drake thought.

'I need something I can tell the press, Ian.'

'Just tell them Gloria Patton's body was discovered in a shop in Llandudno this morning.'

'What about all this?' She tilted her head at the board. 'What am I supposed to tell the waiting public about this?'

'Nothing. Don't tell them anything. It's a police inquiry.'

'Don't be stupid. There'll be people too frightened to sleep at night, terrified to open their doors. This is Llandudno. The average age of the residents is probably over eighty. So I need you to tell me I can reassure the public.'

'We are doing everything we can. Leaving no stone unturned. Every lead being examined.'

Howells gave Drake a sceptical glare.

'This is the first day of the inquiry, so I've got nothing to tell you. The PR department will have to just manage any press flak themselves.'

'No need to get tetchy,' Susan said as she turned

on her heels and stomped out of the Incident Room.

'Damn.' Winder spoke as he stared at the screen. 'The Twitter account was opened by someone called I-am-the-one. Whoever opened it added a photograph of Arnold Schwarzenegger as an avatar.'

'What?' Drake snorted.

Winder continued. 'The email address connected to it is a Gmail account anyone could open.'

'Get a warrant for Gmail to disclose all the details. We'll have to trace the hosting company in the morning. We need to build a picture of who's involved.'

'But ... there won't be anybody available.'

'Just do it.'

Drake left the Incident Room and headed for Price's office. The secretary had left for the day so he knocked on the superintendent's door and, after hearing a shout from inside the room, Drake entered. The soft sheen from an LED table lamp bathed his desk, and in the pastel light the senior officer looked old, his skin pale, the creases deepening. Price and his wife had little family and working was probably his only interest. On an evening like this Drake felt sorry for Price and hoped he could avoid such a fate, but he doubted it.

Drake sat down.

'The PR department are having a fit,' Price said.

'We have to accept that onlookers and weirdoes will have taken photographs. There'll be more of these sort of images on the internet soon enough.'

Price nodded. 'Scourge of modern policing. All this 24/7 media. Any luck with the website?'

Drake shook his head. 'The team are still working on that.'

Price glanced at his watch. 'It's been a long day. That forum meeting today became a ridiculous waste of time – filled with do-gooders and semi-literate local politicians who could barely read their minutes.'

Price sat back in his chair and fixed Drake with a stare.

'Have you met the family?'

'We've seen Gloria's partner and spoken to members of the Orme Arts Festival committee – she was the curator. They gave us the names of some people with possible motives.'

Price scanned the time. 'It's bloody late.'

Drake stood up.

'How are things, Ian?'

Drake knew what he really meant. The superintendent wanted to know how he was coping, living on his own, and that a previous history of counselling wouldn't be repeated.

'Good, sir. Thank you.' Drake wasn't about to share with Price that he missed his family and that too often he blamed himself and his job for his break-up with Sian.

Price settled back to the piles of folders on his desk and Drake pulled the door closed behind him.

Back in the Incident Room, the atmosphere was heavy and lethargic. Winder was arguing with someone on the telephone. Luned was engrossed with paperwork. She had recently been promoted to detective constable; Drake had scanned her curriculum vitae the night before, a worry crossing his mind that she was too young and inexperienced. But two newcomers meant neither of them would know anything about him so he needn't be concerned about comments behind his back. Drake walked over to the board and read the various names underneath the image of Gloria Patton.

Hubert Oswald was pinned to the middle. Tomorrow the team would find out more about him, more about Gloria. Next to him was the name of

Jeremy Ellingham and on the other side Geraint Wood – two of the artists Gloria had rejected from the exhibition at the arts festival.

Winder finished his conversation, stood up, stretched his back and made no attempt to stifle a yawn. 'No luck, boss. Nobody is available.'

'Okay. Nothing more we can do tonight,' Drake said to Winder's obvious relief. Then he turned to Sara. 'We've got the post-mortem in the morning.'

Sara nodded, giving him a tired smile.

It was another hour before Drake arrived home. The answer machine flashed a notification that he had a message. He played it back, listening to his mother, who sounded serious, telling him she hadn't been able to reach him earlier and that she expected to see him on Saturday as planned. Her voice implied he couldn't postpone. Since his father had died he had made every effort to visit her more often and as he wasn't due to see his daughters at the weekend he had no excuse. But Gloria's murder changed everything. It took priority. They always did. It was too late to call her back now, so he promised himself he'd ring her tomorrow.

He had grazed all day and his stomach rumbled. He idly contemplated a takeaway meal but rifling through the freezer he found a fish pie. As it cooked he opened a bottle of beer.

The green glass reminded him of Hubert Oswald's place earlier that morning. He had lived with Gloria for over twenty years but had appeared unmoved by her death. A loving husband would have been inconsolable. So was Oswald's reaction that of a man guilty of murder or guilty of indifference to his partner? As Drake ate, he thought about what their inquiries might discover about Oswald and decided that these artistic types were very odd.

The next morning Drake parked a safe distance away from the nearest car at the mortuary, avoiding potential accidental scratches or bumps to the Mondeo. He reached over for the newspaper on the passenger seat and scanned the Sudoku puzzle, his mind satisfied that he had already managed a couple of squares. He saw the time on the dashboard clock and headed off for the entrance. Sara had completed the paperwork needed for the mortuary assistant who was standing, casting the occasional glance towards her.

'Morning, Inspector.' The assistant hadn't drawn a brush through his hair that morning nor a razor over his cheeks for several days. He let off a faint whiff of unwashed clothes. Drake mumbled a reply.

'The doc's expecting you.'

'Morning, boss.' Sara still had her hair in a tight plait but the navy suit had been replaced by a less formal brown jacket and trousers with sharp creases. Second day in a new job required a more relaxed dress code, Drake concluded.

'Have you ever attended a post-mortem before?' Drake said.

She shook her head.

'Then it'll be difficult, your stomach will turn. If you find yourself nauseous then just leave.'

'Thanks, sir.'

They followed the technician into a corridor and at the end he pushed open the double doors to the mortuary, inviting Sara to brush past him, grinning as he did so. She paused and then shoved open the other door, ignoring him. There was a clinical, antiseptic feel to the place. 'Ian Drake, good to see you again,' a voice bellowed, and Drake and Sara looked around for its owner. Dr Kings emerged from behind a screen, drying his hands. 'I hear this caused a stir.' Kings noticed Sara and raised an eyebrow.

'Lee. This is DS Sara Morgan.'

Kings kept eye contact with Sara. 'Pleased to meet you, sergeant. I hope you can keep Inspector Drake in order.' He shared a conspiratorial smile with her. Another white-coated assistant pushed a trolley into the mortuary and Drake saw Kings' face light up.

'Let's see what she has to tell us,' Kings announced.

Sara coughed loudly as Kings assembled the various shining stainless steel instruments he required. With a flourish he removed the white sheet that covered the body. Drake sensed Sara moving uncomfortably from one leg to another as Kings started on the task of cutting up Gloria Patton.

The pathologist dictated as he worked, occasionally pausing to stare and ponder. 'Rigor mortis was well advanced when I saw her yesterday. It suggests she had been dead for a minimum of eight hours when the body was discovered. The undertakers had to force her arm flat – one of their newbies got a bit squeamish.'

Kings raised Patton's left arm before looking over at Drake. He drew a hand along the bottom surface of the grey, wrinkled skin. 'This discoloration is called livor mortis. It's due to the blood settling in dependent areas. Because her arm was lying on a piece of timber, gravity will have drawn the blood to the side where the limb rested.'

Kings placed the arm back on the trolley and moved nearer Patton's feet. 'The same is true of her feet. She's been stood up post-mortem, allowing blood to settle there.'

Sara cleared her throat noisily. Kings gave a brief, friendly smile before continuing. 'The fact that the lividity is fixed confirms my view that she'd been dead for six to eight hours when you found her.'

Drake nodded. 'Patton was last seen at ten pm and her body found at eleven the following morning. So she was killed between ten in the evening and three the following morning.'

Kings nodded as he walked round to the opposite end of the trolley where he turned his attention to Gloria's head. 'There's evidence of a blunt force trauma to the back of the head.'

'Is that what killed her?'

'Difficult to determine externally; we'll have to look inside.'

He spent time recovering fragments from the wound before reaching for a scalpel. He made an incision around the hairline. Then he peeled the skin back over the face. Drake glanced over at Sara; she had a fist pressed to her mouth and a sickly look on her face. He turned back and watched Kings operating a reciprocating saw to open the skull. Carefully he removed the brain and held it in both hands to admire the mass of tissue. 'Normal brain, no bruising or bleeding that I can see.'

'So the force to the head didn't kill her?'

'Unlikely.'

'But enough for the killer to render her unconscious?'

Kings nodded. He examined Gloria's upper body and limbs before holding up the right arm. He raised his head and looked over at Drake. 'Did she have a history of drug abuse?'

'Not that we know.'

'Because there's a puncture wound here on her arm caused by a needle of some type. It could be anything, from self-inflicted puncture wound to medical treatment or tests. Or something may have been injected to kill her. The head injury didn't kill her. So we can't rule out drugs or a poison of some sort.' He scanned the rest of her body. 'Let's open her up and take a look.'

Once Kings started to open the chest cavity with a saw the sound of bone splintering and cracking filled the air and Sara stepped away from the trolley, coughing loudly. Drake looked over and she mouthed a reassurance that she would be all right and returned to his side.

Kings stood back after a few minutes, frowning. 'There's a lot of fluid on the lungs which suggests pulmonary oedema. She hasn't drowned, and her heart is normal, so it could be negative pressure pulmonary oedema from a partially obstructed airway for a while before death. That could be while she was unconscious from the head injury, but given the puncture wound we should send some samples for toxicology.'

'Do you really think she might have been poisoned?'

Kings stared at the body for a moment. 'We can't rule it out.'

Chapter 6

Sara stared down at her flat white. She dragged a hand through her hair and over her head. It was mid-morning, the café was quiet, more staff than customers. From the sickly look she had developed after the post-mortem Drake decided they needed to pause before their visit to Norma Buckland. He still remembered the feeling of nausea after his first post-mortem. It had been a straightforward case. An abusive husband had lost his temper once too often only to face his wife plunging a kitchen knife into his heart. A full and complete confession followed quickly, the relief palpable at knowing he couldn't torment her any further.

Gloria Patton's murder had a ghoulish quality, and Drake guessed the scene at the shop and the post-mortem would stay with Sara for the rest of her career.

'How are you feeling?'

She looked up at him. The grey tinge to her skin seemed to have made her age visibly since that morning. 'Better now.' She sipped on her drink. 'We are looking for a psychopath aren't we?' she asked quietly.

Drake ran a finger around the handle of his coffee cup. 'We're certainly looking for one very disturbed individual.'

'What was the possible motive for staging her body like that?'

Drake downed the last of his Americano.

'There has to be a link to the artistic world. Maybe it was revenge for rejecting a submission or just plain jealousy.'

'But to stage her body like that is really gruesome. Really sick.' Sara shuddered. 'What if we can't find a link to the artistic world? And it's the work of some ...'

'There's always a motive. That's why we have to

know everything about Gloria Patton. Something about her life will hold the key to all this.'

Sara didn't look convinced. 'We will catch the killer.' Drake hoped he sounded persuasive.

Sara finished her coffee and gave Drake a weak smile, enough to encourage him to beckon a waitress and pay the bill. Drake headed back for the car, pleased Sara had recovered some normality. He started the engine and entered Norma Buckland's postcode into the satnav. The junction for Rhyl was a few miles east on the A55 and the journey took them past Colwyn Bay before skirting along the dual carriageway that ran parallel with the railway line and the wide expanse of shoreline. The flat, open countryside stretched out ahead of Drake and he could see Rhyl in the distance. It almost looked inviting – perhaps it was the seaside or the spring sunshine – but Drake knew the town had one of the worst levels of deprivation in Wales. The amusement arcades and slot machines attracted tourists from Liverpool but now it had become nothing more than a suburb of its near city neighbour.

They passed hundreds of static caravans stationed like obedient soldiers staring out to sea. Then, nearing the town, neat bungalows, net-curtained windows, weed-free drives with small cars, all with proud owners retired from the stresses of Liverpool or Birkenhead. Drake found the old garage Norma Buckland used as a studio easily enough.

The words 'Modurdy Gerwyn' were built into the stonework above the door. Drake doubted Gerwyn was running his garage any longer or that the current owners would be Welsh speakers. The arched opening had been bricked over and in one corner the sign on a door indicated that all deliveries should call a mobile telephone number. Drake pushed it open and from behind a makeshift dividing wall of timber partitions he heard voices and a radio playing a Bob Dylan song.

The plasterboard shook as Drake opened a door in it and stepped into a space occupied by tables of varying sizes and age. Lengths of timber and bits of plywood were stacked on one, and another groaned with tool boxes and wooden crates. Large sheets of paper butted together covered one wall with random patterns in numerous coloured inks.

Two people had their backs to Drake and Sara as they worked, remodelling a sculpture, but they turned when they heard their approaching visitors.

'Norma Buckland?'

'How can I help?' Buckland wore a one-piece boiler suit, a couple of sizes too small from the way it exaggerated everything about her ample figure. She looked up at Drake, tossing out of the way the long dark hair that flowed over her shoulders and down her back.

'Detective Inspector Drake and this is my colleague Detective Sergeant Sara Morgan.' Norma gave his warrant card a cursory glance and spoke to the younger woman by her side.

'Go and get yourself a coffee, Jean.' She folded her arms and glared at Drake. 'I expect you've called about Gloria Patton.'

'Did you know her?'

'Know her?' Norma snorted. 'Everyone in the art world knew her. She was a right cow.'

'I understand she was responsible for rejecting your submission for the Orme Arts Festival.'

'What are you suggesting? If you think—'

'If you could just answer the question, please.'

Norma narrowed her eyes, glaring at Drake.

'She was one of the most thoroughly unpleasant women I have ever come across. Nobody liked her, nobody thought that she contributed anything to the art world and, more importantly, she was full of her own self-importance.' Norma's accent was a watered-down, cultured version of the harsh Scouse drawl prevalent in Rhyl.

'Tell me about your submission to the Orme Arts Festival.'

Norma unfolded her arms.

'It was a piece I had previously exhibited in one of the premier galleries in Vienna. But Gloria Patton didn't know that. She had the gall not only to reject the sculpture but she wrote me a patronising letter of rejection. And that is something never done in the art world.'

Norma walked over to a filing cabinet and yanked out the top drawer. She flicked through some files until she extracted four images she handed to Drake. 'These are the photographs of my piece.'

Drake gazed at the gnarled faces of the small group of figures, cartoon-like, with bloated heads and enlarged feet, surprised that any gallery would exhibit them. He said nothing, although in reality he had little idea what he could have said.

'She had no idea about real quality. She believed art was there to entertain, Inspector. Nothing more than that. For her, it was sophisticated titillation. It never occurred to her that it might stretch the mind, challenge the norm, make people think. After all, art should make people think, don't you agree?'

Drake stayed silent. He was supposed to be the one asking the questions.

Norma continued. 'The Orme Arts Festival was an opportunity to showcase some really exceptional artistic work from everyone in Wales. But she wanted to make it local, parochial. I heard she thought about displaying Victorian bathing huts as though she were running a museum.'

'Are you a full-time artist?'

Norma pouted. 'I have a wide-ranging practice, Inspector. I've been doing this for years. It may not be what you consider to be conventional.'

There was nothing conventional about the letters Drake had read for a second time that morning in the car outside the studio, reminding himself of the comments Buckland had made in them, castigating Gloria Patton.

'I've seen letters you sent to the committee members. Would you say it's conventional to direct abusive comments and insults at them because you were rejected?'

For a second Buckland looked uncomfortable.

Drake waited for her to respond but she stayed silent. He decided to push on, relishing the prospect of asking her about them again.

'When did you last see Gloria?'

Norma shrugged.

'Try and remember.'

'Two or three weeks ago.'

'Well, which is it?'

Norma relented. 'I don't keep track of when I see people. Especially people like Gloria Patton.'

'Did you know her husband?'

Norma shook her head.

'Where were you the night Gloria was killed?'

She stepped nearer Drake. 'I was here, all night. And there is no one to give me an alibi.'

Drake and Sara arrived back at Northern Division headquarters as Gareth Winder tucked into a lunchtime pastry. Luned turned a fork around a plastic container of salad. Drake strode over to the Incident Room board.

'We've finished taking statements from the eyewitnesses who first saw the body, boss,' Winder said.

Luned stopped eating and looked over at Drake.

'It was just before eleven. Two couples walked past the window. They were both taken aback when the curtain fell down. They thought it was a mistake at first so they stopped and stared in. They didn't comprehend immediately they might be looking at a dead body.'

'How did they realise it was a corpse?' Drake said.

'One of the men was a paramedic,' Winder said. 'The more he stared at Gloria the more he became unsettled and aware something was wrong.'

Luned added. 'He called emergency services.'

'But dozens of people had stopped in the meantime, boss. That means photographs and videos of this all over social media.'

Drake spoke slowly when he realised the implication of their comments. 'So if it wasn't for this paramedic, Gloria Patton might have been on display much longer.'

'That's disgusting,' Sara piped up. 'Absolutely sick.'

It was the most animated Drake had seen her so far.

'Presumably that is what the killer wanted. He wanted the whole thing to be a spectacle.' Drake stood back from the board and pointed at the photographs. 'He wanted Gloria Patton to be on display. Gawped at by passers-by.'

'I checked out the unmade bed artwork, sir,' Luned said. 'It was called *My Bed* by Tracey Emin. It sold for £2.2 million.'

The vast sum involved jolted Drake. 'How much?'

Winder and Sara looked equally surprised. Drake

continued. 'So the killer replicates a piece of famous art in the middle of a murder scene. What the hell is he trying to tell us?'

'Maybe he thinks an unmade bed isn't really art,' Winder added.

'Perhaps he was suggesting his art was just as good as *My Bed*.' Luned's soft accent reminded Drake of the rural accents of his childhood.

'So I wonder what he would have called it?' Winder said. '*Dead on Your Feet* or something sick like that.'

Drake gave him a sharp, reproachful glance. 'Did we get anything of value from the eyewitnesses?'

Winder and Luned shook their heads.

'Nothing at all? What about the inquiries with the adjacent shops?'

'That's ongoing, sir.'

'I want progress made, Gareth. Tell the uniformed lads to pull their fingers out. I want reports by later today. Names, addresses of people who might have seen something, anything and find her car – it can't be that difficult.'

Drake left the three officers in the Incident Room. Back in his office he flopped into his chair; he had to fathom out the significance of the murder scene. The interview with Buckland had only confirmed that she had a motive and although she seemed straightforward, Drake wasn't going to dismiss her as a possible suspect.

The possibility the killer might strike again dominated Drake's thoughts. He read through the various reports including the preliminary post-mortem result: it said nothing different from the verbal detail Kings had already given him. A toxicology report would follow in due course. He would have to wait for a definitive answer on the cause of death, but if the puncture wound was anything to go on, it was looking increasingly like Gloria Patton had been poisoned. An email from Mike Foulds reminded him that he still needed to discuss evidence found at the crime scene so he left his desk and threaded his way through the corridors of Northern Division headquarters to the forensics department. He was buoyed by the knowledge that the garments, bedding, clothes and the apparatus at the scene had been handled by the killer, which meant he must have left forensic evidence. Skin samples, beads of perspiration, anything that might give them a DNA profile.

Foulds had the laptop recovered from the crime scene open on a table in the main laboratory. He looked up and pointed to a stool.

'Just in time,' Foulds said.

Drake sat down, waiting for Foulds to continue.

'I would say the killer has a working knowledge of some basic electronics. A timer had been rigged from the laptop to a pulley mechanism. At exactly 10.57 it sent a signal that engaged a motor, which operated the curtains. It means the killer wanted to make certain the scene was presented to the world at a specific time.'

Drake stared at the laptop, thinking it contributed to a profile of the killer as a very dangerous individual.

'Have you made sense of why the body was placed in this upright position?' Foulds said.

'We have no idea.'

'And this unmade bed?'

'There was a famous piece of art a few years ago—'

'I remember. Wasn't it controversial at the time?'

Drake nodded. 'Can you tell me anything else about the laptop? Is there any information on there that can identify the killer?'

Foulds glanced at the screen. 'It looks quite new.

There was nothing else on it, no word processing package, and no internet facility.'

'Any fingerprints?' Drake sounded less than hopeful.

'None. I'm running some tests at the moment but I think one of those computer spray cleaners had been used. There was a faint smell of pine on it.'

'What about the rest of the items recovered from the shop – did you find any evidence that might give us some DNA?'

Foulds gave Drake a worried look. 'The killer has been careful. I would have expected to discover fingerprints, partials at the very least on furniture, but there was nothing.'

Drake sensed the familiar feeling that the inquiry was going to be far from straightforward.

'And that suggests,' Foulds continued, 'that the killer wore gloves. And ... I might be guessing, but it wouldn't surprise me if he wore the sort of protective clothing we use.'

'You mean shoe-coverings, facemask, full one-piece white kit ...?'

Foulds nodded.

'That would suggest he was forensically aware, but also well-prepared.'

'It's going to take time to get all the tests done on every piece of fabric, but we might get lucky.'

'I need the results as soon as, Mike.'

'We're working on it. In the meantime, I'll send you a list of all the exhibits we removed from the crime scene.'

Drake didn't have a chance to reply as his mobile rang. It was Winder. 'I think you should get back here, boss. Something you need to see.'

Chapter 7

Foulds promised to expedite the forensic analysis but Drake knew it might take days, even weeks, to examine each piece of clothing and garment from the crime scene. He marched back to the Incident Room, intrigued by the urgent tone to Winder's voice. Winder jumped to his feet when Drake arrived and walked over to the board, coming to a standstill by the newly added image of a man in his early twenties. Drake joined him, glancing at the photograph: the police national computer mug shot couldn't hide the defiance in the eyes of a young man, clean shaven, but with long, thick hair parted in the centre.

'It's a picture of Roger Buckland,' Winder said.

Drake leant against one of the desks. 'And?'

'He's married to Norma Buckland. He was twenty when he was convicted of murder.'

Drake's pulse leapt. He walked closer to the board.

'I did a PNC search against him,' Winder said.

'What are the details? How old is he now?' Drake tried to fix the face of Norma Buckland in his mind. She must be mid-forties.

'The photograph was taken over twenty years ago. Buckland was in a nightclub in Liverpool. He was really tanked up. He bottled some guy outside at the end of an evening. They had been arguing – all the usual stuff. So Buckland whacked him. Initially he was sent down for murder. He appealed and because it was only one strike his conviction was set aside and he was sentenced to eight years for manslaughter.'

'Not the same MO as Patton. Her murderer was well-prepared and organised.'

'I know, sir. But it's a violent assault and he's older now.'

'Have you spoken to the officer who dealt with the

case?' Drake said, before remembering the lapse of time. 'The senior investigating officer will probably have retired.'

'I've called Merseyside Police already. Someone is going to call us back.'

'So what else do we know about Roger Buckland?'

'He's now a pastor in one of the evangelical churches in Colwyn Bay.'

Winder acknowledged the surprise on Drake's face with a nod.

'Apparently he became a Christian in prison. After his release he became a full-time pastor involved with a church in the Liverpool area before moving to North Wales.'

'Let's build a profile of Roger Buckland. If you don't get a reply from Merseyside Police in the next twenty-four hours we'll make a formal request.'

'Gloria's car has been found too, boss,' Luned said.

'Where?'

'In a side street not far from Canolfan Tudno.'

'Any forensics?'

'Unclear at the moment, but it looks undisturbed.'

'Is there any CCTV available?'

Luned shook her head. 'The CSIs have moved the car to headquarters.'

It meant a full forensic evaluation and more delays. Drake looked at Winder who had returned to his desk. 'Any progress with the website?'

Winder fumbled with some papers on his desk and then double-clicked on his mouse. He peered at his computer monitor. 'Ah … I did speak to one of the civilians in the IT department. He told me that it's very easy to set up this sort of website. It doesn't have its own domain name. It uses Wordpress, which is a common way to establish a website on the cheap and there's no fee to pay. The registration formalities only require an email address without any need to provide personal details.'

Drake stared at the junior officer. 'It has to be traceable. This killer sat in front of a computer somewhere and uploaded these images.'

A silence fell on the room until Luned said what was on Drake's mind. 'Could a Christian pastor be a murderer?'

'It's not the same MO.' Drake knew he was repeating himself, but it worried him that Buckland's conviction years previously gave them scant reason to make him a suspect. If Roger Buckland was a reformed character was he capable of murder? And why? To avenge his wife perhaps? Drake shared a glance with Winder and Luned. 'Do some digging into the Bucklands. It seems unlikely he was responsible for such a carefully staged murder but we need to learn a lot more about them both.'

On one side of *Patton's Fine Art* was a charity shop and on the other a premises selling discontinued clothing, which didn't make for the most salubrious location. Sara followed Drake towards a counter. The woman sitting behind it made no attempt to welcome them as prospective purchasers. Police officers could be spotted a mile off, Drake thought. He barely gave her a chance to read his warrant card before replacing it in his jacket pocket. She had dark grey bags under her eyes; a narrow hand and thin fingers made her handshake lifeless. 'I'm Francine.'

'Is there somewhere we can talk to you about Gloria?' Drake scanned the shop premises, looking for a door to an office or storeroom. A shelving unit against one wall had colourful greetings cards with images of

Llandudno and other North Wales attractions. Another display cabinet had wooden bowls and immaculately turned wooden gifts with fancy labels attached with fine string. Next to the till were ballpoints and fluffy toys all advertising the wonders of a holiday in Llandudno.

'I suppose we could use Gloria's office.' Francine got up and gestured to the staircase at the rear. The first floor extended further back over the rear of the property than Drake had imagined from the ground floor. Large canvases similar to those he had seen in Hubert Oswald's studio dominated one wall. He noticed the price tag on one, almost as much as his monthly income. It surprised him – he would never pay such a sum for what looked like a confused mass of colour. Smaller paintings depicting popular tourist locations all over North Wales hung on another wall. Fine art seemed to be a loose term when it came to describing what Gloria Patton was offering in her premises, Drake concluded. He wondered what made her qualified to be the curator of an arts festival and remembered Norma Buckland had raised similar doubts.

Francine pushed open the door at the far end of the gallery, and Drake and Sara followed her inside to a small office. Drake grimaced at the cluttered desk with papers strewn in no apparent order under the window to his right. Two filing cabinets had been pushed against a wall and alongside them cardboard boxes were piled on a table; underneath were even more boxes, some with leaflets and papers evident. Against the far wall to his left were several plywood shelves, all heaving with books and papers.

'It's a mess,' Drake said, unable to curb his criticism.

'She wasn't the tidiest of people,' Francine said.

Luckily, there were enough chairs for them to sit down near the table.

'How well did you know Gloria?' Drake said.

Francine's bottom lip quivered but she quickly regained her composure. 'I've been working here for four years so I knew her pretty well.'

'What was she like to work for?'

'Fine ... I got on well with her.'

'Did she have any enemies do you think?'

Francine hesitated.

Drake pushed on. 'I know she wasn't very popular with the artists that she disappointed in her role as the curator of the Orme Arts Festival. I understand she received letters from Norma Buckland. Did you know about them?'

Francine jerked her head towards the filing cabinets. 'She kept them filed away. At the time she didn't think too much about them. She certainly wasn't worried about Norma Buckland. It was Geraint Wood she was frightened of.'

Drake recognised Wood's name from the list Rhisiart Hopkin had given him the previous afternoon. He glanced at Sara who already had a ballpoint and her notebook ready. He turned to Francine. 'What can you tell us about Geraint Wood?'

Francine settled back in her chair. 'He came in one afternoon, bold as brass and in a hell of a temper. He started shouting and cursing at Gloria, telling her that she didn't have a clue about art, wasn't qualified to be a curator. He was extremely abusive, and he used foul language towards her.' Francine shuddered.

'How did Gloria react?'

'She was quite calm, until he began to threaten her and jabbed his finger in her face. He even poked her in the shoulder a couple of times.'

'So he got physical with her?'

Sara stopped making notes and used a serious tone. 'Did she report it to the police?'

Francine shook her head.

For the next few minutes, Drake elicited as much detail as he could about the incident with Geraint Wood. Sara nodded to Drake once she had finished recording her notes. Francine slumped, almost withered, in her chair. 'I hope I never have to experience anything like this again.'

'I'll need to see the letters she received from Norma Buckland,' Drake said.

Francine paused, then let out a long sigh. 'Yes, of course.' She stood up and dragged open one of the drawers of the cabinet, rifling through its contents until she produced several folders, which she handed to Drake.

'These are the files relating to Buckland and Wood and that man Jeremy Ellingham too.' She skimmed through the contents absently. 'She thought he had no concept of boundaries in his art.'

She thrust the papers at Drake as a voice called out from the shop below. 'I have to go – there's a customer. Is there anything else?'

Sara replied before Drake had a chance to. 'Thank you. You've been really helpful. We're just going to take a look through Gloria's papers.' Francine left them with a brief nod.

'I'll get to work on some of these other papers, boss.'

Drake mumbled an acknowledgement. He put the blue folder on the table and started reading its contents. Quickly he realised that his initial judgement of Gloria Patton's disorganised office didn't portray the reality. The folder belonged specifically to the assessment she had made of the artwork Norma Buckland had submitted. There was a photograph of the sculpture, the submission form Buckland had completed and another word processed sheet that

Gloria had used to record her comments. She had obviously wanted to apply some objective test, Drake concluded. There was a copy of her letter of rejection to Norma Buckland, which seemed innocuous enough to Drake although for a principled, artistic individual the formality of the rejection might be unpalatable.

The letter from Buckland to Gloria Patton caught his attention. As he read he tried to imagine the thought process going on in Buckland's mind.

> *Gloria*
> *I don't know how to start this letter. There was something completely disgusting, preposterous about your letter telling me that you had rejected my submission to the Orme Arts Festival. You obviously had no idea that it had already been exhibited in Vienna and lauded by the critics there. Roger and I feel utterly betrayed by your misguided belief in the artists that you seek to support. And you have the cheek to suggest that my work doesn't reach the standard you were expecting. This is truly a sign that you have reached into the gutter and become the lowest of the low.*
> *Yours truly*

Drake walked over to the filing cabinet and found the rest of the submissions. Sara was busy sifting through the paperwork from another filing cabinet.

'Something you should see, sir.'

Drake turned and noticed Sara fingering the contents of a buff folder.

'This is a file about her will.'

Drake watched as Sara scanned the document. It did not appear to be lengthy.

'She left everything to Oswald.'

Drake sat back in his chair. 'So that gives Hubert Oswald the perfect motive – her money.'

'He's an artist so he'd know all about Tracey Emin's *My Bed*. Surely? It's a strong link.'

'When we get back to headquarters contact the lawyers and find out what they know about the will. When it was drawn up or if it's been changed lately. We shall have to see Oswald again. He told us he was at home all night – but he could have driven into Llandudno. We'll need to requisition traffic surveillance to check.'

Drake got back to the rest of the paperwork in front of him. Wood and Geraint both had a similar assessment form and another letter of rejection in their folders. Drake wondered whether either of them were capable of murder. He read Gloria Patton's comments about Ellingham's work being 'utterly derivative' and 'lacking in imagination' and as he finished reading the door burst open and Hubert Oswald entered.

'Francine told me you were here,' Oswald said, sounding more aggressive than Drake had witnessed yesterday. 'What the hell do you think you are doing?'

'Why didn't you tell us that Geraint Wood lost his temper with Gloria?'

'She didn't think it was important.'

'She was threatened, he assaulted her. And now she's dead. There's also this letter from Norma Buckland.' Drake held aloft the blue folder. 'Sit down, Mr Oswald.'

Sara stopped what she was doing and sat down near Drake.

'The art world can be a very jealous place, and very competitive.' The chair Francine had vacated creaked under Oswald's weight as he sat down.

'I understand Gloria made a will leaving everything

to you.'

Oswald stammered a reply. 'And I left everything to her.'

'What's going to happen to the gallery?' Drake said.

Oswald frowned. 'I don't know … I mean, it's too early to say.'

'Do you have any debts, Mr Oswald?'

Oswald swallowed hard. 'Surely you don't suspect that as a reason for …?'

'Do you have anyone who could give you an alibi for your whereabouts on the night of Gloria's death?'

'No. I was at home, of course – where else would I be?'

Drake stared at Oswald, knowing it was a short drive through the country lanes from their home to Llandudno.

Sara piped up. 'We've found Gloria's car in a side street. You'll need to collect it from headquarters in due course.'

'That will prove difficult, sergeant. I don't drive.'

Chapter 8

The following morning Sara regretted her decision to offer to drive when Drake turned up his nose as he lowered himself into the passenger seat. She had noticed his fastidiousness yesterday as he stepped awkwardly around puddles in Patton's yard. Sharing this insight with a colleague had elicited a rolling of eyes and she wondered then if there was more to Drake than she knew about. Drake would doubtless think that the inside of her car was disgusting and badly needed a thorough clean. Did the car smell? She couldn't remember when it had been vacuumed last so he was probably right. As he buckled his seat belt he even cast a surreptitious glance at her training bag on the rear seat that spilled out the various bits of her running apparel. In the middle of all the activity in the past two days she had completely forgotten to take it home. Her next five-mile run seemed a long way in the future, certainly not later that day.

She sped along the A55 going west, took the junction off the dual carriageway and crossed the bridge over the Conwy estuary, skirting around the bottom of the fifteenth-century castle dominating the town. She followed the road down the west side of the Conwy Valley but, being unfamiliar with the roads, kept her speed to a minimum. It was off the beaten track, not a route used by the tourists that flooded down the eastern side of the valley with its quaint villages.

The satnav took them along various narrow lanes until they reached a terrace of six houses at ninety degrees to the main road. Each property had a patch of garden at the front accessed from a weed-strewn path. Sara parked on a gravel layby a little distance away. As they walked back Sara noticed the long allotment-like gardens stretching out at the rear of the six properties.

'Where do they park their cars?' Sara said.

Drake stood for a moment. 'These look like old council houses. They didn't think about car parking when they were built.'

Drake led the way, walking gingerly over the muddy path towards the end property. Porches and new PVCu windows were recent additions by two proud owners. Another appeared to be in accelerated decline, garden thick with weeds, a green-and-black wheelie bin upturned.

The words Trem Eryri had been stencilled into an old piece of wood that hung by the door of the end terrace. Drake checked the name of Ellingham's property and nodded at Sara. There was no bell so Drake rapped his knuckles on the door, hoping the occupant could hear him.

No response. Sara peered in through the ground-floor window, over a sink filled with pots and pans and dishes. It looked as though nobody had cleaned inside for weeks. Drake stepped back and looked up at the first-floor windows. The door of the next door property squeaked open.

An emaciated man appeared, slack-skinned and drawing heavily on the remains of a cigarette, a can of cider in his hand. Sara tried to make out his age but he could have been a decrepit fifty or an unhealthy-looking seventy.

'Are you looking for Jez?' The man had a strong Welsh accent.

Sara listened to Drake as he asked the man in Welsh if he knew where Ellingham might be. She knew enough of the language from school and the classes the Wales Police Service offered to understand the exchange.

After thanking the man Drake turned to Sara. 'Apparently he's got a shed at the bottom of the garden.'

She followed Drake's laboured progress around the gable as he placed his feet carefully, like a ballerina on a stage littered with broken glass. She had noticed the occasional idiosyncrasy during her first two days – there wasn't a single sheet of paper out of place on his desk – and she wondered how anyone could manage such neatness. His careful manoeuvring to dodge the muddy areas of the path didn't prevent his brogues from getting dirty nor the hem of his trousers from being soiled. Sara dismissed any concerns. They had a job to do, a person to interview. Clothes could always be dry-cleaned.

Another path crossed the rear of the properties. The gardens that led off it were longer and wider than Sara had expected.

A path of loose gravel lined one edge of Ellingham's garden, which bordered vegetable beds with raised banks of potatoes and wigwam stands ready for runner beans. At the far end stood an old shed, its front step worn thin in the middle. The heavy stink of creosote hung in the air. Drake yanked open the door and yelled. 'Jeremy Ellingham.'

He didn't wait for any response and, indicating for Sara to follow him, he entered.

Immediately the smell of cannabis tickled her nose. Windows on each wall and on the rear gable allowed light to pour in. Towards the back a man was pinning various pieces of newspaper cuttings to a board on an easel. Sara tuned into the only sound, the man's voice humming along to the music playing through his earphones, the cables dangling around his neck.

Drake shouted his name again.

The man turned, startled, leant over to a stereo system and pulled out the earphone plugs. The sound of crashing cymbals and what sounded like a cash register filled the air.

Drake tilted his head, obviously appreciating the music. 'Pink Floyd.'

'Who are you?'

Warrant cards produced, Ellingham stood waiting.

'We are investigating the murder of Gloria Patton.'

Ellingham nodded and now leant over and switched off the music.

'She was the curator of the Orme Arts Festival.'

'I know who she was.'

Drake gave Ellingham a quizzical look. 'She rejected your entry. And—'

'Do you think that would give me a motive to kill her? I'm an established artist. I have exhibitions all over the world.'

Drake paused. 'What sort of art do you produce?'

'Produce? My practice, Inspector, is multidisciplinary. I work in different media. I'm not constrained by one particular discipline.'

'Do you paint?' Sara asked.

He gave a brief snort. 'Painting is dead. It's the visual arts that are the future.'

Just like the unmade bed that surrounded Gloria Patton, Sara thought.

Drake persevered. 'So what sort of work did you submit to the festival?'

Ellingham frowned at Drake, as though to answer was beneath him. 'I can't explain it to you. I'm an artist. You'll have to experience it for yourself.'

Sara glanced around the old shed wondering if it really was the studio of an internationally renowned artist. Garden implements stood upright in an oil drum in one corner. Tools were scattered over workbenches, bits of old plant pots and polystyrene piled in various boxes.

'When did you see Gloria Patton last?' Drake said.

Sara noticed the white of Ellingham's eyes, which seemed to bulge as he rolled them in exasperation. She imagined an artist being much older than the man standing before them. She guessed he was about five foot seven; the T-shirt with a large bicycle printed on its front flapped around his thin frame. His clean-shaven jawline and broad cheeks made him look younger than he probably was, and less eccentric, although his replies were distinctly strange.

'I don't remember.'

Drake folded his arm and took a couple of steps towards Ellingham. Sara sensed his impatience. 'Ok, where were you the night before last?'

Ellingham squinted at Drake.

'I was here.'

'Can anyone vouch for you?'

'My girlfriend. I'll get her to contact you.'

Both men kept staring at each other and for a moment Sara wasn't certain if she should say something. Drake eventually broke the silence. 'Good, we'll need full details of your girlfriend and her address.'

'Of course.'

Sara jotted down the details in her pocketbook.

They left and walked back up the gravel path, leaving Ellingham standing on the threshold.

As they approached the car, Sara turned to Drake. 'What did you make of him, boss?' She had a clear opinion of Ellingham but as she was new to working with Drake she decided to keep it to herself.

'He was an obnoxious little runt.'

'But he has an alibi.'

'We'll check it out. In fact, we can do that now.'

Drake turned on his heels. Sara followed behind him. He hammered on the front door of Ellingham's neighbour's house. The same man emerged still drawing on a thin cigarette at his lips. Drake used more charm than he had with Ellingham. Sara understood most of the conversation and she heard the word 'cariad' which she knew could mean girlfriend and Drake referred to Ellingham a couple of times.

After a few minutes Sara recognised 'diolch' for thank you and they retraced their steps back to the car. 'He's seen a girl there regularly. He saw her arriving there on the night of Patton's death.'

'We'll need to interview her.'

Drake nodded. Sara got in and started the engine, a niggle in her mind that something was odd about Ellingham. 'It's difficult to get a straight answer from these arty types.'

'Let's hope the next one will be more helpful.'

Chapter 9

Drake sat next to Sara on an old sofa in a cramped room of Wood's cottage. The warmth of the spring sunshine had little effect inside the house. An open fire filled the room with a sweet smell and a natural energy. Wood chose an old chair that sank under his weight; his position propelled his strong legs in front of him and Drake could imagine how his physique might intimidate Gloria Patton. His neatly trimmed hair contrasted with the stained pair of ratting trousers he wore.

'Sergeant Morgan doesn't speak Welsh.' Drake forced a friendly tone.

He wasn't certain how much of his initial exchange with Geraint Wood Sara had understood. Many officers in Northern Division lacked the confidence in speaking Welsh but could follow a rudimentary conversation.

Geraint gave Sara a look that turned from sympathy to hostility. 'But I'm sure there's a lot she understands.'

Drake ignored him. 'We're investigating the death of Gloria Patton.'

Wood nodded.

'We've had details of an argument you had with Gloria after she rejected work you submitted to the Orme Arts Festival.'

'The woman was a racist. She went out of her way to reject the work of Welsh artists, favouring her English friends and then only those she thought might attract publicity. The sort of artists that would help *her* make a name for herself.'

'How did you feel when she rejected your work?'

Wood clasped his hands together into a tight, strong fist. 'I hated how I'd been treated.'

'So you threatened her.'

Wood guffawed. 'I didn't threaten. I might have

raised my voice, shouted even. But I didn't threaten. I wanted her to see sense.'

Big men who were bullies never realise the effect they have on people, Drake thought.

'The staff at Gloria's gallery told us about your visit.'

'Gallery? You must be joking. It's a pathetic little shop where she sold trinkets and touristy crap. And some paintings, occasionally. But you can't call it a gallery.'

'But she was curator of the Orme Arts Festival.'

'She wouldn't know how to curate the paintings of a group of five-year-olds.'

Sara butted in. 'Why was she in charge of such an event then, if she was so poorly qualified?'

Wood seemed to relax; he stretched out his hands, showing open palms. 'It would have nothing of course to do with the fact she slept with everybody of any importance.'

Even if Wood's comments were no more than petty jealousy they would have to investigate. 'So who was she having a relationship with?' Drake said.

'There were two men in the council responsible for supporting the Orme Arts Festival. The whole thing couldn't survive without grants. She had been able to persuade them to part with tens of thousands of pounds and in the end she did nothing to support local artists.'

'Do you know their names?'

'One was a guy called Maxwell … something; the other one is called Jackson. I can't remember his first name.'

'How do you know about these men?'

'Everyone knows everybody else's business round here.' Wood smiled.

'What sort of art do you specialise in?' After his

encounter with Norma Buckland and Jeremy Ellingham, Drake expected an evasive, patronising reply. 'I make video installations.'

'Care to elaborate?'

'Dead simple really. I make videos people can watch.'

Sara piped up. 'Where do you exhibit?'

'I am represented by a gallery in Liverpool.' Sara scribbled down the name and the address.

'Can you account for your movements the night before last when Gloria Patton was killed?'

'Of course I can. I was here in bed, all night.' Wood paused. 'And before you ask, I was alone. So nobody can give me an alibi. Does that make me a suspect?'

It was the end of the afternoon when Drake and Sara arrived back at headquarters. Heavy traffic from tourists heading down the Conwy Valley for the weekend had snarled their progress. Sara found a parking space and after locking the car, they headed for the entrance.

'Do we make both Ellingham and Wood formal suspects, sir?'

'All we've learnt is that both men had a motive and that the art world is a fickle place where emotions run deep.'

'There was something odd about Ellingham,' Sara said. 'I couldn't put my finger on it.'

'Female intuition?'

Sara nodded. Drake continued. 'Geraint Wood made clear he hated Gloria Patton. But for now I think we have to concentrate on the Bucklands.'

'Do we spend any more time on Oswald?'

'Find out how much money was involved in Patton's estate and double-check that he was telling us the truth about him not having a driving licence.'

Back in the Incident Room Drake listened to a more confident-sounding Winder telling him about the exact technical requirements to set up the rogue website.

'Everything was done from a public computer in a library in Birkenhead.'

'Any CCTV?'

Gareth shook his head. 'I've called the library and they don't even keep a record of the people who use the computers.'

'So it could be anyone?' Drake looked over at the various images on the board. It was too early in the investigation for things to make any sense. They needed a much clearer picture of Gloria Patton's life. 'Have you made any progress with the checks on Mr and Mrs Buckland?'

Luned replied this time. 'There's nothing suspicious in her background. She's never been in trouble with the courts and there is no intelligence in the system about her. But her husband is a different story. There are two complaints on record about him threatening people he fell out with. He's got quite a temper.'

'I think we need to pay the reverend gentleman a visit,' Drake said.

He turned and saw tiredness in the eyes of his team. It had been a long week. They could make no further progress that evening so an encouragement for them to leave met with grins and thanks. He heard Winder inviting Luned and Sara to his favourite public house later. A pang of jealousy that he wasn't naturally part of this social scene clouded his mind.

So he got back to work.

Once he had tidied away the columns of colour-coordinated Post-it notes from his desk he set out the photographs from the crime scene. He stared at each one in turn trying to fathom out why the killer wanted to replicate a famous piece of art. And wondering whether he had spoken to the culprit that week. After storing the images away he read the reports from the shops-and-offices inquiries, but he wasn't surprised when he read that nothing of significance had been established. They were dealing with a very clever killer.

The statements from members of the public who witnessed the curtain fall away were full of comments about how disgusting the whole business had been and how sick they felt at the sight of a dead body. It occurred to Drake that the killer was deranged enough to be one of the bystanders interviewed. He reached for a list of the names and addresses, making a mental note for Winder or Luned to check them out.

From his inbox, he retrieved the post-mortem report and reread Dr Kings' preliminary findings. He tapped out an email reminder asking for an update on the toxicology results. Another report from Foulds made depressing reading, merely confirming in negative terminology what he had already shared with Drake.

He walked into the Incident Room and gazed at the various names assembled on the board. They had a collection of possible persons of interest, all of whom had the makings of a motive. Oswald had large, powerful hands and inheriting the gallery could be more than enough motive. Money always was, Drake knew, but he didn't drive, which meant he would have needed an accomplice to help with moving the frame and the body. Mentally, he parked Oswald as a suspect for now. He stared at Roger Buckland and the newly acquired image of his wife wanting to believe that a man could change, improve himself, but the conviction and his past hung over him. They still had work to do on Ellingham and Wood so he hoped that the forensic results would help. He scanned the faces in turn, asking himself which of them benefited from Gloria's death and who had the opportunity. He kept staring until he heard his telephone ringing and he returned to his office.

He saw Sian's name on the screen. 'You said you'd call the girls tonight.'

As always, he had lost track of time. 'I'm sorry. I'm in the middle of an important inquiry.'

'Aren't you always? Well, have you time to speak to them now?'

Drake glanced down at the paperwork on his desk, frustrated at the lack of progress.

'Because we're going out in the next five minutes to visit my mother.'

'Of course, sorry. I'll have a quick word with them but I'll try and call to see them on Sunday.'

His spirits lifted when he heard the voice of Helen and then Megan telling him about their day. He sighed heavily when the conversations finished too quickly.

An hour later the sound of cleaners moving around headquarters jolted him into realising he had to leave. In the past when his rituals meant double-checking everything, he had found himself in the office late into the evening unable go home. Counselling sessions helped him realise that he need not work relentlessly and that order and neatness needn't rule his life.

Chapter 10

Drake bought a newspaper as usual that Saturday morning and went straight to the Sudoku, solving some of the puzzle quickly. It always settled his mind. Then he drove down onto the A55 and indicated west. Dipping down into the tunnel underneath the Conwy estuary he emerged on the other side and followed the road as it hugged the coastline. Traffic was light as he passed Penmaenmawr and then powered through the mountain towards Llanfairfechan. Old memories from childhood often resurfaced on Drake's journey to see his mother. Some were welcome, others not, especially those that involved images of his grandfather in his open casket. It had been one of the abiding recollections from his teenage years and one that had triggered the obsessions that could dominate his mind. The ritual of desk-tidying and cleaning had been the worst and the counselling the WPS had insisted on after a difficult case that had scared Drake helped keep his obsessions in check. But it hadn't saved his marriage.

Driving through the scattered communities above the town of Caernarfon made him think of his father and grandfather. Both men reared and hardened by the rural landscape. He recalled as a boy watching wide-eyed his grandfather gathering up stinging nettles with his calloused and powerful hands. Now whenever he returned home to see his mother it reminded him of the day when his father had died: an anniversary, however painful. It meant that the regrets about things left unsaid were still raw.

Drake pulled the car into a gravelled section of the main road before the lane leading down to the family's smallholding. He stared over towards Caernarfon Bay, noticing the wide sand dunes at Llanddwyn, imagining the crowds of visitors flocking to the beach that weekend. He resolved to take Helen and Megan very soon, maybe tomorrow, work permitting.

The sun broke through a layer of cloud, and columns of bright sunshine bathed the countryside. For a few moments he enjoyed the view before driving down to the farmhouse.

As he parked he noticed movement in the kitchen window and then the rear door opened, his mother emerging onto the threshold. Her tone had been practical when she asked Drake to call, telling him she had something to discuss with him. He assumed she was thinking of selling the house and buying a bungalow. After all, the surrounding fields had already been let out to a young couple in an adjacent smallholding. It had enlarged their acreage and made it more likely they could make a living off the land, all of which pleased Drake's mother.

Moving on would be a wrench. But with four bedrooms and two reception rooms she could never use, Drake thought his mother would be better off with a smaller property. Even if she sold up he would still have his memories, of playing in the fields with his sister, watching his father take care of the animals.

Mair Drake walked over to the car.

'Ian, you're looking tired.'

She always thought he looked tired, and frequently she would ask if he was eating enough. Then she kissed him on the cheek. He followed her into the house where she bustled around the kitchen making tea. Mair's conversation kept flitting from one piece of small talk to another, which unnerved Drake.

Eventually she sat down, a china teapot and biscuits on the table in front of them.

'I've been wanting to speak to you for a while.' Mair filled a mug for Drake.

'I thought you had something on your mind.'

'It's about your father.'

Drake frowned. It couldn't be the probate paperwork, which had all been completed after a couple of visits to a local lawyer.

Mair turned a finger around the handle of her mug. 'There's something you need to know.' She looked up at Drake, a plaintive look on her face.

'What's this about?'

'You know that things hadn't always been right between your father and his parents.'

Nothing had ever been said, nothing ever was said about these sorts of things. Caustic comments made by a distant aunt about his grandparents at a family funeral years previously had piqued Drake's interest. At the time his father had dismissed Drake's questions. Now he wanted to learn more.

'I remember asking Dad once. But he didn't want to talk about them.'

'It was all in the past.'

'But things have a habit of coming back, haunting us.'

Mair nodded. She looked up, her eyes watering.

'It was before I knew Tom.' Mair paused. 'We were married a long time and we were very happy. I want you to know that, Ian.'

It was the first time his mother had said anything like that. He had no idea how to respond. What else did she have to tell him?

'When your father was eighteen he left home. There was a terrible argument and your grandfather could be a very stubborn man. He also had a temper.'

Drake remembered a kindly old man, always wearing a waistcoat and a tweed shirt but he had a taciturn nature nurtured by a Nonconformist background.

'Your father mixed with a bad group of lads.'

His father had been in trouble with the police? Even a criminal record maybe. No wonder it hadn't been talked about.

'And he met an American girl.'

Now Drake's lips dried, his throat tightened slowly.

'She was quite a few years older and she was working at the university in Bangor. Your father didn't give me all the details. I didn't pry. After all, it was before I knew him.'

Mair glanced at Drake.

'Your father went to live with her in a flat in Bangor.'

His mother gazed up at him and he could see her measuring his reaction.

Drake imagined that his grandparents would have disapproved. It was a close-knit community after all. He had never thought of his parents as having a relationship with anyone else. It had never occurred to him to ask.

'What did she do at the university?'

'She was a postgraduate student. I think she studied English.'

'Why are you telling me this now?'

Mair returned to fidget with her mug. She lowered her voice, keeping her gaze fixed on a point on the table. 'She had a son.'

For a moment, Drake thought he had misheard.

Then the realisation struck him. 'What?'

'She and your father had a child together.'

Various conflicting emotions ran through Drake's mind. Anger that this family secret hadn't been shared, frustration with a mindset that wanted to conceal things.

Mair brushed away a tear.

'Why did nobody tell me?' Then he thought about

his sister, what she would think. 'Have you told Susan?'

Mair shook her head. 'I wanted to tell you first.'

A dozen questions came to Drake's mind. 'What happened after the baby was born? I mean, did Dad ever see the child? Why are you telling me this now?'

'After the baby was born your grandparents put a lot of pressure on your father. And his relationship with the baby's mother deteriorated. Your father grew up, realised he'd been foolish.' Mair paused. 'Your dad moved back home.'

They were talking about the child in anonymous terms. 'So do you know anything about the girl and the child?'

Another mournful glance.

'After your father left he had no contact with the woman or his son. He thought it was best at the time. Best for everyone. It had been a mistake. He didn't want to complicate the young boy's life.'

Mistake.

Drake was realising quickly that the father he knew was quite different from the man his mother portrayed.

'She moved away from Bangor. He got in touch about a year before your father died.'

'From America?'

A resigned, anxious look crossed Mair's face. 'She worked in a school in Llandudno.'

Drake stared blankly, scarcely able to believe what she was telling him.

'Your brother …' Mair continued. Drake blanked away the incredulity in his mind.

'Your brother made contact with your father after his mother passed. Before she died she had told him about his father. He wanted to try and establish a relationship. But with your father being ill it wasn't the best timing.'

'So did they meet?'

Mair nodded. 'Once, we met him in Llandudno.'

'So, how old is he? What was he like?'

'He's ten years older than you. His mother taught in a secondary school for years but she died of cancer. He has had his fair share of tragedy – he lost his wife recently too.'

'Recently?' Drake hadn't drunk any of his tea. 'You've spoken to him?'

'He's been in touch with me.'

Mair reached a hand over and touched Drake's wrist. 'He wants to meet you.'

He blurted out. 'Why the hell was this kept a secret? I had a right to know.'

Mair gave him a hurt look. 'Your father wanted to tell you. But I stopped him. It would have been too complicated. Your father was ill, I didn't want to upset him. I didn't want the past dragged up.'

'But there must be other people in the family who knew? So it can't exactly be a secret.'

Mair grasped the tea mug tightly.

'What is his name?'

'Huw Jackson.'

'This is all quite a surprise. It's all a bit hard to take in. What did he have in mind?'

'He wants to get to know you, that's what he said. He is going to be in one of the cafés in town at lunchtime.'

'Today?' Drake raised his voice.

'If you don't think the time is right then we can leave it.' Mair hurried her reply

No time was going to be right, Drake thought. So why not do it now? Meeting for lunch in a café – Huw Jackson was his brother after all. He rarely had contact with his sister apart from the occasional telephone call dominated by the diary of her children's hectic activities.

'I know how busy you are. But it was something I had to do. I've been feeling guilty that I didn't encourage your father in having contact with Huw. I realise now that I was wrong. I'm sorry, Ian. Will you forgive me?'

More conflicting emotions overwhelmed Drake, from discovering a half-brother to listening to his mother wanting to exonerate her behaviour from years ago – it was all difficult to take in.

'Lunchtime today?' Drake read the time on his watch. It was late morning already.

Mair gave him a pleading look and he knew that for her sake he had to agree.

Drake parked on the quayside just below the imposing castle walls and waited until he spotted his mother parking nearby. On the brief journey to Caernarfon he thought of all the questions he would have liked to have asked his father. He would have to tell Sian and perhaps even tell his daughters. He could imagine the exasperated reply from his sister and dreaded the possibility that his mother expected him to break the news to her. Not that it would make any difference, Drake thought; she was still going to be furious.

He left the car and joined his mother on the short walk to the centre of town. A crowd of American tourists stood by the statue of Lloyd George, the only Welshman to have been British prime minister, talking animatedly about how important he had been as a wartime leader. A street off the main square led down alongside the medieval walls and after a few yards Mair stopped in front of a café.

She took a deep breath. Then she pushed open the door and stepped in. Drake followed and in one corner, a man stood up, smiling. Drake's mother raised a brief hand in acknowledgement and nodded at Drake.

They stood to one side as a young girl carrying a plate of sandwiches hurried past them.

Mair was the first to reach the table. 'Nice to see you again, Huw.' He shook her warmly by the hand. 'This is Ian.'

They shook hands and Drake sat down.

'I'm sure this has been a surprise,' Huw said.

Huw's small eyes and a thin upper lip were just like Drake's father. He was taller than Drake by a good couple of inches and he still had a head of thick dark hair. There was a singsong lilt to his accent. Drake wasn't certain how to reply. What is the first thing you say to a brother you never knew existed?

'Mam just told me this morning.'

Huw smiled.

A waitress appeared at the table. Drake and his mother ordered sandwiches and tea.

'I've seen your face on television,' Huw continued. 'When those two officers were killed on the Crimea pass.' Huw was making conversation, finding things to say.

'Mam told me that you only found out about Dad a year or so before he died. What happened?' Drake said.

'My mother never talked about my dad. He was never discussed. I must have asked as a child but she always steered the discussion away from giving me any answers. But when she got cancer she realised it had been a mistake. She wanted to make amends somehow.'

Drake sensed his mother's embarrassment.

'Mam came to study English at Bangor University. That's when she met Tom.'

It was odd hearing this man talk about his father as Tom.

'She told me that she loved him very much but his family stood in the way.'

Drake wondered how his mother must feel listening to the description of another woman being in love with his father.

'Why didn't she go back to America?'

Huw shrugged. 'She never said, but I guessed that she wanted me to be brought up in Wales.'

A waitress left their sandwiches with a teapot.

Huw continued. 'Looking back, it was difficult growing up not knowing about your father. I feel a loss now more than I did when I was a boy. I suppose as we get older we value the things we've lost.'

The tea was too milky for Drake's taste so he pushed it to one side.

The café gradually emptied and Drake was conscious he had interrogated Huw. It's impossible to stop being a police officer, Drake thought. Questioning everyone's motive, trying to fathom out why people do certain things gets to be second nature.

Drake's mobile vibrated in his jacket pocket. He read the message for him to call headquarters.

'Perhaps you'd like to meet my family?' Huw said.

'I suppose so ...' Drake looked at his mother. She returned a warm smile.

An uncomfortable feeling crept into his mind that he didn't want to play happy families with a man claiming to be his brother. He wasn't going to make any commitments until he told his sister and Sian.

'In the future maybe,' Drake said. 'I'm separated so I'll need to talk to Sian, my wife. And we haven't spoken to Susan yet.'

Huw nodded. 'I understand.'

Drake's mobile bleeped again: another message,

another request to call. 'You'll have to excuse me.' Drake made for the door just as his mobile rang. 'Area control, sir, you're needed at a crime scene. A man's been murdered.'

Chapter 11

Drake almost tripped over the threshold as he went back into the café. He rushed over to the table where his mother sat with Huw.

'Something's come up. I've got to leave.'

He didn't wait for a reply and hurried for the door, jogging back to his car and dialling Sara. 'I've heard,' she said.

'I'm on my way now.'

'I'll meet you there.'

'I don't want anything done to the crime scene until I arrive. Nothing, do you understand?'

'Of course, sir.'

He was breathless by the time he reached the car. He thrust the mobile phone into the cradle and set up his hands-free. After he input the name of Llanrwst the satnav gave him two alternative routes. The first would take him through Llanberis, past Snowdon, and then over a narrow mountain road. The alternative was back along the A55 before turning south for the Conwy Valley. Deciding that the risk of heavy traffic on the dual carriageway might slow his journey, he chose the first route.

He powered around the edge of the castle, through one of the outer gates of the town walls and then out towards Llanberis. He had no police warning lights to help him clear the road but luckily the traffic was reasonably light. Minutes later he skirted round Llyn Padarn, noticing two small boats bobbing on the surface of the lake. He shot past the terminus of the Snowdon Mountain Railway and floored the accelerator. He reached the top of Pen Y Pass where walkers congregated around the youth hostel, either descending from the top of Snowdon or preparing for a hike.

Drake accelerated down the road cut into the steep sides of the mountain, heading for the Pen Y Gwryd Hotel where he turned left for Capel Curig. A couple of miles later he indicated left, taking a narrow road over the mountain that led down to Llanrwst. It was a gamble but he made good time.

At each corner, he prayed the road ahead would be clear, no caravans or dawdling vans transporting hill walkers. As he neared Llanrwst his mobile bleeped with the exact postcode of the property and he fiddled to punch it into the satnav while driving. In less than thirty minutes he had completed a journey that should have taken him forty.

He spotted the scientific support vehicle in the distance parked by the side of the road, two marked police cars behind it. He scanned for Sara's car but couldn't spot it. He pulled the nearside wheels onto the pavement and stopped the engine. He ran over to the house, carding the uniformed constable at the edge of the crime scene perimeter.

Sara and Mike Foulds were standing by the front door.

'Where is he?'

'In the sitting room,' Sara said.

She led Drake inside the large detached property. A thick Axminster carpet and heavy dark oak furniture in the hallway gave the place a quaint, old-fashioned feel. Drake snapped on a pair of latex gloves before entering. He stared over at the body of Rhisiart Hopkin sitting in an upright leather wing chair.

'Who found the body?' Drake said, taking in the scene.

'He has a housekeeper who comes in on a Saturday to do some of the laundry. She has a key. When she arrived she noticed the rear door had been forced.'

Hopkin had been stabbed several times. His head was slumped to one side, his mouth gaping open, eyes dull, staring blankly, the white shirt a blazing crimson. The more Drake stared the more he noticed the blood splattered over the walls and furniture. It had all the hallmarks of a vicious repeated assault. After the macabre crime scene earlier that week Drake wanted everything undisturbed until he could be present. He had spoken to Hopkin only a few days previously. It was too much of a coincidence not to be connected to the death of Gloria Patton. But this crime scene was completely different. A different *modus operandi*. A different killer?

'It looks like a burglary gone wrong,' Sara said.

Heavy wooden furniture filled the room, all sparklingly clean judging by the dust-free surface of a nearby table. Two bookcases occupied one entire wall with various encyclopaedia and book sets. A morning's broadsheet newspaper lay carefully folded on a table next to Hopkin.

'We'll need to see the housekeeper.'

'She lives in the town, sir. I've got her contact details.'

Drake paced over to Hopkin. The killer had been right there. He turned away and saw, at the rear of the room, a dining table. Noticing the place settings, Drake walked over. Three places had been set out and each place mat showed an image from a different capital city of Europe. The one of the canals of Amsterdam was the first to catch his attention. The cutlery looked unused and cotton napkins had been rolled carefully into silver rings.

'He must have been expecting guests,' Drake said.

'We could ask his housekeeper if she knows anything.'

Drake didn't reply. Laying a table for dinner so

early that morning struck him as odd.

The sound of movement distracted Drake so he turned. Foulds stood in the doorway, a white-suited crime scene investigator behind him.

'Seen enough, Ian?'

'I need a complete picture of everything. Photographs from every angle—'

'We have done this before and—'

'There has to be something here about …'

'Do you think it's the same person that killed Patton?'

Drake fixed his eyes back at Hopkin. The bank manager had seemed out of place in the rarefied and artificial world of the Orme Arts Festival. His world was company balance sheets, profit and loss accounts and making a decent return for his employer. Their support for the arts didn't include the risk of getting murdered. Every part of Hopkin's life would have to be examined: friends and family talked to.

Drake said to Foulds. 'Call me when you're done.' Then he detoured to the kitchen and found a CSI gathering glass shards scattered on the floor.

Drake registered the key in the inside lock just as Sara commented. 'He wasn't very security conscious by the look of things.'

Drake left the house, Sara following. A car pulled up as he drove away and in his rear-view mirror he saw the pathologist scampering up the drive.

Sara directed him to the address on the opposite side of town where the housekeeper lived. It was a bungalow at the end of a cul-de-sac of half a dozen properties, and Drake imagined the conversation she might have with her neighbours, sharing the details of how she discovered the body.

Once he had parked they left the car and hurried over to the front door.

'She's called Fiona Bakewell,' Sara said.

Drake pressed the bell and listened for movement after the chimes finished. There was a delay before he heard the sound of footsteps inside, his impatience building.

'Fiona Bakewell?' Drake said, holding up his warrant card.

The woman in the doorway had thinning silver hair, sunken cheeks and a pasty, off-white complexion. Drake guessed she was early seventies. He didn't wait for an invitation and stepped over the threshold. 'We need to talk to you about Rhisiart Hopkin.'

Bakewell appeared momentarily nonplussed but then she led them into a sitting room. The sofa and chairs must have been bought when she first set up home, Drake concluded from their worn and tatty appearance. Everywhere looked clean though and Drake approved of that. They sat down. What was left of the furniture springs groaned in protest.

He stared over intently at Bakewell. 'Tell me everything you know about Mr Hopkin.'

She blinked repeatedly, brushed away a tear.

Sara pitched in, keeping her voice low. 'It's important for us to build a complete picture of his life so we can work out what happened to him or who might be responsible.'

'I always do a couple of hours for him on a Saturday morning. He likes company. I think he's a bit lonely.'

'What do you do for him?'

'Cleaning, ironing – usual sort of stuff really. I've been with him for over fifteen years, ever since my husband died.'

'Does he have any family?'

She shook her head. 'His mother died about ten years ago. But I've never heard him talk about any brothers or sisters and he's never been married. Well, not that I'm aware.'

'Does he have any friends? People who might know him better?'

She bowed her head. 'He seemed to be very busy with things. He was an important man in the bank.'

'Do you have a key to his house?'

She nodded.

'So what time did you let yourself into the property this morning?'

'Just after nine. The back door was open but one of the panes was broken so I knew something was wrong. I called out and usually he'd be around, pottering, finishing breakfast. But I didn't hear anything. Nobody replied. I got really worried and then I went into the sitting room and … there he was. I was almost sick, I rushed out.'

She swallowed hard and leant back in her chair.

Drake paused.

'Who would do such a thing?' Fiona added.

'Did he ever complain about anybody?' Drake said. 'Mention anyone that might have a grudge against him?'

Bakewell didn't reply; she found a tissue from a box on the table and blew her nose.

'Never, he was a nice man.'

'Does anyone visit the house regularly?'

She covered her face with both hands before rubbing the back of her neck. Drake frowned, and gave Sara a brief glance; she had noticed Bakewell's discomfort too. He softened his tone now. 'It's very important, Fiona, if you can give us full details of anything and anyone that might be of relevance. The dining table was laid for three people. Did he entertain? Maybe a husband and wife?'

She shook her head. 'He did have a couple of

friends. He called them *lady* friends. I don't know who they were, though.'

'Did you see any of them?'

She glanced up, tight-lipped. 'One Saturday morning I saw somebody getting into a car as I was arriving. I didn't say anything, of course. It wasn't my place.'

'Would you be able to describe her?'

Fiona gave a non-committal shrug.

Walking back to the car, Sara looked at Drake. 'What did you make of her, sir?'

'Not much help.'

'She was upset. It might be better to speak to her again when she is more composed.'

Drake opened the door. 'Let's get back to headquarters.'

Drake spent the rest of that Saturday in a blur of activity, knowing the first twenty-four hours after a murder were crucial. He stalked around the Incident Room barking orders, shouting instructions down the telephone to the uniformed officers doing preliminary house-to-house inquiries. It frustrated him that no senior member of the bank was available until Monday to discuss Rhisiart Hopkin's current workload. The meeting with Huw Jackson crept into his thoughts occasionally and he made a mental note to call his mother.

He couldn't ignore the possibility that he was dealing with the same killer. But nothing suggested the scene had been staged with the same theatricality. As Sara had speculated, it looked exactly like a break-in that had gone wrong. But Drake didn't like coincidences. He kept bringing back to mind his discussion with Rhisiart Hopkin a few days previously. He would need a lot more than coincidence to be able to link both deaths together.

By late in the afternoon the crime scene investigators delivered various photographs that Winder pinned to a separate board erected alongside the one dedicated to Gloria Patton. The differences were stark. Hopkin's bloodied figure sat on the chair in an ordinary pose. The furniture surrounding him was unremarkable. Drake moved his attention from one to another, ignoring the activity from the team behind him.

Luned came to stand alongside Drake. 'Do you think they're connected, sir?'

Drake cleared his throat. 'Somebody had a motive to kill Rhisiart Hopkin.' He turned to look at the young officer. She and Winder wore casual clothes. Drake hadn't changed from the jeans and check shirt he'd worn to visit his mother and he felt uncomfortable at his lack of formality in the Incident Room.

Drake looked over at Winder. 'Have we recovered his mobile telephone? What about a computer or laptop?' Winder opened his mouth to reply but Drake continued. 'We'll need details of his diary. I want to establish what his movements were and requisition details about his bank account.'

'I spoke to the CSI team earlier, boss,' Winder said. 'They promised to get me a list of everything they've removed from the crime scene first thing in the morning.'

'Tomorrow morning? Why the hell can't they do it tonight?'

Winder made no reply.

'Take a detailed statement from Fiona Bakewell. And find out when a photofit of the woman Bakewell saw can be organised.'

It was late into the evening by the time Drake finally excused the officers in his team. None of them blanched when he told them to reassemble at nine am tomorrow. He sat at his desk scanning the various Post-it notes and had begun tidying his desk when his mobile rang. His mother sounded concerned.

'I've just heard about that awful incident in Llanrwst.'

His mother had a healthy interest in gossip although Drake had explained many times that he couldn't discuss cases, no matter how much publicity they garnered. 'I'm sorry I had to leave quickly this morning. There was nothing I could do.'

'Of course. What did you think of Huw?'

Clearly, she wanted to gauge his reaction. She seemed to be blaming herself for preventing his father from making contact with Huw over the years. Perhaps she needed reassurance that she was doing the right thing, making amends.

'I was pleased to meet him.'

'Perhaps we can meet up again; he'd like to see more of the family.'

'You need to tell Susan.'

She paused; the silence spoke volumes. 'Yes … I know.'

'You can't avoid it, Mam.'

Drake heard her breathing down the telephone. His sister wasn't the easiest of personalities and he could imagine her overbearing reaction. Having a half-brother wouldn't fit into her circle of Rotary Club friends and dinner parties in the posh suburbs of Cardiff.

'Talk to her tomorrow. I'll speak to Sian as well.'

Drake made no commitment to see Huw again even though he knew it was what his mother wanted. Her call had interrupted his concentration. In reality it was a welcome distraction as otherwise he might have stayed at his desk for longer, persuading himself he had to check and recheck the paperwork and get his desk neat.

On his journey home, he stopped to buy a takeaway curry, making the same choice as he always did. Back in his flat, he found a Joe Bonamassa album on his iTunes and let the guitar hero's chords fill the kitchen as he spooned chicken masala onto a plate. He tore at a naan bread and drank a bottle of lager, forcing his mind to relax. But the image of Hopkin in his chair wheedled its way to the forefront of his mind. Knowing that Roger Buckland had been responsible for a vicious attack as a young man made him an obvious suspect. Drake told himself he had to switch off but the events that morning with his mother and Huw Jackson reminded him that even his father had secrets. Were there more, Drake wondered?

Chapter 12

Despite all the activity yesterday I had slept well. There is something refreshing about making progress, completing the next stage in a plan. Moving forward with my career is about the only thing that gives me focus these days. Enough focus to make everything worthwhile. Seeing the police officers scurrying around my installation had been part of that process, an essential component in sharing my art. Soon, a much greater audience will enjoy my work. This is the important thing about great art: it has to be seen and enjoyed by as many people as possible.

I joined middle-aged couples strolling along the Llandudno promenade that Sunday morning, feeling the warmth of the spring sunshine on my face. As it was north facing it avoided the harsh prevailing winds from the south-west. I took my time, smiling to myself as I pondered my achievement. A woman on a motorised wheelchair buzzed past me but most of the walkers kept a sedate pace.

I swaggered a little, thinking about the sort of comments art historians would make. Nobody could doubt the authenticity of my work from now on or question my rightful place. I stopped to watch families playing on the beach. Two youngsters were building a sandcastle using plastic pots with slots in the bottom that they filled with damp sand. They squealed with delight when they upturned the buckets and the shape of four turrets appeared. Looking down the beach I noticed the tide was already turning. Their sandcastle would be gone in a few hours, it would be a transient memory, lingering from childhood. Permanent things, reminders of work that could be viewed repeatedly offered the only way to fix humanity with great art.

There had to be permanence, a sense of destiny.

Not something subject to the fleeting tides of fashion. That was the challenge: extending the boundaries of how we perceive ourselves as human beings, living together, exposing our frailties.

At the end of the promenade, the lifeboat was being launched for what looked like a regular drill, judging by the lack of urgency among the crew. I paused and watched as the tractor with enormous wheels pushed a cage carrying the lifeboat down into the water. The crew fired the engine into life and it roared away. A small crowd gathered, mostly older retired couples, judging by the blue rinse hairdos and the occasional walking stick.

Perhaps some of them had paused by the shop window when the curtain had fallen. More people should have experienced the installation, of course, and I cursed silently when I thought I hadn't been able to disguise her properly. Somebody had noticed her condition. I became lightheaded, my chest tightened.

Then I realised I was standing on my own.

Some of the lifeboat crew, probably mechanics or volunteers, stood around chatting, killing time. Hurrying away from the promenade I found a café and treated myself to a slice of Victoria sponge with my latte. My work in the past few days had been the culmination of weeks of planning so I felt quite justified in my self-congratulatory indulgence. Eating the cake and drinking the coffee cheered me up too.

After paying, I cut back into the town and discreetly walked past the shop. There was a certain symmetry to the notices plastered on the wooden sheets that covered the glass. But it was a crime scene no one could enter.

Some hooligan had actually spray-painted an indistinguishable image on one of the wooden boards. That gave me a real buzz. My work was being appreciated, enhanced and enlarged. So I needed a record. I dipped into my fleece pocket for my mobile telephone. I crossed over the road, wanting to avoid any possibility that someone might notice me taking a photograph. I fiddled with my phone, ensuring it was ready to take photographs. I even practised walking along holding the camera discreetly by my side, pressing the exposure button. Once I mastered this simple technique I ambled past the shop, snapping away. Back in my car I examined the various images.

I was pleased, really pleased – they were all suitable for me to add to my collection. I still had to catalogue the images from *his* place yesterday. It was one of those other tasks I would have to plan.

I started the car, my mind refreshed from my walk.

Now I had to get back and plan my next installation.

Chapter 13

Drake woke with a jolt. The image of Rhisiart Hopkin sitting in his leather wing chair flooded back to his mind. He had to assume his death was connected to Gloria Patton's even if the preliminary results from the crime scene suggested otherwise. The sound of a baby crying in one of the adjacent flats and then the noise from a television interrupted his rumination. It reminded him of his promise to take Helen and Megan bowling and then for pizza that afternoon. He realised it would be impossible and he dreaded the negative comments from Sian. But now he had another reason to call her, and somehow he had to tell her about Huw Jackson. He reached over for his watch and scanned the time; he would ring her after breakfast before leaving the flat.

After showering, he chose a pair of sombre navy chinos with a dark jacket and a powder blue shirt. His concession to the informality of working on a Sunday went as far as not wearing a tie. He walked through to the kitchen and reached for the coffee. After some experimentation he had discovered that eighteen grams was the precise amount he needed to make a perfect Americano from his machine. He organised a bowl of muesli as the coffee dripped into a mug. He listened to the Welsh language bulletin on the radio – a brief piece referred to the discovery of a body in a house in Llanrwst with confirmation that the Wales Police Service were issuing a full statement later that day. It meant the PR department would be after him that morning.

He finished his breakfast and stared at his mobile on the table.

He reached over and called Sian. She sounded sleepy. 'What time is it?'

'I'm sorry to call so early.'

'You're seeing the girls later this afternoon?'

'That's why I am calling.'

'Oh.'

Sian was the only person Drake knew that could combine menace and criticism with a threatening undertone into a single word.

'Something's come up.'

Now she managed an exasperated tone. 'Nothing changes.'

'I was working until late last night and I'll be at headquarters most of the day.'

'Are you talking about that woman found in the shop? It sounded dreadful.'

Oddly, Drake began to feel relieved as she sounded sympathetic.

'I won't be able to take Helen and Megan this afternoon. But I'll come over and see them later. There's something I need to discuss too.'

'If this is about the house and any of the financial stuff then I don't think—'

'No, I saw Mam yesterday. She ... well, it's best we talk later.'

An embarrassed few seconds of silence followed; Drake wasn't certain what to say next or how he was going to start the conversation with Sian that evening.

'What time will you be calling? I might take the girls out myself. They were looking forward to seeing you.'

She drew out the words of the last sentence, emphasising the guilt Drake felt when his work interfered with family. 'I'll call you later.'

He ended the call, gathered his jacket and car keys and left the apartment. Adhering to his rituals meant he bought a newspaper, completed a few squares of the Sudoku puzzle and then drove off to headquarters.

Sara woke early, determined to have a clear mind when she arrived at work that morning. So after some basic warm-up exercises on the patio area at the back of her house she started running just before seven-thirty am. She kept a gentle pace for the first ten minutes until she got her breathing right. Then she adjusted the length of her stride as her body relaxed into the rhythm she needed.

After five years as a detective constable her promotion to detective sergeant had filled her with pride. The only drawback had been some comments from other officers that Ian Drake was a miserable individual. But the sergeant she had worked with told her he was a good detective, determined and thorough. Drake's handling of a case involving the deaths of two police officers was still talked about in revered terms by the detectives of Northern Division. Her first day on his team had been burnt into her subconscious, barely giving her time to get to know her superior officer. No matter how hard she tried to shake off the image of Gloria Patton standing upright in the shop premises, the crime scene still dominated her mind. She felt she had let herself down at the post-mortem. She was a detective now; this was the life she wanted and blood and guts would be a part of it.

Still, it worried her that she hadn't been able to switch off the evening before and wondered if it happened to every detective.

She decided on a route that took her out of the village into the countryside with narrow lanes lined with thick hedges. Occasionally a car passed and a group of cyclists met her as she slowed her journey on one of the steep ascents. She stopped when she reached the brow of a hill and, pausing, looked down at the coastal area and out towards the windfarms dotted over the horizon.

She had googled *psychopath* the previous evening, reading a simple article accompanied by various images that explained the steps used to identify the disorder. She had no expert basis for suggesting Gloria Patton's killer was a psychopath and regretted it soon after saying it. Drake probably thought she had overreacted. The sheer coldblooded audacity of the way Gloria's body had been staged suggested a level of depravity that frightened her. She had even clicked onto the Hare Psychopathy Checklist, reading all about the symptoms of a psychopath. By midnight her eyes burnt and she went to bed praying she would sleep.

A car rounded a corner nearby and sounded its horn. Sara set off again and soon found the exercise was doing her good. She settled into a steady rhythm, managing her breathing effectively by the time she finished eight miles. Back home she completed a routine of stretches and lunges that helped her body recover and warm down. Once showered and caffeinated she left for headquarters.

Winder and Luned were sitting by their desks when Drake walked into the Incident Room.

Luned wore a pair of denim jeans with a pale green blouse, no make-up. The occasional streak of grey in her thick hair made her look older. Winder had tidied his appearance over the past few months, a result Drake put down to a live-in girlfriend. It meant his blue striped shirt was neater than usual, although Winder hadn't shaved that morning.

'Good morning, boss,' Winder said.

Drake looked around the Incident Room. 'Any sign of Sara?'

Winder and Luned shook their heads.

Drake paced over to the board, staring at the various images from Hopkin's home. 'I want both of you coordinating the house-to-house enquiries in Llanrwst this morning. Sara and I spoke to Hopkin's housekeeper yesterday. We'll need a detailed statement from her. And we need to go through all of Hopkin's possessions at the house – make sure we aren't missing something there.'

As Drake finished, the door into the Incident Room opened. Mike Foulds followed Sara inside and their discussion drifted into silence as they saw Drake and the other two officers.

'Sorry I'm late,' Sara said.

Drake mumbled an acknowledgement.

'I thought you'd like to see these,' Foulds said, holding up a plastic evidence pouch with two mobile telephones inside. 'We found them in Hopkin's place. They've been dusted and examined for DNA. You can access them without pin numbers.'

Drake stared at the handsets. 'Why would he have two?'

Foulds shrugged.

'Anything else from the crime scene? Any fingerprints?'

'Lots of prints. The vast majority belonged to Rhisiart Hopkin of course. There were others unknown as yet, and a few partials too. One set in particular was all over the place. Did someone clean for him?'

Drake nodded.

'We'll get the results processed later today.'

'Get back to me as soon as you can.'

Foulds left, quickly followed by Winder and Luned. Drake returned to his office and Sara joined him, sitting in one of the visitor chairs. He scanned the room, pleased nothing seemed to have been moved from the night before. He opened the plastic evidence pouch and emptied the contents onto his desk.

'My guess is one of these is for work,' Drake said.

Both mobiles were modern smartphones. Drake handed Sara an iPhone. 'I suggest you work on this one.'

She trooped off. Drake switched on the remaining handset. He turned his attention back to the large display of the iPhone. He surveyed the various icons and apps. There were symbols for three different weather forecasting applications, a typical British fascination, Drake thought.

He turned to the text messages Hopkin had received and sent. They were ordinary, day-to-day banter about football scores, arrangements for him to see friends, reminders about meetings – Drake noticed a series of messages from Gloria Patton. He knew that each one would have to be transcribed, checked and referenced against Patton's own telephone.

It hadn't occurred to him until mid-morning that he might have expected a message with the #Iamtheone. Suddenly, he froze. If it was the same killer then surely one of the phones would have such a message?

'Sara,' he called out. 'Have you seen any messages with hashtag Iamtheone?'

Moments later she appeared in his office doorway. 'The mobile I've got is the one from the bank. It's messages from his superiors in the Cardiff head office and then messages from him to his juniors.'

'Download all the details. We can ask the bank about Hopkin's work.'

Sara returned to her desk and Drake carried on scanning the messages, looking for something to link Hopkin to the death of Gloria Patton. He noticed the names of the two committee members he had met and wasted time reading the banal exchange about dates and times of meetings. A record of messages always helped an inquiry, although Drake had found too often that compromising messages were deleted. Hopkin had kept dozens going back several months. He probably didn't know how to delete them, Drake thought.

He made a list of everybody who had called Hopkin in the last seven days – contacting them all meant hours of work. Drake laboured for the rest of the day using different-coloured highlighters to build a picture of Hopkin's friends and colleagues and also trying to establish what the bank manager had been doing the day before he was killed. A call to one of Hopkin's colleagues established that he had spent Friday afternoon compiling his regular weekly report to the bank's head office. Hopkin had made three calls on his mobile on Friday evening and Drake spoke to each person in turn. But they told him nothing to help the inquiry – one had been about the railway society Hopkin belonged to and another about the arrangements for a walking club's monthly hike. None of his friends had ever been for dinner nor did they know who might have been the guests.

Drake stalked around the Incident Room staring at the images on the board. Reports from the house-to-house team in Llanrwst proved a distraction although the lack of any eyewitness evidence added to his frustration.

It was early evening by the time Drake parked outside the house he had called home for many years. Sian's BMW was in her usual place. He noticed the lawn had been cut and immediately he wanted to know who was cutting the grass for his soon-to-be ex-wife. It had been something he had done and enjoyed mostly.

He pressed the front door bell and heard Sian's footsteps.

'I expected you much earlier.' She turned and went back inside the house.

She wore a pair of her expensive trousers that accentuated her slim build. Helen and Megan ran from the sitting room when they realised Drake had arrived and he hugged them both. 'Look, I'm really sorry about today.'

'Is it an important murder case?' Helen said.

'You know I can't tell you.'

'Dad.' She had inherited her mother's ability to inject a single word with enormous meaning.

'I need to speak to Mam.'

'Are you going to read to us later?'

'Of course.'

Drake went through into the kitchen and found Sian preparing her evening meal. There wasn't an invitation for him to join her.

'Coffee?'

He shook his head. 'Look, I'll keep this brief. I saw Mam yesterday. She's been wanting to discuss something with me for a while.' He kept his tone serious, matter-of-fact and it had the desired effect; Sian sat down at the pine table. She stared over at him intently.

'It was about Dad.'

'Are there problems with the legal papers?'

'No, that's straightforward enough.'

Sian threaded the fingers of both hands together and leant forward slightly on the table.

'Mam told me stuff about Dad I never knew. It came as a complete shock.'

'Get on with it, Ian.'

He gave her a sharp, reproachful look. 'She told me Dad left home at eighteen and started a relationship with an American woman. She was a lot older than him and my Nain and Taid disapproved – apparently there were blazing arguments between Dad and Taid.'

Sian crossed her arms and raised her eyebrows.

'They had a child, a boy.'

Sian's mouth fell open in disbelief.

'Tom was a father when he was eighteen?'

'I know, it is hard to believe.'

'So why haven't you been told about this before? Your family are useless about sharing personal details. They are so secretive and why did she tell you this now? The man involved must be in his fifties by now. Does your mother know where he lives in the States?'

'I met him yesterday.'

'What!' Sian's chair squeaked against the tiled floor as she sat upright.

'He lives in Llandudno.'

'I don't believe this. You've got a brother in Llandudno?'

'He wants to meet more of the family.'

'Don't be stupid. You don't know anything about this man. Have you thought about checking him out? Having a DNA test done? And what is it he wants? After all these years. I don't think it's fair on your mother. You're definitely not involving the girls in any of this.'

Drake floundered, uncertain how to respond. Sian continued. 'What does your sister think? I can imagine she would tell you to have nothing to do with him.'

'Mam hasn't told her yet.'

'Now she is completely mad. She needs to tell Susan straightaway.' Sian stood up, walked over to the worktop, and flicked on the electric kettle. 'What's his name? Is he Drake too?'

'Huw Jackson.'

As he said his brother's surname Drake sensed that he had recently heard the name -Geraint Wood had mentioned a Jackson being involved with Gloria Patton. Drake knew exactly what he was doing the following morning.

Chapter 14

'There's someone to see you, Inspector.' The woman behind reception smirked and tilted her head towards the faux leather sofas nearby. Drake glanced over. 'She's been waiting for half an hour.'

Although it was a Monday morning, Drake felt as though it were midweek already.

He walked over, stretching out a hand. 'Good morning. Detective Inspector Ian Drake.'

'Jeremy said you wanted to see me. I'm sorry, I should introduce myself. I'm Valerie Reed, Jeremy's girlfriend.'

The husky voice matched the blonde hair styled into swirls that suggested it had been cut randomly but in reality had been carefully constructed. The eyelashes were heavy and almost as long as the artificial nails painted a bright red that grazed Drake's skin as they shook hands. Ellingham's neighbour described her as a film star. It was probably what the old man thought such a person might look like.

Drake led Valerie Reed to one of the conference rooms and waved a hand at a chair around the table. The red dress she wore seemed to float around her and the high heels gave her legs a sculpted appearance.

'We are investigating the murder of Gloria Patton.' Drake sat down; Valerie did the same.

Valerie nodded. 'It's all very sad.'

Drake continued with his preamble. 'Jeremy's name came up as a person of interest because work he submitted to the Orme Arts Festival was rejected by her.'

Valerie tilted her head and gave Drake a concerned look. 'Yes, I know. He was very surprised and angry, poor thing. It affected him really badly.'

'We're looking into everybody associated with Gloria Patton and her life. So I need to be able to establish Jeremy's movements on the night Gloria Patton was killed.'

Valerie crossed her left leg over the right knee and smoothed the folds of her dress as she did so. 'That's easy. We were together during the evening and ...' she paused. 'All night.' She lowered her voice just a notch, making it even huskier.

It confirmed what Ellingham's neighbour had told him.

'How long have you been in a relationship with Jeremy Ellingham?'

'Almost two years now.'

'What do you do for a living, Miss Reed?'

'I'm a graphic designer. I have my own business, which means I can work from home.'

'What does that work entail?'

'I design letterhead and brochures.'

Nothing to link her conclusively to either murder, Drake thought.

'I'll need your contact details, Miss Reed, in case we have any more questions for you.'

'Of course,' Valerie purred, before dictating her number.

'And your address?'

'You can reach me at Jeremy's place.'

Drake's mobile buzzed and he fished it out of his jacket pocket, sending Superintendent Price's call to voicemail; he would return the call once he was finished. Realising that Ellingham had an alibi for Patton's death and knowing he had other priorities that morning, he cut the interview with Valerie short. Winder or Luned could be delegated to take a more detailed statement. He stood up.

'Thanks for your time.'

From reception, he watched her leave headquarters. He rang Price, who sounded business-like. 'I'm going out this morning. But I want an update when I'm back this afternoon. I want the latest on these two murders. Are they connected, Ian? Have we got some insane serial killer stalking the streets?'

Drake was accustomed to the occasional rant from his superior officer.

Price didn't wait for him to reply. 'Call Hannah to arrange a time.'

After Price finished the call Drake took the stairs to the Incident Room and noticed the inquisitive glances from Sara and Winder; Luned stared at her computer monitor.

'Jeremy Ellingham's girlfriend was waiting in reception.' Drake walked up to the board. He moved Ellingham's photograph to one side, rearranging the various images. 'She confirmed what Ellingham's neighbour told us.'

'Does that mean he's no longer a person of interest, sir?' Sara said.

'I still want a full background check but he's got an alibi.' He peered at the other faces. 'Let's concentrate on Buckland and Geraint Wood.'

Drake turned back to the team, looking over at Winder and Luned. 'Did you make any progress with the house-to-house near Hopkin's place?'

'Nothing, sir,' Winder said. 'He just seemed normal, a single middle-aged bloke. Some of the neighbours knew him quite well. Others were nodding acquaintances only.'

Drake continued. 'The housekeeper says he had *lady* friends that visited him. She saw someone leaving one Saturday morning. So concentrate on identifying who they might be.'

An hour later Drake and Sara were heading towards the council offices in Llandudno. It occurred to him as he drove that he should explain to Sara his suspicion that Huw Jackson might be the person named by Geraint Wood. But it meant sharing with her personal details about his family. And that wasn't easy. In any event he had nothing to confirm Jackson *was* implicated so Drake decided to say nothing about him.

They drove on to the council offices where Drake parked near the old rambling building that stood overlooking the West Shore beach. In the distance, Drake could see Conwy Castle and the medieval town alongside it.

Drake showed his ID to the receptionist, asking for the manager of the human resources department. Moments later a woman emerged into reception, a fierce but frightened look on her face. She was mid-forties, with short, shocking-turquoise hair. 'How can I help you?'

'We need to establish the identity of some people who work for the council.'

She led them through a maze of corridors until eventually she reached an office. A small metal plaque on the door said 'Principal Officer'. She sat at her desk, pointed to two chairs in front of her and started clicking with her mouse.

'What information did you want?'

'Does the council employ someone called Maxwell?'

'Christian name?'

'That's his Christian name, we don't know the surname.'

She squinted at the screen. 'There's a Maxwell Owen in finance.' She scribbled down the contact details. 'Anyone else?'

'Jackson – that's probably the surname.'

Drake expected an inquisitive glare, querying how he knew. But the woman just kept on clicking. 'There are two. Huw Jackson works in the economic development and public support department. There's a Jane Jackson in environmental health.'

She dictated the contact numbers for each of the employees named. After thanking her they made their way back to reception where Drake spoke to Sara. 'We'll start with Maxwell Owen.' At least it meant he could postpone having to explain to Sara about Huw Jackson for a little longer.

One of the staff dialled Maxwell's direct number and Drake heard her explaining that two police officers wanted to speak to him. She rolled her eyes at Drake and Sara as she listened to Maxwell. Eventually she said, 'I think you'd better come down to reception.'

Maxwell was well over six feet tall with an enormous thick beard. His thin blue shirt strained at the bulk around his shoulders, arms and stomach. There were large damp patches under his armpits and a tang of sweat and body odour. Drake and Sara followed Maxwell to a nearby conference room that was hot and airless. Maxwell fiddled to open a window, then sat down across the table from Drake and Sara.

'We're investigating the death of Gloria Patton,' Drake said.

He nodded. 'What's that got to do with me?'

'I understand the council support the Orme Arts Festival.'

'The council support a lot of things.'

'Just tell me about *your* involvement with the festival.' Drake knew he sounded irritated. He wanted straight answers, quickly.

'I was the finance officer. We told Gloria exactly the extent of the financial support we could give. We're not a charity, Inspector. She had to manage our grant and then get match funding from other bodies in order to make the festival a success.'

'How often did you meet with her or the committee?'

'I met her once and she was really difficult. You should talk to the officer who actually coordinated the grant.'

Drake waited for Maxwell to confirm who was responsible.

'Huw Jackson did all the groundwork.' Apprehension at the prospect his brother was involved filled Drake's mind. Maxwell continued. 'He attended all the meetings. But once she had my name and my email address, I got bombarded with copies of minutes and business plans. It was nothing to do with me.'

'Do you remember when you actually met?'

Maxwell rolled his eyes. 'I would have to check. I can't possibly remember that sort of detail. Speak to Huw about her.'

Drake nodded.

Maxwell reached for the telephone on the table. 'I'll call him now. Then perhaps you'll leave me in peace.'

Drake and Sara listened to Maxwell tracking down Huw Jackson to the office of a colleague. 'There are cops from the WPS here who need to speak to you. Get down here now. I've got work to do.'

Maxwell stood up. 'You can wait here. Hopefully he won't be long.'

After Maxwell left, Drake had to say something to Sara. 'I know this Huw Jackson. We met on Saturday.'

Sara tilted her head to one side, raising her eyebrows. But Drake paused, got up and walked around the desk staring out of the window, letting the fresh air cool his face. They didn't have to wait long until Huw entered.

'Hello, Ian. Nice to see you again.'

Drake returned to sit alongside Sara as Huw took the seat Maxwell had vacated.

'I heard about Rhisiart Hopkin last night. It was on the news this morning. Are you involved in that case? It's terrible.'

'I wanted to speak to you about Gloria Patton.'

'Do you think both deaths are linked?' Jackson leant forward over the table. 'I met him a couple of times and he was a really nice man. Have you any idea who killed him?'

'The WPS are going to be issuing a statement later today about his murder.' Drake used a formal dismissive tone and continued. 'I understand you were responsible for coordinating with Gloria Patton about the Orme Arts Festival.'

'I administered the council's grant.'

'Would the festival have survived without the council's contribution?'

'Unlikely.'

'When did you see Gloria Patton last?'

Jackson hesitated, averting his eyes. 'Last week. We had a meeting. It was .... unscheduled. She wanted to see if the council was prepared to increase its contribution.'

'What was the reason for that?'

'She mentioned financial problems around the cost of setting up the various exhibits. Getting the artists to agree fees, etc.'

Sara stopped scribbling in her notepad and looked up at Jackson. 'So what did you say?'

Jackson raised his eyebrows. 'That there was no chance of any additional funding.'

'We'll need to see any documents that you've got relating to the festival.'

'Of course. I'll send them over.'

'And all the emails and correspondence from the council.'

Jackson nodded. 'Her paperwork was pretty chaotic. The festival was supported by one of the local councillors. He thought it would raise the profile of Llandudno, develop the art scene. Bring in more visitors.'

'Did you agree?'

'Not up to me, Ian. The business plan Gloria submitted initially was completely inadequate. We had to send it back to her, suggest amendments.'

Drake peered over at Jackson. It was an odd sensation knowing this man was his half-brother. Sian's exasperated comments from the day before, challenging him about Jackson's authenticity, raised doubts in his mind.

'So what was the nature of your relationship with Gloria Patton?'

Jackson frowned. 'What do you mean?'

'Just that. Did you meet socially?'

Jackson crossed his arms over his chest. 'We did meet a couple of times away from either the formal setting of the council offices or her gallery. They were minuted, of course.'

'Where did you meet?' Drake's voice sounded sharp.

'In the one of the cafés in town—'

'Did you ever meet her at her home?'

'No, of course not. Don't be absurd.'

'Did you know where she lived?'

Jackson paused again. Drake barely knew this man, but instinctively he wanted to trust him, despite there being something evasive about his replies. The fact they might share the same father didn't mean he was going to treat him to any less scrutiny than any other person. They needed a complete picture of

Gloria's life and Jackson knew her. It was a matter of finding out how well.

'I've got her address somewhere I suppose. What are you trying to establish?'

Sara butted in. 'We need to learn everything about Gloria and anything you could tell us about her might help.'

Jackson glared over at Sara. 'Well, quizzing me about her isn't going to help. Do you think someone connected to the council or the festival had anything to do with her death?'

'We're looking at everyone who had contact with her. It's routine.' Sara's emollient tone managed to make Drake's interrogation sound plausible.

Abruptly Drake stood up. 'Send everything you've got to us, Huw.'

Jackson scanned the details on the card that Drake thrust at him. Drake left with Sara and trudged back to his car. The whole meeting had disturbed him. He found himself on edge. He liked order and Jackson's wish to get to know him better, meet the family, was unnerving.

They reached Drake's car. 'You gave him a hard time, sir. Do you suspect he might be involved?'

Drake pointed the remote at the car. It thudded open.

'I thought you knew him?'

Drake jumped into the car and looked over at Sara. No point delaying the inevitable.

'I met him Saturday for the first time. He claims to be my half-brother.'

Drake read the stunned look on Sara's face easily enough.

Chapter 15

Drake appeared more sullen than usual as they drove away from the council offices. He cursed a couple of times at dawdling cars even though they were still in the thirty miles per hour speed restriction limit. Sara grabbed hold of the door handle tightly when Drake shot out in front of a car on a roundabout near the junction for the A55. Something was troubling Drake, so she decided on the direct approach.

'So you didn't know Jackson might be your brother until Saturday?'

Drake glared through the windscreen, his eyes narrowed. Sharing this information must have been difficult, Sara thought, but he had no alternative.

'Yes, that's right. It has all come as a surprise. My father had ...' Drake blasted the car horn at a van ahead of them on the slip road. Then he floored the accelerator. Heading east on the dual carriageway he slowed as they reached the speed restrictions near Colwyn Bay before speeding up again. A few minutes passed silently, Sara wondering what else she could say, until Drake indicated for the business park and the area office of the bank that employed Rhisiart Hopkin.

Sara pondered what it might feel like to discover you have a half-sibling you knew nothing about. It might be quite interesting, rather exotic.

Expensive German saloons, all under two years of age, filled the car park. Drake found a slot for visitors and switched off the engine. He turned to Sara. 'It has all come as a surprise.'

'Of course.'

'We don't know anything about Jackson really.'

'Do you think he is involved with Gloria Patton in some way?'

Drake looked perplexed, as though he was

struggling to find an answer.

Sara continued. 'He did sound evasive. Perhaps he had a relationship with Gloria and she threatened to tell his wife. Is he married?'

'Widowed.'

Sarah frowned. 'Then we treat him like a person of interest, someone to help in the inquiry. But if he is involved, why the macabre crime scene?'

Drake reached for the door handle and left the car. The business park was a modern collection of purpose-built offices. Sara followed him towards the building the bank shared with a marketing agency that occupied the ground floor. They took the stairs to the first floor. Workstations filled the open-plan office with employees staring at flickering screens. A woman nearby looked over before leaving her desk and walking over to them. The bank's logo was stitched into the fabric of her cream blouse, and her skirt, a neutral blue, matched the corporate colour scheme.

'Can I help?'

Drake flashed his warrant card; Sara did likewise.

'We have a meeting with Roger Finch.'

'Please wait – I'll tell him you're here.' She tilted her head at the upright visitor chairs behind Drake and Sara. They sat down and waited. Sara wondered if every bank had offices as anonymous as this one. She looked around and saw the woman who had spoken to them deep in conversation with a man who shot an urgent glance at them. Moments later, he strode over, carrying various files and sheaves of paper.

Roger Finch had a healthy stock of red hair. He kept it fashionably short, the edges of his hair trimmed close to the skin. Finch peered down at them after they stood up. Sara noticed the vigorous handshake he gave Drake before he did the same to her.

'Come this way.' He waved over to a door with

'Conference Room' in large letters printed on a stainless steel sign. Inside, the room was cool, the cream walls bare. Finch gestured at the plastic chairs surrounding the table. Drake ran a finger along the table's surface before sitting down.

'This is the most dreadful news about Rhisiart.'

'How well did you know him?' Drake asked.

'He was a work colleague.'

'And away from work? Did you know anything about his private life?'

'Very little.' Finch pushed a buff folder over the table. 'This is a copy of his personnel file. It has all the relevant details on Rhisiart.'

'Does he have any family?'

'I don't think so.'

Drake reached over and flicked through the paperwork. It gave Sara an opportunity to ask her first question. 'Who were his closest work colleagues?'

'This is a small office. We all knew each other quite well.'

'But you don't know anything about his family.'

Finch shrugged. Sara persevered. 'Did he ever discuss his personal life? For example, did he mention whether he ever went to football games, support a particular team?'

'Sorry ...'

'Does the bank have any connection with the Orme Arts Festival?'

'We were providing a modest amount of sponsorship, no more than a few thousand pounds. The public relations department in headquarters approved it all. It's part of the bank's policy to raise its profile in the community.'

Drake closed the folder and looked over at Finch. 'We will need all the records of Rhisiart Hopkin's customers.'

Finch put a hand on a pile of papers in front of him. 'This is a list of the customers he dealt with in the last three years. I thought that you might ask for that sort of detail.'

'Did he have any difficult customers?'

'What do you mean?'

'People who may have complained about him. There must be some disgruntled individuals who weren't happy with some of the decisions he made.'

'Only one I can think of.'

Sara stopped making notes and stared over at Finch.

'A couple of years ago Rhisiart withdrew the credit for a farmer who was in business with his son. Their farm wasn't particularly prosperous and neither was a sideline in agricultural contracting. We did everything we could but in the end we couldn't continue supporting the venture.'

'So what happened?'

'They came here one afternoon. Barged in, threatening Rhisiart and some of the staff. When they became abusive, we called the police but by the time they arrived they had already smashed his car. When the case came to court both men were given suspended prison sentences.'

'I'll need the names and addresses,' Drake said.

'I've highlighted their details on the top of this list.'

Finch dragged a hand over his double-cuffed shirt and read the time slowly enough to signal he wanted to finish. 'Is there anything else?'

'Can we see his office?'

Finch looked surprised. 'I can show you his work station. I don't think you'd call it an office.'

Drake and Sara followed Finch out into the main office area. She noticed the averted glances from the occasional member of staff, all in similar colour-coordinated uniforms.

Finch reached a section of a long bench and stopped. He drew a hand in the air. 'This is where Rhisiart worked.'

It amazed Sara that the desk was so small. She was expecting something altogether more grand, more bank-like, more prosperous.

Drake scanned the desk and Sara guessed he thought the same as she did. 'Does he have a secretary?'

Finch shook his head. 'We do all the admin ourselves these days. Rhisiart was a good typist and very proficient with IT. So we don't have secretaries and we organise our own diaries. It is all on the computer.'

Sara peered down at the desktop, bare apart from a desk lamp, a pot of pencils and biros all in the corporate colours of the bank, a keyboard, a mouse and twin monitors. A stack of Post-it notes had been pushed under a monitor.

Drake tugged at the chair – it was one with a tall back and additional lumber support. He sat down and then turned to Finch. 'Is there a password?' He reached for the mouse.

'We unblocked it this morning once we were told to expect you. Are you looking for anything in particular?'

Drake had speculated whether Rhisiart Hopkin recorded in his diary who his guests were to be on the night he died. Finch stood motionless by his side as Drake scanned the various entries for the last two weeks. Drake clicked on the mouse and seconds later there was a whirring sound from a machine nearby.

Sara turned to Finch. 'Did he ever entertain customers at home?'

'Not that I know of.'

'Did he ever mention difficulties with the Orme Arts

Festival?'

'I don't think he was happy with the way that Gloria Patton or some of the other people in charge were running things. I read the last minutes of the meetings he sent me. I suspected things weren't going as he anticipated.'

A young bank employee appeared with various sheets that Finch surveyed quickly before handing them to Drake.

Drake peered at them carefully, shaking his head slowly as he passed them to Sara. They had hoped for the identity of his dinner guests – two people crucial to the inquiry.

Drake stood up. 'Thanks for your help.'

Finch accompanied Drake and Sara out of the bank's offices and down into the spring sunshine. He paused for a moment, enjoying the fresh air. 'I hope you find Rhisiart's killer.'

'So do we,' Drake said.

An hour later Drake stood in the kitchen at headquarters staring at the electric kettle, waiting for it to boil. He tipped the exact measure of ground coffee into the cafetière and set the timer on his phone before heading back to his office with the coffee and a clean mug. The coffee had to brew for no more than two minutes and by the time he reached his office and sat down the mobile bleeped and he plunged the filter.

Following the same routine always settled his mind. It had a calming effect. An email from Superintendent Price had arrived during his absence that morning requesting a meeting at the end of the day. Drake gathered his thoughts together. Blanking out the activity from the Incident Room he poured his coffee, then rearranged the Post-it notes into appropriate columns – those that needed urgent and less urgent attention.

He'd just finished his first mouthful of coffee when the telephone rang.

'I thought you should be the first to know,' the pathologist said. 'The toxicology report came back today. The death made me think about a case several years ago. An anaesthetist in Newcastle got fed up of his wife and used a drug called suxamethonium to kill her so he could marry his mistress. He thought he'd get away with it but his pharmacology wasn't that good; they couldn't detect the suxamethonium but found a metabolite – a breakdown product of the drug. So I asked for some additional tests on blood and tissue samples to be done. Gloria Patton had a high level of a breakdown product of succinylcholine in her system. It's a substance used as a muscle relaxant as part of an anaesthetic.'

'Did it kill her?'

'It relaxes the muscles, stops the nerves communicating with them, so one effect is that the patient can't breathe until it wears off. They usually give sux in theatre and then take over the patient's breathing, but without them doing that the patient will suffocate and die.'

'So how was it administered?'

'There was a puncture wound in Gloria Patton's arm, remember?'

'I remember.'

'It reminds me of medical students who used to have 'sux runs' where they'd inject themselves in the muscle and see which one could run the furthest before passing out. One of the group wouldn't take part and had oxygen and a mask and bag ready for the runners until the sux had worn off.'

'That sounds dangerous.'

'And stupid.'

'So it's possible she was alive when he began to assemble the wooden frame on which she was standing and the unmade bed and all the other crap in the shop window.'

'Once the sux is administered the patient would have a few minutes, ten at most, depending on the dose and how it was administered, before they'd suffocate. Unless you know when the sux was administered I cannot answer your question.'

Drake shuddered. 'So where could he have got this drug? Presumably they are heavily regulated.'

'It was probably stolen from a hospital. Or maybe from the pharmaceutical company that supplies it.'

'Was there any suggestion from Rhisiart Hopkin's post-mortem that he might have been poisoned?'

'I've sent a blood sample for a toxicology test but there is no sign of a puncture wound.'

Price would need to be informed, Drake thought.

'I'll email you the full report.'

Drake finished the call and sank back in his chair, wondering what progress he could actually report to Superintendent Price. His stomach hardened at the prospect of being quizzed by his superior officer. He called Foulds, hoping for progress on the forensic examination of the Patton crime scene.

'Have you been able to make any progress with the rest of the exhibits?' Drake couldn't think of a better word for the unmade bed; he didn't want to call it an artwork. A woman had been killed. No one would want to associate her death with artistic endeavour.

'The place was a shop, Ian. There are fingerprints all over the doors, door handles, door frames. But nothing on the bed or the bedside cabinet. The preliminary results of the bedding drew a blank. But it could be weeks before we can finalise every test. It suggests someone who was forensically aware.'

Every fingerprint would need to be eliminated in due course. It meant a mountain of paperwork. Drake pinched his lips together before shaking his head in frustration. 'Whoever this is, he is a sick bastard.'

After the call ended he sat for a moment gathering his thoughts before walking over to the coat stand and reaching for his jacket. On the way to the senior management suite he detoured into a bathroom to adjust his tie, put a comb through his hair. He needn't have bothered; Superintendent Price looked dishevelled, tired. He sat behind his desk and sighed heavily when Drake sank into a chair opposite him.

'I hope you've got some news.'

Drake opened his mouth slightly but Price continued. 'Every councillor for the entire county has been on the phone asking me about progress with the inquiry into Gloria Patton's death.'

'She was poisoned, sir. Apparently she had an abnormally high dosage of a muscle relaxant in her system. So the cause of death was suffocation.'

'I suppose you're going to tell me there is no DNA evidence so far ...'

'It's proving difficult. The crime scene investigators believe the killer was forensically aware.'

'For Christ sake, *forensically aware.*'

'I don't think there are any traces that are likely to provide us with any DNA.'

'Next you're going to tell me Patton's death is linked to that bank manager.'

'Well, it's too early—'

'One of the local hacks has been sniffing around looking for a story, suggesting we might have a serial killer on the loose in North Wales. Can you imagine those headlines? I think we should issue a press statement along the lines that the death of Rhisiart

Hopkin is wholly unconnected with Gloria Patton and we are treating them entirely independently.'

'I'm not certain—'

'What do you mean? Is there anything to connect them?'

'Not at the moment.'

Price reached for the telephone. 'Then I'll tell public relations to draft something up for release to the press.' He read the time. 'We might even be able to get it into the evening news.'

'Don't you think that might be a bit premature?'

'Fuck's sake, Ian. Is there *anything* to connect them?'

'They were both on the committee that organised the Orme Arts Festival.'

Price placed his fingers on the handset. 'Coincidence. Nothing more than that.' He cocked his head to one side, lowering his eyebrows. Drake began to regret that the tone he used sounded a little too aggressive. He had worked with Price for a long time and he hoped the superintendent valued his opinion.

Before he could say anything else the phone on Price's desk rang. He snatched the handset out of the cradle. He listened for a few seconds, gasped and his mouth fell open. 'You won't believe this.'

Chapter 16

Price and Drake rushed over to public relations. Price shouted at various officers and civilians who got in his way as he jogged through the corridors of headquarters. He leant a shoulder against the door, kicking the bottom at the same time. Drake followed him inside and saw the startled look on the faces of two women sitting by their monitors. He recognised Susan Howells as the most senior. She could always be a calming influence on Price.

'You need to see this immediately, Wyndham,' she said. In the hierarchical world of the WPS it still grated when Drake heard a civilian using the superintendent's Christian name.

They stood looking over the shoulder of Susan Howells. Drake noticed a blood vessel pumping under Price's right ear. Susan started clicking with her mouse and seconds later a YouTube channel appeared on the screen. It had the words #Iamtheone over a photograph of the promenade at Llandudno on a fine summer's day.

'Jesus.' Price's voice sounded throttled.

'This must be your suspect,' Howells said. 'He's put together this YouTube channel so that everybody can look at his work.' She clicked on the static image of the inside of the shop and quickly it filled the screen. 'It's exactly the same video that he uploaded to his website.'

'Can't we do something about this?' Price made a grinding sound with his teeth.

Howells looked up, sharing an are-you-serious look with both Price and Drake.

'The video has already had one thousand hits.'

'There has to be something we can do.'

'There are two more videos.' Howells clicked away

from the first and onto the static image with the now-familiar #iamtheone in large Gothic-like font. 'You won't like this.' She lowered her voice.

Once she had clicked on the image the screen filled with the word 'Pursuit'. Then a montage of still photographs of Gloria Patton, outside her gallery, visiting the supermarket, walking her dog. Abruptly they ceased, replaced by images of her getting into her car. Nobody said anything. Drake stared dumbfounded.

Once it had finished Howells moved to the next video.

Drake caught his breath, unable to believe what he was watching. The orchestral theme played through the speakers. Drake didn't recognise the music but he recognised the scene being recorded. It was inside the shop and they watched in disgust as a white-suited figure busied himself around the unmade bed. He adjusted the props, ruffled the sheets, stepped back and admired his handiwork. The camera was on a tripod in a corner, Drake thought. The images looked high quality, professionally assembled.

Price leant forward, squinting. 'Fucking hell,' the superintendent said eventually.

'There's more,' Howells said.

She clicked on the third and final video. After the opening scene the word 'Observation' appeared before cutting to the moving images of the pavement the morning the murder was discovered.

'Stop that image now,' Drake shouted. 'Where the hell was he filming from?'

'My guess is he was in a car or a van.'

The video continued until the first police officers arrived at the scene.

Then Drake saw hands raised to mouths, disbelief shared among the onlookers. The oddest part of this sick scenario was watching himself arriving, followed by Sara. He could remember talking to the police officer but had little recollection of speaking to the civilian by his side who he remembered as the property manager. There was something hideously entrancing about the whole thing.

'What do you want me to say to the press?' Howells said.

Price didn't reply; he kept staring at the images.

Howells switched off the last of the videos.

'I have to draft a press release. Is this connected to the murder at the weekend?'

'Of course it's not,' Price snapped. 'Use all the standard wording about wanting as much help from the public, particularly anybody who might have been in the area around the shop on the day Gloria Patton was killed.'

'But I'll need more detail than—'

Now Price sounded angry. 'Email me a draft straight away.' He turned to Drake. 'Let's go.'

'The filming looked very professional, sir.' Drake hurried to keep up with Price. Was it too much of a coincidence that Geraint Wood was an artist who specialised in video installations? 'One of the persons of interest makes videos for a living.'

Drake almost bumped into Price as he stopped mid-stride.

'Well, arrest the sad fucker. Take his place apart, seize all his equipment.'

Price was overreacting; he often did. Common sense would have to prevail.

Price continued. 'Speak to the lawyers about whether there's anything we can do about the YouTube videos. It was a crime scene, for Christ's sake. There must be something we can do.'

'Yes, sir. I'll get the team organised to arrest Wood.'

'Keep me informed. It could be a long night.' Price marched away.

Back in the Incident Room, Drake addressed the team, his voice raised. 'There's been a development. Our killer has launched a YouTube channel so the whole world can see his sad little life.'

Winder clicked on his mouse. Moments later he opened up the YouTube channel and Sara and Luned watched in stunned silence as he played the various videos. Drake saw the disgust and shock on the faces of his team. Once they finished he walked over towards the board.

'They all look professional. The only person of interest so far who makes videos is Geraint Wood.' Drake pointed a finger at the photograph of the artist. 'So let's dig a little deeper into Wood's life.'

Drake allocated the task of establishing the details of Wood's finances to Winder and Luned while Sara scoured for intelligence about his family background. Back in his room Drake typed 'Geraint Wood artist' into the search engine on his computer. The first entry was Wood's website and the second that of the gallery that represented him. Drake read the biography and profile for Wood, blanking out the conversations in the Incident Room. He reread a quote from Wood, wondering what the hell he meant:

I am a seeker. Searching, aching for that essence of neutrality. When everything baffles the paradigm and sends challenging and ultimately masked and deeply disturbing messages to the subconscious about one's true self. The rhizomatic discipline needed to conquer existence and its existential reality is only a small part of what challenges me.

A page on the gallery's website featured two of Wood's videos. Drake clicked on the first, called *Truth or Lies?* The video involved twenty minutes of blurred images of individuals; it was difficult to tell if they were male or female sometimes, crossing railway lines and tracks from different countries all over the world. Then there were cows in static locations and then men in suits, wearing bowlers and homburgs staring at the animals.

My Castle was the second and had various faces grinning and gawping at the camera with stretched mouths in exaggerated smiles. Suddenly it flicked to images of people wearing masks walking through a city street. It could be London or Birmingham, and then it cut to what looked like Paris and then Berlin.

After they finished he sat back wondering if the last hour had been worth it. Modern art had a narcissistic quality, Drake decided. Or perhaps he simply didn't understand. A painting seemed easier to enjoy, something he could look at and appreciate.

Sara appeared in his doorway with a steaming mug. Drake turned up his nose but said nothing. She was new after all.

'Gareth's making progress, boss.'

'Good.' He sipped on the drink. Decent coffee would have to wait.

Sara left and Drake turned his attention back to Wood's website. He wondered how many people paid the equivalent of a month's salary for a video. You couldn't hang it on a wall or display it on a shelf.

A call to one of the intelligence officers that covered the area where Wood lived produced little useful information but eventually Drake tracked down a district inspector.

'I remembered when he was younger,' the officer

conceded. 'He was wild. There was something odd about him. As though he couldn't see the consequences of what he had done.'

Drake jotted down the details of possible other contacts the inspector dragged from his memory. It was the sort of run-of-the-mill police work that might contribute to a breakthrough.

Drake's desk lamp cast a soft glow over his desk as the evening darkened. Sara appeared in the doorway holding various papers. 'I've got the results of the police national computer search against Wood.'

Drake waved her into the room.

'He was convicted of common assault when he was fifteen. And that led to two more court appearances before he was eighteen.'

It didn't surprise Drake. The rate of juvenile reoffending was far too high.

'I've done some research on psychopaths too, sir.'

Drake waited for Sara to continue.

'It is often the case they have troubled childhoods and numerous convictions before reaching adulthood. They have no concept of guilt or of accepting the consequences of their actions.'

For the second time someone had suggested Wood's inability to accept guilt.

'When we spoke to Wood he told us that he had been at home all night. He was quick enough to challenge us then. Maybe it was a way of pushing us into a corner, forcing us to arrest him prematurely,' Drake said.

Sara furrowed her brow. 'I think that could be stretching it, sir.'

It was a little before ten pm when Drake walked through into the Incident Room. Winder stretched self-consciously and Luned suppressed a yawn but without trying to conceal it.

Drake cleared his throat. 'Sara has discovered that Geraint Wood has several convictions for assault from when he was younger. We know he threatened Gloria Patton. We know that he does video installations as an artist. The YouTube channel is highly undesirable.'

He looked over at Luned. 'Anything on his family?'

'He comes from a classic broken home. Father abandoned his wife and children when they were toddlers. One of his brothers was taken into care and it almost happened to Wood. His mother got into abusive relationships with different men. And his father's convictions are a long list of serious offending.'

Drake nodded. 'When we spoke to him he certainly had a hell of a grudge against Gloria Patton. Especially about the way he thought she favoured English artists.'

Winder had stood up as Luned spoke and Drake wondered if he was anxious to make a quick exit or whether he had something constructive to add. He nodded at the junior officer.

'The stuff I got from a financial search is very revealing. The Inland Revenue sent me copies of his accounts. The man barely scratches a living.'

'So having an exhibition in Llandudno would have helped?' Drake said.

'Looks like it, boss. His bank account is overdrawn and has been for months. The bank has threatened to foreclose on his mortgage. But the biggest surprise is that the bank involved is Rhisiart Hopkin's.'

'Really?' Drake paused. The others in the team stared over at Winder. 'So that makes him a person of interest in that inquiry too. Something else we can ask him about tomorrow.'

Drake glanced at his watch. 'We assemble again at six am. I've already warned the custody suite to expect a visitor. A search team is ready. Once we've got Wood in custody they'll take his house apart. Let's get some sleep. It's going to be a long day tomorrow.'

Drake slept badly. He was back in Northern Division headquarters by five-thirty drinking coffee and eating a breakfast bar. Before leaving the apartment he had listened for a second time to a message his sister had left on his machine the night before. Her tone had been increasingly hysterical about Huw Jackson. He would call her back later that day.

Sara was the first to arrive. Her hair still had that freshly laundered look as though she could step out of bed without having to spend hours in front of the mirror with straighteners and a brush. She shrugged off a fleece and when Winder arrived soon after he offered to make coffee and sauntered off to the kitchen, returning minutes later with three mugs, deep in conversation with Luned.

Drake walked over to the board and stood alongside a map of the village where Wood lived. It took him only seconds to outline the plan. His mobile bleeped and he smiled as he read confirmation from the search team who were ready to leave.

'Let's go,' Drake said.

He led the way in an anonymous pool car, Winder and Luned following close behind. Drake pressed his handset into the cradle, engaging the hands-free function before calling the marked police car already parked near Wood's property.

'No sign of any movement, sir,' one of the officers responded.

Winder tucked in behind Drake as they drove down the A55. Behind Winder Drake caught sight of a marked police car in his rear-view mirror. The traffic was light as they followed the route to Wood's cottage.

Drake parked a few yards from the gate that led to

the front door. The cottage had probably been built for farm labourers a century previously. A makeshift fence of thin, tall shards of slate lined the road. Drake recalled his grandfather calling them 'pileri' – a Welsh word borrowed from the English pillar. It was quiet. No passing traffic. Winder and the second marked police car pulled up a short distance behind Drake.

Drake's mobile rang. It was the search team supervisor. 'Just pulling up now, sir.' Another glance in the rear-view mirror told Drake the final piece of his arrest jigsaw was in place.

He turned to Sara. 'Let's go.'

They streamed out of the cars and over to the front door. Drake gesticulated for Winder and Luned to go round the rear. He hammered on the door. 'Geraint Wood, open up, police.'

There was no response so Drake hammered on the front window as Sara called Winder, warning him Wood might try and escape through the back door. Drake noticed the curtain on the window moving. He shouted again.

He heard movement as an old-fashioned lock shifted open.

The door opened against a chain. Geraint Wood peered out. 'Be fwc ti eisio?'

Drake guessed Sara would understand Wood's foul-mouthed demand to know what they wanted. 'I have a warrant to search the property. You're under arrest—'

The door slammed in his face. Drake waited for a few seconds hoping to hear the chain fall away. Nothing. Looking over his shoulder he saw a uniformed officer, one of the search team, holding the battering ram quaintly called the big key. Drake nodded. The officer's relaxed pose changed quickly; his jaw tightened, he adjusted his hands in his thick gloves.

Drake stood to one side. 'Get it done.'

It took one swing for the door to crash open. Drake and Sara darted in followed by two officers from the search team. Wood stood in the sitting room swinging a baseball bat. This time he resorted to English so everyone understood. 'The English say that every man's home is his castle. Now this Welshman is not going to tolerate intimidation by the English state.'

He raised the bat behind him and took two steps towards Drake and Sara.

The next few seconds seemed to happen in slow motion as the two officers by Drake's side launched themselves through the air like rugby players. They crashed into Wood. The baseball bat clattered on the slate hearth and three bodies came crashing down, demolishing a coffee table. He continued to shout obscenities as handcuffs snapped over his wrists.

Drake and Sara watched from the front threshold as Wood was bundled into a marked police car. Back inside, Drake reached down and picked up the baseball bat. He tossed it onto an old sofa. The search team supervisor joined them. 'Where do you want us to start?'

'Take the place apart.'

Chapter 17

After depositing Geraint Wood in a cell in the area custody suite Drake and Sara returned to the first crime scene. Drake strode back and forth along the pavement outside the shop that still had yellow tape draped across the door. He gesticulated with his hands, pointing to possible locations from where the video could have been filmed.

'Did you notice a van parked over there?' Drake said, nodding towards the opposite side of the street.

Sara shook her head.

Drake scanned the various shops across the street. He wondered if the camera had been set up inside one of them. A brief forensic analysis by Mike Foulds had established clearly that the recording had been taken from ground level.

Drake searched in vain for any CCTV cameras. This side of Llandudno obviously wasn't a priority. Crime rate in the town was low; murder only happened on television dramas. He jogged over the road, encouraging Sara to follow him. Then he stared back, hoping to pinpoint the exact position where the vehicle had parked.

He walked a little further down the pavement and beckoned Sara over.

'It was here, he was parked here,' Drake sounded breathless.

Sara lifted her iPad and pointed towards the crime scene. She pressed play and the images from the video filled the screen. 'Yes. This is the spot.' Drake turned and looked at the shops behind him.

He entered the nearest: a charity shop. Display rails heaved with second-hand clothes and a musty smell hung in the air. Shelving had been pushed against the walls displaying various glassware, vases –

Drake even spotted an old 35mm camera. A woman in her sixties stood behind the counter and, once she finished serving a customer, smiled at him. Her name badge had *Jean* printed on it.

He held up his warrant card. 'Detective Inspector Drake and this is Detective Sergeant Morgan. We're investigating the murder of Gloria Patton. She was found last week in the old shoe shop opposite.'

Jean's smile disappeared. 'It was awful. Everyone is talking about it. Nothing like this has ever happened before.'

Drake paused. Instinct told him not to share the details of the videos on YouTube even though it was common knowledge. 'We're looking for any possibility that somebody may have filmed the police arriving on the morning the body was discovered.'

Jean seemed to get paler.

'What time did the shop open that morning?'

'I wasn't working that day,' she whispered. 'Maureen was volunteering.'

'Is she here?'

'She's sorting through stuff in the back.'

'We need to talk to her.'

Jean gestured towards a man in his early twenties, giving him strict instructions to call her if a customer had to be served.

They walked through to the storeroom where a woman with steel-grey hair was digging through a pile of old clothes. She stood up straight; long, thick plastic gloves covered her hands and forearms.

'This is the police, Maureen,' Jean said. 'It's about the murder.'

Maureen stared over at Drake and Sara. 'Everyone is talking about it.'

'You were working on the morning the body was discovered?' Drake said.

Maureen nodded.

'Somebody filmed the police arriving. When did you open the shop that morning?'

'At the usual time – about nine.'

'Did you notice anything unusual? Any cars or vans parked outside?'

She shook her head and frowned. 'It was quiet. Nothing much happens here until coffee time. Come to think of it, there was a van outside. It was one of those shop-fitting companies. We had one here when we first opened years ago.'

Drake's chest tightened slightly: a step a nearer to the killer. 'Do you remember the name printed on the side?'

'No, sorry.'

'Did you see anybody in the van?'

'No, of course not. I didn't look in. Do you think I'm some sort of busybody?'

'Well what about the colour?'

'I can't remember.'

'Come on. It's important. Was it red or black or white?'

Maureen gave Drake a frightened look as he raised his voice.

'I can't remember …I suppose it was white.'

'Can you remember what make it might have been?'

Drake sounded desperate. It was the nearest they had got to the killer, but the terrified look on Maureen's face told him he had pushed her too hard already.

'I'll get someone to show you some photographs so that you can identify the make.'

Maureen relaxed.

Drake lowered his voice. 'Was there anybody else working with you that day?'

'No. Just me and I'm only a volunteer. I worked

until lunchtime that day. Other weeks I might work in the afternoons.'

Drake turned his back on Maureen and walked back into the shop area followed by Sara. He made for the front door and noticed the CCTV camera clipped to the top of one of the shelving units. He turned to look at Jean. 'Why didn't you tell me there was CCTV?'

'It doesn't work,' Jean replied. 'It was put in a couple of years ago after we had a problem with a few customers coming in drunk and arguing. There was no money to have it fixed.'

Drake left the shop and stood on the pavement with Sara. They both stared at the cars parked nearby.

'He was here,' Drake said. 'I'll get Gareth to show her images of every possible van. Hopefully that might narrow it down.'

'It was probably stolen.'

'But he would have needed some stencilling for the livery on the side of the van. We'll have to contact all the local companies that do that sort of thing.'

Drake gave the row of parked vehicles one last look and then turned to Sara. 'Let's go and talk to Wood.'

The smell of bleach and air freshener hung in the windowless atmosphere of the area custody suite. The whippet-thin custody sergeant wore trousers a size too small and his eyes seemed to hover above hollowed-out cheeks. Drake signed for the tapes he needed as Sara discussed with the sergeant which marathon he was doing next.

Drake entered the interview room and saw Wood sitting on one of the upright plastic chairs. The lawyer sitting by his side stood up and reached out a hand. 'Hywel Williams.' He had a strong North Wales accent and immediately started talking in Welsh with Drake.

'If you don't mind we'll conduct the interview in English; Sergeant Morgan isn't bilingual.' Drake nodded towards Sara.

Williams looked over at Wood who nodded. Expediency always meant it was easier to conduct interviews in English. Drake loaded the tapes into the recording machine and once he clicked it on, a screeching noise filled the air for a couple of seconds.

'I'm investigating the death of Gloria Patton,' Drake said once the formalities were completed.

Wood looked over the table impassively.

'I understand that you had a difficult relationship with her.'

'I didn't have any relationship with her.'

Drake reached for the papers in front of them. 'Were you angry with her when she rejected your work for the Orme Arts Festival?'

'No. I was fucking incandescent.'

Drake paused. Wood continued. 'She should never have been in charge of running the arts festival. It was public money, and all she did was spend it on some of her favourites, people she knew, English people, English artists.'

'Why did you visit her in her gallery?'

Wood sat back and scowled. 'She didn't have a gallery. She had a shop. I went to her fucking shop.'

'Is it true that you threatened her?' Drake took the opportunity of reminding himself of the exact words one of the eyewitnesses used. 'You said that you would sort her out, make certain that she would never be involved with an arts festival ever again.'

Wood shook his head back and forth. 'I was angry. I didn't say anything wrong. I never threatened her. Whoever said that is lying.'

Williams made his first contribution. 'My client

admits having an argument with Gloria Patton, but that isn't evidence he killed her.'

The lawyer was right. Drake scanned his watch. He was still waiting for details from the search team.

'When we first spoke you told me you make video installations.'

Wood stared at Drake, but said nothing.

'I assume you are experienced in using video cameras?'

'The visual arts are the way forward. Everybody wants videos. Can't you see that? There are videos everywhere. On Facebook, on YouTube. It's the only realistic artistic medium that has a future.'

'You make a living from selling your installations?'

Drake fingered the reports from the Inland Revenue service that indicated Wood earned less than the equivalent of the minimum wage.

'I don't judge my success against normal conventions.'

'You haven't sold a piece of art for almost two years.'

Wood managed a shocked look. 'I don't know what the hell you're talking about.'

'When did you last sell a piece?'

Wood looked at his lawyer, rolling his eyes in despair.

'Let me turn to your current financial position. Did you know a man called Rhisiart Hopkin?'

Wood seemed puzzled. Williams butted in. 'Where are you taking this line of questioning? Are you suggesting my client is involved in that murder too?'

Drake ignored the lawyer and looked straight at Wood. 'Rhisiart Hopkin worked with the same bank where you have your bank accounts as well as your mortgage.'

Drake paused, hoping Wood could see exactly

where his line of questioning was heading. 'Your mortgage is in arrears and the overdraft you have with the bank has been called in.'

Wood leant on the table, peering over at Drake. 'I had nothing to do with Hopkin's death.' His voice trembled.

'Where were you last Saturday night when Rhisiart Hopkin was murdered?'

Drake saw the colour draining from Wood's face.

'This is a conspiracy. A fucking stitch-up.'

A message on his mobile from the custody sergeant interrupted Drake's train of thought. 'We'll suspend the interview at this point.' He glanced at Sara who completed the formalities of sealing the tapes.

'How long is this delay going to be?' Williams said.

'Inquiries are ongoing. It is difficult to say,' Drake said.

'I must protest. This is quite unconscionable.'

Drake was on his feet, Sara behind. He gave Williams a benign smile and traipsed through to the custody suite where the sergeant was processing a drunk driver. The man scooped up his keys and personal items from the desk and then signed the custody record. The sergeant jerked his head towards the door into the area control centre. 'There's a woman at the main reception. Apparently, she's hysterical. She's demanding to see you about Geraint Wood.'

The interruption gave him the chance to call the search team supervisor. A pile of clothes and boxes full of video equipment, cameras, and an ancient laptop had been recovered. It meant more work for the forensic team. He called Gareth Winder. 'Have you been able to trace any vehicles owned by Geraint Wood?'

'We've just had the report in, boss,' Gareth replied. 'Apparently he owns a fifteen-year-old Ford Fiesta.

Nothing else is registered in his name.'

Drake finished the call as Sara joined him. 'What's up?'

'There's a witness in reception demanding she speak to us about Wood. And I've just spoken with Gareth. He doesn't own a vehicle apart from his Fiesta.'

'He could have stolen one and then added the livery.'

Drake nodded. After talking to the witness he'd make a decision about what further progress they could make with Wood.

A few minutes later they sat around a table in one of the smart conference rooms just off reception in the area custody centre. Amber Falk, sitting opposite them, wore a multicoloured thin sweater, and long dreadlocks cascaded down her back. She chewed on her nails, her eyes restless. It surprised Drake when she had introduced herself as Wood's girlfriend. He would have expected a Welsh girl but Amber had a harsh Geordie accent.

'He's not killed anyone. It's not in him. He's not capable of it.'

Drake opened his mouth to say something but she continued.

'He can be stupid but he's no killer.'

'How long have you known him?'

She gazed over at Drake, focusing hard on his face as though she were trying to fathom out exactly what he had asked.

'We are life-partners.'

More exciting than just partners or boyfriend/girlfriend, Drake thought.

'Where do you live?' Sara asked.

Amber gave her an angry look. 'I've got my place of course. Everyone needs a little independence.'

Sara smiled. 'Of course.'

'Does Geraint stay with you?'

'Sometimes.'

Sara leant forward, attempting to put this anxious woman at ease. 'Did he spend last Saturday night with you, for example.'

Amber relaxed. 'Yeah, always on Saturday night. We went down the pub.'

'We'll probably need a few more details from you, a proper statement.'

'Anything I can do to help. Geraint's not a bad man.'

Drake hoped he could get more detail now that Amber appeared to be more amenable. 'Was he with you last Tuesday?'

Amber almost winced in concentration as she cast her mind back. 'No. I was with my mother. She likes to watch the repeats of *Downton Abbey*. She's old.'

'So you didn't see Geraint that evening?'

'I've just said. Anyway he was with me first thing the following morning. He got to my place by seven. We went up the hills for a long walk.'

'What time were you back?' Sara asked.

'After dinner, about two.'

Drake looked over at Amber. Years of experience told him that finding the truth meant looking beyond clothes or the appearance of a witness. She had struck him as truthful. It didn't mean that Wood was innocent; it meant they had to dig a little further.

'Are you going to release him now?'

'I don't make that decision.' Although it was not strictly true, it helped Drake to avoid answering directly.

'I'll wait for him.'

Drake and Sara left Amber in reception and threaded their way back to the custody suite.

Sara organised two weak insipid coffees which

they drank in one of the bare interview rooms. 'At least she confirmed what he told us about the night Gloria Patton was killed,' Sara said.

'Doesn't make him innocent.'

'And she gave him an unprompted alibi for the time the videos were filmed.'

'But he could have set up everything remotely.'

Sara nodded.

'Everything suggests Wood is our suspect. The way Patton's body was staged and the YouTube videos. And now his girlfriend comes in and offers an alibi. It could be carefully planned.'

'We don't have enough to justify charging him.'

Drake nodded; he knew as well as Sara they had no alternative other than to release Wood on bail. Drake finished the last of his coffee, grimaced at the disgusting taste, crushed the plastic in one hand and dropped it into a bin.

'Let's go and break the good news to Mr Wood and his lawyer.'

Chapter 18

Luned relished every minute of the inquiry. The speed, the urgency and the intensity had been intoxicating. All the activity yesterday had left her feeling winded. Nothing in her previous role in one of the regional CID units had prepared her for the frantic pace of Wood's arrest and the fallout from his subsequent release. Last night she had fallen asleep on the sofa at home, exhausted but also pleased that at last she was getting to do some real policing.

The only drawback was working with Gareth Winder. But it was less than a week since she had met him for the first time and she persuaded herself that her genial nature had to give him the benefit of the doubt. He was her senior officer by age if not rank and that morning she determined that she would absorb how he worked. Learn from his experience.

Winder had insisted they leave headquarters before she had even opened her emails.

He drove to Llandudno with Radio 1 playing in the background. She hated the music the station played so by the time they reached the charity shop to interview Maureen her nerves were on edge.

Winder parked a little way down the street and switched off the engine. After leaving the car, he reached for the laptop in the rear seat and they walked over to the shop.

A faint musty smell from the clothes that hung from the display carousels tickled her nose. Luned squeezed past a heavily pregnant woman pushing a wheelchair with a toddler inside.

Winder reached the counter first, warrant card in hand.

'I'd like to see Maureen, please.'

The woman gave Winder a frightened look before

darting a glance at Luned, who forced a reassuring smile.

'That's me.'

'Is there somewhere we can talk in private?'

Maureen nodded towards a door at the back of the shop and after shuffling out from behind the counter she threaded her way past a stand full of greetings cards until she pushed open the door. Inside, another volunteer was sifting through piles of old clothes.

'I need to ask you about the van that was parked outside last week.'

'Yes. The inspector told me.' Maureen seemed to have relaxed.

Winder glanced over at the table. 'Can we sit here?'

'Yes. I'll find some chairs.'

Luned helped Maureen to release three plastic chairs stacked untidily in one corner. Winder leant over the table, laptop booting up.

All three sat down and Maureen stuffed her hands under her thighs, staring at Winder and the screen.

'I need to show you some images of various vans.'

Maureen nodded. Luned struggled to tell how stressed Maureen was but she had already decided that if Winder was going to be too rude then she would butt in. Winder fiddled with the mouse and the screen came alive with the various images from the internet pages Winder had bookmarked.

After half an hour Winder had shown Maureen various images of different makes of vans, but they all drew a non-committal reply. The image of a red VW Transporter filled the screen, which Luned thought unhelpful as it was a different colour from the vehicle Maureen had seen.

'Imagine it in a white colour,' Luned said, using her best schoolteacher tone. Winder clicked onto the next image, oblivious of Luned's comment. Sometimes he could appear quite disinterested, Luned concluded.

'It was quite old,' Maureen announced before Winder had a chance to show her the next image. 'It was rusty, I'm sure.'

She quickly dismissed a van made by Mercedes that obviously looked expensive and which Luned doubted would be the likely choice for a killer. Then Winder showed her a van made by Nissan and one by Citroen and she shook her head.

'You don't recognise any of these. At all?' Winder sat back in his chair sounding frustrated. Maureen gave a worried look.

'Can you show me the photographs again?'

Winder gave her a disdainful look and dragged himself back to the table.

Volunteers drifted in and out of the storeroom, casting the occasional quizzical glance towards the laptop.

'If the van was quite old maybe we should concentrate on older versions of some of these makes,' Luned suggested. It seemed obvious and it troubled her that Winder hadn't thought of it.

He tapped something into the browser and then dozens of brightly coloured images of various vans filled the screen. Maureen leant over and stared with more interest at the selection Winder had found.

He scrolled down until he clicked on the second page while Maureen stared at the images.

Another few minutes passed until she pointed quickly to the image on the screen. 'That looks like it.'

The relief in Winder's face was palpable as he focused on the image of an old Ford Transit.

'I remember that it had a rusty scratch mark on the wheel arch just like that one.'

'Is there *anything* else you can remember?' Winder

added.

'I told the other police officer that I couldn't remember the number and I didn't see anyone.'

'Not even the name of the shop-fitting company?'

'Sorry.'

Luned decided to butt in. 'Do you remember seeing anyone get into the van – anyone acting suspiciously?'

Maureen swallowed hard and blinked a few times before stammering a reply. 'No ... the shop was busy. There were customers ... I mean, I didn't see anyone.'

'You've been really helpful already.' Luned smiled at Maureen. 'Please contact us if you remember anything that might be of assistance.'

Maureen nodded as Winder closed the laptop.

The shop thronged with customers as they made their way to the exit.

On the pavement outside Luned stood alongside Winder who seemed to be deep in thought. 'At least we know it was a Ford Transit.'

'Let's visit the other shops.' Winder jerked his head towards the row of shops behind them.

Luned had expected this. Someone might have noticed the van arriving or leaving. Someone might have seen the killer. All they had to do was find that someone.

But after an hour of shaking heads and blank faces Luned realised it was a hopeless task. Winder sat in the car and blew out both cheeks in desperation.

Drake kept his office door firmly shut for most of the morning, emerging only to make a coffee. Apart from a brief nod of acknowledgement and a mumbled greeting he ignored Sara. It reminded her that last evening Drake had scowled and said very little when Geraint

Wood stood by the custody sergeant's desk as his release on bail was processed. Now she guessed that his disappointment that the arrest hadn't led to Wood being formally charged contributed to his sullenness that morning. She remembered too the words of a fellow officer who warned her Drake could be annoying and 'impossible to work with'.

She wasn't going to make any snap judgements. Perhaps she was being too petty-minded. Nothing had been found to suggest Wood was working on any projects, or that he had any exhibitions in the pipeline. It added to the niggle in her mind that suggested he was desperate for a chance to exhibit at the Orme Arts Festival. Sara gazed over at the board and let her thoughts drift back to the interview with Wood, realising soon enough she was wasting time. She shook off her malaise and got back to the papers on her desk.

Sara trawled through the names of Rhisiart Hopkin's customers. The list went back many years. Each entry had a summary of the customer and the business sector in which they operated. She began with the most recent. There were new accounts for dot.com companies and several for farmers and dozens for hotels and guest houses. A colour-coded system flagged reminders about the dates for reviews and the contact names for the owner, and sometimes the word 'director' appeared.

It was mid-morning by the time Sara had read back two years. None of the details caught her attention until she started on the older accounts. The name Mr and Mrs Buckland soon focused her mind so she scanned the particulars quickly, but there was scant information. She picked up the telephone handset and dialled the bank.

'I'm afraid Mr Finch is in a meeting.' The receptionist's tone suggested the conversation was at an end.

'Interrupt him.'

'That won't be possible.'

Sara bristled at the veiled disdain in the voice.

'Let me explain something. We're investigating the murder of Rhisiart Hopkin. Mr Finch has the details of Mr Hopkin's files. I need to speak to him; you are obstructing me in doing so, and that could well be a criminal offence. So I suggest you interrupt Mr Finch, asking him to call me in the next five minutes. Otherwise, I'll request a warrant from the senior investigating officer to search the bank's premises and open a file about your uncooperative attitude.'

Sara slammed the handset down. It took her a few minutes to draft a formal letter addressed to the bank. Then after making a few minor adjustments she trooped off to the kitchen. Returning with a steaming mug of tea she plonked it down on the coaster near a small metal-framed picture of her two nieces as the telephone rang – it seemed to have a more insistent ring than normal.

'Sergeant Morgan.' Sara's tone was measured, calm.

'Roger Finch, I understand you want to speak to me.' His voice betrayed none of the apprehension Sara might have expected.

'I need the complete files of a number of customers Rhisiart Hopkin handled.'

'We'll need a formal written request.'

Sara had already anticipated this request. 'What's your email address?' She typed the details into her email system and attached the letter she had drafted earlier. 'There's a letter on its way as we speak. Can you email the papers immediately?'

'I have to return to a meeting so it may—'

'When I say immediately, Mr Finch, that is exactly

what I mean. Will that be a problem? If it is I shall have to speak to my senior officers.'

Sara could hear his breathing down the telephone.

'No, of course not. I'll see to it.' Sara smiled at the sound of his strangled voice.

The next hour dragged. She had sent Finch a list of a dozen customers but it was only the Bucklands that were of interest, at least for now. Sara heard Drake having a long conversation in his office. An email arrived from Finch. Its tone was conciliatory, offering his assistance and the bank's IT department if there were any problems with accessing the documentation. The email was the first of a dozen or so, each with numerous attachments. She would need hard copies but for now the electronic versions would have to suffice. She scanned the first for any reference to the Bucklands. Frustration turned into a knot of annoyance by the time she reached the fifth attachment.

There was a Hennessy, two Williams, a Jones: eventually she saw the names of Roger and Norma Buckland. After opening the folder she read Rhisiart Hopkin's notes. Initially, everything seemed positive. Hopkin summarised the youth club venture and community centre the Bucklands were hoping to start. Sara noted the occasional observation from Hopkin that Norma Buckland was 'idealistic' and 'with her head in the clouds' and she wondered if he recorded similar remarks about Roger Buckland. But the complimentary remarks reinforced for Sara that Hopkin was a typical chauvinist. She printed off a copy of the initial business plan that formed the basis of the application for a substantial loan to develop an old building. There were promises of funding from a local authority and indications that various charities were prepared to support the venture.

Hopkin made no critical comments, limiting his notes to observations about how the business could be a success. Sara skirted around the internal memoranda forwarded by Hopkin to Finch and his area office – it had far too much technical jargon. If it became important, somebody from the economic crime department would have to untangle its significance, Sara thought. For the time being she wanted to gauge the relationship between the Bucklands and Rhisiart Hopkin.

She ignored the grumbling hunger pains in her stomach and gradually got into the stride of following the language Hopkin used. Within a year of the loan being advanced the tone of the minutes chilled. Hopkin was covering his back, Sara concluded, as she read a memorandum to Finch highly critical of Roger Buckland. None of the promised funds from the third parties had materialised.

By the final meeting Roger Buckland was being described as 'aggressive' and 'argumentative' and there followed a stream of emails from the area head office demanding an assessment of 'the likelihood of default'. Once Sara read the letters from the bank's lawyers, formal repossession proceedings looked inevitable.

Sara sat back and read the time on her watch. It was late morning and she had to talk to Drake. She strode over to his office and knocked on the door. He waved her in. There were three columns of coloured Post-it notes on his desk. An empty cafetière sat neatly alongside a china mug. Idly she looked for a coaster and it surprised her that he didn't have one.

'I've been through the various files from the bank.'

Drake waved to the visitor chair.

She sat down, drawing a hand through her hair, gaining a few seconds to compose herself. 'Mr and Mrs

Buckland had a business loan with Hopkin. It looks as though everything had gone wrong. The bank allege they had been misled by Roger Buckland to believe that the local authority and various charities might contribute but apparently it was all a lie.'

Drake threaded the fingers of his hands together and steepled them on the desk. 'Why would that give him a motive to kill Hopkin?'

'He blames Hopkin for calling in the loan, which means they would be insolvent, bankrupt even. So he seeks revenge.'

Drake raised his eyebrows. 'And his wife isn't selected for the arts festival thereby losing the opportunity of more exposure for her art.'

Having her conclusions acknowledged pleased Sara; it dispelled her apprehension that the enthusiasm of Superintendent Price and Drake for arresting Geraint Wood the night before and the resulting embarrassment might temper his response.

'I don't think we have evidence to—'

Drake held up his hand. 'Just enough to talk to him. We'll go and see him this afternoon.'

Before Sara could reply they heard Winder and Luned's voice from the Incident Room and Sara and Drake joined them. 'We spoke to Maureen at the charity shop and she reckons the van was an old white Ford Transit with a scratched wheel arch.'

'Good. At least that's some progress.'

'But neither Maureen nor anyone in the shops nearby could remember seeing anybody parking the van or driving it away.'

'I'll get public relations to announce we're looking for this sort of van. Good work both of you.'

It was late afternoon when Drake pulled out of the car

park at headquarters. Several drafts of the press release about the white van had been emailed back and forth from the PR department before he was happy with the wording. He anticipated that the switchboard would get some crank calls but hopefully there might be a nugget of useful information too. He had given Sara's shoes a surreptitious glance when she sat in the passenger seat. It was a hangover from his experiences of Caren leaving soil and gravel from the farm she shared with her husband. It always meant he had to vacuum at the end of the day. He couldn't bear the thought of the car being left dirty overnight.

'It's hard to comprehend the possibility that a man of the cloth might be capable of murder,' Sara said.

'I suppose it's the old cliché that everyone is capable of murder. But in the case of Roger Buckland we know he is.'

Sara nodded slowly.

Drake hurried along the dual carriageway, reaching a flat section where he could see the beach alongside the road stretching out into the distance. Soon he indicated for Rhyl and they passed row after row of static caravans. Eventually he slowed as they reached the thirty mile an hour speed restriction.

Rhyl was divided by a railway line. To the north were the bedsits and pubs selling cheap lager next to slot machine arcades that reflected a town dedicated to the instant amusement of its visitors. The opposite side had the occasional tree-lined avenue where the crime rate was lower. The River Jordan Community Centre stood in a narrow backstreet. Drake found a parking spot behind a rusty Land Rover and they made for the entrance.

The hinges of the battered old door creaked as Drake pushed it open. A nasty pungent smell of urine clung to the air, from the toilet to their left. A radio played somewhere beyond another set of double doors, in need of a coat of paint. Drake hesitated for a moment as he reached for the handle, contemplating how contaminated he might feel after touching it, but not wanting to embarrass himself in front of Sara; he pushed the door quickly. Luckily, it flew open and they entered another corridor that led down one side of the building. Music drifted out of the first room they found and he peered in through a glass section. Three people were huddled around the desk in the centre of the room. Drake entered, Sara following.

'I'm looking for Roger Buckland.'

A man in his thirties, purple hair and nose ring, looked up at Drake. 'He's in the gym, mate.' He nodded towards the opposite end of the building before returning his gaze to the papers taking his attention.

Scuff marks covered the walls, and the lino on the floor was cracked, curling up at the edges. One of the windows they passed had a pane missing, a piece of plywood pinned to the outside.

'I can see now why the place needed so much work,' Sara said.

'It's a right dump.'

Drake inspected two more rooms, both empty, one of which had large damp stains discolouring the walls around the window. At the end of the corridor a staircase led up to the first floor. They heard sounds of feet scuffling and instructions from raised voices.

Calling the place a gym stretched the imagination. It had three tattered and ragged boxing punchbags hanging from the ceiling. A dozen elderly pieces of equipment stood neglected underneath a television screwed to a bracket high up on the wall, the music video muted.

A man in his late forties, give or take a few years, directed three men in their twenties punching the bags enthusiastically. He spotted Drake and motioned for them to stop. Drake scanned the three boxers, who had turned to stare at them; there was a flicker of recognition as he held the gaze of the taller. The man walked over to Drake and Sara, deep sweat patches around his neck and armpits.

'Roger Buckland? Detective Inspector Ian Drake and this is Detective Sergeant Sara Morgan.'

'Yes, how can I help?'

No matter how often Drake heard a Scouse accent it still sounded harsh, crass, even from the pastor.

'Is there somewhere we can speak privately?'

Buckland frowned. Then he nodded towards the far end of the gym. 'My office.'

Drake and Sara followed him into another room reeking of damp and decay.

Buckland sat down on a hard wooden chair and motioned at two similar chairs, inviting them to sit down.

'Is this about the murder of Gloria Patton?'

'We are investigating both the murder of Gloria Patton and the death of Rhisiart Hopkin.'

Buckland scowled. 'I didn't think they were connected.'

'I didn't say that they were.' Drake stopped, gauging the reaction.

Buckland didn't react, except to stare at Drake.

'I understand that Rhisiart Hopkin was your bank manager. Tell me about your relationship with him.'

Buckland nodded. 'I see where this is going. You think I have a motive to kill Rhisiart Hopkin. And because your searches have told you about my background you think I am the natural suspect. So, tell me, Inspector, what do you think about the power of forgiveness?'

'What exactly do you do here?'

'It's sad that society jumps to conclusions. Everybody deserves a second chance. Don't you agree?'

'Just answer my question, Mr Buckland.'

Buckland smirked, managing to notch up Drake's irritation.

'Second chances, Inspector Drake, that's what we offer here. The ability for youngsters, young adults, anyone who has fallen by the wayside, to experience the redemptive power of the Gospel.'

'And how does boxing do that?'

'I'm a qualified coach. Everyone who comes here knows they don't get judged. I treat everybody the same.'

'Did Rhisiart Hopkin understand what you are trying to do?'

Buckland shook his head. 'We had an agreement.' He waved a hand in the air. 'This place has to be refurbished. We put together a detailed business plan, secured extra funding and had the whole project on a secure footing. We made commitments based on the bank's promises and they changed their minds.'

'Is it going to cause you financial problems?'

'It will be sorted.'

'Do you blame Rhisiart Hopkin for your predicament?'

Buckland raised his voice. 'What you're really asking is – did I kill him?'

Drake opened his mouth to reply but Buckland continued. 'Because I've got a previous conviction you think you've got a compelling case. Well I can tell you now, Inspector, you're dead wrong.'

'The bank tell us that various promises of additional funding never materialised.'

Buckland sighed, as though an explanation was beneath him. 'I've already been in contact with my lawyers. They say we've got a cut-and-dried case against the bank. I'm not going to let Hopkin and the bank stand in the way of this project.'

'What did you think of Rhisiart Hopkin?'

Another contemptuous shake of the head. Even though he might be a reformed character Buckland still had a conviction for manslaughter, had been through the interview process, appearances in court, being banged up in a high-security jail. And that made him hard.

'For what it's worth I didn't like him. I didn't trust him.'

'Tell me why you didn't trust him?'

'He promised us the bank's full support and then we discovered that he'd been talking about how the project was going to fail.'

'How did you find that out?'

'The owner of the next door premises has been after this place for years. He told me he'd heard the building was going to be repossessed soon.'

'That must have annoyed you.'

'What do you think?'

Drake turned to Sara. A prearranged nod and on cue she asked. 'Can you account for your movements on the night Mr Hopkin was killed?'

'Am I a formal suspect?'

'It will help our enquiries if we can eliminate you.'

Buckland guffawed. 'Next, you'll want to suggest that I killed Gloria because of what she did to Norma.'

Buckland was buying time, Drake thought.

Buckland drummed the fingers of his right hand on the desktop. 'I was here, probably. After leaving here I usually go home, write a sermon or prepare for one of our Bible study groups.'

'Is there anyone apart from your wife who could confirm that?'

'You really are good cop, bad cop aren't you? Or at least you're trying very hard. I didn't kill him.' Buckland stood up. 'Now, if you don't mind.'

Drake glanced at Sara, his nod telling her they had to leave.

'Thank you for your time, Mr Buckland,' Drake said, reaching out a hand.

Buckland stared at it without reacting.

Drake and Sara left and outside they paced over to the car.

'What did you make of that, boss?' Sara said before Drake started the car.

'He's an obnoxious character. Difficult to imagine him offering pastoral care. And he's got the motive to kill Patton and Hopkin.'

Sara nodded.

Drake continued. 'I recognised one of those lads in the gym. He was a regular wife beater. I was the SIO on a case when he was sent down. He's not the sort to seek forgiveness – more like revenge.'

'I'll do a search on him, boss.'

'Something about Roger Buckland doesn't ring true.' Drake sounded like a jaded, distrustful police officer. At that moment that was exactly how he felt.

Chapter 19

'I've been trying to get hold of you for days.'

Susan, Drake's sister, sounded at her wits' end. Drake sipped the dregs of his breakfast coffee and reached over to switch off the voice of a politician avoiding answering questions about the negotiations for the United Kingdom to leave the European Union. Drake shared the exasperation of the interviewer about the evasions.

'I've been busy.'

'What do you think it's like for me? The boys are doing exams, George has just taken on a new client and he's frantic at work. Now, Ian, the business with this … man. I mean, it is preposterous. Does he want money? Does he want to make a claim against Dad's estate? Does he realise the effect all of this is having on Mam?'

His mother had been remarkably phlegmatic about the situation, Drake thought. She accepted Huw Jackson's sincerity. Susan reflected her concerns and not her mother's, but telling her that might be tricky.

'I hope you're not going to have anything to do with him.'

'Well, it's not that simple—'

'George thinks we should get lawyers involved.'

'Lawyers?'

'Yes, to warn him off.'

'He doesn't want anything.'

'How can you possibly know that?'

'If he is our brother then—'

Susan almost choked. 'Brother?'

'Wouldn't you like to know something about him and his family?'

Susan kept her voice hard. 'I think it would be in everyone's best interest if we closed this little episode.'

'What, pretend it didn't happen?'

'Well, I suppose so.'

'Don't be daft, Susan.'

'Don't involve me or mention it to the boys.' Now she sounded edgy. 'What does Sian think? I am sure she agrees with me.'

Drake left a heavy pause hang between them. Her marriage to an accountant from Pembrokeshire who barely concealed his disdain for their upbringing in the Welsh-speaking rural community of North Wales estranged them even more. Drake was torn between wanting to learn more about his new extended family and his loyalty to Susan, even though it felt very thin at that moment. In the past, he would have discussed it with Sian. What was the right thing to do?

Drake checked the time. 'Look Susan, I'm going to be late for a meeting with a witness. Why don't you come to stay with Mam for a few days?'

He could hear the impatience in her breathing.

'Then you can talk to her yourself. You might even meet Huw and make up your own mind.'

'Really, when you're in one of these moods you are impossible.'

She rang off before he could say anything else.

Drake found the papers he had collected from headquarters the night before and headed out for his car. After a brief journey along the A55 he indicated left for Llanrwst. Over to his right Conwy Castle dominated the estuary that curved away in front of him down the valley.

He had wanted to visit the home of Rhisiart Hopkin again. This time alone. He was missing something and intuition told him the murders were linked although the crime scenes were different. But gut instinct was never good enough. For now he had no idea how to justify to Superintendent Price his conviction the two deaths were connected.

The house looked forlorn when he parked in the drive. He stared out through the windscreen. The windows were old wooden casements with nets hanging from the top half. Chosen by Hopkin's mother probably, Drake thought. Weeds pushed their way out through the surface of the ageing tarmac and dirty grey streaks discoloured the pebbledash.

He let himself into the house. The place smelt of a mixture of old furniture and the chemicals the CSIs had used. He walked into the sitting room and noticed a film of dust on the mantelpiece. It was never the same visiting the crime scene a second time. Now he had more time to order his thoughts as he scanned the room.

Hopkin had watched television here, read the newspaper, and entertained his friends. Drake turned around and stared over to the dining table still laid out with three places. He stepped around the chairs and stood wondering who the guests were or even if there had been intended guests the evening Hopkin died. He skirted round the table, its place settings and napkins undisturbed. The cutlery looked old but clean. He reached the sideboard at the end and saw the books and several binders of photographs. He recalled noticing photographs and postcards from a summer holiday in an open album when he first arrived at the crime scene. He picked up one of the albums but a noise from the kitchen disturbed him. It was the sound of the back door opening and then a voice.

'Hello.'

'Good morning.' Drake made his way into the kitchen and recognised Fiona Bakewell.

'Good morning, Inspector. I was going to start cleaning. The lawyers handling his estate wanted me to tidy the place up before they sell the house.'

Drake nodded. 'I was looking at the photograph albums on the sideboard. Did he enjoy travelling?'

'He liked to go to Europe mostly. He always went on the train. He loved them. His father worked on the railways, as did his grandfather who was the night stationmaster in Llandudno Junction years ago before the war. Mr Hopkin collected photographs of the railways.'

'I'm sure I saw a postcard from the US.'

Fiona frowned. 'He never mentioned going to America. I thought he was afraid of flying.'

Drake retraced his steps into the dining area and idly flicked through the album he handled earlier. As he searched for the postcards, he heard Fiona entering the room behind him.

'He left everything to a charity so I guess the old place will be sold.'

The postcards were of an airport and Drake removed one from its sleeve. 'Chicago Airport' was printed in small letters at the bottom.

Fiona continued. 'I wonder who he was going to entertain. He was always a private sort of man. He could be dead funny too – making jokes about different people.'

'You mentioned a 'lady friend' when we first talked to you.' Drake replaced the postcard and closed the album. 'Would you recognise her?'

'Well, which one?' Fiona sounded embarrassed.

Drake found his mobile and called Sara, asking her to send him an image of Gloria Patton. Seconds later a message arrived; he tapped it open, and the face of Gloria Patton filled the screen. He showed it to Fiona. 'Oh yes, I saw her leaving a couple of times. A friend of mine has seen cars parked near the house at odd times.'

Drake's concentration immediately sharpened.

'Has your friend spoken to any of the uniformed police officers?'

'I don't think so.'

'I think it might be helpful if I talked to her. Could you call her?'

Fiona gave a puzzled look. 'I suppose so.'

Fiona fumbled with her mobile. Drake's impatience grew. Eventually she found the right number and called her friend. 'The police want to talk to you about Mr Hopkin.' She paused. 'I don't think …'

Drake reached over a hand, inviting Fiona to give him the mobile. She cowered slightly but did as she was told. He pressed it to his ear. 'This is Detective Inspector Ian Drake. I'm investigating the murder of Rhisiart Hopkin. I'd like to speak to you.'

The tone, which suggested he wasn't arranging a business meeting, did the trick and having taken a postcode and address he handed the phone back to Fiona. He scanned the sitting room one last time, deciding he had seen enough.

Five minutes later he arrived at the home of Zandra Tonks. Her appearance matched the exotic nature of her name. Her hair was a bright purple, her complexion fine and, being tall and slim, it was difficult to make out her age. Drake guessed she must be the wrong side of sixty-five and the right side of seventy. Two greyhounds, both a shimmering dark silver, stood by her side as she opened the door.

'Inspector Drake, come in.'

She led Drake into a small conservatory at the rear of the property and sat down, pointing to one of the soft chairs for Drake to do likewise.

'Did you know Rhisiart Hopkin?'

'Not really.' Tonks shook her head.

'Fiona said you mentioned noticing cars outside his house.'

'I regularly walk the dogs. Twice a day, in the morning and in the evening, sometimes quite late. I take the same route every time. There is a footpath that leads through the woods near Hopkin's property. A week or so before he was killed there was a car parked in a layby not far from his house. Struck me as odd. I could see the man sitting inside and when I got close he looked down as though he wanted to avoid me.'

'Do you remember the exact date?'

She shook her head again. 'Sorry.'

'And was this morning or evening?'

'Evening.'

'Did you notice anything else?'

'Nothing, and the only reason it stays in my mind is that when I returned he was still there. But he started the car and screamed off.'

'What make was the car?'

'I think it was a Ford.'

'And colour?'

'Red.'

'Were there other occasions when you noticed cars parked at odd times?'

She nodded and adopted a more serious tone. 'There was a car in the same place the night Mr Hopkin was murdered; I can't be certain it was the same one but it was definitely red.'

Looking for two red cars would be an impossible task, Drake knew.

'It's really important if you can remember whether they were the same car. Did you notice the registration number?'

'I'm not normally a busybody, Inspector. But because of what happened the week before I paid a little bit more attention. It was RTF, or something similar.' Drake moved forward slightly in the chair; this was progress – he hoped that Zandra could drag more details from memory. 'Can you remember the three numbers at the beginning?'

'The letters RTF were at the beginning.'

It made the vehicle very old, at least eighteen years old, Drake thought. Someone with limited means, which included all the artists in the inquiry so far.

'Can you be certain both vehicles weren't the same?'

'I don't think so.'

Drake stood up, making to leave.

'Thank you, Mrs Tonks. Is there any reason why you didn't come forward sooner?'

'I did. I went to the mobile incident room and gave them my details. It surprised me when I didn't hear anything. I do hope I won't get anyone into trouble.'

He left Mrs Tonks and headed back to his car, reaching for his mobile telephone at the same time. He would give the officer in charge of the Mobile Incident Room a dressing down.

Winder was finding it hard to become accustomed to working with Luned. It had been so much easier when Dave Howick had been the other detective constable in Drake's team. But with Howick now a sergeant in Wrexham, Winder struggled with the different dynamic in the Incident Room. He couldn't make out Luned, or Sara Morgan for that matter. It was going to take time to find the right rhythm for his working relationships. It might have been easier had their first case been a burglary or a missing person. Everything about the murder of Gloria Patton suggested a very sick individual was responsible. The death of Rhisiart Hopkin seemed unconnected even though they were running both inquiries simultaneously. Hours trawling through the statements from eyewitnesses outside the shop had produced nothing. And despite the grotesque scene there was no useable evidence. So Winder turned his attention to the direct cause of death: succinylcholine.

His first call was to the main hospital in North Wales and after several telephone calls he eventually spoke to a member of the pharmacy team.

'It's kept in the theatre area in a drugs cupboard.'

'Who has access to it?'

'What do you mean?'

Simple question, Winder thought. 'What system do you have in place to monitor who can access the drugs?'

'We don't.'

Wading through mud would be easier than talking to this man, Winder thought. Before Winder could respond he continued. 'Succinylcholine is a common drug that is used in operations and medical emergencies. It would make the running of the hospital impossible if the surgeons or doctors had to sign for every phial. In an emergency the medics need instant access to it.'

'So anyone could swan in and pick up some supplies.' Winder regretted his flippant language but the man had annoyed him.

Winder heard an audible sigh over the telephone. 'It's not *that* easy. We do have some security procedures in place. I suggest you come and see for yourself.'

Two hours later Winder sat in his car barely able to believe what the hospital described as 'security procedures'. Every member of staff had a personal identity card that had to be swiped before accessing the theatre area. In a period of ten minutes Winder had noticed several nurses in blue and green uniforms and orderlies in mauve polos and cargo pants walk in as the door was propped ajar by staff members going about their daily duties. When the pharmacy manager told him that the other general hospital in North Wales didn't have a swipe card system and that they 'all knew each other' Winder stopped thinking about the possibility of identifying a member of staff who could have stolen the sux needed. Basically anyone with a confident manner wearing the right clothes could waltz in and help themselves.

His work that morning justified a lunch hour with his girlfriend in a burger bar in the middle of town. Afterwards, on the stairs to the first floor of headquarters he started to regret the large portion of fries as indigestion got hold of him.

It only got worse when he entered the Incident Room and three pairs of eyes turned to stare at him. Detective Inspector Drake stood by the board, Sara and Luned sat by their desks.

'I sent you a message.' Drake glared at him.

Winder flushed. He wanted to reach into his pocket, grab his telephone, check the screen, as if somehow the handset was to blame. 'Sorry, boss.'

He sat down, trying to compose himself. Drake said. 'Let's hear about the progress you've been making, Gareth.'

Winder cleared his throat noisily. 'I've been to the general hospital and basically anyone can walk in and take the sux used to kill Patton.'

'But they'd need to know what they were looking for?'

'Yes, boss. But that doesn't take much. Just a Google search.'

'Even so they'd need to play the part. You'd better circulate all the hospitals on the off-chance that someone noticed missing supplies of the drug.'

Winder scribbled on his pad as Drake looked over

at Luned. 'Anything from inquiries around the premises round the shoe shop?'

Luned launched into a detailed narrative almost listing each individual that had been interviewed.

'A couple of individuals confirmed they saw the office refurbishment van outside the property the night before Gloria Patton was killed. We still have a number of people to interview. And—'

'Focus on whether you can identify this vehicle through the CCTV system.'

'Yes, sir.'

Winder could see Luned preparing to launch into another detailed analysis. Drake stood up and tapped a ballpoint on the picture of Gloria Patton.

'I've interviewed an eyewitness this morning. She's given me the details of two red cars that were parked outside Rhisiart Hopkin's home. Gareth, you do a search against the registration number – she only gave me a fragment. And Luned, I want every CCTV camera checked out for the route down to Hopkin's house on the afternoon he was killed.' Drake turned, looking intently at Winder. 'Gareth, help Luned, because we'll need to scour the CCTV records for the previous week. The same witness saw another red car about a week before.'

Winder's enthusiasm sagged as he contemplated the hours of work ahead of him.

Chapter 20

Sara clipped her seat belt into place and Drake drove out of headquarters, passing a team of landscape contractors busy on the open parkland with strimmers and sit-on lawnmowers. Once they reached the dual carriageway Drake accelerated on towards Llandudno.

'We've had the results of the financial checks against Roger Buckland and Gloria Patton's husband,' Sara said.

A large Mercedes saloon sped past Drake, easily exceeding the speed limit. The unmarked police cars on the A55 would make certain the driver was stopped if he continued speeding.

'So what are the details?'

'Roger Buckland has a small regular income from the church where he works. It's less than the average salary. But he's got massive debts. He's got a dozen various credit cards, as well as the bank loans we know about. He seems to have a hand-to-mouth existence.'

'So what's his motive? Killing Hopkin doesn't get rid of his debts.'

'Buckland has a hell of a temper.'

'He discovers that his wife is having an affair with Hopkin. The red mist descends. He can't control his anger, they argue. And ...'

'And Gloria Patton? Is he responsible for her death?'

Drake indicated towards Llandudno and slowed at a roundabout. Norma Buckland certainly had a motive to kill Gloria Patton. Their financial position necessitated not losing a money-making opportunity, and not appearing at the Orme Arts Festival must have been a blow to their plans. But how was killing Patton going to help?

Sara continued. 'It's too much of a coincidence that Hopkin was on the committee with Gloria Patton. There's nothing to link both deaths together. There's no similarity and we haven't had any messages.'

Drake nodded. He could almost hear Superintendent Price making the same points at the meeting arranged for later that afternoon.

'I don't like coincidences,' Drake said.

'Of course not, sir.'

Drake found a place to park in one of the side streets near the gallery where the Orme Arts Festival was launching in two weeks' time. A large banner hung outside the entrance announcing the prestigious guest line-up for the opening. Various gallery owners and critics from Vienna and Berlin were due to attend.

The committee had requested the meeting and Drake hoped the press would be kept far away. He wanted to avoid any awkward questions linking the death of Hopkin and Gloria Patton.

The open window of a second-floor room let in some badly needed fresh air. At one end three tables had been pushed together with half a dozen chairs behind them. Drake scanned the room. He recognised Marjorie and Julie from the first meeting immediately after the death of Gloria Patton. Each gave him a brief nod. Jeremy Ellingham sipped from a plastic cup while deep in conversation with Amber Falk who now had a two-tone hairstyle, the top half a vibrant cream colour, the long shards below it a golden auburn. Nervous-looking individuals, occasionally sharing comments with their immediate neighbours, sat in the main part of the room. Others tapped away on their mobile telephones.

A tall man with the air of a funeral undertaker walked in. Judging by the ceremonial chain hanging limply over the shoulders of his dark business suit,

Drake guessed him to be the mayor. He joined the committee members, greeting each warmly. Drake and Sara found a couple of empty chairs at the back of the room and as they sat down Huw Jackson arrived. He diverted over towards Drake.

'Hello, Ian.' Jackson reached out a hand, which Drake shook. 'The head of my department wanted me to attend.'

'Of course,' Drake said.

'Perhaps we can talk at the end of the meeting.'

Drake nodded before he turned his gaze towards the luminaries gathering at the main table, wondering what Jackson had on his mind. Much to Drake's annoyance, as the mayor called the meeting to order, a man in his fifties entered – overweight with ruddy cheeks and a dishevelled suit with a tie that hung limply from an open-necked shirt. He mouthed apologies. Drake knew him as a nosy journalist.

'Who's that?' Sara whispered.

'He's the local hack. Last person we wanted to see here.'

The town mayor rapped two knuckles on the tabletop like a makeshift gavel. 'I think we should start. The tragic events surrounding the death of Gloria Patton have made us all realise the great contribution she made to the development of the arts in Llandudno. The Orme Arts Festival was her brainchild; it inspired her every day. I know some of you believe the festival shouldn't continue. Members of the public are rightly concerned about safety and security bearing in mind the horrific circumstances surrounding her death.'

For the next half an hour various voices expressed their concerns that Gloria Patton's death, so soon before the launch of the arts festival, would attract trolls and adverse publicity. The mayor and the committee members seated alongside him nodded respectfully, frowned at the appropriate times and occasionally scribbled a note.

'Detective Inspector Drake is here from the Wales Police Service and perhaps he could share with us the latest information about the inquiry.'

The mayor gave Drake an encouraging, rather pleading look. Drake could see that he wanted to deflect any further comments about the cancellation of the festival.

Drake stood up, buttoned his jacket and, sensing many pairs of eyes following him to the front of the room, composed his thoughts. He had been accustomed to speaking at press conferences, and being bilingual often made him a natural choice for the Welsh language news broadcasts. But usually he had time to prepare; now the mayor had surprised him.

Drake reached the end of the tables. The mayor nodded again and gave an encouraging smile. Drake scanned the room, noticing the journalist adjusting his position, ballpoint poised, ready to scribble down Drake's every word.

'Thank you, Mr Mayor. The investigation into the death of Gloria Patton is still in its very early days. We have appealed for witnesses who might have been around the shop premises the night before she was killed or during the morning when her body was found.'

'Are there any suspects?' It was the journalist.

Drake tried not to give him a hard stare, instead looking at no one in particular, but all he could see were dozens of pairs of eyes staring at him expectantly. 'I'm sure you appreciate I cannot divulge details of the inquiry. Any of you who are involved in the art world will know that the circumstances of Gloria Patton's death were unusual. Anybody with any relevant information should contact us as soon as possible.'

Drake didn't wait for any further questions and returned to his chair.

'Thank you very much, Detective Inspector. I'm sure we all appreciate you taking the time to be here today.' The mayor was already on his feet.

'When are we going to discuss cancelling the festival?' A voice from the middle of the audience piped up. 'Gloria's death was like something out of a horror film. We're going to get all sorts of weirdoes coming to the festival because of what happened.'

Drake noticed several heads nodding in front of him.

'I think we need to have a period of calm reflection,' Marjorie declared.

Another voice, more strident this time. 'Gloria Patton has been killed, for Christ's sake. She was strung up like some exhibit in a funfair.'

Drake became increasingly uncomfortable with comments made by some of the audience who wanted the arts festival cancelled. An elderly woman even stood up, her voice trembling. 'None of us feel safe in our beds. There's a madman loose. From what that inspector was saying earlier...' She raised a hand and pointed towards Drake. 'They haven't got any suspects.'

Drake felt like jumping to his feet, telling her that that was far from the truth.

'I'm sure the police are doing everything they can,' the mayor responded. 'As for the arts festival, I'm sure we can all agree Gloria Patton would have wanted it to continue.'

It had the desired result and the tone of further questions softened.

Drake admired the mayor's skill in getting them to rally around Gloria Patton's memory and that evil shouldn't defeat the pursuance of art. Once he declared the meeting over, small talk exploded around the room.

'Did you expect that?' Sara said.

Drake shook his head.

They got up and made to leave but Julie waylaid Drake, taking him by the arm. They joined the mayor as well as Jeremy Ellingham and Geraint's girlfriend Amber Falk, both looking pleased with themselves.

'I thought you should be introduced to the latest members of the committee,' Julie said. 'We won't be able to appoint a new curator in Gloria's place so we've decided that Jeremy and Amber will be on the committee to help move things forward.'

Drake paused, staring at Ellingham and Falk in turn, trying to read the expression on their faces. 'Congratulations.'

'We don't want anything to prevent the festival from being a fantastic success,' Julie continued. 'We've got Milos Fogerty coming to the opening event, which is simply wonderful.' She rattled off other names Drake didn't recognise. 'Jeremy was taught by Milos in art school.'

'I'm looking forward so much to seeing him again,' Ellingham said. 'I shall be doing my utmost to make the festival a great success.'

Falk piped up. 'I really love Milos' work. It's such an honour to be on the committee.'

Drake searched her eyes for the irony he wanted to believe was present. But she seemed genuine enough and Drake wondered what she had been discussing with Geraint Wood. They were an odd couple and having these two on this committee felt even odder.

'Perhaps you might come along to our next meeting and brief us about progress.'

Brief us.

Drake could scarcely believe her request. He was standing next to possible suspects in the inquiry. But Ellingham had an alibi. And Falk had given Geraint Wood an alibi without prompting but it still didn't rule him out. But what about Falk? Was she a person of interest?

'Yes, of course,' Drake said through gritted teeth.

Drake nodded at Sara and they left.

On the pavement outside, Huw Jackson caught up with Drake. He motioned for Sara to go on without him and turned to Jackson.

'I know you can't talk about the case, but the council are very concerned about the whole business. It's probably too late to pull out but given half a chance there are councillors who want us to cancel and take the financial hit. They believe that the publicity is going to be bad for the town.'

Drake didn't reply.

'Ian, I appreciate that recent events are a bit of a surprise. I didn't want it to happen like this.'

Drake stared over at Jackson.

'I've got a family party this Sunday at lunchtime and I was hoping that you might come. It would give you a chance to meet my children. I'll send you the address. I'd really like you to meet my family.'

Susan's words rang in his ears. She would be furious if he attended. That might be reason enough to be there.

'Thanks. I'll let you know.'

Jackson smiled. The invitation seemed genuine, Drake thought. He walked back to his car wondering if the day could get any odder.

Chapter 21

Drake returned to headquarters by lunchtime that Friday after his visit to the father and son who had smashed Hopkin's car. Hopkin's death had left them unaffected ... even pleased.

'We hated him,' the father had said to vigorous agreement from his son.

'Did you know Gloria Patton?'

'Who?

'She was involved with the Orme Arts Festival.'

The father guffawed. 'Is that some poncy arty-farty thing with paintings?'

Drake had opened his mouth but decided that explaining about fine art would be a complete waste of time. When both men had launched into a detailed itinerary of their holiday in Tenerife for the time of Hopkin's and Patton's death, including the names of the bars they visited each day, Drake knew he was wasting his time.

Their farmhouse stank and Drake detoured back to his apartment to take a shower. The smell had got into his nose and even clung to his clothes.

The Incident Room had an end-of-the-week feel. It was going to be a day of tidying the loose ends in the hope that by Monday the investigation would have minds fresh from the weekend. Drake settled into reading the complete forensic report from Hopkin's home, which only confirmed the paucity of evidence. Fiona Blackwell's fingerprints were all over the property as well as Hopkin's and two others from the bedroom that weren't on record. The glass shards scooped up by the back door yielded no evidence, which troubled Drake. If it was a typical burglary he expected some forensic trace, a piece of fabric caught on the door, soil or gravel brought in on the soles of shoes. It meant the culprit was well organised and forensically aware: exactly like the Patton scene.

Finally, he read again the post-mortem report on Hopkin. Unlike the report on Patton it used the common language for a violent murder and death from a repeated attack with a large knife and massive blood loss. They had no murder weapon and no DNA evidence to help them. After a final catch-up session with the rest of the team Drake headed home. On Saturday he was taking his daughters bowling and for pizza.

He woke that Sunday morning refreshed from a good night's sleep, knowing his time yesterday with his daughters had done him good. He recalled the smiling faces of Helen and Megan as they squealed with delight as the pins fell to their accurate bowling. And their disappointment that they couldn't play for longer. Afterwards, over pizza and ice cream, Helen had asked if he was searching for a serial killer, and he'd realised his daughters were growing up too quickly.

After breakfast he couldn't stop thinking about the culprit as a deranged artist whose tweets and YouTube videos really did reflect what he thought. Or else he was a sick individual who wanted to deflect the attention and make the WPS think it was an artist at work. So he decided to spend an hour at his desk.

In the Incident Room he scanned the images of the persons of interest as he mentally ticked them off. Buckland had a motive for both killings, enough of a temper and a history of violence to make him a prime suspect. Drake couldn't help but think they had missed something important in his background.

The excitement at the arrest of Geraint Wood had been short-lived. His girlfriend had provided the crucial alibi Wood needed for the morning after Patton's death but it still meant he might have killed Hopkin. Or had Amber been involved? Or perhaps both of them? There was no image of Amber on the board so his gaze drifted to Jeremy Ellingham, the other artist disappointed by Patton. But his girlfriend had given him an alibi, too, and he and Falk were now the two new committee members ensuring the festival would continue.

He walked over to his room and booted up his computer before carefully moving the piles of Post-it notes to one side. He found Ellingham's website easily enough and watched again some of the videos. None made any sense. None had anything he associated with art. An email from Luned caught his attention alongside one from Superintendent Price. He scanned Luned's message referring to a gallery that had rejected Ellingham's work as disgusting and sordid before she summarised a background search on Amber Falk that told him nothing new. Returning to read Price's email, he saw with alarm his suggestion that if there was nothing connecting Hopkin to Patton it might be prudent in due course for another team to take over the Hopkin inquiry. It annoyed Drake intensely that Price was even contemplating such a thing. It was too early to involve another team.

Grudgingly Drake acknowledged that nothing obvious connected the deaths. The crime scenes were different and the lives of Hopkin and Patton never crossed – except for the festival, and that niggled in Drake's mind.

His thoughts returned to the Patton crime scene and he remembered that Luned had pinned to the board a photograph of it. That the Emin *My Bed* had sold for two million pounds shocked Drake. Where would someone exhibit it? Why would anyone want to buy it?

He typed 'unmade bed' into a Google search and scanned the results. He followed various links and read comments about *My Bed* by Tracey Emin being described as iconic and representative of the irreverent British art of the nineties. Modern art had no boundaries and there was little chance he would ever understand it. How many ordinary people enjoyed this sort of art, Drake pondered.

He spent another hour following the results of the search for modern art. The screen filled with dozens of images of multicoloured canvases. One article described Tracey Emin as one of the top-ten woman artists and so he searched other women artists and feminist art until he reached a page on the internet that he promised himself would be his last. This time he clicked on the images button and the screen filled with an eclectic mixture. Drake scrolled down, deciding he would spend only a few more minutes on this task, knowing he had wasted far too much time already.

He closed the browser, overwhelmed by a feeling that he had missed something. Years of policing had taught him to follow his instinct. So he reopened the browser and searched again for feminist art. It was on the fourth line that he stopped and looked at the images of an elaborate dining table. Then he recalled Hopkin's dinner guests, who they hadn't been able to trace. Fiona Blackwell had never heard of him entertaining people.

He followed the links to the Wikipedia page of Judy Chicago – the artist responsible for *The Dinner Party* piece. The place settings for *The Dinner Party* were for famous women in history. Drake's enthusiasm waned.

Chicago.

A picture of the city's airport had been tucked into the album on the sideboard.

Yet Hopkin had never visited the place.

Drake stood up, pushed his chair away from his desk and marched into the Incident Room. He had to remind himself of everything about the scene in Hopkin's home. Things had to make sense. He squinted at the framed photographs on one of the shelving units. It was an image of Gwynfor Evans, one of the most prominent Welsh politicians of the previous century.

An idea formed in his mind.

He scoured more of the images the CSIs had taken. On the table was a discarded blister pack and at the time Drake thought nothing of it. But what if it had some symbolic meaning? Then from the depths of his memory he recalled a history professor from university speaking at length about the three greatest Welsh men of the twentieth century. He already had a link to Gwynfor Evans. Perhaps – though it was a weak link – the blister pack might signify the creation of the NHS and its founder Aneurin Bevan.

All he had to do was find the reference to the third man.

Behind the image of Evans on the shelves were books by David Lloyd George, the wartime prime minster – the third eminent Welshman? Drake counted the books quickly. At least two dozen. His pulse quickened and his mouth dried.

He yanked the telephone off its cradle and found the home number of the lawyer handling Hopkin's estate. 'Don't touch the house until we've been there again.'

The voice sounded startled. 'Of course. Can you tell me what this is about?'

'Just do as I say and call Fiona Blackwell and tell her not to go inside.'

Drake rang off without replying.

He looked over at the board, convinced that now he had a link between Hopkin and Patton's murders.

Chapter 22

'I hope this isn't a waste of time.' Foulds wore a casual shirt over a pair of washed-out blue jeans. He stood next to Drake on the drive at Hopkin's home waiting for the rest of his team to arrive. It was Sunday. Children were shouting in a nearby garden and an elderly couple walking a Labrador both gave Drake and Foulds a long, inquisitive glance.

'The finance department have been complaining about the overtime last month. So this exercise this morning had better be a valuable use of my team.'

Drake hoped so too. A van pulled into the drive in front of them and two investigators got out. Once pleasantries were exchanged they trooped off towards the house. Drake opened the rear door and led the others inside. The living room smelt of old furniture, but as Drake surveyed it, he noticed nothing else had been changed. He turned his attention to the shelving at the far end of the room.

'Did you dust all the Lloyd George books?'

Foulds looked puzzled. 'We would have dusted the shelves but not each book.'

'I want all the Lloyd George books dusted for prints.'

'What? Every book?' Foulds said.

'Drake nodded. 'And all the photograph albums and any personal items you find.'

'Is there a purpose to all of this?'

Drake looked at Foulds, wondering what his reaction might be to his theory of a connection between Hopkin and Gloria Patton. He doubted Mike Foulds would be persuaded by his notion the killer had staged the dining room to mimic a work of feminist art.

'I need a complete picture of all the forensics from this room – make sure we haven't missed anything.'

Foulds frowned. The look in his eyes told Drake he guessed there was more to it. Drake decided against risking further interrogation from Foulds and he reached for his mobile, excusing himself. 'I need to speak to Hopkin's housekeeper.'

He had tried calling her three times on the journey down to Llanrwst but each time the call had gone to a messaging service. His fourth attempt failed too. He returned to the living room and spoke to Foulds. 'I have to speak to a witness. I'll be back shortly.' He didn't wait for a reply, turned on his heels and left.

Drake jogged down to his car. It was a short drive to the home of Fiona Bakewell. The streets were quiet although Drake spotted a couple of walkers with hiking poles sauntering through the town. He parked outside her bungalow and walked up the drive. The doorbell rang out; the place sounded empty. He found a small gate that led to the rear of the property and pushed it open. An old wooden patio set stood on a random collection of concrete slabs, weeds poking out between the joints.

He hammered on the back door but there was no sign of life. He heard someone shouting from the neighbouring garden. He turned and saw the face of a man in his seventies peering over at him. 'What do you want?'

'I wanted to speak to Fiona.'

'She's not home.'

'Do you know where she is?'

'Who exactly are you?' The man folded his arms.

It wasn't the time for belligerence. Drake found his warrant card and walked over to the boundary fence. 'Detective Inspector Drake, Wales Police Service. Do you know where she might be?'

'Try her ... friend.'

This man was trying his patience. 'Just tell me the

address. It's police business.'

The man gazed again at Drake's warrant card as though he wondered if it was a fake. He gave Drake the name of an estate in the town but was vague about the precise number although he identified Fiona's friend's name – Joe Yates. It took Drake another half an hour to find the small estate, knocking on two front doors before he was pointed in the direction of a bungalow, two galvanised planters either side of the front door with sweet peas climbing over a wooden trellis pinned to the wall.

'Joe Yates?' Drake had his warrant card ready as the door opened. 'I need to speak to Fiona Bakewell.'

Yates stared at Drake but shouted over his shoulder. 'Fiona, someone to see you.'

Drake heard movement in the house behind Yates, who filled the doorway. Moments later Fiona appeared. Drake didn't bother with pleasantries.

'I need you to come and look at something in Rhisiart Hopkin's home.'

She gave him a puzzled look. 'It's Sunday.'

Yates added in a deep voice. 'We're going out now. Can't this wait until tomorrow?'

Despite himself, Drake forced a pleading tone to his voice. 'It would be very helpful if you could spare a few minutes.'

It did the trick; Yates moved to one side as Fiona found her jacket and walked with Drake to his car. Foulds and his team were still hard at work when Drake entered the living room with Fiona. She looked, open-mouthed, at all the activity.

Drake turned to Fiona. 'Take a close look at these books. Have they always been there? Is there anything unusual about them?'

'I don't know what you mean. Surely you don't expect me to remember all the books he had on the shelves.'

'You must have noticed if he changed the books when you cleaned?'

She shook her head. 'It's difficult … I mean. I dusted, of course. And I cleaned. But I didn't keep track of every book.'

'Take a good look. This is really important.' Drake glanced over at Foulds whose expression had now turned to incredulity. An edge of self-doubt crept into Drake's mind.

'He had lots of books. He did a lot of reading.'

Volumes on Welsh history, and various textbooks about the Second World War and the history of various famous families filled the shelves. There was not a work of fiction in sight, not a single Ian Rankin novel or even one of the classics from the nineteenth century.

'Take a step back; I want you to look really hard. Do the books look familiar or are some new?'

Fiona swallowed, stumbled over her words, obviously getting flustered. 'It's difficult. I know he made a record of when he bought every book.'

'A record? What do you mean?'

'I was here one day when a delivery of books arrived. He noted down in pencil inside on one of the first pages when he had bought them.'

Drake stared back at the bookshelf. There was only one thing to do.

He snapped on a pair of latex gloves. Returning to the bookshelf, he removed delicately a biography of Winston Churchill. He placed it on the table, taking care not to finger the cover too much as he opened the book. On the title page he found in a neat pencil – 'January 2013 Arden bookshop'.

Then he reached for another book, which recounted the Eighth Army's campaign in North Africa during the Second World War. The relief in his mind was palpable when he found another pencil annotation.

The next was one of the books written by David Lloyd George.

Blood thumped in his neck as he took it to the table.

Excitement built as he flicked past the title page and on to the first pages of the book without finding any annotation. He glanced round the investigators. There was a mixture of bewilderment and uncertainty on their faces. Methodically he worked through another two volumes authored by David Lloyd George. The earlier excitement turned to certainty and exhilaration.

He gazed at Fiona who was chewing her lip. His belligerence had given way to greater clarity. He stared over at the memoirs of David Lloyd George. Was he right that the killer had constructed the living room as another sick and deranged piece of art?

Drake turned to Mike Foulds. 'I want every book catalogued, and notes made of whenever a book has a pencil record added by Rhisiart Hopkin.' Foulds narrowed his eyes.

'Maybe you think all this is necessary.' Foulds crossed his arms. 'There had better be a good reason for this extra work.'

Drake owed Foulds an explanation. For now, it could wait.

'Let me have a full report once you're finished.'

Drake looked over at Fiona. 'I'll take you home.' Drake retraced his route to the home of John Yates. As Fiona left the car Drake leant over. 'Thank you for your cooperation.'

On the journey back up the Conwy Valley Drake pressed a Bruce Springsteen greatest hits album into the CD player and found one of his favourite tracks – 'Thunder Road'. He had made progress. He tried to forget the probable, inevitable objection that Price might raise to his notion about the Rhisiart Hopkin crime scene. For Drake it answered that simple question – both deaths were connected. They were looking for the same killer.

A message reached his mobile as he neared the Black Cat roundabout. It was Huw Jackson reminding him about the party and telling him he was looking forward to seeing him later. Drake hadn't mentioned the invitation to his mother or to Sian and definitely not to his sister. It intrigued him; part of him wanted to know about the family he never knew existed, but another part was wary, uncertain how he might feel, how he would react, how it would affect his memory of his father. What would his father have wanted? He knew the answer, so when he got back to his flat he showered and changed his clothes.

He stood in front of the mirror in the hallway and checked his appearance. There were bags under his eyes. A few good nights' sleep might help, Drake thought.

The following morning restful sleep had eluded Drake. He yawned as he drove the short distance into headquarters his mind still thinking about the events of the day and evening before. Huw Jackson had been welcoming and his children, a man in his twenties and a daughter a couple of years younger, had been courteous and kind. They had also made him feel welcome and he had chatted easily to Jackson's late wife's family. The time had flown until he had made his excuses and left. On the doorstep Jackson had thanked Drake, grasping him firmly by the hand, telling him how pleased he was to see him.

Drake pulled up by a traffic light as early morning shoppers crossed in front of him. His father would have approved and he would call his mother later and tell her about the evening. But Sian and Susan would be different. For now he postponed any decision about what he would tell them.

He parked the Ford away from other cars before walking over to the main entrance. A smell of furniture polish hung in the air of the Incident Room and immediately he worried the cleaners might have disturbed the neatness on his desk. It pleased him that nothing had been moved, although the bin had been emptied.

He sat down and got straight into summarising yesterday's events in a report for Price. He felt justified that the gut feeling Price had disparaged was vindicated.

Sara was the first to arrive and he acknowledged her greeting but carried on with his report. Gareth and Luned arrived soon afterwards and Drake tried to block out the noise drifting into his office.

He heard Gareth and Luned joking with Sara. Then the telephone starting ringing in the Incident Room. He heard Luned advise that Inspector Drake was in his office. He resented being interrupted so early.

The phone on his desk rang. 'An officer wants to speak to you.' There was a loud click on the line. Drake kept staring at the screen. He had written a clumsy sentence that didn't make sense. It had to be changed.

'DI Drake?' It was a man's voice, shaking. 'Constable Geoff Williams.'

Drake heard shouting in the background and the sound of a woman sobbing loudly.

'What is going on?'

'There's another body, sir.'

Drake stood up abruptly.

'I've never seen anything like it. It's sick and

disgusting.'

'Give me the details.'

Chapter 23

Drake accelerated hard out of the car park at headquarters. He jammed on the brakes as they reached the junction with the main road, their progress slowed by a funeral cortege. He slammed an open palm against the steering wheel.

'Nothing you can do, sir,' Sara said.

'Who the hell gets buried on a Monday morning?'

As soon as the words left his lips he realised it was an idiotic statement. He glanced in the rear-view mirror and saw the scientific support vehicle drawing up behind him. Moments later he nudged the car into the traffic, flashing his headlights and waving at the oncoming drivers. It did the trick, they slowed and allowed him in. Luckily the hearse wasn't heading for the A55 so Drake managed to accelerate down to the dual carriageway.

Once he was in the outside lane, he floored the accelerator. He heard the sirens from patrol cars and an ambulance. He didn't need the satnav to tell him the length of the journey to Conwy. Drake ignored the speed restriction signs and raced past the traffic before indicating for the turn-off for Conwy.

'Did the officer give you any more details?' Sara said.

Drake clenched his jaw as he recalled the description from the officer. 'It sounds just like the scene of Gloria Patton's death.'

Drake sped over the bridge towards Conwy and then through the one-way system until he found a marked police car parked at an odd angle. A second patrol car parked, blocking the traffic, two officers directing people away from walking up the street. Drake pulled up near the shop and switched on his hazard lights. Behind him a third patrol car arrived. Two police officers emerged.

'Make sure nobody gets anywhere near this building,' Drake shouted.

Sara strode ahead of him as they made for the entrance.

An ashen-faced uniformed officer stood in the narrow hallway. 'Geoff Williams. You won't believe this, sir.'

'Show us.'

Williams led them upstairs to the first-floor office. The off-white colour of the bare wooden floors created a dirty-looking effect. Each wall had been covered with a similar white paint. Against the wall immediately in front of Drake was a table, its surface covered with CDs scattered in no apparent order. Williams walked over to the front window and grimaced as he nodded towards the far end of the room.

Drake stared in disbelief at the spectacle. His heart pounded against his chest. Williams had been right; whoever was responsible for this had a sick and disgusting mind. A man's body stood upright in a large Perspex box. He wore blue jeans and his shirt had the logo of an expensive designer brand. But what took Drake's attention was the plastic shark's head pressed over the upper part of the man's torso.

'Jesus,' Sara gasped.

The shark's teeth glistened.

'Another body dead on its feet,' Sara mumbled through a hand clasped to her mouth.

In a corner a few feet away from the shark-headed man a monitor played edited scenes from the film *Jaws*. Robert Shaw and Roy Schneider embarked on the final part of the movie where they destroyed the giant fish.

Drake turned as he heard the sound of footsteps approaching over the wooden floor. He glanced over at

Mike Foulds.

'Fucking hell,' Foulds said as he stared, open-mouthed. 'It's got to be the same killer.'

'There has got to be some evidence, something that might tell us who this madman is.'

Foulds scanned the rest of the room. 'Who found the body? Has the place been contaminated?'

'A woman employed by a contract cleaning company found him sir,' Williams replied.

'Where is she now?' Drake asked, moving away from the body.

'Downstairs with my colleague. She was very distressed.'

Three more crime scene investigators entered the office as Drake and Sara made their way to the ground floor. Another uniformed officer introduced a woman in her fifties sitting in the staff area of the second-hand clothes shop on the ground floor. She wiped away tears as she saw Drake approaching. The colour of her skin reminded Drake of the floorboards upstairs.

'I'm Detective Inspector Ian Drake, and this is Detective Sergeant Morgan. We need to ask you some questions.'

She gulped for breath and grasped a plastic beaker tightly.

'Did you see anyone when you arrived?'

She blinked furiously. 'I swapped shifts. I was only doing Jennie a favour.'

'Did you have a set of keys for the office?'

'Yes.' Her eyes opened wide. 'The boss gave them to me. The place was supposed to be empty. I was only supposed to clean. Make sure everything was neat and tidy.'

'Who do you work for?'

Sara jotted down the name of her employers. It would be the next thing on the lengthening to-do list that morning. As Drake left the shop, a message from Mike Foulds reached his mobile – *Est id. Contact me.*

'Let's go back upstairs; they've been able to identify the victim.'

Drake took the stairs to the first-floor office two at a time, Sara following. A white-suited Mike Foulds stood by the window thumbing another message on his mobile. He looked surprised when Drake walked in. 'That was quick. Your victim is one Noel Sanderson.'

The name Sanderson rang a vague bell and Drake tried to drag the recognition from his memory. Drake turned to Sara. 'Ring area control. Find out if a Noel Sanderson has been reported missing. And tell Winder to contact the cleaning company.'

Drake remembered the video taken from the van near the shop where Gloria Patton had been found. 'Outside now,' he said to Sara.

He bounded back downstairs, almost falling onto the pavement. Sara stood by his side. 'Look for a van. Anything where he could be filming.'

Drake quickly scanned all the cars parked nearby and then jogged a few metres along the road, lowering his head so that he could peer inside each vehicle, but there was no sign of any camera equipment. He turned back and ran towards Sara who scanned the buildings on the opposite side of the street. 'No sign of anything, boss.' Drake loosened his tie. His mobile rang and he fumbled for it from his jacket.

'I'm on my way to see the owner of the cleaning company,' Winder said.

'Call me as soon as you have anything.'

Drake noticed an estate agent's To Let board fixed to the front elevation of the building. Drake tapped the number into his mobile and once his call was answered he demanded an address. He finished the call. 'Let's go and talk to the estate agent.'

They found the offices easily enough after a brisk walk. The place had a professional, busy feel with staff in colour-coordinated uniforms. A slim woman in her early thirties, with long hair and precise make-up got up and walked over to Drake and Sara. She smiled at them, obviously assessing their value as potential purchasers.

'I need to speak to the owner.' Drake showed his warrant card. 'This is police business.'

The smile disappeared. She returned to her desk and picked up the telephone. Moments later a man appeared from an office at the far end of the room and hurried over to them.

'Detective Inspector Drake and this is Detective Sergeant Sara Morgan. A body was found this morning in an office that you have to let.' Drake turned to Sara who gave the estate agent the address.

Drake lowered his voice. 'Is there somewhere we can discuss this?'

'Yes, of course. Come through.'

He waved Drake and Sara to a couple of chairs and sat down behind his desk.

'What happened?' he asked in hushed tones.

'We need details of who owns the property and who had access.'

The agent made no reply but started clicking with his mouse as he stared at the monitor. 'The property is owned by an investor who lives in London. We've been offering it as a self-contained office suite for the past six months. We've had six people show interest in it. We accompanied a prospective tenant only last week.'

'Do you have a name?'

'Damien Hirst.'

'What?' Drake spluttered. 'You can't be serious.'

'That was his name.' The agent gave Drake a puzzled look.

'Don't you know who Damien Hirst is?'

'I've never heard the name before, but I've got an address here.' He scribbled the details on a Post-it note and thrust it over at Drake. Drake frowned, showed it to Sara.

'Have you got a contact number?'

The agent stared at the screen again. 'No …sorry. Normally we do take a number, but we didn't this time for some reason.'

'Can you describe him?'

'He had a full beard, really thick, and he was dressed very smartly. He had a heavy navy pinstripe suit and dark rimmed spectacles.'

The description didn't fit any of the suspects but the beard and glasses could all be props used as a disguise and Drake imagined Buckland or Wood or even Ellingham dressed like this.

Sara made her first contribution. 'We'll need a complete list of everyone else that you have shown around the property.'

'Yes, I understand.' The agent paled before their eyes. He clicked a few times with his mouse, and the printer behind him whirred into life. He picked up the printed sheets and handed them to her.

'We may need to speak to you again.'

The agent looked startled. Drake and Sara stood up.

'What if he contacts me again?'

Drake stared at the estate agent. 'He won't.'

Moments later they were standing on the pavement outside the agency when Drake's mobile rang. 'You were right, boss,' Winder said. 'Noel Sanderson was reported missing last night.'

Chapter 24

As Drake drove out of Conwy heading for the tunnel through the mountains towards Penmaenmawr, a message reached his mobile sitting in the cradle on the dashboard.

'It's a missing persons report.' Sara stared at his screen.

The journey only took a few minutes to the nearby town and Drake found the address without any difficulty.

Drake parked and read the report, lodged late the evening before by Sanderson's husband, Jack Smith. Reading that Sanderson was an artist, he made the connection. 'I thought I recognised his name. He was one of the artists exhibiting at the Orme Arts Festival.'

Sara raised her eyebrows. 'Someone has it in for them.'

Drake decided against sharing with her his theory regarding the death of Hopkin. He had a grieving husband to see. 'Let's go.' Drake left the car and they crossed over to the black painted front door.

Jack Smith had a long chin and protruding eyes that stared at Drake and Sara in turn. His thick jet-black hair glistened.

Drake introduced himself and Sarah. 'I'm afraid we have some news about Noel Sanderson. May we come in?'

Smith's eyes filled with tears, his lower lip quivering. Drake didn't need to say any more; the look on their faces must have told him instantly what he feared. They followed him through into a seating area with a high, vaulted ceiling and two immaculate leather sofas, one black and one white. They sat down opposite Smith.

'He's dead isn't he?'

'I'm so very sorry,' Drake replied.

Smith covered his face with the strong fingers from his broad hands. He brushed away the tears before finding a handkerchief and blowing his nose, composing himself.

'Can you tell me where Noel was going yesterday?'

'He …' Smith faltered. 'He was supposed to be going to see a new gallery owner, someone who wanted to exhibit his work locally. Somebody willing to offer Noel a much bigger share of the sale proceeds. When he didn't return home I knew something was wrong. We were supposed to be going out for dinner. I called his mobile dozens of times and I called all our friends.'

'Do you have the contact details of the person he was meant to be meeting?'

Smith shook his head. 'Noel said he seemed to be well connected. He name-dropped various artists he knew. The man knew all about Conwy and gave Noel some flannel about it being an up-and-coming destination resort. Noel could be gullible sometimes.'

Colour slowly drained from Smith's cheeks.

'Where was he? I mean who found the … Jesus, I can't believe I'm saying this. Did he suffer?'

Drake thought about the grotesque scene in the office building. 'Noel's body was found in a first-floor empty office suite.'

'Can I see him?'

'We'll need you to make an identification later. But it would help us now if we could see Noel's personal effects. Did he have his own studio? What sort of artist was Noel?'

Smith drew in deep breaths to calm his nerves but his voice shook as he spoke. 'He's …I mean... was an abstract artist. He liked to work on large canvases; he sought inspiration from the mountains and the sea and the wild open countryside around us.'

Smith stood up and led Drake and Sara to a room at the rear of the building. Sunshine flooded in from the skylights. A personal computer sat on a desk in one corner near a laptop. 'Did Noel have a mobile telephone?'

'You didn't find it?'

'We'll need to remove the laptop and computer,' Sara said. 'I'll arrange for another officer to collect them.'

Smith gave her an insipid nod.

Drake scanned the shelves of books as Sara continued. 'A family liaison officer will call in due course. I'm sure you will find their assistance helpful. And if you find Noel's mobile telephone then please let us know.'

Once they were finished Smith led them back to the front door. Drake could see the sadness in his eyes, despair at the death of a loved one.

'He seemed genuine enough, boss.'

Drake nodded.

During the journey back to headquarters, Drake explained his theory about Rhisiart Hopkin's dining table. Sara questioned the logic, challenged the very basis for him making such assumptions. After all, Rhisiart Hopkin had an extensive library of history books.

'If it was the same killer then why didn't he or she publish messages on Twitter or Facebook or post a video to YouTube?'

It was the biggest flaw in his argument.

'Maybe the killer isn't ready to publicise the Hopkin killing. There is some perverted logic in his mind that says he needn't boast about it. But he leaves enough clues to tease us.'

'I still think it's a different killer. What you're suggesting is quite fanciful, if you don't mind me saying so, sir. The deaths of Gloria Patton and now Noel Sanderson are similar. Famous pieces of art have definitely been copied.'

'That's exactly what he's trying to do with Rhisiart Hopkin.'

'I don't … what does the superintendent think?'

Drake fell silent.

'I need to discuss it with him later.'

But he wasn't expecting a positive response. Price would probably snort in disbelief, dismiss his notions as lacking any evidential value.

Drake slowed the car as they drove through the tunnel under the estuary. Moments later they emerged and he accelerated towards Colwyn Bay.

Drake walked through headquarters, his mind troubled by the prospect of a meeting with Price, when his mobile rang. Drake hoped Mike Foulds had something to report from the scene that morning.

'I thought you should know the results of the fingerprint analysis of the books was inconclusive.'

Drake paused as a stream of uniformed officers left a conference room ahead of him. 'I'm sorry?'

'No fingerprints on any of them.'

'Nothing? I mean, that's odd isn't it?'

'You're the detective. All I can tell you is that we didn't find any trace of prints on the books. Maybe Hopkin handled them with gloves, some people do that with valuable books.'

Or maybe Hopkin hadn't handled them at all – just the killer. He was forensically aware after all.

Drake reached the senior management suite and finished the call. At least it was progress of sorts. It confirmed what he believed, that the books had been planted and didn't belong to Hopkin, but could he persuade Price?

Drake smiled at Hannah who nodded at the door to Price's office. 'He's expecting you.'

Price stood by his desk clutching the telephone handset when Drake walked in. The superintendent gestured to a chair. Drake sat down and noticed Price's jaw twitching.

'He's with me now,' Price said, glancing at Drake.

He nodded his head, growled and rolled his eyes at Drake as the one-way conversation continued. Finally, he slumped into his leather executive chair and blew out a mouthful of breath. 'That was ACC Jones. He wants regular reports about the investigation. Did I tell you that I worked with him as a DI in Cardiff?'

Price hadn't made eye contact and Drake worried that the involvement of senior management would mean more interference.

'He was good to work with back then. A real team player, but now …'

Price could be abrupt – diplomacy didn't come easily – but Drake had never heard him making any derogatory comments about a superior officer before.

'So tell me about the latest murder.' Price shuffled papers around on his desk.

'It looks like another staged killing.'

Price creased his forehead and raised an incredulous eyebrow as Drake explained about the shark's head and the images of the *Jaws* movie.

'Wasn't there a controversial piece of art involving a shark?' Price said.

Drake nodded. 'It was a piece by Damien Hirst. He preserved a tiger shark in formaldehyde in vitrine. It's called *The Physical Impossibility of Death in the Mind of Someone Living.*'

Price spluttered. 'What? A dead fucking shark?'

'It must be the same killer.'

'Dead right and a sick bastard at that. Who was the victim?'

'Noel Sanderson. We've just seen his husband.' It surprised Drake that Price didn't even raise an eyebrow. Years ago there would have been a non-politically correct comment. 'Sanderson was an artist. He specialised in big abstract canvases. And he was one of those exhibiting in the Orme Arts Festival.'

'So was he connected to Gloria Patton?'

'At the moment the only thing in common is the festival.'

Drake decided to discuss Hopkin with Price. Something connected all three deaths. 'I had some more forensic work undertaken at Hopkin's home yesterday.'

Price's telephone rang and he gave a brief acknowledgement to the caller. 'I'll look at it now.' Then he turned to Drake. 'Go on.'

'I think that Hopkin's death was staged too.'

Price stared at the screen and clicked on his mouse. 'What do you mean?'

'It was intended to mimic a famous piece of art by Judy Chicago.'

'Really?' Price wasn't listening, his eyes still peering at the monitor.

'Hopkin's housekeeper says he had never been to Chicago.'

'Chicago, what's that got to do with anything?'

'It's the artist's name and we found a postcard of Chicago on Hopkin's dresser.'

Price didn't respond so Drake paused, but it had little effect.

Drake persevered. 'Judy Chicago built an enormous dining table to represent famous women. I believe the killer was trying to represent famous Welsh politicians.' Drake continued with his explanation, watching as Price looked over at him with increasing incredulity. But he pressed on.

'Why the hell would the killer want to do that?'

Drake shrugged. 'Why did he build the …' Drake struggled for the right word to describe the scene in the shoe shop. 'Display? It was sick. Now there's the death of Sanderson.' Price had turned his attention back to the monitor. Drake persisted. 'We've got another macabre death. They are all connected.'

Price looked over at Drake. 'You've got nothing to suggest Hopkin's death is the same sort of set-up as the other two. He was stabbed for Christ's sake.'

'But the evidence about the table—'

'That's stretching it, Ian.'

'None of the Lloyd George books had any fingerprints. As though they had all been wiped clean.'

Price cocked his head. 'I grant you that might be odd but it doesn't give you any basis to suggest it was the same killer.'

'But, sir, it makes sense if you …' Drake stopped when he noticed Price had returned to stare at the screen on his desk.

'The public relations department have sent me a draft press release. A local journalist has got hold of the fact the body was covered in a shark's head,' Price announced as he stood up and walked over to the printer that spewed out sheets of paper. He handed one to Drake who scanned the standard bland phrases assuring the public everything was being done to identify the killer and to interview witnesses, adding the special dedicated helpline number. It disheartened Drake when he guessed that within hours there would be dozens of crank calls.

'Forget the Hopkin link, Ian. It's a waste of time.'

Chapter 25

Someone said that politics was the art of the possible. I wonder what he would have said about my art. It is accessible and readily discernible by everyone. Except those with no understanding of the concepts behind my work and what it means and how it affects people. I didn't risk taking another video, even though I was sorely tempted. I have so much more to achieve and I needed to be careful so I watched the charade from a distance. I wanted to laugh aloud when that detective came out of the office and looked around the street like some frightened rabbit caught in the headlights of a car.

He scurried around with his sidekick like something from a pantomime.

I almost pissed myself laughing as they ran up the road staring into cars and gazing up at the windows of the buildings. Then I lost sight of them. I tried to guess where they would go first. I cut through to a side street and saw them entering the estate agents that handled the letting of the property.

Damien Hirst. Using his name had been inspirational. The agent had no idea. He didn't flinch when I gave him the name and a phoney address. He was typical of the ill-informed, uneducated masses. Society had a lot to learn about how it saw itself and how it should appreciate fine art. They were taking so long and I wondered what they could be talking about with such a nonentity? Eventually they came out and I followed them back to their car.

I guessed they would visit the grieving family next. Preparation was key to all of this, of course, and I'd binged on all the television detective favourites for weeks beforehand just to get into the mindset of the police. I couldn't leave anything to chance.

The war mongers would call Sanderson collateral damage. Nice phrase that. Makes me think of that film with Arnold Schwarzenegger where he slaughters a bunch of Colombians who killed his family.

I drifted back into the crowds milling around in the centre of town. I ate a late breakfast and drank bad coffee. A customer at the table next to mine spoke loudly about the SWAT teams arriving in the middle of Conwy. Everyone knows SWAT teams only exist in the US so he was another person whose whole life experiences had been formed by watching rubbish television.

A woman with a broad Liverpool accent shouted behind me. 'Two people have been slaughtered. There's blood and guts all over the place.'

For an instant I wanted to turn round and correct her. But I had to be careful. Not even that estate agent would recognise me if he came into the café and sat down by my side. So I enjoyed a contented feeling that despite the commotion I knew exactly what had transpired and that I was responsible. It was surely only a matter of time until I could share my success.

After paying, I left and spent an hour walking through the town. Seagulls squawked and shrilled around me and I found myself wandering down to the quayside where I stopped and watched the pleasure craft bobbing up and down on the sea. I walked over towards the castle and paid the entrance fee. I declined the offer of a guide book. King Edward I built the castle and imported English people to live in the new town constructed inside the castle walls in the hope of colonising Wales. Listening to all the various English accents that morning, I knew nothing much had changed.

You had to admire the sheer audacity of the king responsible. The castle cemented his place in history.

As powerful art is remembered for centuries. Just look at van Gogh and all the great masters. A breeze picked up by the time I was on top of the battlements looking down into the town and over the estuary. Everywhere looked still and tranquil.

I retraced my steps through the narrow passageways of the castle, running a hand occasionally against the damp, cold walls. Outside, I sat on a low wall in the warm sunlight, wondering if I had to rework any of my plans for the next installation.

I paced over to the end of the grassy section, passing the remains of the royal apartments before I followed the passageway into one of the inner chambers I had chosen. As I entered, I stopped abruptly, shocked. A dozen or more children were shouting and bawling. This wouldn't do at all. It was my space and I needed it exclusively. My chest tightened. I left and stood outside, my back to a wall, gently letting my breathing return to normal. I calmed as the kids barged past, followed by their parents calling out warnings to the sprogs to be careful as they ran around.

I relaxed as I stepped back inside.

The empty room.

I closed my eyes and imagined the place full of English knights and Welsh servants from the thirteenth century. I had carefully thought out each step of the installation's construction. I rehearsed it again in my mind. The sound of approaching voices broke my concentration so I headed for the exit.

After all, I had tweets to send.

Chapter 26

Reports from the crime scene in Conwy filtered back to the Incident Room where Winder had been unable to concentrate on the work in hand, much to Luned's annoyance. After Drake and Sara had rushed out earlier that morning Luned focused on the to-do list on her desk.

She wanted to convince herself that settling into a working routine with Winder was going to take time. She needed to be patient, but he was so annoying. She hoped that monosyllabic answers to his comments would encourage him to get back to work. It didn't seem to have any effect; he even rang the area control office and flirted with one of the girls. Then he called the police station in Conwy, managing to waste twenty minutes gossiping with the officer about the discovery of the body. So she focused intently on the unfinished tasks Drake had allocated from the week before.

There were hours of CCTV coverage from various cameras covering the route from Llandudno to Llandudno Junction and down the Conwy Valley. It had been difficult knowing exactly where to start. But the village of Glan Conwy had a strictly enforced thirty mile an hour limit so she decided it might offer the best opportunity for recording the number plates of vehicles.

She took a moment to reread the various statements and remind herself that she was looking for a red car – possibly with the letters RTF, uncertain age.

She settled on a date fourteen days before Hopkin's death despite Drake's suggestion she go back only seven days. Even if it meant working late that evening and every other evening that week she was determined to make an impression on Inspector Drake.

It took her a couple of hours to become

accustomed to the angle of the cameras and she settled into a routine of fast-forwarding the coverage so that she could spot red cars without having to watch in real time. By mid-morning she rubbed her temple, hoping that the developing headache would disappear.

She stared at images of various vans and trucks, including oil and fuel delivery tankers. Builders merchants' lorries passed back and forth regularly during the day. She finished the first day and sat back in her chair before deciding to organise a coffee. She looked over at Winder. He was chewing gum energetically, clicking on his computer while staring at the screen.

'Coffee?' Luned said.

'Great, thanks and bring that packet of pastries I left in fridge this morning. I'm starving.'

In the kitchen Luned readied two mugs as the electric kettle boiled. Winder had previously warned her that Drake was fussy about his coffee so she was careful not to disturb the small cafetière and his cup and saucer. Sellotaped to the inside of a cupboard door was a list of the team's preferences so she checked for Winder's choice. Then she returned to the Incident Room and dropped the bag of confectionery onto Winder's desk before putting his milky coffee alongside it.

A smile creased his face as he pulled out a Danish pastry before offering her one.

'No thanks, I'm not hungry.'

'Suit yourself.' Winder made a contented sound as he ate through his first mouthful.

Luned went back to her desk. Another hour took her towards the end of the second day and idly she calculated it might take her two full days to watch the coverage from each day. A nagging doubt filled her mind that going back fourteen days hadn't been such a wise choice.

She recognised some of the familiar builders merchants' lorries by the third day. There were more caravans and cars with bicycles strapped to carriers on roofs and tailgates. It surprised her there hadn't been more red vehicles. She noted the number of each one and then requested the details of every registered keeper from the DVLA system. Nearly all had been from visitors with addresses across the border in Cheshire or Liverpool. She assembled a list of the local cars and called various startled members of the public, mostly happy to tell her the nature of their business in Glan Conwy.

By lunchtime, Winder wandered over to her desk.

'How are you getting on?' He didn't wait for a reply. 'Have you heard about the latest body?'

She shook her head.

'Some sad bastard has dressed up the victim with a plastic shark's head.'

Luned raised her eyebrows. 'What do you mean?'

'The body was standing up in a tank. That's what the sergeant in Conwy told me. We are dealing with a right psychopath.'

'It sounds like a piece of art by Damien Hirst.' Luned couldn't remember the title but guessed Winder didn't know who Damien Hirst was. He gave her a quizzical look.

'The boss will tell us all about it when he's back.'

'Of course'

'I'm going for a sandwich, are you coming?'

Luned shook her head. The prospect of watching CCTV coverage seemed more enjoyable than spending time with Winder. 'I want to finish this, bring me a sandwich back.'

Luned got back to work.

By the evening of the fourth day she had another

half a dozen cars to be eliminated. She sat back and stretched her arms over her head. Another red car appeared onscreen; this time it held her attention and she couldn't immediately think why. So she reached for the pause button and rewound the coverage five minutes. She stared at the monitor, wondering if she was going completely mad. The lunchtime sandwich Winder had brought lay half-eaten on her desk.

A red car returned. She paused the coverage. She frowned and did a double-take. Then she realised it wasn't the red car that caught her attention but the orange vehicle with a black roof in front of it. Gloria Patton had an orange car. She drew herself tightly up to the desk. She scribbled down the registration numbers for both vehicles and punched them into the system.

Now she had registration numbers for two red cars. By now Winder should have checked the details Drake had given him of the car that the witness had seen outside Hopkin's home. Luned guessed Winder had forgotten. He had disappeared somewhere after lunch so she decided to get it done herself. She found the details from the witness statement of Zandra Tonks and typed the letters RTF into the system.

Her hands shook slightly as she waited.

The results of her search for the orange car and the fragment RTF appeared moments later. The search for the owner of the red car, still frozen on her screen, was pending.

It pleased her that she was right in checking the orange car as the result confirmed Gloria Patton as its owner. She clicked on the details for the red car with the fragment RTF. It was registered to a local business, Apollo Fruit and Veg. A Google search quickly established they were a wholesaler in Rhyl. Winder had still not returned so she seized the initiative and rang the number, knowing he might be irritated that she had been doing his work.

A girl with a singsong voice answered the call.

'I'd like to speak to the owner of the business, please?'

'I'll put you through to Reg.'

Luned got into her stride; nobody had asked her who she was or why she wanted to speak to Reg.

'Reg Walker,' the voice announced. 'How can I help?'

'I'm Detective Constable Luned Thomas.' She liked the way the title sounded. 'We want to establish the ownership of a red Ford Fiesta.' She glanced at the screen, citing the full registration details.

'What about it?'

'The car is registered to your company and I'd like to know who has the use of the vehicle.'

'It's a knackered-out old car. We use it occasionally if deliveries are late or if some of the other cars are broken down.'

'It would help, Mr Walker, if you can tell us who has been using the car in the last couple of weeks.' Luned tried to sound as relaxed as she could.

'What was the registration number again?'

Luned repeated the details.

'Give me a minute, love. I'll check.'

She heard a hand over the mouthpiece and Walker bellowing something she couldn't quite make out. Then the sound of conversation with another person. 'Are you still there?' Walker said. 'Sorry about the delay. I wanted to check that that's the one I gave Roger to use.'

Luned's lips dried. She was a step closer to identifying the driver who was following Gloria Patton. The hours in front of the computer monitor might well be worth it.

'Do you have his full name?'

'Of course. Roger Buckland. He is the pastor of my church. I gave him the car to use because his was broken.'

It stunned Luned into silence. She swallowed. 'Can I check the name again?'

'Roger Buckland.'

Luned knew there were formalities she needed to complete. 'We may need to take a formal statement from you.'

'Is he in any trouble?'

'It's all part of a routine enquiry. Thank you for your time.' She rang off, anxious to avoid any further questions.

Winder arrived back in the Incident Room as she finished the telephone conversation and he raised an eyebrow. 'Progress?'

She wondered how she might share the discovery with him. Winder held a photograph in his hand and walked over to the board, pinning it alongside the image of Gloria Patton.

'One of the crime scene investigators gave me the photographs of Noel Sanderson.'

'Is he the—'

Luned was interrupted by Drake and Sara marching in.

'The body of Noel Sanderson was found by a cleaner in an office in Conwy this morning.' Drake tapped the image Winder had just stuck on the board. 'It looks like the same killer who was responsible for Gloria Patton. I want to know everything about Sanderson.' Drake turned to Winder. 'Did you talk to the cleaning company?'

'Yes, boss. They didn't have anything of any assistance. It was a one-off job. Paid for by the letting agency.'

Luned pondered how she could tell him about her discovery. He might not even remember he had asked Winder to research the fragment of the number plate. She couldn't waste any time. 'I found the details about the red car with the RTF letters.'

Drake stopped in his tracks and turned towards her, nodding for her to continue.

'It belongs to a fruit and veg distributor company based in Rhyl. I've spoken to the owner.'

'I thought Gareth was …'

Winder flushed as Drake shot him a glance. 'Go on,' Drake said to Luned.

'He lent the car to Roger Buckland.'

Drake raised his voice. 'Bloody hell!' He paced back to the board, moving Buckland's image so that it was directly underneath Gloria Patton. 'We shall have to talk to Buckland again, very soon. Gareth—' Drake glared at the junior officer. 'Get hold of any CCTV in Conwy. Today. And get the house-to-house organised.'

Luned looked down at her screen realising she still hadn't read the results of the search for the vehicle that followed Gloria Patton. Drake started a conversation with Sara so Luned clicked onto the result.

She peered down at the screen, hardly believing what she read. She clicked back into the CCTV footage to check she had recorded the number plate correctly and then read the name of the registered keeper.

'Boss, something you should see.'

Her tone cut across Drake's conversation and he and Sara turned sharply towards her.

'I've discovered a red car that followed Gloria Patton in the week before she was killed.'

'Who is the registered keeper?'

Luned blinked rapidly as she glanced from Sara to Drake. 'It was Huw Jackson.'

Chapter 27

Coordinating the work on the crime scene in Conwy should have been Drake's priority. But the involvement of his half-brother began to dominate his mind. Even so, he spoke to Price, brought him up to date with the details on the Sanderson case, and made certain the house-to-house inquiries in Conwy got started. Luned and Winder were trawling through hours of recordings hoping to establish if Jackson had driven down towards Llanrwst on other occasions.

By late afternoon Drake knew he had to confront Jackson. Until he did so he couldn't concentrate. After grabbing his suit jacket he left his office and spoke to Sara.

'I'm going to see him.'

'Do you think he's involved in killing Hopkin?' Drake could hear the incredulity in Sara's voice.

He paused and glanced at the board.

Sara continued. 'What could be his motive?'

'Jealousy,' Drake said after pondering Sara's comment. It sounded unconvincing. 'Geraint Wood thought Jackson was having a relationship with Patton. Maybe ...' But without eyewitness evidence or forensics Drake's explanation was thin. Too thin even to justify talking to Jackson?

'Are you sure this isn't premature?' Sara said.

She was right of course and Drake valued her contribution; it meant she was growing in confidence. But he had to tackle Jackson and he had to do it alone. Leaving headquarters, the various questions he wanted to ask Huw Jackson swirled around his mind. He broke into a jog as he made for his Mondeo. Sitting inside he let the smell of the recently used dashboard cleaning wipes tingle his nostrils. It had become one of his latest rituals. It reassured him that the car was clean.

He started the engine before gripping the steering wheel tightly. Only two days previously he had been at a family party in Huw Jackson's home. Then he had felt welcomed. He tried to picture what his father might say, realising that Huw Jackson was caught up in a murder investigation. You have to do the right thing, his father would say. Now he regretted not having spoken with his mother; at least he could have told her he had met Jackson's family. This latest development muddied everything.

He shook off his malaise and drove out of the car park. He rehearsed the questions to ask Jackson but they all came back to one – are you involved? Part of him didn't want to hear the answer. He made his way through the light evening traffic in Colwyn Bay and the sedate detached properties of Rhos on Sea towards Llandudno.

He parked a little distance away from Jackson's property and gazed over. There was a silver car in the drive and Drake wondered if it was pure coincidence that Gloria Patton was in front of Huw's car as it was driven down the Conwy Valley.

A woman in her fifties left the house next door to Jackson, a spaniel on a lead barking at her feet. She appeared vaguely familiar, probably a guest at the party, Drake thought. She ignored him and once she walked past the car he paced up to Jackson's front door. He rang the bell and waited. A second attempt to raise a response failed.

He peered into the sitting room. The sound of beating drums seeped through the glass. Drake knew Jackson shared his taste in music but he couldn't make out the band.

At the side of the property a gate led to the rear. Drake unlatched it and walked through. He remembered the well-kept garden from his previous visit. Then he saw Jackson seated in the conservatory, his head bobbing in time with the music. Jackson took a long drag from what looked like a cigarette and tilted his head back.

Drake walked over to the window and rapped his knuckles on the glass. Jackson jumped up wafting his hand in the air frantically. He pointed the remote control at the stereo system and 'London Calling' by The Clash abruptly stopped. Jackson jerked a hand towards the rear door and seconds later met Drake.

'I wasn't expecting anyone,' Jackson said.

When Drake smelt the plumes of cannabis surrounding Jackson it explained his initial reaction.

'It's personal use only.'

Drake raised an eyebrow, said nothing.

'Ever since Jean died, things have been difficult. I couldn't cope.'

Both men were standing on the threshold. 'Can I come in?' Drake said.

'Of course, I'm sorry.'

Jackson stood to one side and gestured for Drake to enter. In the conservatory, Jackson opened a window, and put the remains of the spliff in a glass ashtray.

Jackson slumped into one of the chairs covered in pink floral material. 'Jean loved this room. It was her favourite place.'

'It's very comfortable.'

'Do you want something to drink?'

Drake shook his head. 'I need to ask you about Gloria Patton.' Drake noticed Jackson's eye contact drift away. 'Were you having a relationship with her?'

Jackson reached over for the bottle of beer. He took a long gulp and nodded slowly at Drake. 'She got under my skin.'

'When did it start?'

'A while ago.'

'Was Jean still alive?'

Jackson rubbed the back of his neck. 'I never meant to hurt her.'

'Did Jean find out?'

'I don't think so.'

Drake should have been angry, knowing his brother had been capable of cheating on his wife but he wasn't going to judge a man he barely knew.

'Are you the owner of a red Ford Fiesta?'

Jackson tilted his head at Drake. 'I think you know the answer to that.'

Drake recited the registration number and Jackson nodded. 'It's in the garage.'

'The car was seen in Glan Conwy following Gloria Patton. We believe she was on her way to see Rhisiart Hopkin. Why were you following her?'

'I couldn't stop myself. We argued. She told me our relationship was over. She could be a callous bitch. Marjorie from the festival committee thought Gloria was having an affair with Rhisiart Hopkin. I couldn't believe it. He was a smarmy bastard. Saying all the right things, agreeing with those middle-aged women. They all fawned over him because he was rich and single.'

'But why did you follow her?'

'I wanted to be certain. I had to know for myself.'

'Tell me what happened.'

'She went to his place. She stayed for hours.' Jackson curled a lip, recoiling at the memory. 'I even saw him draw the curtains in one of the bedrooms.'

'What did you do?'

'I sat outside.'

'Why did you wait?'

Jackson shrugged.

'How long did you wait?'

'A couple of hours.'

'Did you ever follow Gloria again?'

Jackson gazed at the floor. 'A couple of times. She noticed me and then she stopped and called me on my mobile, telling me that if I followed her again she would call the police.' Jackson finished the last of his beer.

'Why the hell didn't you tell us about this before?'

Jackson stared at Drake blankly. 'Things haven't been easy.'

'For Christ's sake, this is a triple murder investigation.'

Jackson reached for an unopened bottle of beer on the table. It fizzed as the opener sprang the cap. Drake imagined once he'd left that Jackson would be drinking a few more and finding another spliff. Drake stood up. 'I'll get one of the other constables to take a formal statement from you.'

Jackson looked pale and rather sad as Drake made for the back door. He reached for the handle as his mobile rang. It was Winder. 'Get back here pronto, boss. The internet has gone mental.'

Chapter 28

Drake pushed open the door to the Incident Room and strode over towards Winder's desk. Sara gazed up at him. He could see the worry in the creases on her forehead and in her tight lips. Winder kept staring at the screen, clicking his mouse. Luned stood looking over Winder's shoulder, twisting a lock of hair around two fingers.

'You need to see this, boss,' Winder said.

Drake stood behind him.

'This crazy bastard has posted another video on YouTube. This time it's a completely new page. He's called it – The Impossible Life.'

'Show me.'

'And there are dozens of tweets.'

Luned sounded serious. 'It's a play on the title of the artwork Damien Hirst constructed.'

Drake nodded.

Luned continued. 'I did some research on the original installation. It was supposed to remind us that in life we are always close to death.'

Winder finished clicking and glanced up at Drake. 'Here it is, boss.'

A white-suited individual filled the screen. Drake peered in ever-increasing disgust as the man paraded in front of the camera like some demented clown showing the various props he was about to use. His facemask looked like the image of a joker from one of the *Batman* movies.

Drake heard the door crash open. 'Where the hell have you been, Ian?'

He turned to face Susan Howells from the public relations department. 'I've been trying to contact you for hours.'

'I've been busy,' Drake snarled. 'I need to watch

this video.'

He turned his attention back to the monitor, sensing Howells standing behind him. He guessed she had already seen it.

This madman must think this is entertaining, Drake thought. For the next ten minutes, they stared at him constructing the murder scene. But the footage kept cutting to cinematic shots of the North Wales countryside including images of Conwy Castle, the Menai Strait and the promenade in Llandudno.

'What the hell is happening?' Drake said when the film cut to an image of the promenade at Llandudno.

'There are lots like this, boss,' Winder said.

He must have been filming as he walked along Llandudno prom, Drake thought. Somebody would have noticed. Then the sheer impossibility of identifying an individual using a video camera on the promenade in Llandudno struck Drake with depressing clarity.

After a couple of minutes the image cut back to the inside of the office. By now, the body of Noel Sanderson was erect. Three sides of the Perspex box surrounded him. The killer sat watching the *Jaws* film. He made an exaggerated laughing gesture at the scene where a swimmer was eaten.

Then the coverage switched to a video, obviously taken by a drone over Conwy Castle. The camera panned around to show the ancient castle walls surrounding the medieval town before switching to a speedboat travelling up the Menai Strait, underneath both the Menai Bridge and the Britannia Bridge.

'Don't you need a licence to use one of these?'

Winder replied. 'A friend of mine has just bought one. There are no restrictions. Anyone can use them.'

Drake frowned at Winder, scarcely able to believe these drones were unregulated.

At the end of the Menai Strait the drone hovered

over the eighteenth-century Fort Belan before moving over to Aber Menai point. Drake could see the power of the tide as it ripped past the sand dunes.

'It looks like a tourist information video,' Howells said.

'How the hell is that supposed to help us?' Drake said without looking at her.

Just as abruptly, the coverage switched back to the inside of the office. It churned Drake's stomach to see the plastic shark's head stuffed over the upper part of Noel Sanderson's body. For five minutes, they viewed the coverage in complete silence, no one moving in their chairs, those standing remaining utterly still. The killer finished erecting the box surrounding Noel Sanderson and stood back to admire his handiwork. Then he fiddled with the laptop and the *Jaws* clip restarted.

Then the man stepped towards the camera and bowed.

'For fuck's sake,' Drake said. 'Switch the damn thing off.'

Nobody said anything. They stood in silence for a few seconds although it felt like much longer. Drake paced over to the board.

'We need to find this bastard.'

He stared at the faces of Wood and Falk, linking them together, and then Roger Buckland and finally Ellingham.

'What's the motive for killing Sanderson?' Drake said.

Sara gave a pensive look.

'Killing Gloria might have been revenge,' Winder said.

Drake nodded. 'But Hopkin and Sanderson? Maybe the motive is about creating an opportunity to show off.' It sounded outrageous, of course. Howells interrupted his thoughts.

'What do we tell the press? Every news agency in the UK has asked me to comment. I even had one of the US networks calling because they'd learnt we had a serial killer on the loose. I need to write a press release.'

'And I need to find this killer,' Drake replied. 'Put out a statement denouncing this appalling crime. Including an appeal for anybody who was in Conwy on the night Sanderson was killed to come forward with any helpful evidence. And also include an appeal for eyewitnesses who might have seen someone using a video camera or videoing on their phone on Llandudno prom.'

'Come off it, Ian, without dates and times that will be impossible.'

Grudgingly Drake acknowledged she was right. 'Okay. But add that we have active lines of inquiry.'

'Will you organise a press conference?' Sara said.

Howells paused before replying. 'The superintendent will make that decision tomorrow.'

It was late in the evening by the time Drake got home. He played the recorded messages on his home phone from his mother reminding him he had an arrangement to take the girls to see her next Sunday. She always reminded him, at least three times. Another message left by Sian asking if he could collect the girls from school one afternoon. It was too late to reply to either. He sat playing 'Dark Side of the Moon', a glass of whisky in one hand, trying to relax, but it was difficult.

The images from the YouTube videos kept replaying themselves in front of his eyes. He had read dozens of tweets that included #Iamtheone. Once the initial few tweets had been broadcast various sick individuals had retweeted, sharing the original. The killer was out there revelling in this attention.

When the Pink Floyd CD finished Drake left his drink and walked over to the window, staring out at the street outside, sensing sleep would elude him. He dragged on a coat, closed the flat door behind him and headed into town. Revellers poured out of a late-night bar, girls in short skirts giggled and hobbled around in high heels. It made him realise he hadn't spoken with his daughters for a couple of days. He wondered how he would feel when they would be old enough to visit night clubs, have boyfriends. He shuddered at the prospect and hurried on past the closed shops and cafés.

Eventually his eyes started to burn so he retraced his steps back to the apartment. He propped a scribbled note against the coffee machine to remind him to call the girls in the morning.

When the alarm woke Drake the following morning he couldn't remember which day it was. He calmed his unease by reaching for the mobile telephone and reading the day and date. He showered, chose a navy suit from a German designer he had bought years previously when living with Sian meant more disposable income for purchasing an expensive suit. He draped the jacket over the chair in the kitchen, fingered the note from the night before and smiled to himself. He dialled his old home number: it was still difficult to think of it as just Sian's number.

'Hiya Dad,' Helen said. 'Are you going to be on TV again?'

'What do you mean?'

'Like that last time when you were in that press conference.' Helen was older than Megan by two years but at ten she sounded like an adult.

Drake asked her about school but got monosyllabic answers. He registered Megan's voice in the background and Helen passed the handset to her.

'You haven't forgotten about Sunday?'

Even at her tender age Megan could get reproach into the simplest of questions. 'Of course not. I had a message from Nain last night. She's looking forward to seeing you.' Drake's mother adored both girls and they enjoyed their time with her. 'Let me speak to Mam.'

Megan bellowed for Sian.

'I got your message. I'm in the middle of—'

'You're always busy.'

Drake paused.

'Will you be able to take them on Sunday?'

'Of course.'

'Don't disappoint them, Ian. Surely you can take one afternoon off work.'

'I'll call you later this week about the arrangements.'

'I'd better get going or else the girls might be late for school.'

After finishing the call Drake felt little appetite so he drank a coffee and left for headquarters. He squinted against the spring sunshine as he walked over to his car.

Half an hour later he was parking outside the mortuary. He waited for the final bars of 'Born in the USA' to finish and left the car. The assistant still needed a personality transplant, but it must be depressing work shifting dead bodies around all day, Drake thought as he nodded him through.

Dr Lee Kings cast a glance behind Drake. 'Your beautiful new sergeant not with you this morning?'

'You are not supposed to say things like that, Lee.'

The assistant wheeled a trolley towards them.

'Come on Ian. She's gorgeous. Don't be such a

prude. You can't be politically correct all the time.'

Drake folded his arms, ignoring Kings' comments.

'I saw the photographs of the crime scene,' Kings said, lowering the tone of his voice. 'You're looking for one sick individual.'

'Have you seen the videos on YouTube?'

Kings shook his head.

'He's been tweeting using the hashtag #Iamtheone. So I want you to tell me it's the same killer.'

Kings pulled back the sheet covering the body. Drake saw the intensity in Kings' gaze, looking forward to the task ahead. Attending post-mortems as the senior investigating officer had always been the most challenging part of Drake's work. The smell and the sound of saws and drills were the hardest to forget.

'The killer might have used the same drug that caused Gloria Patton's death. So we need to find the puncture wound,' Kings said.

The pathologist started a detailed examination of Sanderson's legs, then his arms, before turning to the shoulders and neck. Then he smoothed his hands over the fleshy, flabby stomach. A few grey hairs protruded from Sanderson's chest but otherwise he had little body hair.

Drake cringed silently as Kings cut Sanderson open. Kings dictated aloud his conclusions as he worked, oblivious of Drake. Once he had finished Kings stood back. 'Again, he has pulmonary oedema with no obvious cause other than possibly negative pressure oedema.'

'Is that the same as Gloria Patton?'

Kings nodded. 'Build-up of fluid in the lungs was probably caused by a partially obstructed airway. The sux was administered directly into the muscle via the puncture wound on her arm.'

'Does that mean he had medical experience?'

'Not really. This sort of technical stuff is available on the internet these days. All you need to do is click on Wikipedia and it'll give you a dozen ways to kill somebody without leaving much of a trace.'

Kings paused before giving Drake a troubled glance. 'I can't find a puncture wound.'

Drake nurtured a worry.

'We'll have to wait for the toxicology report,' Kings added. 'At least this time we'll know which drugs to look for.'

Kings leant over the body one more time, moving the head to one side. 'There's no sign of any bruising similar to the wound sustained by Gloria Patton. That suggests the killer was able to overcome Sanderson by administering some sort of drug, possibly something like flunitrazepam if he managed to slip it into a drink.'

'In English?'

'Rohypnol'

Drake nodded.

'Again the toxicology reports will tell us.' Kings warmed to the prospect of such an explanation. 'That might make sense. Rohypnol is mixed into orange juice or something to hide its taste. Once he's unconscious the killer can administer the muscle relaxant.'

'But there was no puncture wound.'

'He could inject into the muscle from inside the mouth.' Kings looked over at Drake.

'So we're looking for one clever individual.' Kings made no reply. 'When will you finish the report?'

Kings rolled his eyes.

'I need it yesterday, Lee.'

'All right, I get the message. I'll do what I can but I can't promise anything.'

Drake left Kings whistling along to a piece of classical music and once he was outside in the fresh morning sunshine he stood for moment, taking a couple of long, deep breaths. The ease at which anyone could access succinylcholine had disturbed him. He surveyed the sprawling hospital building. It meant the killer had probably disguised his identity by wearing scrubs and had walked around the theatre area with a confident swagger. But how would he have known where to look, what ampule to remove from the relevant fridge? Once they found that link it would only be a matter of time before they caught him.

He drove back to headquarters and then straight for the crime scene investigators lab where he found Mike Foulds busy completing the forensic analysis of Sanderson's clothes and his personal effects.

'I've just come back from the post-mortem.'

'Anything of interest?'

'It was the same cause of death as Gloria Patton. He suffocated. The pathologist is going to organise toxicology tests. He might have been drugged too.'

Foulds walked over to the clear panels of the Perspex box that encased Sanderson's body. Drake knew the crime scene manager well and the dark, intense look on his face troubled Drake.

'I watched the YouTube video. He must have taken a lot of time to get everything prepared. Describing him as forensically aware is an understatement. I can't find anything, no skin fragments, or grit or soil and definitely no fingerprints. A couple of my team have been reconstructing the mechanism he used to keep Noel Sanderson upright. It was a simple wooden frame screwed to the floor once Sanderson was upright. He must have used some additional pieces of timber to brace the whole thing.'

Drake stepped towards the wooden frame. Noel Sanderson had been strapped to it as he slowly suffocated. Drake chilled at the thought.

Foulds turned up his nose. 'You're looking for a clever man, practical and very determined.'

Drake turned to leave and glimpsed a television at the far end of the worktop. The screen had been frozen on the final frame of the YouTube video. Something took his attention. 'Can you play that video again?'

Foulds joined him. Drake tensed as he saw the white-suited killer preening himself around the office. Drake stared at the table in the background. On its surface were two glasses.

'Can you enlarge those tumblers?'

Foulds fidgeted with some of the controls until both glasses dominated the screen. Drake leant forward; the remains of an orange liquid was evident at the bottom of each.

'Bastard.'

Chapter 29

It had been almost midnight the previous evening when Sara left headquarters, pleased to escape the fractious atmosphere. Drake had been abrasive, barking out instructions, making it difficult to know exactly what was on his mind. That morning the alarm woke her earlier than normal. She was determined to start the day pounding the tarmac. After a few warm-up exercises she set off for a brief run around the country lanes near where she lived. It cleared her thoughts, helping her prepare for the day ahead.

Something niggled about the initial meeting with Jack Smith, Noel Sanderson's husband. Perhaps it had been too rushed, or it might have been Drake's abruptness; she decided to visit Smith again, and with Drake at the post-mortem it was the perfect opportunity. Routine maintenance work in one of the tunnels under the Conwy estuary delayed her journey as the trucks with registration numbers from all over Europe heading for the port at Holyhead slowed to a crawl. Eventually she emerged on the western side of the estuary and powered the car towards Penmaenmawr.

After parking, she looked up at the old building owned by Jack Smith and Noel Sanderson. It looked drab, in need of render and a fresh coat of paint. From the outset of the investigation Sara had realised artists paid very little attention to the normal conventions of society. It was probably exactly that which made them artists, Sara thought, reminding herself of the apparent squalor in which Gloria and her partner lived.

She walked over to the entrance and rang the bell repeatedly before Jack Smith dragged open the door. His stubble was a dirty white colour, the edges of the bags under his eyes edged in black. He wore the same dishevelled T-shirt and a pair of heavily stained jogging pants.

Smith gave her a blank look. 'What do you want?'

Sara caught the tinge of alcohol on his rancid breath.

'I wanted to talk to you about Noel.' Sara smiled.

Without saying anything further he turned his back on Sara, so she followed him inside and closed the door. Smith walked through into the main part of the building and Sara followed him into the large kitchen area. There was a makeshift table and benches constructed from recycled planks of wood. A daily newspaper lay in a heap by an old Lloyd Loom chair, a coffee mug had been plonked on the floor. Sara shivered; it would be the end of the afternoon before any sunshine found its way into the room. Until then it would be uninviting.

Smith stood by the kitchen worktop staring out of the window. Overnight his skin had paled, the bags deepened. 'Do you want a coffee or tea?' He flicked on the electric kettle without waiting for her to reply.

'Coffee, milk, no sugar, thank you.'

'I can't believe how you can do your job.'

Sara paused, uncertain how to respond. Smith saved her the need.

'Seeing all those dead bodies. This morning I woke up and all I could smell was decaying flesh from that room where I identified Noel.'

The kettle switched itself off. Smith put a generous slug of whisky into his mug, poured water over the instant and then walked over to Sara. He sat on one of the benches opposite her. 'You don't want a ...?' He held up the whisky bottle.

Sara shook her head.

'It's been difficult.'

'I can't imagine what it must be like.'

Smith looked up at her as though he were checking her sincerity.

'I'd like to ask you a little bit more about Noel.'

'I gave a statement to one of the other officers. Was he killed by the same person who murdered Gloria Patton?'

Sara fingered her mug and leant over the table slightly. 'That's one of the things we need to establish. What did Noel tell you about the man he was meeting?'

Smith drew breath and released it slowly before replying. 'I don't know how much more I can help.'

'Anything really, Mr Smith. The slightest details might be of value. For example, was Noel pleased he had been selected to exhibit at the Orme Arts Festival?'

Smith smiled. 'He was delighted. He couldn't believe it. There is some hotshot art critic coming from London or one of those European cities. Noel thought it was a fantastic opportunity to have his work appreciated.'

'Did he ever meet any of the other artists?'

'The art world is very small. They all know each other. They all think the work done by the rest is rubbish.'

'Did he mention Gloria Patton?'

Smith winced as he took a mouthful of coffee. 'Yes, I think so … He kept a diary.'

Sara's concentration sharpened. 'Diary?'

'Yes, he was a bit old-fashioned. He liked to keep things on paper.'

Sara couldn't recall any reference to a diary from the schedule of Sanderson's belongings. Perhaps the officers from operational support were satisfied with the computer and a laptop, Sara thought, although she knew Drake would be unhappy the diary hadn't been mentioned yesterday.

'Do you know where he kept it?'

Smith nodded. 'I can probably find it.'

He led Sara into a study lined with plywood shelves. A small stereo system sat at one end, alongside it boxes all neatly labelled and numerous paperbacks. A quick glance told Sara they appeared to be in alphabetical order based on the author's surname. Sara approved of the collection of television period dramas including the entire *Downton Abbey* series. Smith searched through the shelves and boxes until he found a collection of hardback diaries.

'How far back do you want to go?'

'Say, the last three years?' Sara was only interested in the last few months in reality but decided three years sounded reasonable.

Smith handed her three bound books. 'I hope these will be useful.'

Back in the kitchen, Sara no longer noticed the chill. She declined another offer of coffee and thought about Sanderson's link to the Orme Arts Festival. Establishing who had a motive for killing Sanderson and Patton was the priority now.

'I understand the festival committee has been discussing the possibility of cancelling the event. They have asked Amber Falk and Jeremy Ellingham to join them on the committee.' Sara hoped she could elicit some response without Smith realising they were persons of interest in the inquiry.

'The name Ellingham rings a bell vaguely. I seem to recall Noel mentioning his name. Perhaps he'd met him at one of these openings. Check the diaries.' Smith pointed at the books piled in front of Sara.

Smith organised a refill for himself, whisky not coffee, and sat down opposite Sara visibly relaxing as she asked him about Noel's background. He'd had an idyllic childhood, the son of a vicar on the south coast of England. An only child, his parents had doted on him. His mother had died of cancer when he was in his early twenties. Her death had hit Sanderson hard as, without her, telling his father about his sexuality was difficult. But Noel's father had been killed in a car accident before he could tell him.

'I suppose moving to North Wales was escaping his past. He found it difficult to live with the guilt that he hadn't been able to share something so intimate with his parents.'

'What do you do for a living, Mr Smith?'

'I write children's fiction. It doesn't make me a fortune, but it pays the bills.'

Sara made to leave but remembered she had to ask about the two others whose images had been pinned to the Incident Room board.

'Do you know if Noel ever met Norma and Roger Buckland?'

Smith bridled. 'No, I can't say I do. But he did come here.'

'I beg your pardon?'

'Roger Buckland. He came here last night.'

'Why did he call?'

'He said he wanted to pray with me.'

Sara frowned, wondering what had lain behind Roger Buckland's visit.

'What did you tell him?'

'I told him to fuck off.'

Sara shrugged off a light fleece as Drake walked into the Incident Room. He acknowledged her smile and breezed over towards the board. He turned to face the team. 'I've just got back from the post-mortem. We'll have to wait for a toxicology report for a definitive cause of death but the pathologist reckons it could be the same modus operandi as Gloria Patton.'

He scanned the faces, recognising the concentration in their eyes.

'The killer probably administered Rohypnol – the date rape drug – to render Sanderson unconscious before giving him a massive dose of some drug that caused him to suffocate. In the video posted on YouTube there are two glasses that seemed to have the remnants of orange juice, one of which could easily have been contaminated.'

'Did the investigators find the tumblers?' Sara said.

Drake shook his head. 'The whole crime scene is devoid of any DNA.'

'I blame all these TV cop dramas,' Winder said, leaning back in his chair, hands threaded behind his head. 'Everyone gets to be an expert on crime scenes and police procedure.'

'Mike Foulds even thinks the killer used a vacuum cleaner to make absolutely certain he didn't leave any trace.'

'Every killer leaves a trace, isn't that the principle?' Luned piped up.

'Not if you can't find it,' Winder said.

'Bring me up to date,' Drake said.

'I'm going back to Conwy this afternoon, boss,' Winder said. 'One of the lads from the local station thinks some of the shops have CCTV coverage.'

Drake's mobile rang and he fumbled for the handset from his inside pocket.

'Detective Inspector Drake, there's a couple in reception demanding to see you.'

'Who are they?'

'Odd-looking woman – Amber Falk and a Geraint Wood. I've told them that you're busy and ...'

'I'll be down directly.'

Drake glanced over at Sara, nodding towards the

door. 'Downstairs, we've got someone to interview.'

Sara caught up with Drake as he hurried down the corridor towards the stairs for reception. 'I saw Jack Smith again this morning, sir,'

Drake mumbled an acknowledgement.

'Smith gave me Noel Sanderson's diaries for the last three years.'

Drake was on the final flight of stairs, Sara a couple of steps behind him.

'I thought operational support had recovered all the relevant paperwork?'

'Evidently that wasn't the case.'

'How can we be expected to do a job if the basics aren't done properly?'

At the bottom of the staircase, Drake turned for the door to reception and held it open for Sara.

'Roger Buckland went to see him last night.'

'Buckland? Really?' They reached reception and saw Amber Falk and Geraint Wood pacing around. Drake whispered to Sara. 'You can tell me about Buckland later.' He neared Amber and Geraint, reaching out a hand.

'I understand you want to speak to me?'

Amber gave his hand a single, brief, limp handshake. In contrast, Geraint's handshake was firm and brisk.

'We need to discuss things in private,' Amber said.

Drake gestured towards a conference room. A catch of a window eventually gave way after Sara struggled with it and fresh air streamed into the stuffy room.

Amber and Geraint sat upright against the table, their elbows leaning on its surface.

'It's about Noel Sanderson,' Amber said.

Opposites attract, Drake thought, but Geraint was such a belligerent Welshman and her accent made her so obviously English.

'Do you have any information that might be of interest?' Drake said.

Alongside him, Sara opened her notepad, a ballpoint at the ready. Drake sensed her staring over at Amber and Geraint.

'It is most dreadfully sad about Noel. It must be terrible for his family,' Amber said.

'Do you have anything to add to the enquiry regarding the death of Noel Sanderson?' Drake wondered why they had turned up at headquarters.

'We knew him, of course. We liked his work.'

Geraint butted in. 'Fuck's sake, Amber. Just get on with it.'

She gave him a dark stare that had barely left her face before she turned back to look at Drake. 'What Geraint means is there was a bit of an incident.'

Geraint groaned. 'Stop this malu cachu woman.'

That Amber understood the Welsh word for bullshit amused Drake. But living with Geraint probably meant she knew a lot more common words.

'What Amber is trying to say is that we had a blazing argument with him. When the committee told me I wasn't going to get a place to exhibit I completely lost it. Well and truly fucking lost it.'

Amber cut in. 'We went to see him. Tried to reason with him. Pleading that Geraint had to have an opportunity. Noel was old for God's sake. It should have been our turn.'

'Where did this argument take place?'

'We saw him when he was talking to Gloria Patton in her gallery. I did my best to talk Geraint out of confronting him. They were sharing a glass of wine, passing the time of day.'

'I'm not proud of what I did, Inspector.' Geraint's accent deepened as he launched into his confession. 'I called him a weasel. I told him his art was shit. I made some comments about him going back to live in England and if he had any interest in Wales he could at least learn the language.'

Drake sensed that both had more to get off their chest.

'When did this happen?'

'Earlier this month,' Amber said.

'I take it there were other witnesses present?'

'That's why we are here,' Geraint added in a slow voice. 'I wanted you to hear the details from us before you heard it from anyone else.'

'All you've told me so far is that you had an argument.'

Geraint cleared his throat. 'I may have said something a little stronger … I think I may have told him that he'd be better off dead.'

Chapter 30

Back in his office Drake sat by his desk as Sara recounted Jack Smith's reaction to Roger Buckland's offer to pray with him. He chuckled but quickly enough his mind turned to motive. There was a motive for everything.

'Why did Buckland really visit Smith?' Drake said.

'If he killed Sanderson it would be pretty macabre visiting his husband.'

'Roger Buckland is an oddball character. We know he's got a violent temper so he's probably quite capable of acting completely irrationally.'

Sara rolled her eyes, unconvinced by Drake's logic.

'What did you make of Amber Falk and Geraint Wood?'

'You'd better talk to the staff at Gloria Patton's gallery. Try and find out if anyone recalls the argument. If they are involved I suppose they think themselves terribly clever, coming in, confessing to an argument that clearly gives them a motive for Sanderson's death.'

'Amber seemed genuine enough.'

'I don't trust any of these artistic types.'

Sara scooped up her papers and left Drake.

He reached over and switched on his computer. Seconds later the screen lit up. He dreaded the prospect of having to trawl through dozens of emails needing his attention. He couldn't simply delete them; each one had to be read and contemplated.

Drake pondered the meeting between Roger Buckland and Jack Smith. Sara had been wise to see him again but he was still annoyed that the diaries had been missed so he fired off an email of complaint to operational support. He felt a growing unease that he had insufficient detail about Buckland. They knew about his criminal conviction and his violent temper but Drake had to spend more time getting to know Buckland. He found the file from the Merseyside Police. Buckland was the product of a broken home. He had never known his biological father and his mother had several failed relationships that resulted in three half-siblings. Drake took a moment to reflect that he now had the opportunity to build a relationship with his half-brother. He wondered whether Buckland regretted his fractured family relationships. It might only be a matter of time before those questions could be asked, Drake thought, starting to relish the prospect of an interview with Buckland.

The reports from the social workers described the family as classically dysfunctional with major inter-generational issues. The only constant factor in his life had been the same secondary school. Buckland's interest in the school's amateur dramatic group grabbed Drake's attention. The drama teacher praised his dedication and his stage presence that contributed to a production of Macbeth.

Confidence was one thing he shared with Patton and Sanderson's killer.

Drake stood up, pushed his chair back and paced out into the Incident Room. He stared at the images of the two crime scenes broadcast on YouTube. It was more than confidence. It was a sick, menacing paranoia. The description from the estate agent of a man with an immaculate pinstripe suit and bushy beard suggested the killer enjoyed a certain theatricality: the dressing-up, performing in front of the camera. But the scene at Hopkin's murder was different. Was Superintendent Price right? Was it simply a burglary gone wrong?

Once he read the basis of Buckland's appeal

against the original murder conviction the more Drake realised it was bound to have succeeded. Although Buckland had launched an unprovoked vicious attack on the victim, it was clear the intention to kill couldn't be sustained. Drake skipped onto the various parts of the documentation that dealt with Buckland's imprisonment. An eight-year sentence for manslaughter resulted in his release on parole after six years supported by reports from probation officers that spoke of him as a reformed personality. The chaplain at the open prison where he had served his final few months spoke warmly of his committed Christianity.

After his release from prison information about him was scarce. Drake turned his attention to the website of the church where he was now a pastor. His biography conveniently avoided any reference to his criminal conviction. There were references to various churches in the Liverpool area and to his training at an evangelical college.

Another hour flew by as Drake read the details of each congregation. Luckily, the churches spend little time updating their websites and Drake found a bio page for a young-looking Roger Buckland. He read the details and section that made reference to Buckland's work supporting a hospital chaplain.

It meant he was accustomed to hospital procedures. He would have talked to doctors, gossiped with nurses, shared a joke with them. Would he have known how to access sux, Drake wondered.

He stood in front of the Incident Room board, ignoring the activity around him, and stared at the image of Buckland. Then his gaze fell on Wood, and Drake replayed in his mind Wood's confession earlier that morning.

Wood had admitted that he wished Sanderson dead. Geraint Wood and Norma Buckland both hated

Patton. Revenge as a motive for either of them sat uncomfortably for Drake. Perhaps they hoped to gain by getting their work exhibited at the festival with Sanderson out of the way. With Amber Falk on the committee that option fitted more easily into implicating Geraint Wood.

The oddity of the whole arts festival committee baffled Drake. He stared at the face of Jeremy Ellingham. Despite Ellingham's work being rejected he was now on the committee. Drake could even see his work being exhibited. That pointed the finger of guilt at Ellingham. Drake knew from Sara that Sanderson had met Ellingham. It reminded him that Sara had left Sanderson's diaries on his desk so after returning to his office he sat down and opened the diary for the current year.

Peering into a person's life had become second nature for Drake, and Sanderson's diary made the task easier. Every day had an entry for some event in his life, however insignificant, and Drake groaned to himself at the prospect of having to work through every piece of information. Sanderson had jotted down his appointment at a barbers and discussions with colleagues and friends. He scanned for Ellingham's name, knowing he might miss something important. He found the name and alongside it a mobile number.

Drake reached over and double-checked it against their contact number for Ellingham. They were different. Drake paused, focusing on why Ellingham needed two telephone numbers.

He reached for the mouse on his desk and googled Jeremy Ellingham.

A glossy website appeared and Drake clicked on a tab with the title 'performances' and watched Ellingham prancing around an empty stage acting two roles. The sound of taped laughter added to the absurdity of the whole scene. Another video had Ellingham walking in a deserted street, avoiding the cracks in the pavement. Drake clicked away and found a video of Ellingham hard at work in his studio. The camera panned slowly over pieces of ceramics and pottery on shelves and cupboards. Drake barely recognised the garden shed where he had first seen Ellingham. Drake guessed his girlfriend must have helped him tidy. He couldn't immediately recollect her name so he surfed through the records to discover Valerie's name.

He silently cursed that her contact details were incomplete, so he instigated a search against her name.

He sat back in his chair. Thinking.

He let his mind go right back to the start and Gloria Patton's death. It had taken careful planning to avoid any forensic trace and to gather the resources to complete the macabre scene inside the shoe shop. Drake pondered the motive for her death. Convinced there would be something in her life, something about her background to point them in the direction of the killer, he decided to revisit everything about her.

He found the papers removed from Patton's gallery office and spread them over his desk in neat and orderly piles. After half an hour he opened the file with her comments on the rejected artworks for the Orme Arts Festival. The description of Ellingham's work as 'utterly derivative' and 'lacking in imagination' made him realise he hadn't paid enough attention to Ellingham as a suspect. It meant learning more about Valerie Reed, who had provided his alibi.

The telephone rang as he wondered about his next conversation with Valerie Reed. He grabbed at the handset. 'Yes.'

A disinterested voice from area control announced. 'A white van has been found in woods near Betws y

Coed. You were to be notified.'

Drake stood up abruptly. His chair fell over. He muffled the microphone and bellowed. 'Sara.'

He finished scribbling the details on a sheet of paper when Sara appeared on the threshold of his office. 'Some hikers have found the white van.' Sara turned on her heels and scampered back for her jacket. They left headquarters and raced for Drake's car.

'What do we know, sir?'

Drake thrust his notes in her direction. 'Uniformed officers are at this postcode.'

He accelerated hard out of headquarters and switched on the blue flashing lights of the pool car.

Sara tapped the postcode into the satnav then rang area control to track down the contact details for the officers at the scene. Drake ignored the speed limits as he raced down the Conwy Valley. The satnav took them up through the lanes and towards a thickly wooded landscape. Drake's frustration increased as Sara struggled to make sense of the directions.

Eventually Drake turned into a gravelled car park next to a ramshackle dilapidated toilet building. A tall officer ran down the track leading up into the forest, his high-vis jacket flapping by his side.

'Follow me, sir.'

Drake nodded and they followed the officer, their shoes crunching on the loose gravel, a thick smell of pine and earth filling the air.

Sara read the message that bleeped her mobile to life. 'CSIs should be here in three minutes.'

Drake acknowledged the information with a cursory nod.

As the track narrowed a left-hand fork led up through the forest. In the distance, no more than three hundred yards, another uniformed officer stood, wide legged, hands on hips. Behind him were two hikers in grey walking trousers, holding poles propped against rucksacks at their feet. Drake increased his pace and by the time he reached the officer his chest was tight, his breathing shallow.

'Over there, sir.' The officer nodded through the thickening trees and shrubbery.

Drake stared over and saw the green tarpaulin straddling something in a thicket nearby.

He glanced at Sara standing by his side. 'We should wait for the CSIs.'

'The scene might have been contaminated already,' Sara said, referring to the hikers.

'Let's talk to them.'

Drake made his way over to a man in his forties who stood next to a woman of the same age. Both were slim, with short hair and healthy complexions, an outdoorish look in their eyes.

'This is Russell and Diane Wright,' the officer said.

Drake dispensed with formalities. 'Can you tell me exactly what happened today?'

Russell Wright gave a brief, frightened look before replying. 'I had a call of nature. I went off the track and into the trees when I spotted the tarpaulin. I was intrigued why anyone would leave anything in this beautiful woodland. Then I noticed the tyre tracks and they looked recent. So I got curious and I went over and peeked at the van underneath. I'd read all about the white van with the removal livery so once I read the letters on the side I called 999.'

Drake stared at him. 'Did you see anyone?'

Russell shook his head.

Drake turned as he heard voices approaching. Mike Foulds and two crime scene investigators walked towards him. He turned back to Diane and Russell. 'I'll need your exact movements today with a precise route. And details of anybody you passed.' Drake paused and lowered his voice. 'This is important. I need your full cooperation not to tell anyone about this. Do you understand?'

Two startled faces nodded in turn.

Drake left them and met Foulds who peered into the thicket of trees.

Foulds cast a wary glance around the woodland. 'What do you want me to do?'

Drake gazed over to the trees. 'We can't leave the van undisturbed on the off-chance he might return. There could be valuable evidence. So we do a full forensic analysis of the van and replace the tarpaulin. I need fingerprints results as soon as you can.'

'I know the drill.'

Drake was already three paces down the track. 'Let me know if you make progress.' Drake turned to Sara. 'Talk to operational support – get them to allocate a constable and a probationer to keep an eye on this van overnight.'

She reached for her mobile as Drake did likewise.

He dictated clear instructions for triangulation to be completed on three telephone numbers for the last two weeks with specific attention paid to the woodland they were walking through.

The killer had hoped the van would remain undiscovered and Drake hoped that when he had parked it his mobile telephone would have been switched on.

Chapter 31

Drake left headquarters the following morning, annoyed that Foulds still had nothing to report about possible fingerprints from the van. A call chasing the results of the triangulation analysis had earned him a petulant response. So he determined to spend as little time as possible at the Orme Arts Festival committee meeting. The now-familiar Julie paced around the room in Canolfan Tudno like a scalded cat, adding to his frustration. She chewed furiously on one fingernail after another. She even paused to gnaw off a large piece before continuing her pacing. Marjorie looked as though the colour in her cheeks had been mechanically extracted.

Drake checked the time on his watch. He had priorities to manage. His presence was an exercise to assure them that the WPS was doing everything it could.

Drake noticed the slight tremor in Marjorie's voice as she raised it and beneath her posh accent he heard West Country rhythms. 'How the hell are we supposed to continue?' She didn't wait for a reply. 'Are we next?'

Julie simpered before slumping into a plastic chair. 'I'm terrified.' She reached over for the glass on the table in front of her and grimaced as she knocked back a mouthful of the whisky-coloured liquid.

Drake glanced over at both women. 'Did either of you know Noel Sanderson?'

Marjorie was the first to reply. 'Of course. He's a fixture in the North Wales arts scene. Brilliant, brilliant.' Her voice trailed away.

'Awkward bugger,' Julie said. 'I never liked him. Too much of a posh git for my liking.'

'Julie, how can you say that? He's dead.' Marjorie reached for a handkerchief and blew her nose.

'Will you still exhibit his work?'

Julie stared at Drake but she looked straight through him. Marjorie thrust her hand to her mouth. 'I hadn't thought about it. What can we do? We can't exhibit now. After what has happened.'

Julie's voice sounded shrill now. 'And Rhisiart is dead too. There's only us two left from the original committee.'

'And now Jeremy and Amber,' Marjorie said.

'Where are they?' Drake said, his interest piqued by their non-attendance.

'I sent them a text and left a message on their voicemail telling them you'd be here.'

Julie stood up abruptly, nearly losing her balance in the process. She paced around the room again. 'Can you protect us?'

Drake opened his mouth to reply but Julie cut in.

'I mean, this mad man has killed Gloria and now Noel Sanderson.'

Drake wanted to establish who might replace Sanderson, and whether that person might have the perfect motive. 'Will you be inviting some other artist to exhibit instead of Noel Sanderson?'

Julie screwed up her eyes at Drake, as though she couldn't understand the question. 'We simply don't know. It's too soon. There's so much to discuss.'

Julie stopped and stared at Drake. 'Oh my God. You don't think that Rhisiart was killed by the same man?'

Drake cleared his throat, deciding to follow the official WPS line. 'We believe that the death of Hopkin is unrelated to that of Gloria Patton.' He hoped he sounded convincing even if he couldn't convince himself.

Marjorie lowered her voice to a whisper. 'I can't believe it. Wasn't it a burglary that went wrong?'

'We—'

'Jesus, this is awful. I can hardly bear to think about it. I think we shall have to cancel the arts festival.'

Julie leant over the table. 'We can't do that. Everything has been arranged.' Julie continued. 'There are so many people depending on us, Marjorie. We can't simply give up.'

'I know, I know. But everything's changed.'

'We have the support from the bank. And the local council.'

'Somebody else might be killed. It could be one of us. For Christ's sake, Julie. We might be next.'

Drake decided to interrupt. 'All I can suggest is you take reasonable precautions, be careful. Please don't make arrangements to meet anybody you don't know alone.'

Both women stared over at him, wide-eyed.

'We will find this killer; it's only a matter of time.'

Before either woman could reply the door crashed open and Amber Falk entered. 'It's the most terrible news about Noel.' Drake searched for insincerity in her voice, reminding himself again that Geraint Wood, Amber Falk's boyfriend, had been rejected by the committee.

She didn't seem to be exaggerating and she seemed genuinely distressed. Behind him Drake heard voices approaching and Huw Jackson walked in; noticing Drake, he gave him a sombre nod. Following immediately behind was Jeremy Ellingham.

Huw sat down alongside Drake. 'Good morning, Ian.'

Drake didn't reply but allowed his gaze to follow Ellingham as he greeted Julie and Marjorie and then Amber.

He heard Huw say something but he wasn't

listening. Drake stared over at Ellingham. He and Geraint Wood had alibis for the death of Gloria Patton. Drake's chest tightened at the possibility that the results of the triangulation of the mobile telephones for both men might place them in Betws y Coed in the last week. Eventually Huw raised his voice. 'Ian, how is Jack Smith?'

Drake looked at his half-brother. 'As you would expect.'

Ellingham had found a seat next to Marjorie and the exchange of condolences had slowed. The older two women stared over at Drake and Huw Jackson blankly, expecting them to say something, take the initiative.

Huw cleared his throat. 'This is terribly sad. The leader of the council and the town mayor called me this morning offering their support. The local authority wants to ensure the festival continues despite all the recent tragic events.'

Drake recognised the sincerity in Huw's voice. Watching Julie and Marjorie, he saw the tension on their faces slacken. He listened as Huw regurgitated platitudes. Meaningless clichés, Drake thought.

'I've spoken with the important sponsors including the bank and they all agree the festival should continue. I appreciate emotions are raw and you may feel it would be best to cancel but I'm sure that Noel Sanderson and Gloria Patton would want the festival to be a success.'

Amber Falk and Jeremy Ellingham nodded immediately but Drake sensed reluctance from both women.

'In the end it must be a decision for the committee. But we are doing everything we can to track down the killer,' Drake said.

'I am very worried ...' Julie said.

Marjorie nodded now. 'There are three deaths all related to the Orme Arts Festival. I think we'd be crazy to carry on.'

'Three deaths?' Ellingham said. 'What could possibly lead you to suspect that Rhisiart was killed by the same person?'

Drake ignored the question but stared at Ellingham for a moment. Was it a performance?

Drake stood up and made to leave. 'I hope I've given you as much reassurance as I can. I'll be asking officers to interview you about Noel Sanderson in due course.'

He scanned four frightened faces. Even so, a niggle of doubt crept into his mind. How many of these artists could be genuine, Drake thought.

Uninvited, Sara followed Drake into his room and made herself comfortable in one of the visitor chairs. The hour she had spent that morning at Patton's Fine Art interviewing one of the staff felt wasted and from the drained look on Drake's face she suspected his meeting had been equally unproductive.

'I spoke to a girl at Gloria Patton's gallery this morning.' Drake pitched his head up and stared over at her. His eyes looked tired. 'She confirmed Wood's version of the argument with Sanderson.'

Drake exhaled a long breath. 'He's still a suspect until we can exclude him.'

Sara nodded. Drake could be infuriatingly rude and brusque but she had learnt that he was single-minded and thorough. 'How did you get on, boss?'

'Have we had the results of the triangulation analysis I requested?'

She shook her head. Avoiding answering questions was another affectation she put down to his impatience.

'Jeremy Ellingham and Amber Falk were both there. As were the committee members.' He paused. 'They're frightened.'

Sara could easily see why that was the case.

'We'll need to speak to Ellingham again. There's an entry in Sanderson's diary suggesting they met.' Drake adjusted his position on the chair, straightening his tie before continuing, as though he'd been able to shake off some thick veil. 'Buckland, Wood and Ellingham could all be simply wreaking revenge for having their work rejected by the committee, which would give them a motive to kill Hopkin and Patton.'

'And Sanderson?'

'He took a place in the arts festival one of them thought he didn't deserve. Money and greed are the oldest motives known to mankind.'

'But that implies that Hopkin's death is linked to the other two. Although they are completely different.'

Drake became silent again and she wondered if he was being pressurised by senior management about his theory explaining Hopkin's death. It was just a theory after all.

'We keep an open mind. Until we are ordered to do otherwise we'll run both investigations together, and assume it is the same killer.'

Sara nodded and shared a steely determined look with Drake.

Drake glanced over at his monitor and she noticed the concentration on his face as he read an email.

'I know that name,' Drake announced.

Sara waited for him to continue.

'The CSIs found fingerprints inside the van. They are a match to a Michael Spencer.'

Drake drew his chair nearer the desk. Sara could see him opening the link for Spencer's details. He sat back abruptly. 'Spencer was the man in the gym with Buckland. I arrested him years ago for beating his wife.' Sara watched as Drake read from the screen. 'He's got a dozen convictions for violence.'

'He could be Buckland's accomplice.'

'Exactly.'

Before Drake could add anything else Winder appeared at Drake's office door. 'You need to see this, boss.' He stumbled over his words in excitement. By the time Drake and Sara had reached Winder's desk the junior officer was clicking open CCTV coverage on his monitor.

'I managed to recover a lot of CCTV recordings from the middle of Conwy.'

Drake stared at the screen. The filming had been taken from a camera perched high above street level. It had obviously survived the cutbacks imposed by cash-strapped town councils.

'It's mid-morning two days before Noel Sanderson was killed,' Winder said, clicking his mouse. The screen filled with pedestrians milling around the town centre. A timer at the bottom told Drake it was 11.36 am.

'There it is: watch the two people coming out of the café.' Winder moved away from the screen, allowing Sara and Drake an uninterrupted view.

The seconds passed as they watched Norma Buckland deep in conversation with Noel Sanderson. She laughed at something he said and he smiled broadly. She touched his forearm. They focused on each other, neither paying any attention to the passers-by.

They embraced before exchanging an intimate kiss.

'Now that changes things,' Sara said.

'That was a snog, boss. If you don't mind me

saying so,' Winder said.

Luned, sitting next to him, sniggered.

Drake stared at the screen. Sanderson and Norma parted lips. Only to kiss again moments later. They were artists, they'd have some plausible explanation, Drake concluded.

'You won't believe what happens next,' Winder said

Norma Buckland and Sanderson walked up the street and out of the immediate view of the camera. Then the image of Roger Buckland appeared. There was no disguising the tight jaw and the fiery anger in his face.

'He doesn't appear too happy,' Drake said. 'We are well overdue another discussion with Roger and Norma Buckland.'

He strode over to the board and tapped a ballpoint on Buckland's image. 'Let's see what he has to say for himself.'

Sara stared at the face of Roger Buckland, ignoring the first two rings of the telephone on her desk. Then she grabbed at the handset and listened to the chilling news.

She looked over at Drake. 'There's another body.'

Chapter 32

A police motorcyclist led the way, siren blazing, every light flashing. Drake gripped the steering wheel tightly, the engine squealing in third gear as he accelerated for the A55. It was a short journey to Llandudno and no sooner had Drake reached one hundred miles an hour than he braked hard for the junction. Traffic cops cleared the exit slip road. Sara relayed instructions for the quickest route to Llandudno pier.

Having an outrider ahead of him certainly helped.

The wailing sound of the siren filled the cabin.

'Find out when the CSIs are going to arrive,' Drake barked.

He listened to Sara's brisk one-sided conversation.

'They are three minutes behind us.'

Drake nodded. He reached the end of the promenade, the rev counter peaking as he changed into third and almost collided with a small roundabout. Eventually he jerked the car onto the pavement near a marked patrol car.

Drake and Sara jogged down towards the pier entrance, waving their warrant cards at several uniformed officers who were ushering the public off the pier.

Drake's shoes clattered on the wooden decking. Squawking seagulls perched on the railings and underneath Drake could hear the Irish sea lapping against the cast-iron columns. They passed several shopping booths: worried faces peered out from a Welsh gift shop, a leather goods seller and a retro and memorabilia store. Marching down the pier brought back old memories for Drake of family trips as a child. Buying candy floss and pestering his parents to let him ride the funfair attractions.

This visit was entirely different. He wondered how

many of the nail-chewing worried-looking customers and tourists realised they might have passed a murderer, mingled with somebody capable of three – possibly four – gruesome deaths.

'How far is it to the end?' Sara said.

He glanced at her, noticing the wide beach and promenade stretching out behind them. It made him realise why people loved the Victorian elegance of the town. That afternoon it was peaceful and tranquil. He shuddered, thinking what might be facing him in one of the booths at the end of the pier.

'Not far,' Drake said.

At the end, the pier widened and Drake noticed the main amusement arcade in the middle and then two officers in high-visibility jackets, obviously relieved to see him. Two women sat on a bench nearby, cleaning equipment, including an industrial vacuum, next to them.

'DI Drake and this is DS Sara Morgan.'

The uniformed officers introduced themselves as Ellis and Charleston; Drake recognised Ellis from a previous case, and the officer nodded at Drake. 'Their job was to clean the shopping booth ready for new tenants.' He tilted his head towards the whitewashed windows a few feet away. 'When they opened the door there were two bodies sitting there.'

'Have you checked for life signs?'

Ellis shook his head. 'There's blood everywhere. And it smelt. You can tell they've been dead for hours.' Charleston nodded his agreement.

Drake turned to both women. 'Did you see anybody suspicious when you arrived?'

Two faces gazed up at Drake, wrinkled, pallid complexions. Drake guessed they were mid-forties. 'Did you touch anything when you went inside?'

Two heads shook in unison.

The sound of heavy footsteps on the planking drew his attention and, turning, he saw Mike Foulds and two crime scene investigators approaching.

Foulds arrived by his side. 'It's much further out than I thought.' He stood, catching his breath, beads of sweat on his forehead. 'What have we got?'

Drake gestured towards the heavy wooden doors, their white paint shimmering in the sunshine.

'After you,' Foulds said. The crime scene manager dictated instructions to his investigators as Drake walked over to the empty shopping booth, snapping on latex gloves. He shared a serious look with Sara and then pushed open the door.

Two bodies sat in wooden framed deckchairs at the far end, a pile of sand scattered by their feet. The man seemed to be in his seventies, a knotted handkerchief on his head, a pair of Ray-Bans, popularised by Tom Cruise decades earlier, perched on his nose. The dark flannel trousers and heavy shoes looked out of place. Blood stains smeared one wall and the heavy clawing smell of decay hung in the air.

Drake's mobile rang. Angrily he dipped a hand into his pocket; reading Gareth Winder's name he declined the call. Foulds stepped towards him, the CSI photographer immediately behind him.

Drake gazed at the woman sitting under the window. She was slim and tall, again another pair of sunglasses hid her face. A multicoloured scarf was draped around her head. The sound of Sara's mobile distracted him. He glanced at her as she killed the call.

Foulds took another step nearer.

Now Foulds' mobile rang. And Sara's again.

A second later Drake's mobile rang. Winder again. This interruption was going to earn him one hell of a reprimand. He answered the call, preparing a sharp comment.

'You're on a live YouTube feed, boss.'

Drake glanced around. Foulds knelt by one of the deckchairs. Drake spotted the CCTV camera high up in the corner. He threw his mobile at Sara and then brushed past Foulds, ignoring the possible contamination of the crime scene. He ripped the camera from the wall, tossing it out of the door.

Foulds was on his feet when Drake turned back to him.

'Your man is a real joker. These are fucking mannequins.'

Chapter 33

My only regret was being unable to link up a camera on the outside of the other shopping booths at the end of the pier so that I could watch and share with an appreciative audience all the activity at my beach hut.

There was a nice ring to the title – *My Beach Hut*. The whole installation and its subsequent discovery had a holistic feel. I felt a sense of achievement that I had been able to construct it in such a short period. As with all my work it had required complex planning, attention to detail. Leaving an ice cream to melt overnight would remind everyone of the sheer transient nature of our existence. They would probably have the remains forensically analysed. I chuckled to myself, thinking what the police officers would make of a melted Cornetto.

Specificity. Such an expressive word. The sunglasses were originals from the sixties and all the clothes had been sourced from shops selling retro designer gear. More sand would have been good but it had been hard enough getting everything else in place. The bucket and spade added an authentic touch. As did the Cadaverine that I produced with my makeshift chemistry kit. It really did create the disgusting smell of death.

The certainty of chaotic scenes at the end of the pier was all part of the installation, an extension, a performance carried out by the officers without them realising they were part of the artwork itself.

I settled down at my computer, content my work was complete and hopeful nothing would prevent the installation being shared. When the two cleaners opened the door my pulse exploded. I started broadcasting, sharing to the world, knowing people could appreciate me at last.

Even without the sound, I sensed their screams. Hands clasped to mouths, standing rigid for a moment until the frightened looks turned to a sickening realisation of what they might be facing. One of them dropped a broom, before fleeing out into the sunshine. The second camera I had rigged up gave a narrow but effective angle out onto the wooden decking immediately in front of the shopping booth. It wasn't perfect but it would enhance everyone's enjoyment.

Two fat policemen arrived within minutes. One held his hands on his knees to gasp for breath. I even contemplated he might have a heart attack.

And die.

In my installation.

That possibility hadn't occurred to me.

My increasing anticipation that *My Beach Hut* would have an added dimension was dashed as the officer gathered his breath. They kept talking on their radios clipped to their uniforms and soon enough Inspector Drake and his sergeant appeared. I edged closer to the monitor hoping to register the slightest facial expression. Annoyingly, they talked to the two women sitting on the bench and then the police officers. I guessed they must be waiting for the white-suited investigators.

When Drake walked over to the doors, I almost squealed in excitement. My chest tightened. My breathing slowed. I hoped my audience were enjoying this is as much as I was. I switched to the camera inside and watched as he took those first tentative steps through the doorway.

I held my breath. This was the most challenging and engaging part of the whole piece.

He stared down at the deckchairs. How long would it take him to realise what was really taking place? He dipped a hand into his pocket and I saw him stab a finger at his mobile telephone. The girl standing behind him picked up a call too and then an investigator fumbled inside his pocket as well. Impossible. My worst nightmare. Someone warned them they were being filmed. I despaired, my heart sank.

When his mobile rang again he answered. He glanced up and I knew then it was finished. I cursed. I suppose I knew there was a risk the broadcast would be spotted. But why so soon?

He scrambled up towards the camera and the coverage abruptly stopped.

I slumped back into my chair. My initial elation thwarted.

I turned to the filming from the second camera but it lasted no more than another few seconds.

Chapter 34

'*My Beach Hut* – what kind of bloody title is that?' Drake crossed his arms tightly and scowled at Winder's monitor as they watched the coverage a second time.

'*My Bed* and now *My Beach Hut* – not very imaginative,' Winder said.

'There's something weird and voyeuristic about the whole set-up, as though the whole thing is one big performance,' Sara added. 'And that we're a part of it.'

'Switch the damn thing off,' Drake said. 'Where the bloody hell are the results of the triangulation requests?'

Drake glared at Winder as Sara and Luned exchanged a glance.

The sheer futility of the masquerade on the pier clouded his judgement as his anger and frustration built. He had to make progress.

Winder cleared his throat noisily. 'They should be available later today.'

'In the meantime the internet is awash with this madman's handiwork. And get the CSIs to expedite the tests on the chemical they found that was responsible for the smell.'

Drake turned his back on the team and stared directly at the face of Roger Buckland on the Incident Room board. 'Michael Spencer,' Drake said to no one in particular.

Winder again. 'I ran a check on him, boss, as you wanted. He's been clean for the past four years although he keeps some nasty company.'

'That includes Roger Buckland.' Drake's tone was sinister.

'I did some more digging around into the theatre group Buckland has been involved with.' Luned sounded positive. 'He's been doing some filming.

And—'

'Filming?' Drake raised his voice a couple of decibels. 'Where the hell is he doing that?'

'I checked the papers we received from the bank about his loan. He owns a smallholding in the country.'

Drake stared over at Sara. 'Buckland's connection to Spencer gives us enough to bring him in for questioning and Norma can explain to us all about her relationship with Sanderson.' Drake turned to Gareth and Luned. 'Both of you go and arrest Norma. We'll get them all into the custody suite and interview them separately.'

Before leaving, Drake stood over his desk, telephone thrust to his ear, dictating instructions for a warrant to authorise a search of Buckland's property before finding a suitably qualified officer to be in charge. Then he found officers to arrest Spencer and deliver him to the custody suite. Once Drake finished he headed down to the car park with Sara.

Drake drove out of headquarters towards Rhyl, Winder and Luned following. Sara rang the area custody suite and Drake listened to her side of the conversation warning the sergeant in charge he'd have three customers that afternoon.

The journey passed quickly as Sara jotted down Drake's thoughts about their interviews with Norma and Roger Buckland. 'I'll do Roger Buckland and you interview Norma with Gareth. Luned can deal with Spencer.'

It would give Sara her first taste of interviewing a suspect in a murder inquiry. Drake relished the opportunity of talking to Roger Buckland. After all, he was experienced at police interviews and Drake steeled himself for an aggressive confrontation. Lawyers would be called to attend, which meant more delays. Drake could easily see the interviews not happening until later into the evening. It looked like being another long day.

He pulled up outside the River Jordan Community Centre.

Drake spoke to the officers tracking down Spencer. They had arrested him in his flat on the outskirts of town. Moments later Winder rang to confirm they were outside Norma's studio.

'Let's go.' Drake finished the call and left the car.

Drake dragged open the dilapidated front door and entered, Sara following. The rooms on the ground floor were empty so Drake hurried on up the stairs and into the gym where he saw Buckland supervising two young men hammering a punchbag.

Buckland stared over at them as they approached.

'Roger Buckland. I'm arresting you on suspicion of murder.' Drake made it sound as neutral as possible.

Buckland gave a non-committal shrug, and left without a word to the boxers.

The drive to area control was punctuated with messages from Winder confirming Norma Buckland's arrest and a text telling him Spencer was already halfway to the custody suite.

Once the Bucklands and Spencer were sitting safely in a cell each, Drake assembled his team in one of the interview rooms and ran though their strategy. Neither Norma nor Roger had requested a lawyer, which meant they could move ahead quickly.

'Why haven't they asked for a solicitor?' Luned said.

'That's their choice,' Drake said. 'It doesn't change anything.'

'Lawyers just get in the way.' Winder sounded dismissive.

Drake nodded at Luned. 'I want you to interview Spencer. We need to know about the fingerprints.'

'Yes, boss.' Luned sounded pleased, business-like.

Drake left first, heading for an empty interview room, tapes and notepad in hand. A uniformed officer delivered Buckland to the room and he sat down opposite Drake. Buckland smiled but his eyes flickered disdain.

'I'm investigating the death of Gloria Patton.'

'Of course.' The understanding tone to Buckland's voice disarmed Drake who paused to glance at him.

'Tell me where you were on the night of her murder.' Drake scanned his notes before announcing the date.

'I don't keep an exact record of all the events in my life. I could have been in the centre or my office at the church. I know Norma was busy in her studio – she often works through the night. She finds that time of day tranquil and she isn't distracted.'

'If you can remember Norma was working how is it you cannot recall your whereabouts?'

'Inspector, I lead a very hectic life and I have so little time to myself. Personal details like that seem distracting.'

'Gloria Patton was known to you?'

'Yes, of course.'

'And to Norma?'

'Indeed.'

'So it must have come as a shock when you learnt of her death?'

'Dreadful. Absolutely dreadful. I called to see Oswald and offered to pray with him in the hope I could offer some solace.'

This was a new version of Roger Buckland – silver-tongued and condescending. Drake sensed him crawling under his skin already.

'So when did you learn about her death?'

'Well, I cannot be certain.'

'Was it the day her body was discovered?'

'Quite possibly.'

Even Buckland's accent had lost some of its rough edges.

'So let's go back. Can you remember where you were when you heard the news?'

Buckland smiled at Drake as though he were a child to be scolded.

'I want to assure you, Inspector, I had nothing to do with poor Gloria's death.'

Drake sat back and folded his arms. 'I find it hard to believe you cannot remember that one thing. After all, she was in the art world where your wife works and she had rejected Norma's work. You would have known suspicion might fall on you and Norma.'

'Of course. But Inspector, I have done nothing wrong. And while my past may give you the perfect justification to suspect me I have left that world behind. I have experienced God's forgiveness and the healing power of his love.'

Drake paused and gazed into Buckland's dark eyes, wondering how thin the veneer of sincerity really was. He expected the aggression he had seen at the gym, read about in the police reports, so Buckland's charm offensive took Drake aback.

'Let's move on.' Drake managed not to grit his teeth but it took some willpower. 'I want to clarify some personal details.'

Drake spent time getting Buckland to confirm where he was born and where he grew up and all about his schooling and teenage years. Buckland answered without hesitation, cooperating fully as Drake trawled through his life.

Drake shuffled the papers on the desk in front of him and drew out a photograph of the red car parked outside the River Jordan Community Centre. He pushed it over at Buckland.

'Is this the vehicle you drive?'

'Yes.'

'Is it registered in your name?'

Buckland sighed as though the whole process was tiresome. 'You know full well it belongs to one of the members of my church.'

'And you drive it with his consent.'

'Yes, of course.'

Drake sat back, wondering if Buckland could guess where he was going next.

He scanned a sheet from his file, checking the dates. Then he stared at Buckland. The eye contact would be direct – he wanted to measure his reaction.

'Do you know where Rhisiart Hopkin lived?'

Buckland swallowed. Of course he did but would he admit it? Would he risk a lie?

'No, sorry.'

'We have an eyewitness who testifies she saw the car outside Rhisiart Hopkin's home several times in the days before his death.'

Buckland blinked now.

Drake continued. 'And she gives a description of the driver.'

Buckland forced himself to keep Drake's eye contact until he couldn't manage it and he looked away.

Buckland kept staring at the table top. Drake waited for him to look up.

'Rhisiart Hopkin was brutally killed in his own home. He was your bank manager. When he refused to support your business ventures you decided to take revenge. You have history of being unable to control your temper. I think you went to see him and there was an argument.'

Still no eye contact from Buckland. Drake continued.

'The argument got out of hand and you lost your temper. And you killed him.'

Buckland raised his head and then stared directly into Drake's eyes.

'Yes, you're right.'

For a moment, the confession caught Drake by surprise. If his theory that Hopkin's killer was the same person it meant Buckland had murdered Gloria and Sanderson.

'It *was* revenge.' Buckland's confidence crumpled. 'But I didn't kill him.'

Drake cut in. 'What? Then why were you outside his home?'

'I was going to complain to his superiors about him. I was desperate and I wanted to do everything to keep the community centre running. I learnt a lot about Hopkin. He was an unprincipled, promiscuous man with no moral compass. He had affairs with women in exchange for supporting their businesses. I have proof. You have to believe me.'

For the next twenty minutes, Buckland gave Drake a commentary of Hopkin's life.

'I was going to build a dossier and send it to the bank. I wanted them to see sense and change their mind about my project.'

Drake sipped from the plastic water bottle on the table, wondering if what he had just witnessed was another performance, more smoke and mirrors. He gathered the papers on his desk deciding he had to move forward.

'Did you know Noel Sanderson?'

'Yes.'

'How did you know him?'

'He's a local artist. And ...'

Drake paused. Buckland wanted to tell him about Norma and Sanderson but something held him back. Truthfulness didn't come naturally to Buckland, Drake thought, no matter how much he might have changed.

Drake waited.

Buckland faltered and stared at the desk top again.

Drake reached over for the laptop and, opening it, found the CCTV coverage from Conwy. 'How well did your wife know Noel Sanderson?'

Buckland coughed.

'When did you discover Norma was having a relationship with Noel Sanderson?'

A smile flickered over Buckland lips but it soon died.

'I forgave her.'

'Answer the question.' Drake had tolerated Buckland long enough. He wanted answers.

'A few months,' Buckland whispered.

Drake clicked the laptop into life. 'This is coverage we found from the centre of Conwy when you followed her.'

He swivelled the monitor so Buckland could watch the scenes. Drake stared at him. From swagger to crushing realisation his world had been exposed. Buckland gawped blankly at the images.

'You look pretty angry to me.'

Buckland said nothing.

'Angry enough to kill someone. And that someone was Noel Sanderson.'

'I forgave her.'

'But you couldn't forgive Sanderson. That's why you killed him.'

Buckland shook his head.

Drake continued. 'I need to establish your whereabouts on the Sunday evening Sanderson died.'

Buckland looked over at Drake, his eyes opening

wide.

'I was ...' he stammered. 'I know exactly where I was. I was preaching in a church in Macclesfield and the following morning there was a prayer breakfast.'

Drake frowned. 'It's convenient you can remember your whereabouts that evening but not for the night Patton was abducted and murdered. I'll need the full details of anyone who can support your alibi.'

Buckland reeled off names and addresses but he couldn't recall telephone numbers. Drake scribbled on his notepad.

'What's going to happen now?'

Drake sat back. 'We need to check out what you've told us. While we do that you go back to your cell.'

Sara enjoyed every minute of her interview with Norma. The anticipation of her first interview in a murder inquiry was a welcome change from burglars and petty thieves who would lie repeatedly without compunction. Although Norma hadn't been classified as a formal suspect yet, it didn't matter. She was involved somehow and that meant the interview was important.

Norma repeated what they already knew: she had been working on the night of Gloria's death. She made no attempt to hide her hatred of Rhisiart Hopkin. Sara had even asked if Norma was sorry he was dead, and she had laughed out loud. Sara had glanced over at Winder, registering his disbelief at the reaction.

Norma had no idea the questions were coming about Sanderson and she clammed up immediately. Showing her the scenes on the street in Conwy shocked her.

'It's not what it seems.'

Sara sighed to herself. It sounds like something

spouted by a philandering spouse in a cheap romcom movie, Sara thought. Then she tackled Norma about her relationship with Roger and the shutters came down.

After Sara finished, she and Winder trekked through to the canteen to wait for Drake. They met up in a room on the first floor of the area custody centre, enjoying the early evening sunshine after the oppressive atmosphere of the windowless interview rooms. Drake stood by the window, his mobile pressed to his ear when they entered – his conversation monosyllabic. Sara had been working with Drake long enough to realise it wasn't helpful news. Drake tossed his phone onto the table. 'Nothing from the search of Buckland's smallholding.'

Drake waved them to visitor chairs and spoke to Winder. 'Any news on the triangulation of the mobile telephone numbers?'

'Any time now.' Winder had been chasing the results ever since they had finished the interview with Norma.

Luned bustled in and slumped into a chair.

'Tell me about Spencer,' Drake glanced over to Luned.

'He was terrified he might be involved in a murder inquiry. Started sweating like a pig. Then he told me he'd been working for a double glazing company on the quiet – all cash-in-hand jobs. Eventually I got hold of the owner of the company who confirmed the story and told me the van had been sold about six months previously. I spoke to the garage—'

Drake put up his hand. 'I get it – it looks like he's in the clear and that means we cannot link the van to Buckland.'

Sara pitched in. 'Norma refused to answer any questions about her relationship with Sanderson. But she clearly admitted she'd been happy to see Hopkin dead. How did you get on with Roger, boss?'

'He's given us the names of various people as an alibi for the night Sanderson was killed. I'll need them checked out.'

Winder's mobile bleeped and he read the message before looking over at Drake. 'Triangulation puts Wood and Ellingham near the van in the five days before we found it.'

'And Buckland?' Drake said.

Winder shook his head.

Chapter 35

The evening light was drawing in when Drake returned to the Incident Room at headquarters. He needed to think. Although Norma and Roger Buckland were sitting in the cells at area custody centre Drake knew they'd be released in the morning. Buckland's alibi would check out – it sounded too plausible not to. But he didn't want to dismiss them as suspects. He perched himself on the edge of one of the desks and peered over at the board. Both Wood and Ellingham had alibis. But the triangulation of their mobile telephones meant that in the morning they both needed the full attention of the team.

Drake's mobile rang as he pondered and he recognised Huw Jackson's number.

'Hello, Huw.'

'I thought you should be the first to know. Jack Smith came to a meeting of the committee this afternoon. He got very abusive, told us all he hoped we would rot in hell and nothing would ever persuade him to agree to Noel Sanderson's canvases being used.'

'It doesn't surprise me. From what Sara told me he was pretty cut up.'

'It's been decided that Noel's work will be replaced by Jeremy Ellingham and Geraint Wood.'

Drake let his mouth fall open. 'But Ellingham and Amber Falk are on the committee.'

And suspects.

'The festival is to start this Saturday, for Christ's sake. Somebody had to replace Sanderson.'

Drake finished the call. Now both Wood and Ellingham benefited directly from Gloria and Sanderson's deaths. The board was missing a photograph of Valerie Reed to match the image of Amber Falk alongside Geraint Wood and more nagging uncertainty filled Drake's mind that establishing her identity had been overlooked.

Behind him Drake heard the door squeak open and Superintendent Price walked in. He looked over at Drake.

'Working late, Ian?'

'We've just finished interviewing Norma and Roger Buckland.'

Price nodded. 'Any progress?'

'We need to check out his alibi but …'

'I've decided the inquiry into Hopkin's death will be conducted by another DI. On Monday you'll conduct a briefing for DI Metcalf from Western Division. She'll have her own team and I expect you to give her your complete cooperation.'

'We still need to finalise our inquiries into Wood and Ellingham. They could both be implicated.'

'I thought they had alibis?'

'Yes sir, but we've had the results of triangulation analysis of their mobile telephones and—'

'I appreciate you believe we are dealing with one killer but there is far too much at stake and I'm not persuaded they are linked. This whole case, including that fiasco over the video this morning, is having an effect on you. You should go home. You look like shit.'

Drake narrowed his eyes. His lips dried. He searched for the right words, to persuade his superior officer he was in charge and that he was capable of clear thinking.

After Price left, Drake sat in his office for several minutes staring at his desk. They had missed something, he was convinced. He got up and left his office. Everything about the Hopkin case told him it was linked to the other murders, but was he the only one who could see that?

He found the images from Hopkin's home and set

out them out on an empty table before creating a panoramic view of the room on the board. It started with the dining table and its three place settings and then alongside it were two images of the bookcase with the Lloyd George volumes. Moving his gaze into the living room where Hopkin had been found, Drake stared at the newspaper folded carefully. Had he missed some meaning in the visible page?

The chair where Hopkin sat was streaked red. The gallery continued with the footstool and some watercolours hanging on the walls. Then the mantel appeared, a piece of green ceramic in the middle alongside two pieces of cranberry glass. Drake spotted a brass companion set on the hearth before the images of old, heavy second-hand furniture near the window.

He yawned as he went over the familiar images again. He was too tired to concentrate, but instead of going home, he drove into Llandudno.

He parked opposite the shoe shop and walked over to the spot from where the killer had filmed him arriving at the scene of Gloria Patton's death. The streets were quiet. The sodium streetlights cast a dull yellowy pallor over the pavement. Drake looked into the charity shop. He noticed the blinking light of a CCTV camera clipped to a wooden display stand. The staff had told him the system was broken so he made a mental note to double-check.

He skirted around the rear of the shops and down towards the entrance where the killer had parked the van used to move Gloria Patton. It was dark now; the lights from the flats above the shops the only illumination.

Drake retraced his steps and stood at the junction of the main road. Parked on the opposite side was a delivery lorry for a large department store. Cigarette smoke wafted out of the driver's window.

He walked over, pointing his warrant card at the driver who yanked the cords of his iPhone out of his ear.

'Are you a regular with deliveries to Llandudno?'

'Every Monday, Tuesday and Wednesday. I don't get here until much later but I started early tonight.'

'Do you always park here?'

'Usually, is there a problem?'

Drake paused; the possibility that this was an eyewitness dispelled his tiredness.

'Two weeks ago on a Wednesday morning a woman's body was found in one of the shops nearby.' Drake nodded at the arcade. 'We believe she was abducted the night before.'

'That's terrible.' The driver straightened his position in the cab.

'We are trying to trace a shop fitters' van seen in the vicinity.'

'I remember. I was having my break. I'd just started on my sandwiches.' The certainty took Drake by surprise. 'It stuck in my mind because he was wearing one of those one-piece suits you see on the TV cop dramas. The van was really battered. The front panel was done in. I notice those kinds of things because my wife runs a van hire business.'

Drake stared at the driver. He needed a written statement. Now.

'I'll need you to come with me to police headquarters.'

'No chance. I've got deliveries to make.'

Drake took a pace backwards and stared inside the cab. 'It wasn't a request.'

Chapter 36

Drake arrived home a little after two am. He gazed at his reflection in the bathroom mirror realising Price was right but knowing a few hours of sleep wouldn't improve his complexion. Drake patted the folds of skin under his chin. The whites of his eyes looked grey and stray hairs grazed the top of his ears.

When he woke the following morning, he couldn't remember getting into bed.

He had work to do. A killer to catch.

Sara and the rest of the team were already at their desks when he arrived.

He went straight over to the board. 'We've got an eyewitness.'

He moved his gaze between each of the officers, measuring the significance of his announcement. 'I found a lorry driver who spotted the white van.'

'Where, boss? I mean, when did this happen?' Sara said.

'He was parked last night near the shoe shop. There's a photofit.'

Drake pulled the artist's impression from a folder and pinned it next to Buckland's image.

'The driver of the van smoked and wore dark black-rimmed glasses and a one-piece white suit.'

'That ties in with him being forensically aware,' Winder added.

'As neither Buckland nor his wife smokes it rules them out,' Sara said.

'I know,' Drake said.

The image of Amber Falk and Geraint Wood stood out from the Incident Room board. Underneath, relegated to a secondary position, was Jeremy Ellingham. Both Wood and Ellingham benefited from the death of Noel Sanderson, each now exhibiting at the Orme Arts Festival. In reality, the photofit description could have fitted either of the men.

Drake cleared his throat before continuing. 'Whoever it was visited the pier Monday and Tuesday this week.'

Drake kept staring at the board, trawling through his memory, searching for something to make the pieces fall into place.

'I thought Ellingham had an alibi for the death of Gloria Patton?' Winder said.

Drake turned to Sara. 'I'll go to the pier. There might be eyewitnesses that could identify Wood or Ellingham. I need you to visit Wood. Find out where he was earlier this week. Then we'll think about Ellingham once we find his girlfriend. That's your job, Luned.'

Drake glanced at his watch. 'Back here as soon as.'

Drake drove to Llandudno pier and parked on double yellow lines. He reached over to the passenger seat, picked up his carefully folded jacket and the folder underneath with the artist's impression. The smell of fresh coffee drifted from one of the booths as he walked towards the entrance of the pier so he bought an Americano. Statements from all the concession owners along the pier would be taken in due course but he had to check as many as he could himself.

Taking a moment to savour the surprisingly fresh and strong coffee he gazed over the bay. TripAdvisor recently voted Llandudno the most popular seaside resort in the United Kingdom. On a morning like this he could see why.

Two young women were busy in the first booth, arranging stands of retro-merchandise. One had long purple hair and the other various body piercings of different size and shapes.

Drake flashed his warrant card. 'Were you here yesterday when there was an incident at the end of the pier?'

Both girls nodded. Drake pulled the artist's impression from the folder. 'Whoever was responsible must have passed you. He might have been carrying two deckchairs.' The tension on their faces showed as they grasped what Drake was suggesting. He scoured their faces for any glimmer of recognition.

'Is it the same person that killed that woman in the shop?' The pronounced Scottish accent came as a surprise from the purple-haired girl. 'Do you mean the killer actually walked passed us?' She shuddered, drawing her arms around her chest. 'We get hundreds of people walking the pier every day.'

The other girl nodded and her piercings shimmered in the morning sunshine.

'Take another look at this picture.' Drake held up the photofit once again. They shook their heads. Drake thrust them a card. 'If you think of anything let me know.'

By the time Drake was halfway along the pier the responses had been the same. Everybody was too busy making a living, making certain youngsters didn't pilfer from their stalls, to pay any attention to the people walking past. At the end of the pier he stood looking at the booth he had visited the day before – yellow crime scene tape covering the door. Remembering the fiasco, he fisted his right hand before telling himself that anger wasn't going to achieve anything. Behind him a woman's voice shouted in delight and he heard the trickle of coins crashing from the slot machine. Inside he saw a glass-enclosed booth offering change. A young girl sat at a counter reading a magazine, filing her nails absently.

Drake produced his warrant card again. 'I want to talk to you about what happened yesterday.'

Luckily, the amusement arcade was quiet and the girl left the booth and stood with Drake.

'What's your name?'

'Tina James.'

Drake tried to put Tina at ease, keeping his voice low. 'Tina, we thought what happened might have been a murder scene.'

She blinked furiously.

'It was a hoax but we really want to find the person responsible. Do you work here full-time?' She gave a frightened nod.

'I'm looking for this man.' Drake showed her the photofit.

'It looks a bit weird.' Tina peered at the artist's impression. 'It's them glasses that look strange.'

'Did you notice anybody resembling this man?'

Curiosity turned to recognition as she stared at the image. Progress at last, Drake thought. 'There was this strange old man here this week. He was fishing off the pier and he had a deckchair with him.'

'What was he wearing?'

'He had one of them jackets without sleeves and lots of feathers and fluffy things sticking out of the pockets. He wore a hat with fancy ribbons. I saw him when I was on my fag break.'

'Tina, it's very important. Can you remember what he looked like?'

'It was like that picture you showed me. He had thick heavy-rimmed glasses.'

'Did he smoke?'

'Yeah, come to think of it. I saw him flicking butts into the sea.'

'How long did he stay?'

She curled her lips. 'I can't say. All morning?'

'How old was he?'

'Dunno, maybe forty.'

Really old then.

Tina soon got into the swing of providing information. The man was dressed to be completely convincing. Tina even remembered the fresh bait wrapped in newspaper lying by his feet. She had described him as having chubby cheeks and Drake guessed the spectacles, like the wispy beard and the clothes, had been a prop. Satisfied she had dredged her memory, Drake walked back to the car. Passing a billboard advertising the opening event of the Orme Arts Festival the following afternoon, Drake recognised the name of Milos Fogerty. It promised to be a busy weekend of events.

Arriving back at his car Drake cursed when he saw the parking ticket stuck to the front windscreen. He glanced around for the traffic warden before ripping it off the glass. He tossed it onto the passenger seat and drove back to headquarters.

Sara drew up a short distance from Wood's cottage. Opposite, the branches of a large sycamore reached out over the road. She opened the window a couple of inches and a chainsaw clattered somewhere in the fields. Looking out through the windscreen, she saw the rear of Geraint Wood's vehicle. With Buckland eliminated as a suspect Sara focused on Wood, forcing clarity into her thoughts. Wood had a motive for Patton's death and a flimsy alibi. She dismissed the explanation from Amber Falk that she had been with Wood for most of the morning after Patton's death, which ostensibly ruled him out of a connection with the shop fitters' van and the recording broadcast on YouTube. Now he would benefit from Sanderson's murder by exhibiting his work.

But it still didn't explain the death of Rhisiart Hopkin. Sara had respected Drake's opinion that Hopkin's home was an elaborate copy of a famous piece of art just like the other two crime scenes. Even though she wasn't convinced. She doubted she would ever have his single-minded approach.

She left the car and walked towards the cottage. A pile of cigarette butts littered the paving slabs near the front door. It confirmed her recollection of the smell inside. She grabbed the knocker and banged on the door. Immediately she heard a shout and recognised the voices of a man and a woman. Good, both Falk and Wood were home, no time to concoct alibis, Sara thought.

The door squeaked open and Wood stood on the threshold. He glared at her. 'What do you want?'

'I need to ask you some questions.'

'Am I under arrest?'

'I need you to assist my inquiry.' Sara smiled.

Wood glanced up and down the road, assessing what prying eyes might have been looking out on the scene. Wordlessly Wood pushed the door open and Sara stepped inside.

In the kitchen at the rear of the property Amber Falk sat by a table nursing a large mug of a steaming clear liquid. A chamomile and mint odour hung in the air. She gave Sara a surprised look as she entered. Wood went to stand by Falk's side. There wasn't an invitation to sit down.

'I'd like to know your whereabouts for the early part of this week.'

'For fuck's sake, do you still think I'm a suspect?'

'It would be helpful if you could clarify exactly where you were Monday and Tuesday mornings between eight and midday.'

'If you're going to arrest me then shouldn't I have a lawyer? Shouldn't you be reading me my rights, like they do on TV?'

'Tell her Geraint,' Falk said. 'Don't play games.'

Wood baulked. Cooperating with the police was the last thing Wood wanted, Sara thought. Slowly, Wood let out a long breath. 'We were in Buxton. We only got back this morning. Amber and me had our first joint show. Satisfied now?'

Sara paused. 'Can someone confirm your whereabouts?'

'Jesus, you people never stop.'

Amber raised her voice. 'Just tell her.'

'We worked twelve-hour days from first thing Monday constructing an installation for the show.' Wood reached for his mobile on the table, scrolling through the various numbers until he found one in particular. Then he thrust the device towards Sara. 'Nick can confirm, we were with him all the time.'

Chapter 37

'Does that mean Wood is in the clear?' Luned said, an edge of incredulity to her voice.

Drake sat behind his desk, staring at the junior officers in his team after Sara shared with them the details of her meeting with Geraint Wood.

'It means he wasn't around this week to put the beach hut scene together,' Drake said. 'But it's only his word and that of Amber Falk that they were busy on Sunday preparing for their show in Buxton. It's similar to the alibi they offered for the day after Patton's death.'

'Wood might have had an accomplice,' Luned said.

It was the last sort of observation Drake wanted to hear. He began tapping the ballpoint on the pile of paperwork in front of him. He reached over and adjusted the photograph of his daughters a few millimetres.

'The scene at the end of the pier might have been a copycat.' Winder seemed determined to make unhelpful comments. 'Buckland didn't get back from Macclesfield until late Monday and on Tuesday he was working in the church's charity shop all day.'

'So that just leaves Ellingham.' Drake turned to look at Luned. 'How did you get on tracing his girlfriend?'

'Nothing, sir. I can't find her on the electoral roll. She doesn't have any financial records I can trace with any of the credit reference agencies. And no National Insurance number.'

'Try the banks direct.'

'Already done, sir. But I won't have the results until tomorrow.'

Drake paused. 'Luned, go and talk to her. Call at Ellingham's place. That's the only address we have for her.'

'How do we link Wood or Ellingham to the murder of Hopkin?' Sara stared at Drake, willing him to reply. He felt Winder and Luned's gaze boring into him too. Superintendent Price's intention to remove the Hopkin inquiry from his team still rankled and until Monday the case was his.

He turned to Winder. 'Gareth, fresh eyes on Gloria Patton. We've missed something. Now we've got a photofit, get around; talk to the eyewitnesses and go into as many premises near the shoe shop as you can. Somebody must have seen him, he must have bought a packet of cigarettes, a soft drink, chocolate bar.'

Winder nodded.

Drake looked at Sara. 'Let's focus on Wood and Ellingham.'

Sara focused on building a complete picture of Wood and after an hour, she called Drake over to see the various works of video art Wood displayed on his website. Rather than it being a distraction, Drake welcomed the interruption. He had barely finished working his way through the eighty-two new emails in his inbox without much enthusiasm.

Sara's monitor flickered into life as the images of figures walking along the beach while the tide lapped at their feet filled the screen. Then it cut to the same faceless figures near a mountain lake.

'That's Cwm Idwal,' Drake said. 'Near the Devil's Kitchen.'

Sara nodded.

Then they were back to the seashore where the water covered the man's shoes, the damp spreading up his trousers.

'How do they make a living from video art?' Drake

said.

'From what we know of his financial position I don't think he makes much of an income. It's a hand-to-mouth existence.'

'So the chance of exposure at the Orme Arts Festival might be a big thing.'

'Wood had some exhibitions in galleries in Scotland and he began a course in some fancy art school in Germany but dropped out after a year. Then he dossed around various European capitals for two years before returning to Wales.'

Back in his office, Drake got back to the emails. There were two reminders from Superintendent Price chasing a briefing memorandum for the new detective inspector taking over the Hopkin enquiry. Hurriedly, Drake tapped out a reply before peeling off a yellow Post-it note and scribbling on it the words – *urgent – memo to WP*. It went at the bottom of his column of yellow Post-it notes. That evening he would sit down and finalise all the details.

Susan Howells from public relations sent a link to the recent news report carried by the Wales television channels featuring the photofit image. He wasn't expecting the telephone to ring off the hook but a second email from her told him the usual cross-section of eccentrics and weirdoes had telephoned. One even suggested she had seen a man dragging two bodies along the pier.

Once satisfied he was up to date with his emails Drake turned his attention to the background of Jeremy Ellingham. Alibis from girlfriends and friends can be suspect, Drake thought. Nothing suggested Valerie Reed was unreliable and her presence in Ellingham's home had been confirmed by the neighbour. Reading Ellingham's curriculum vitae, Drake realised some dates were missing when he calculated Ellingham was twenty-eight graduating from the National Art College of Wales. But what had he done after leaving school? Drake's instinct distrusted an incomplete picture so he googled Ellingham's name and on the second page of the results the name of a gallery in Cardiff appeared. Once he clicked onto the site he discovered they represented Ellingham. Words like 'innovative', 'exciting young artist' and 'candidate for Welsh artist of the year' littered his biography. But Drake could find no recent reference. When he noticed they also represented Noel Sanderson his interest heightened.

He found a contact name – Egon Wentworth – and called him.

'My name is Detective Inspector Ian Drake of the Wales Police Service, Northern Division.' Drake indulged himself with the full formal introduction. 'I'm investigating the death of Noel Sanderson.'

'We were all so shocked. Have you arrested the culprit?'

'The inquiry is still ongoing. I was wondering if you could tell me anything about Noel Sanderson.' Drake knew it sounded vague; it wasn't the purpose of his call but Sanderson was a convenient excuse. Drake made scribbled notes, interrupted when appropriate, making Wentworth entirely comfortable.

'I couldn't help notice on your website that you represent Jeremy Ellingham. He is on the committee for the Orme Arts Festival.'

Wentworth guffawed loudly. 'What? We represented Ellingham for about a year. He came here and got very abusive when I told him he should be looking to change career. I didn't think he was an artist. I told him to find another way of making a living. I've been meaning to remove his details from my website but I never get round to doing it. He is completely flaky; I'm amazed he is on a committee dealing with anything. He's got some really weird ideas.'

Drake took a deep breath. 'I've only met him a couple of times.'

'That'll be more than enough. When he was at the art school he had a hell of a row with his tutor. I know Milos very well.'

'Milos?' The name of the art critic opening the Orme Arts Festival at the weekend heightened Drake's interest.

'Milos Fogerty was one of his tutors. He thought that Ellingham was utterly unsuited to being an artist. His criticism of Ellingham's work was harsh, brutal even. It was only because of pressure from Ellingham's family he actually scraped through the course.'

'He's had a colourful career then, hasn't he? I know he mentioned training to be an accountant but it's quite a change to be an artist.' Drake threw a wide fishing net. It worked.

'Accountant, is that what he's saying? He did a year of a history degree at Aberystwyth, wanted to do everything in Welsh, refused to speak to tutors unless they spoke in Welsh, refused even to acknowledge their existence. Accountant? I find that difficult to believe.'

'The Orme Arts Festival is giving him the opportunity of exhibiting his work.'

'Then he's dead lucky because nobody else will.'

'Thank you for your time,' Drake said, eventually finishing the call.

He sat and thought about his first meeting with Ellingham. Something had been out of place at the time but he couldn't put his finger on one thing.

'Why do you possibly think that would give me a motive to kill her? I'm an established artist. I have exhibitions all over the world.'

Drake replayed the last statement, knowing it to be

a lie. Why would Ellingham have challenged him so abruptly about the purpose of his visit?

He read again the comments from Patton that his work was derivative and lacked imagination. No boundaries, Francine had said about Ellingham when they spent time in the gallery, and a sickening realisation dawned that he was the priority now. It was late in the evening by the time Drake finished building a complete picture of Ellingham. He cajoled school records from the local authority, and threatened a university administrator with the full power of the police before she would promise to email details of Ellingham's attendance at Aberystwyth University.

A civil servant working in the human resources department of the National Art College of Wales was more cooperative. 'We're in the middle of digitising all our records so we might not get everything to you until tomorrow morning.'

'Thanks,' Drake said, making a mental note to call them again in the morning.

It was early evening when Winder and Luned returned to the Incident Room. They both stood in the doorway to Drake's room.

'There was no one at Ellingham's place,' Luned said. 'I spoke to the neighbour again who sent me on a wild goose chase into Llanrwst and then Betws y Coed because he thought Ellingham's parents lived there.'

Drake recalled the emaciated man drawing on a thin cigarette next door to Ellingham's home and it didn't surprise Drake that he was unreliable. Winder stood behind her.

'Nobody could recognise the photofit boss. And the charity shop was closed.'

Drake nodded. 'We'll call in the morning.'

After both officers had left, the yellow Post-it note demanded Drake's attention but he was reluctant to give up on the Hopkin inquiry, so once the Incident Room was quiet he stood by the board scanning the panoramic image of Hopkin's sitting room. Something had been missed. Something that linked the scene to his theory. Something to point them to the killer.

He spent the final hour of his working day with the yellow Post-it note stuck to the side of the monitor as he typed the draft of a memorandum to Detective Inspector Metcalf and Superintendent Wyndham Price. His interpretation of the crime scene sounded eccentric when exposed to the harsh light of objective policing. Metcalf would probably think he had gone completely mad. When his eyes started to burn and the small of his back ached and a yawn escaped he decided to leave for the night.

Chapter 38

The launch of the Orme Arts Festival merited a brief piece on the Welsh television news the following morning. The artificial light from the film crew glistened on the chain hanging around the mayor's neck as he spoke about the council's ambitions for developing the arts in Llandudno.

Drake chose a navy suit, clean white shirt and a tie with a ruby red stripe, all on the off-chance Price would want a progress report, perhaps even a discussion about the briefing memoranda he had emailed the night before. He left for headquarters and, after buying a newspaper, spent five minutes in his car challenging himself to try the fiendish Sudoku puzzle but his frustration turned to annoyance when he found himself stymied after only one square.

He kept thinking about the photofit image of a man with large heavy-rimmed spectacles who smoked. The glasses could be false but why would he wear them driving a van away in the middle of the night from the crime scene? Arriving early at headquarters he set out a copy of the photofit image on his desk alongside the images of Wood and Ellingham. It looked nothing like either man and, momentarily deflated, Drake clicked open both suspects' websites. Wood wore glasses but Ellingham did not, and a disguise might change a man's image. He watched the video from Ellingham's studio that showed him at work. Ellingham put on a serious face and pouted occasionally before launching into a monologue about modern art that made no sense to Drake. The camera toured the inside of his studio. It was comfortable, familiar, as Drake had viewed it before. He had stood there speaking to Ellingham but the artworks on the shelves were different, as were the posters hanging on the wall.

When he heard movement in the Incident Room he left his office, glancing at his watch.

He looked at Sara shrugging off her coat. 'Let's go and visit the charity shop.'

Sara jiggled the coat back onto her shoulders as Winder and Luned sat down. Drake stared at the board.

'He's a good actor,' Drake said. 'He likes performing.'

'That suits Ellingham and Wood,' Sara said.

Drake kept staring at the board, picturing Wood or Ellingham dressed up as an imitation Damien Hirst or as a clichéd fisherman. His mind turned to the anaesthetic the killer had used. 'Is there anything in the background of Jeremy Ellingham or Geraint Wood that gives them a connection with a hospital?'

Three pairs of eyes stared over at him blankly.

'Ellingham has a sister,' Luned announced in a slow, determined manner. 'I'll find out about her.'

'And Geraint Wood, his best friend from school might be a doctor or a nurse.'

Sara piped up. 'Not everybody has the gumption to walk into an operating theatre and know where to steal the right drugs and be convincing in whatever role he chooses.'

A nagging doubt wormed its way back into Drake's mind as he stared at Ellingham's face. 'And we still need more information on Ellingham's girlfriend?'

The silence from the team behind him unsettled Drake.

'By the time we're back I want to know everything about Jeremy Ellingham's family and his girlfriend.' He nodded at Sara and they left.

Drake took the stairs down to reception two at a time. His mobile rang as he approached the car. It was Superintendent Price. 'I want to meet this afternoon.'

Drake opened the Mondeo, and Sara climbed into the passenger seat.

'We're going back to interview a possible eyewitness this morning.'

'I'll expect you at one o'clock.'

From the brevity of the conversation Drake couldn't make out Price's mood, which only added to his anxiety. He started the engine and left headquarters for Llandudno. After five minutes he turned to Sara. 'The super's bringing in a new team on Monday to take over the Rhisiart Hopkin case.'

Sara didn't hide the surprise on her face. 'I didn't know.'

Sara asked nothing further about Hopkin, which pleased Drake, and their conversation was dominated by going over everything they knew about Wood and Ellingham.

Two nights earlier Drake had stood outside the shop noticing the flickering CCTV camera and now he had to recheck himself whether the system was working. He parked on the side streets nearby. Passing an optician's, he noticed the advertisement for contact lenses, disposables with a special offer for a month's trial.

Focusing his mind on Jeremy Ellingham brought flooding back to his memory the image of the artist rubbing his eyes: and they had protruded slightly.

'Are you coming, boss?' Sara said.

Drake realised he was staring into the window. 'Ellingham wears contact lenses.'

'I beg your pardon, sir?'

'When we first met him his eyes protruded and they were bloodshot, you know, like people who have ill-fitting contact lenses.'

'It could be hay fever or maybe he's allergic to something.'

Drake ignored her reservations. 'The eyewitnesses who saw him driving the shop fitter van says he wore glasses. We've been working on the basis that they were a prop. But they were real. He was avoiding the risk of losing a contact lens.' Energised by his new zeal, Drake followed Sara towards the charity shop.

A single customer flicked through a carousel of blouses. The saxophone introduction from 'Baker Street' by Gerry Rafferty played in the background. The woman behind the till smiled as he neared. 'How can I help?'

'I'm Detective Inspector Drake and this is Detective Sergeant Morgan. We're investigating the murder of Gloria Patton. We spoke to two other members of staff last week.'

'What day was that?

Sara consulted her pocketbook. 'Tuesday.'

'Then it was probably Jean or Maureen. We have lots of volunteers and they all work different days. I'm Penny, the manager. I was away last week on holiday.'

Drake produced the photofit identikit picture. 'We're looking for somebody who matches this description. Does he look familiar to you? Did he come into the shop at all?'

She took a moment to stare intently at the image. 'Yes. There was someone who called – he was selling CCTV cameras. But we told him ours was broken and that headquarters wouldn't pay for new ones.'

Drake struggled for a moment – it sounded so matter-of-fact. The killer had been in the shop. It meant they were closer now. Drake's pulse hammered. 'Can you describe him?'

'I don't know – ordinary, I suppose.'

'When was this? How long ago?'

'I can't remember. It was quite a bit before Johnny got the cameras fixed.'

'Fixed?' Drake almost shouted. 'What the hell do you mean? I was told they were broken.'

'Keep your shirt on. You can ask Johnny.'

'Who on earth is Johnny?'

Now she sounded offended. 'No need to take that tone with me. He helps out two mornings a week.' She lowered her voice. 'He isn't quite right. But he's great with the electronic stuff.'

Sara piped up. 'Is Johnny here? It is very important.' She gave Drake a smile that combined a gentle chastisement and grudging respect.

The woman disappeared into a room at the rear of the shop, appearing moments later, gesturing over to Drake and Sara. They weaved past carousels of old clothes to join her.

'This is Johnny. I hope he can help you. I've got to go back and look after the till.'

Drake could hardly contain himself. Johnny was trying to grow a beard but his hormones weren't allowing him much success. He had an open, inquisitive sort of face that gave Drake and Sara an innocent smile. Sara dragged over two chairs stacked in a corner. They sat down. Drake tried to reassure him. 'I understand you're an expert with the CCTV coverage.'

'Somebody at head office sent an engineer to have a look at the system. Everyone thought it was broken. But I fixed it. I go to this day release course in the local college and we did some electronics and computer. It's my favourite subject.'

Sara leant over. 'So, which mornings do you work?'

'Thursday and Friday, and I go to college two afternoons. The rest of the time I help to look after Mum.'

Sara again. 'Penny tells us you've been able to fix

the CCTV cameras.'

Johnny nodded, pleased with himself.

'When was that?' Drake said.

'Two weeks ago. I know cos it was just before that woman was killed in the shop opposite. And it was before I repaired those stereo systems over there.' He jerked his head at a shelf of hi-fi equipment.

'Do the recordings have a date?' Sara continued.

'Of course, would you like to see some?'

'What we would really like to see would be the coverage for the day after the woman was killed.'

Sara spoke in clear, measured tones that disguised the urgency. Drake held his breath.

Johnny fiddled with the mouse and eventually his monitor came to life. It took a few minutes to find the right recording.

'Here we are.'

An image of the shop floor filled the screen, as did the window and the street beyond. Sara was the first to respond. 'There's the van, boss.'

Drake stared at it. 'Fast-forward the damn thing.'

Johnny pouted and Drake regretted sounding so brusque.

The minutes seemed to stretch interminably as the counter on the screen clicked forward. It wasn't until twelve-thirty pm that a figure walked quickly across the shop front, unlocked the van and got in. Drake knew exactly who he had seen. Sara turned to him, wide-eyed in acknowledgement.

Chapter 39

Drake called Mike Foulds after formally telling the shop manager he was seizing the computer equipment. She looked stunned, Johnny beamed. Drake's mobile rang; it was Winder.

'You won't believe this, boss,' Winder said. 'We've been able to trace Ellingham's sister. She's a hospital nurse.'

'Bloody hell. Did you find an address?'

'Yes—'

'Is she working, today, now?'

'Luned is checking at the moment.'

'We have a recording of Ellingham getting into the van outside the charity shop.'

Winder whistled down the telephone; Drake heard him bellow over at Luned, whooping with delight.

Drake finished the call and joined Sara in his car, heading back to headquarters only after a uniformed officer had arrived to wait for Foulds.

He raced back, knowing he had to build a cast-iron case against Ellingham. After parking he made his way with Sara to the main entrance and then up to the Incident Room.

Drake beckoned the team into his office. Sara plonked herself on one of the visitor chairs, Winder and Luned standing behind her.

He looked over at Luned. 'So have you found Ellingham's sister?'

She nodded. 'She started a twelve-hour shift this morning at eight am.'

'Good. Now we need to find out if Ellingham is at home.' Drake snatched at the telephone on his desk and called the nearest police station. He dictated clear instructions for uniformed officers to drive out to his home, establish his whereabouts and if he moved, to follow him.

As he finished, Sara sounded a cautionary note. 'We can't prove the video was actually taken from that van.'

'The forensic analysis is strong compelling evidence. And we have the vehicle. And one of his mobiles was triangulated to an area near the van.'

Luned made her first contribution in a measured tone. 'So what would be his motive?'

'Revenge – Gloria Patton had rejected his work. And with Noel Sanderson out of the way he gets a slot in the art festival.'

'Rhisiart Hopkin?' Sara said

Drake sat back. Hopkin's murder didn't fit into the pattern for the other two. Drake had to face the reality that his explanation was looking too far-fetched.

Drake looked up at Winder. 'Have you been able to trace his girlfriend – Valerie?'

Winder glanced at Luned. They both shook their heads in unison. 'It was probably his sister,' Winder added.

Drake read the time on his watch, reminding himself of his appointment with Superintendent Price. Glancing at his inbox, he saw the attachments to emails from Aberystwyth University and the National Art College of Wales. Filling in the blanks on Jeremy Ellingham's past meant he could plan an arrest.

'We need to know everything about Ellingham's sister.' Drake dismissed his team, pleased there was a renewed determination on their faces.

Drake recognised the name of one of Ellingham's tutors from his own studies in Aberystwyth. Ellingham had proved to be a difficult student, aggressive and uncooperative. His failure to attend lectures had been largely ignored but failing to sit an examination at the end of his first year meant he had to re-sit. The record of Ellingham's meeting with the senior tutor recorded 'unprovoked aggression' and 'foul and abusive language' and eventually he was expelled. An obsession with Welsh history to the exclusion of other topics had ensured his university career was short-lived. So Drake focused again on the scene in Hopkin's home. If he was right then everything was intended to refer to prominent Welsh politicians. People who had made a difference to the lives of other people. Just as artists aspired to do. It was another link to Ellingham but how could he prove it?

The justification for artists who scraped a living relied on their self-serving rationale that their work could only be valued if it was in a museum and enjoyed by everyone. Drake wondered if he was overdue an interview with Ellingham.

Winder brought Drake coffee in his usual cafetière. Drake stared at it suspiciously, hoping it had been made properly. But he had more important things to worry about than correctly brewed coffee. He plunged the filter and poured the drink.

An officer called him after driving past Ellingham's home. 'It looks like he's in, sir. The lights are on.'

At least they knew where Ellingham was that morning and they had traced his sister who must have provided him with the drugs he needed or else told him how to get them. He pictured her image from the initial meeting when, as 'Valerie Reed', she had offered Ellingham an alibi. He smiled to himself as he savoured the prospect of interviewing her. Preparation was the key now they had two prime suspects. He turned to Ellingham's website again and the video he had watched earlier. After five minutes he almost switched it off, a worry developing, but then he caught sight of something on a shelf. The noise from the Incident Room died to a whisper. He managed to zoom in, before squinting at the screen.

He jumped out of his chair and jogged out to the board.

Grabbing the photograph of the mantelpiece from the panoramic image, he paced back to his room, nodding for Sara to follow him. He sat down and drew himself up to the desk. He held up the photograph alongside the monitor.

'There, can you see it?'

Sara stared at the screen, realisation dawning on her face. 'Jesus, it's the same piece of ceramic.'

'Ellingham left it there. He must have done. It was a record of his work. The whole thing was a sad reflection of a twisted mind.'

'He overlooked this video.'

Drake nodded. 'Now we've got him.'

The rest of the morning disappeared in a flurry of telephone calls and brief, snatched exchanges with Sara and then Winder and Luned before Drake left the Incident Room for his meeting with Superintendent Price.

In the senior management suite he remained standing. He couldn't sit still. He kept glancing at his watch, realising that for Price this appointment was routine. The door to Price's office glided open. The superintendent waved over at Drake. 'Ian, good, you're prompt.'

The large conference table was strewn with papers and folders. Price sat down by his desk, gesturing at one of the chairs.

'We've made progress, sir.'

Price stared at the monitor, making Drake feel like a distinct bystander.

'Good. I saw your briefing memorandum for DI Metcalf. I suggest we have a formal meeting on Monday. I'll send it to her over the weekend.'

Drake cleared his throat. 'We've now got a clear suspect. And enough to make an arrest.'

It was the hard tone to Drake's voice that got Price's attention. At last, Drake thought. The superintendent narrowed his eyes, blinked several times. He leant both elbows on the desk and gazed over at Drake. It took Drake no more than a few minutes to summarise most of the evidence implicating Ellingham. Price scribbled the occasional note, curling his lips, but didn't interrupt.

'There's still no link to Hopkin's death.' Before Drake could reply, Price continued. 'We can't prove definitively that the filming was taken from the van, so the fact that Ellingham is seen driving it away may not help you.'

'We found video evidence that one of Ellingham's ceramics was in Hopkin's home. It's a direct link.'

Once Drake finished, Price sat back, scratching his head before taking a deep breath.

'I suppose you want my agreement to make an arrest?' Price paused. 'I'm not convinced about motive – suggesting he's killed a man to immortalise the whole thing as a piece of art installation is sick. Really fucking sick.'

Thinking like a defence lawyer made policing so much more difficult, Drake thought.

'The fact that he is a performance artist is a tenuous link to suggest he might pretend to be Damien Hirst and wear a dark bushy beard around Conwy. Or indeed dress up as a fisherman at the end of Llandudno pier.'

'We've got enough to justify an arrest.'

Price sighed. 'You're hoping a lawful arrest will lead you to discover more evidence.'

No shortcuts. And definitely nothing to help any half-decent defence lawyer.

Drake had said everything he wanted to say. As the superior officer Price had to make the call. The superintendent scanned his notes again. He cleared his throat.

'If I'm right, sir, this man is a danger. He has killed three times already. He won't stop at killing again.'

Price drew his chair back to the table. 'You're right, arrest Ellingham and his sister.'

In his haste to leave, Drake bumped into two civilians who had arrived to see Superintendent Price. He mumbled apologies and jogged back to the Incident Room, taking the stairs two at a time.

Winder was pinning a grainy image to the board. Luned and Sara were emptying boxes of pre-packed sandwiches and soft drinks from a bag, which reminded Drake he felt hungry; it was lunchtime after all.

'How did you get on?' Sara said.

'Both arrests authorised.'

'We've found the driving licence image of Rhian Ellingham,' Winder said.

Drake stepped towards the board and dropped his gaze to the photograph. He stared at it intently. 'There must be some mistake.'

'What do you mean, boss?'

'This isn't anything like the woman I saw.' Suddenly Drake realised that 'Valerie Reed' wasn't Rhian Ellingham after all. He had been stupid to even contemplate the possibility a brother and sister would embark on a killing spree. A dark reality struck him. Ellingham had dressed up for his performance as Damien Hirst and for his performance as the fisherman at the end of the pier. Maybe he had dressed up for another performance: as Valerie Reed.

It annoyed him to think that Ellingham must have enjoyed dressing up, taking time with the make-up, getting the hair just so.

'That bastard Ellingham pretended to be a woman.' Drake clenched his jaw, trawling through his memory for details of his interview with Valerie Reed. She – he – had given Ellingham an alibi and Drake had been completely fooled.

He fisted a hand.

'Difficult to believe,' Sara said.

'He must have some other premises somewhere where he kept all this stuff.' Drake paused, letting his anger abate. 'All we have to do is find it.'

Chapter 40

Drake sat at one of the spare desks in the Incident Room.

'It's hard to believe he could dress up so convincingly as a woman,' Sara said.

Winder wore an amused expression as though the idea of a man walking around in drag was totally alien.

'He's been planning this for months,' Drake said, recalling his discussion with Ellingham's neighbour. Drake flopped back in his chair and let out a long breath. Sara offered Drake one of the sandwiches. 'You should eat something, sir.'

Drake fiddled with the packaging of a chicken salad sandwich. A soft drink can fizzed when Winder cracked it open. The priority would now be to arrest Jeremy Ellingham, find a cell for him in the area custody suite and execute a search of his premises. At this stage Drake couldn't afford to have doubts. The evidence was compelling, his team had worked well, and Superintendent Price supported his decision.

He leant over the table. 'We've got a lot to do.'

Drake and Sara would arrest Ellingham, and Winder and Luned were delegated to arrest Rhian.

It took Drake half an hour to reach Ellingham's property. A patrol car followed.

Drake parked outside. Behind them a marked police car came to a halt.

Sara reached over and dragged two stab jackets from the rear seat. They were taking no chances. They left the car and Drake strode up the path to the front door. He had rehearsed in his mind the first words he would say to Ellingham. The standard phrases about his arrest and then the caution. He hammered on the door. He heard the sound of footsteps on a quarry tiled floor.

The door opened. 'How can I help?'

Drake stared at the woman, trying to fathom out whether it was Ellingham. He pushed out his warrant card. 'I'm looking for Jeremy Ellingham.' He craned to look over the woman's shoulder.

'He's not here. Take a look for yourself.'

Drake barged past her, Sara following. They went into every room before returning to the kitchen. Drake jogged out to the old shed, rattling the chain and padlock that were keeping it securely locked. He put his hands to the window, peering in, but saw nothing.

Back in the kitchen, Sara jotted down the name and full details of the mysterious woman.

'This is Ann,' Sara said

Ann piped up. 'He's a friend of my brother's. He told me I could stay here; I was kicked out by my partner last week.'

Drake stared at her, tempted to pull her hair just to be certain. But she had no make-up on, and having paid attention to the way she looked, it was clear it wasn't Ellingham. She was thinner, smaller. 'Where is he? Drake demanded.

'How would I know?'

'Well, he bloody well lives here.'

'He comes and goes at all hours. He's been dead busy last couple of days. He said that he wouldn't be around much. Complained that he had a lot of work to do. But he's a bit weird if you ask me.'

Drake raised his voice. 'I want to know exactly when you saw him last.'

She recoiled slightly, blinking rapidly. 'I can't remember. You can't talk to me like that. I haven't done anything wrong.'

Drake nodded at Sara and they returned to the car. Sara kept up with his brisk pace. His mobile rang, it was Winder.

'Bad news, boss. Rhian Ellingham is in theatre and can't be disturbed.'

Drake cursed silently. He finished the call as he reached the car. 'Where the hell is he?' Drake paused, recalling Ann's comments. 'He must have been referring to the arts festival when he mentioned work. I'll speak to Huw; he might know Ellingham's whereabouts.'

Drake fumbled with his mobile and after the third ring, Jackson answered.

'Hello, Ian.'

'I need to speak to Jeremy Ellingham. Do you know where I can find him?'

'Sorry, I know he was busy this afternoon. He told the committee he couldn't attend the performance.'

An invisible vice tightened itself around Drake's neck. 'Performance? What do you mean?'

'There's a performance in Conwy Castle. It's private, invitation only. Not my cup of tea.'

'Who's going to be present?'

Jackson reeled off various names: the members of the arts festival committee, councillors and local politicians. It was a collection of the great and the good associated with the festival. Before he finished, Jackson mentioned one other name, a name Drake recognised.

'Did you say Milos Fogerty?' Drake said slowly.

'Yes, he's flying in from Vienna. The committee were delighted he was going to attend.'

A knot of bile spun around Drake's stomach. Drake dredged his memory for the comments Milos Fogerty had made about Ellingham: 'utterly unsuited to being an artist' and 'his criticism of Ellingham's work was harsh, brutal even'.

'Thanks, Huw.' He tried to sound calm. Ending the call, he turned to Sara.

'We need to get in Conwy Castle. Now.'

Drake hammered the car along the narrow country lanes back to Conwy. He had to slam on the brakes to avoid colliding with a tractor, which meant the passenger side wheels careering into a shallow ditch. Sara grabbed hold of the car door before he accelerated away.

'He's going to kill Milos Fogerty. He's big in the art world. Fogerty tutored him at art school. Ellingham hated his guts apparently.'

'Why would he want to kill him?'

'Because he's fucking mad. It must be the last part of some perverted show.'

Another car came round a blind corner. The wing mirrors of both cars clipped each other with a loud crack.

'But it's in the middle of the castle. Other people will be there.'

'He'd have thought of all that.'

Drake had to stop a fourth murder, another person killed by this madman. But what if Fogerty had already been injected with the same muscle relaxant as Patton and Sanderson? 'Call an ambulance or one of those paramedic cars to the entrance of the castle. Tell them it's a matter of life and death.'

Sara fumbled for her mobile.

They reached the outskirts of Conwy where the traffic thickened. Drake blasted the car horn, flashed his lights. Most of the cars cowed to one side and allowed him through. Occasionally a bad-tempered driver raised a middle finger, gesticulating angrily. 'Get that guy's registration number,' Drake said. 'We'll report him after this is finished.'

Sara did as she was told.

They dropped down past the town walls and through one of the old gates. There was little prospect of overtaking any traffic in the narrow street so he curbed his annoyance. Near the castle he drove the car diagonally onto the pavement over double yellow lines and sprinted to the entrance.

He had to hammer on the door to gain the attention of an assistant in the office. Barely concealing his anger, he pressed his warrant card against the glass. 'Just bloody well open the door.'

The flashing light of a first response vehicle was reflected in the window. He turned as it parked and he paced over to meet the paramedic who jumped out. 'What's the emergency?'

'Have you got oxygen in the car?'

'Yes. Why, is there someone unconscious?'

'How many bottles have you got?'

'Two.'

'Get them out now and follow me.'

Drake legged it up to the entrance and confronted a uniformed attendant. He drew himself up, about to deliver Drake a lecture. The inspector pushed him to one side. 'You can't come in, it's a private function.'

Drake ignored him and grabbed a printed castle guide as he passed the ticket desk. He ran over the footbridge towards the castle and then raced up the path to the ruins of the main gate. Drake stood for a moment catching his breath. In one corner at the far end of the courtyard a group stood talking around a table underneath a pergola that was held rigidly in place with tent poles and guide ropes. 'This way,' Drake said to Sara and the paramedic.

They sprinted over. Drake recognised Marjorie and Julie from the committee. He caught his breath as he reached them. 'Have you seen Milos Fogerty?'

Both women scanned the group. Then their brows furrowed. 'He was here a minute ago,' Marjorie said. 'Once the performance had finished I saw him talking to the mayor.'

Drake turned his back on them and surveyed the castle layout before frantically opening the castle plan and staring around, trying to get his bearings. He spotted a uniformed guide and marched over to him.

'We're looking for a room or a space. Somewhere private where a man could be killed.'

The guide turned a sickly colour. 'Well … that could be a lot of places.'

'Quickly. Show us.' Drake thrust the sheets of the castle plan at him.

'The Prison Tower behind us has been refurbished but the Chapel Tower …' He gestured to the far corner of the castle. '… is probably the most likely.'

'We'll have to split up.'

'I've done a first aid course, boss,' Sara said.

'Good, you take the Prison Tower. And take one of the oxygen canisters.' Drake turned to the paramedic. 'You're with me.'

Drake turned to the guide again. 'When did this performance finish?'

He managed a frightened sort of croak. 'Not long, five minutes maybe.'

They still had time, Drake thought.

'Let's go,' Drake said.

Drake jogged towards the site of the drawbridge between the Outer Ward and Inner Ward as Sara headed with a stunned-looking guide for the Prison Tower. Heading down a passageway, Drake could see the bridge over the estuary ahead of him. He darted into a walled enclosure, seeing an entrance at the base of the Prison Tower.

He ducked his head to avoid the thick lintel.

The room had a display cabinet but nothing else.

He turned on his heels and almost barged into the paramedic following him.

'Upstairs,' Drake gasped.

He quickly retraced his steps until he found a steep staircase that took him to the first floor of the Prison Tower. When he entered the thick castle walls the temperature dropped. The atmosphere was damp and clammy. His footsteps echoed over the wooden floor but the room was empty.

Despair that they were running out of time to resuscitate Fogerty clawed at every nerve in his body.

His mobile rang. It was Sara. 'No sign of him, boss.'

'He's got to be somewhere.'

'He might have taken Fogerty out of the castle.'

The possibility had occurred to Drake but he didn't want to consider it. 'Someone would've seen him, surely,'

'I'll call you when I finish in the tower.'

It had given Drake a valuable few seconds to gather his breath. Drake turned to the paramedic who was breathing heavily. 'Let's go.'

He spotted the narrow passageway and headed up the staircase. It wasn't designed for easy access or for carrying oxygen around easily – Drake sensed the paramedic behind him struggling. The castle stairwells had been designed so that right-handed swordsmen defending the castle were able to wield their weapons against attackers. Ellingham was probably long gone by now and even if he came down he wouldn't be wielding a sword. Probably a syringe, just as deadly as a sword, Drake thought.

He yanked on the rope hanging from the circular wall to heave himself up the stairs more quickly. The first room they reached was empty apart from a few pieces of old furniture. From a narrow window he gazed down over the town. Cars were threading their way towards the bridge. He returned to the stairwell and bounded up to the next floor. There was no sign of Ellingham or Fogerty. 'Where the bloody hell has he gone,' Drake said aloud. Sweat dripped down his armpit. He loosened his tie and undid his shirt button.

Ellingham knew the place was going to be empty today, Drake thought. Nobody would disturb him.

Drake hauled himself further up the narrow staircase to the top floor, his heart hammering. Time was marching on, seconds turning into minutes. Time was running out for Fogerty.

Drake found renewed energy as they reached the top. He looked inside and caught his breath.

Strapped to a wicker lounging chair was the limp body of a man in his early fifties. Drake rushed over, followed by the paramedic who immediately searched for a pulse. Drake stood back, scanning the room, and found the camera tucked out of reach above an old fireplace.

He cursed, looking around for a chair, anything. He dragged over a heavy, wooden upright chair towards the fireplace and jumped up, yanking the camera away from the wall. He dropped it onto the floorboards and smashed it with his right heel. The paramedic was busy administering oxygen but when he turned, Drake recognised the wary frown on his face.

Chapter 41

Two paramedics rushed past Drake as he reached the lawned area near the entrance. He watched Mike Foulds and two crime scene investigators hauling boxes of equipment into the castle.

'Well done,' Foulds said.

'I hope you find some forensic evidence this time.' Drake sounded unconvinced. Foulds hurried away and Drake turned to Sara. 'We need to find Ellingham.'

'Where would he go? How could he possibly hope to get away with this?'

'He believes that Milos Fogerty is dead, so he'll be building an alibi.'

'Somebody will have seen him here, surely.'

Huw Jackson's comments came to his mind. Ellingham had made excuses about not attending the performance. What did he mean? He must have been planning to be somewhere else. Drake reached for his mobile. He tapped in the details of the Orme Arts Festival and found the programme of events.

'He'll be nearby,' Drake announced.

He read the brief mention of the private opening performance and then reference to a film being shown that afternoon. Drake's pulse hastened. He knew exactly where Ellingham was going.

'There's a film being shown in the one of the cinemas in Llandudno Junction,' Drake said as he jogged towards the exit.

'That's going to be his alibi?'

'Not if we have anything to do with it.'

A dozen uniformed officers milled around the pavement outside. Drake shouted over at them to stop any further traffic crossing the bridge. Three of them galloped over the road, raising their arms at the oncoming vehicles. It meant Drake and Sara had a clear road across the estuary. It was no more than a mile, Drake thought. Ellingham wouldn't have used a car and walking would have been too slow. Drake drove off the pavement with a thud, ground the gearstick into first and accelerated hard for the bridge. Drake knew the cinema complex well; he and the girls had been there frequently. He reached the roundabout on the eastern side of the estuary, flashing at oncoming vehicles, and swung the Mondeo around and then up towards an elevated section and down to his left and the car park.

Sara announced after searching her mobile telephone. 'It's a French art film: "genre defining", whatever that means.'

Cars disgorging families visiting the cinema for the afternoon matinees and the restaurants nearby delayed Drake's progress. He slowed to a crawl but it only increased his anxiety. Drake double-parked near the cinema.

They headed inside, warrant cards at the ready. Two members of staff blocked their way before they reached the door. 'I'm sorry, sir. You can't go in now.'

Drake pushed his warrant card into the man's face. 'Get the lights on. Now. This is official police business. There's a killer inside.'

Using the word killer did the trick. An ashen-faced usher spoke into an intercom as Drake hauled open the door. Seconds later the lights inside flickered on and voices started mumbling protests. Heads moved, peering towards the rear. Drake started down one aisle, Sara the other.

Drake scanned the audience, some on their feet blocking his view. Others were milling around in the aisle ahead of him. The film continued to run on the screen. It occurred to Drake that if he was wrong it was an embarrassing waste of his time. His pulse pounded in his neck and he had to move slightly to his left to see more clearly the faces around him.

As he looked over at Sara she shook her head and carried on checking the people passing her.

Drake's chest tightened as he noticed Ellingham chatting to a woman, as though he had few cares in the world. He smiled, rolled his eyes, joked and looked towards Drake.

Drake's gaze met his.

Ellingham froze. He turned and in a moment Drake had lost sight of him. Gesturing to Sara, Drake pushed his way through the crowd. But Ellingham was nowhere to be seen. Sara was by his side now.

'He was here right enough. He made a run for it when he spotted me. There must be an exit through the toilets.' Drake nodded at the illuminated signs above a door. 'Do a search for him. I'm going outside.'

Sara sprinted down the aisle as Drake jostled through the audience and the people assembling in the foyer. Outside he ran round to the rear of the building. A door flapped ajar, Drake jerked it open. The empty passageway led into a service area full of napkins and paper towels and toilet rolls.

He raced back to the parking area. For a fraction of a second, he contemplated the possibility they had missed Ellingham. More cars were arriving. He craned to spot the man, walking, running, anything.

Drake started off towards the main road, reached a pizza restaurant and paused; he caught his breath then set off again, scanning every car, every parking slot. His mobile rang; it was Sara. He pushed the handset to his ear. 'We've lost him.' Drake sounded desperate. 'Where are you?'

'I've just left the cinema.'

Drake jogged towards the roundabout on an elevated section, furious Ellingham might have given them the slip. He reached the road. He put his hands on his knees, drawing in deep lungfuls of breath.

If Ellingham had been able to make good his escape he might be heading east into England or west for the port at Holyhead. Drake looked over at the stationary cars on the slip road emerging from a large supermarket. One car in particular caught his attention. It was small and red and the driver was looking down at his feet.

Sara joined Drake. He pointed at the car. 'There he is.'

Cars accelerating off the roundabout prevented Drake from running towards Ellingham's vehicle and he had to watch helplessly as Ellingham left the car and raced away. Drake and Sara ran after him on the other side of the road, hoping they could cross as the traffic thinned.

But Ellingham was a lot fitter than Drake imagined and he raced ahead towards the bridge for Conwy. Once Drake and Sara were on the same side of the road they sprinted after Ellingham. A stitch burnt in Drake's side. Sara kept up with him but she slowed.

Suddenly, Ellingham disappeared from view. Moments later Drake reached the section of the bridge where he last saw Ellingham. He peered over the railings and watched as the figure ran onto a path by the side of the estuary. It was a drop of ten or twelve feet. Drake hesitated.

'He's gone down to the river,' Drake shouted at Sara, gesticulating downstream.

Then he clambered over the railing.

'It's a big drop, boss …'

Drake let go and fell clumsily, scratching his palms as he broke his fall. He took a couple of seconds to compose himself before running after Ellingham. The footpath took him under the road bridge and then underneath the adjacent railway bridge. A train rattled overhead. In the distance, Ellingham ran towards the nature reserve that occupied a spit of land on the estuary.

Drake picked up speed and the gap narrowed. But Ellingham's figure disappeared so Drake increased his pace. Moments later he saw Ellingham fiddling with the rope tethering a small wooden dinghy.

Drake was within a few yards when Ellingham realised how near he was. He jumped into the dinghy and reached over for the outboard motor. But Drake was too close. He launched himself at Ellingham. Both men crashed into the bottom of the dinghy. Drake, breathless but determined, had the advantage. He turned the man over onto his face.

Moments later, he saw Sara on the bank. She threw him a pair of handcuffs.

He snapped them onto Ellingham's wrists and sat down in a heap, slowly gathering his breath.

'Jeremy Ellingham, I'm arresting you for murder ...'

Chapter 42

Drake arrived at the area custody suite after a fractious half an hour in accident and emergency. A nurse had warned him the wait would be three hours to see a doctor. Her attitude had soon changed when he explained why he had to be seen immediately. His wounds were promptly cleaned and dressed and after twenty minutes he was driving to the area custody suite.

A message reached his mobile – *Fogerty conscious and out of danger*. Relief washed over Drake and he shared a slow smile with Sara who was standing with the custody sergeant.

'Fogerty's going to pull through.'

'Great news, boss. Rhian Ellingham is in interview room three.'

'Let's see what she has to say.'

Rhian Ellingham sat cowering behind a table: blond hair drawn into an untidy bun behind her head. She wore her green nurse's uniform. She had a round, kindly face, her gaze following Drake and Sara intently as they sat down. It wasn't an interview under caution, not yet. Drake wanted her cooperation so he smiled.

'Why am I here?' Rhian stretched out a trembling hand to a plastic beaker of water and took a sip.

'I'd like to ask you some questions about Jeremy.'

'What has he done? I'm sure there's been a mistake.'

No mistake: three deaths.

'Where do you work in the hospital?'

'In theatre.'

'Have you always worked there?'

Rhian ran her tongue over her lips. 'I was in accident and emergency for five years. But it got too much for me.'

Drake nodded. 'Did you ever discuss your work with Jeremy?' Drake leant forward. 'Did you discuss treatment procedures? You know, how the doctors deal with patients needing anaesthetics.'

'No, never … I mean … I don't remember … Perhaps I talked about work sometimes. What is this all about?'

'You're familiar with Rohypnol and succinylcholine?'

Rhian nodded. 'Sux is used regularly.'

'Have you ever accessed that drug for doctors when it was needed in an emergency?'

She frowned. 'Yes, a few times. Why?'

'Did you ever describe for your brother how muscle relaxant drugs are stored?'

The barest hint of recognition filtered across her eyes as the colour in her cheeks drained away.

'There was this one time when we watched a cop series on TV. They used drugs to put someone into a sort of suspended animation.' Rhian paused. 'He wanted to know how easy it might be to get those sorts of drugs. All you have to do is look on the internet. Google it.' She stared at Sara. 'Are you talking about that poor woman who was killed in Llandudno?'

Drake broke in. 'Can you tell me about Jeremy's girlfriend?'

'He's told me about her and showed me a photograph, one of those passport photographs he kept in his wallet. I never met her. They haven't been going out very long.'

'How long has it been?' Drake lowered his voice.

'I don't know, few months maybe.'

'Didn't strike you as odd that you've not met her?'

'She's a quiet person, private, doesn't want a fuss. That's what he told me.'

'Of course. Has Jeremy had many girlfriends?'

'No, Valerie was the first one he ever talked about. He was never good with relationships.'

'Have you met many of his friends?'

'Like I said, he's not good with people. He tends to live on his own, you know, off the grid, as they say in those TV dramas.'

Drake took a moment to scan some of his notes. It gave Sara the chance to ask a question. 'We'd need to talk to Jeremy. We've been to the house but he wasn't there and the shed at the back was locked. He mentioned his other studio but I didn't make a note of the address. I was wondering if you could help?' Drake looked over, mildly surprised, admiring Sara's audacity. At least it wasn't a taped interview.

'He used Mam and Dad's old place near Betws y Coed.'

Drake hoped that she wouldn't notice the intensity of his stare and Sara's. And knowing Ellingham's mobile could be located to that area fitted another part of the jigsaw together.

Sara managed an interested tone. 'Perhaps you've got the full address and directions.'

'Well done,' Drake said as they scampered over to their car.

'Thank you, sir,'

Drake's mobile rang as he unlocked the car. It was Mike Foulds. 'You'll never guess.'

'Forensically aware – there's nothing from the castle.'

'Top of the class, Inspector.'

Drake threw Sara the car keys. 'You drive. I need to get all the formalities done.'

Drake called Superintendent Price as Sara drove, explaining in detail why he needed a search warrant. Price listened without interrupting. Once Drake finished there was a pause, which unnerved him. 'Get it done, Ian. I'll organise a full team.'

'Thank you, sir.'

Sara slowed for the speed limits in Glan Conwy. Sunshine flooded through the clouds, glistening on the surface of the river that appeared through openings in the trees as they accelerated down towards Llanrwst. Minutes later an email arrived on Drake's smartphone confirming the warrant. His superior officer had a tame magistrate, Drake thought.

Having no postcode rendered the satnav redundant so Sara relied on Drake dictating the instructions Rhian had given them earlier. Drake directed Sara through various turns, each marked by some landmark before a right-hand turn took them down a narrow lane. It led to a farm and then beyond it to an old barn and cottage. They were a little more than a mile or so from the van hidden in the forest. Rhian had explained that the cottage was let on a long tenancy to an elderly couple. They drew the car into the yard. Drake jumped out and began to scout around the premises. Moments later two police cars arrived with a posse of officers.

The sergeant had shoulders like bags of cement and hands like shovels. 'What needs to be done, sir?'

Drake nodded at the barn doors. 'Break it down.'

The sound of wood shattering and splintering filled the air as the heavy black battering ram made quick work of the doors. 'Are we expecting someone to be inside?' The sergeant asked, a contented look on his face.

Drake shook his head.

He made straight for a door at the far end. It led through into a long narrow room. Against one wall, a computer with two monitors and a complicated sound system stood silently on a purpose-built desk. Sara walked over to a cupboard and opened it. 'Wow.'

Drake turned and saw the collection of CCTV cameras and cables and wires. The search team leader appeared behind Drake. He had a purposeful, workmanlike attitude. 'You want to remove this kit?'

'Everything.' Drake headed to a door on the other side of the room. Behind it was a makeshift bedroom, single bed and a washbasin and tap. A large double wardrobe pushed into one corner drew his attention. He glanced over at Sara. She raised an eyebrow, sharing his expectation at what hung inside.

He walked over and placed a latex glove on the handle.

Chapter 43

The following morning Drake walked up to the two uniformed police officers seated near Milos Fogerty's room and who stood as he approached. He had one simple question to ask Fogerty. For today at least. A more detailed interview would follow.

'He's had a comfortable night, sir,' one of the officers said.

'Good.'

'And he's eaten breakfast.'

Drake nodded and opened the door to let himself into the private ward.

Fogerty turned to look at Drake but he struggled to recognise him.

'Detective Inspector Drake.'

Fogerty nodded. 'I owe you my life. Thank you.'

Drake drew up a plastic chair near the bed.

'I need to ask you about the attack.'

Fogerty was in his late fifties but his sickly complexion made him look much older. 'Can you identify the person who assaulted you?'

Fogerty managed a nod. 'Of course. Jeremy Ellingham.'

Drake had to be certain. 'No doubt in your mind?'

Fogerty shook his head and took his gaze to the window. It was a warm spring day. Drake sat back. Now he had the conclusive evidence he needed.

Drake returned to headquarters and entered the Incident Room. He walked over to the board, knowing the team wanted to hear the result of his conversation that morning.

'Positive ID for Jeremy Ellingham,' Drake said.

Winder punched the air, Sara beamed and Luned nodded sagely. The tension ebbed away at the news.

He turned to Sara who took the prompt. 'We've been through all of the clothes we found at Ellingham's barn yesterday. They match the descriptions of the clothes the fictitious Damien Hirst wore and there was fisherman's gear too. And test tubes and chemicals in a shed in the garden.'

Winder butted in. 'CSIs have found a copy of the recording made outside the charity shop on the morning the body of Patton was discovered.'

'Good,' Drake said.

Winder continued. 'We're still digging but it could be some time before we finish. What we did find was a receipt for a purchase on eBay for various books. Exactly the same ones lined up on Hopkin's shelves.'

Drake said nothing, letting the significance sink in.

Sara broke the silence. 'They don't directly link him to Hopkin.'

Drake spoke slowly, emphasising each word. 'But the books and the ceramic piece together are powerful circumstantial evidence.' He turned and stared at Ellingham's photograph. 'But I want him to tell me what his motive was, in his own words.'

For the rest of the morning and early afternoon Drake listened to the results of background checks on Ellingham. Nobody had been able to find a record of any exhibition by him in any gallery in Wales or London and definitely not Vienna.

By the afternoon Drake had arrived at the area custody suite ready to interview. Drake made a habit of choosing one of his better suits for an interview: today it was a sombre navy, narrow lapels, two buttons. The dusty pink shirt had the elasticated cufflinks he preferred, his tie dark with pink polka dots. He detoured to the bathroom on his way from finalising the interview plan with Sara. He took time to scrub his hands. He would feel grubby at the end of the interview so he wanted to start it feeling clean, sanitised. Looking at the reflection, he resolved to get a decent night's sleep. And with the investigation at an end he might even be able to plan a couple of afternoons off with Megan and Helen.

Drake joined Sara in the small, confined interview room.

He heard Ellingham joking with his solicitor as they approached along the corridor. Once inside Ellingham strolled towards the table and sat down nonchalantly. His lawyer dropped a blue legal pad and a fountain pen onto the table.

'Good afternoon, Inspector.' Jason Fox had perfect manners, a thorough understanding of every aspect of police procedure and a terrier-like attitude to defending his clients.

'Jason,' Drake said. 'You know Detective Sergeant Sara Morgan.'

Fox gave Sara a perfect-teeth smile.

Ellingham threaded the fingers of both hands together and started turning each thumb around the other. Drake stared at him, wondering exactly how he might respond.

Once the formalities were completed, Drake got down to the questioning.

'I understand you're a well-known artist?'

Ellingham nodded, preened himself, as though it were common knowledge.

'Tell me about your work.'

'I don't have to tell you about my work, I'm an artist.'

But you can't help yourself, Drake thought. He fingered a biographical summary the team had discovered.

'This is from an article I found about your work. "My work examines relationships between mind and empirical objects with a special emphasis on everyday beliefs, political and social realities in which I seek to implicate myself personally."'

Drake looked up at Ellingham. 'It must have come as a disappointment when Gloria Patton rejected your work as inadequate for the Orme Arts Festival. She called it "utterly derivative" and "lacking in imagination".'

Ellingham's smugness evaporated into scorn.

'As a well-respected gallery curator surely Mrs Patton's view of your artwork riled you.'

'She wasn't a curator. She had no place being involved in the Orme Arts Festival.'

Drake sat back, waiting for him to continue, but he shut up.

'Everyone we have spoken to in the art world speaks very highly of her.'

Ellingham blanked Drake.

'Her gallery has exhibited some very well-known artists.'

Now Ellingham's posture stiffened.

'And she had made some inspirational decisions in choosing the cross-section of artists. A critic we spoke to thought she could have built a very successful business representing artists from her gallery.'

Drake gave Ellingham a kindly smile. He forced a reply through clenched teeth. 'Her judgement was flawed, her taste pedestrian.'

Jason Fox leant over, whispering in Ellingham's ear. Drake guessed the lawyer was warning him not to overreact.

'Where were you on the night Gloria Patton was killed?'

'I was with Valerie.'

'Your girlfriend?'

Ellingham nodded.

'Where is she now?'

Ellingham shrugged. 'We split up.'

'I'll come back to her later. I've spoken about your work with the Anderson Gallery in Cardiff.'

Ellingham sighed heavily.

'Tell me why they terminated their relationship with you?'

Ellingham said nothing.

'Is it true your relationship with them broke down because of your behaviour?'

Ellingham shook his head in feigned disbelief.

'The owner says that you became abusive and threatening once he had criticised your work, suggested you should seek a career other than in the art world.'

Drake continued to repeat the various comments about the quality of Ellingham's work, his artistic integrity and, more importantly, his violent mood swings. By the end Ellingham's nostrils flared widely and it looked as though his eyes wanted to jump out of his head. 'They know nothing about art,' Ellingham hissed.

At last, this interview might be going in the right direction, Drake thought.

'Your career was over, wasn't it? You were finished. Nobody wants to display your work. Now you'll have to work for a living.'

'I've got galleries all over the place eager to show my work.'

'Name them,' Drake snapped.

'The negotiations are at a delicate stage. I have to keep everything confidential.'

'This is confidential, Jeremy. If you had any galleries interested you'd tell me straight away.'

Ellingham flushed slightly. 'Everything is at the pre-contract stage. I've already had some significant offers for my last three pieces.'

Drake shuffled his papers once again and found Ellingham's latest tax returns. Drake had spent an hour calculating how much Ellingham's meagre income represented as an hourly rate. He pushed the printed sheets across the table. 'Can you confirm these are your tax returns?'

Ellingham swallowed and then pushed them back as dismissively as Drake had.

'Assuming you work a forty-hour week your equivalent hourly rate is about half of the minimum wage. You could earn more working behind a bar.'

'And your question is, Inspector?' Fox said.

Drake addressed Ellingham directly. 'In the last two years you've made barely enough to pay your rent, pay your electricity bill or buy food. Would you agree with my description that you are desperate for money?'

'I'm an artist, I don't do things for money. I live for my art. I prefer to live as a pauper than prostitute my work.'

'Your work was described by Gloria Patton as "utterly derivative" and "lacking in imagination". And she's an expert so she would know.'

Ellingham picked at his lips and gave Drake a spearing glare.

'The scene in the shoe shop where Gloria's body was found was the work of a twisted mind.' Drake arranged various photographs of the scene on the table and Fox peered over at them. Ellingham glanced at them impassively but Drake thought he caught a glint of admiration or even pleasure. He lowered his voice and slowed his delivery. 'I think you hated Gloria so much that you killed her. Nobody would do this to her unless they were really perverted. Because she rejected your work you decided to show her body as some sick, distorted representation of art. You knocked her unconscious by a blow to the head before administering a muscle relaxant causing her to suffocate. It was a brutal and inhumane way to die.'

Drake sat back. A silence filled the room.

Ellingham tilted his head and sneered.

'Did you hope the world would appreciate looking at a dead body?'

Ellingham ignored him.

'Nobody in their right mind would think arranging a corpse as you did could be construed as art.' Drake paused. 'It's murder. So explain to me why you killed her?'

Ellingham ignored him.

Drake leant over, jabbing a finger at the images on the table, raising his voice. 'Look at them. Now, Jeremy. The scene was intended to mimic *My Bed* by Tracey Emin, considered to be a great example of British art. So you built the scene at the shoe shop to copy her work – making it utterly derivative and lacking in imagination. That summarises your art, doesn't it?'

Ellingham straightened. 'Who the fuck do you think you are to tell me about art?'

Drake shared a look of incredulity with Sara, who continued the questioning as planned. 'Is it true you have an interest in Welsh history?'

Ellingham folded his arms and stared at Sara with hooded eyes. Drake saw the faintest glimmer of recognition, acknowledgement in his eyes.

'It's a fascinating period of history.' Ellingham sounded patronising.

'Did you know that Rhisiart Hopkin was on the committee that turned you down for the festival?'

Ellingham made a brief ineffective shrug.

'That must have annoyed you?'

He stared over at Sara, an annoying grin playing on his lips.

'We found a receipt in your computer for books you bought. The exact same books were left at the home of Hopkin the night he was killed. Why did you leave them there?'

Ellingham opened his mouth but thought the better of replying.

'Is that the only evidence you have to link my client to Hopkin?' Fox said.

Sara ignored him. Be patient, Drake thought.

From a box by his feet Drake fished out a laptop, which he opened on the desk. A few seconds later he clicked on the film from Ellingham's website. 'You can confirm that this is a video from your website?'

Ellingham and Fox stared at the monitor.

Ellingham nodded. Drake moved the screen away from Ellingham's gaze and let the coverage run on until it came to the image of the green piece of ceramic pottery; he froze the images. 'What sort of art do you make?'

'My practice is multidisciplinary.'

'Do you paint?'

Ellingham sighed in disgust.

'Pottery or ceramics?'

'Never.'

'So, to be clear, you don't sell paintings or ceramics at all?'

'Yes, Inspector,' Ellingham drawled.

Drake then produced the photographs from Hopkin's home and spread them out on the table.

'This is the inside of Rhisiart Hopkin's home.'

Ellingham and Fox leant over the photographs.

'You can see the books Sergeant Morgan mentioned. Please look at the mantel.'

Drake stared at Ellingham and saw the surprise in his eyes and the descent into paranoia approaching. 'Is the green ceramic piece familiar?'

Ellingham parted his lips but no words came out.

'It belongs to you, Jeremy. It's the same piece we just saw on the video from your studio.' Drake spun round the laptop and pointed at the screen.

A strange pout crossed Ellingham's face.

'You left it there when you killed Hopkin.'

'Really, Inspector,' Fox said. 'You haven't shown any motive.'

Drake ignored him. 'You killed Rhisiart Hopkin because you wanted to prove how great an artist you are. Let me tell you what I think about the scene at Hopkin's home. It's your sad and perverted idea of a piece of art. You left three clues, something that suggested three famous Welsh politicians. You wanted it to be your piece of work – a copy of a famous piece by Judy Chicago. You even left a postcard from Chicago airport. But Hopkin had never been there. What you didn't realise was that Rhisiart Hopkin annotated every book in his library, usually with the date when he bought them and details of the seller. All the ones you left were clean, and no fingerprints.'

Ellingham tut-tutted and rolled his eyes at his lawyer, pretending to be tired of listening to such mumbo-jumbo.

'It was going to be your secret masterpiece.'

Ellingham reached forward and took another sip from his water bottle.

'You left the piece of green ceramic for posterity. But you had forgotten about this video. And because Hopkin was on the committee that rejected your work you wanted revenge.'

Drake glared at Ellingham who glared back.

Drake continued. 'Do you know Noel Sanderson?'

Ellingham adjusted his position in his chair but made no reply.

'I understand he's a highly regarded artist with

exhibitions and shows all over Europe.'

'Bullshit,' Ellingham spluttered through gritted teeth.

'He was another artist chosen ahead of you for the Orme Arts Festival. How did you feel knowing he was a better artist than you?'

Ellingham settled into an intense stare.

'He's represented by the Anderson Gallery. So they obviously think he is a better artist than you. It must be galling to think that someone who has come to live in the area, and an Englishman, could get a place ahead of you. Did that make you angry?'

Drake pushed over the photofit picture of the man described by the girl at the end of the pier and the pinstripe-suited bushy-bearded individual who introduced himself as Damien Hirst to the letting agent in Conwy. 'These are photofit images of the two persons of interest in our enquiry. Do you know who they are?' Ellingham didn't respond.

From underneath the various papers Drake produced the photographs of the dresses and wigs discovered in Ellingham's barn the previous afternoon.

'We recovered these items of clothing from your property. Do they belong to you?'

'I don't know what you're talking about.'

'Now, tell me about your girlfriend. Where does she live again?'

Beads of sweat appeared on his forehead. Ellingham stared through Drake.

'Is she an artist too?'

'You don't know anything. I don't want her involved.'

'Does she have a number where we can reach her?'

'Keep away from her. I've told you. It's private.'

Drake paused, waiting for Ellingham to elaborate.

He kept fidgeting with his hands. 'How many girlfriends have you had, Jeremy?'

Ellingham clenched his jaw; his eyes burnt contempt. 'You can go and fuck yourself.'

'Valerie doesn't exist, does she?'

No response.

Drake pushed over the image of the dress 'Valerie Reed' had worn. 'This dress and various wigs were found in a property near Betws y Coed that belongs to you.'

Drake paused, hoping for a response. When it didn't come he continued.

'Do you admire installation artists?'

'You don't know the first thing about art.'

'What would you prefer – to sell frequently or have your work in a museum?'

'I cannot begin to explain to you what true art means.'

'Try.'

'You haven't got the open, inquisitive mind that's needed.' He waved a hand in the air, dismissing Drake.

'Your work is "utterly derivative" and "lacking in imagination".

'Bollocks.' Jeremy adjusted his position in the hard plastic chair.

'Gloria was right to reject your work because you're not an artist.'

Ellingham hissed a reply. 'Don't ever say that. You have no right to say that.' He shrugged off a calming hand Fox placed on his arm.

Drake pushed over the images from the Patton murder scene. It shocked him to witness the admiring look in Ellingham's face. He was enjoying all of this. Perhaps in his sad world this interview was part of his sick idea of art.

'The scene where Gloria died is a sick and

disgusting fantasy. It will never be seen by anyone. Never be shared and it is a testament to your sick and perverted mind.'

Ellingham raised a fist and let it crash down on the desk.

Drake ignored the tantrum.

'The same is true for the scene at Noel Sanderson's death.' Drake found the CSI photographs and with a flourish set them out on the table. 'You copied Damien Hirst's work and killed Sanderson because he took your place in the festival and … because it was another …. performance to satisfy your sickness.'

Ellingham stood up and shouted. 'It's society that cannot comprehend what I'm doing, what my work really means.' He slumped back into his chair.

'Jeremy, take a look at this last photograph.' Drake tried a more upbeat tone, friendly, almost as he slipped the image of Ellingham outside the charity shop over the table. 'Can you confirm this is an image of you outside the charity shop opposite the premises where you murdered Gloria Patton. You are entering a van from which recording equipment was used to broadcast on YouTube.'

Ellingham stared at the image. His lawyer did likewise. Ellingham looked up but behind his eyes there was nothing but a vacuum.

'Finally, did you know Milos Fogerty when you were at art school?'

Ellingham drummed his fingers on the table. 'He falsely accused me of all sorts of things. He made up allegations. It was all lies. And he was a crap teacher. His work belongs in the middle ages.'

'And last night you tried to kill him.'

Ellingham shook his head.

'The scene where we found Fogerty is exactly the

same MO as the deaths of Patton and Sanderson. Once we have the toxicology reports I guess it will be the same drug too.'

'I was in the cinema.' Now Ellingham started to fidget with his fingernails. Drake curbed his desire to reach over and grab this lunatic by his collar.

Drake paused long enough to make Ellingham and Fox realise he had something important. 'Fogerty identifies you as his assailant.'

The blank look of a mind utterly unable to comprehend his own failings returned to Ellingham's face.

'Jeremy Ellingham, I believe that you murdered Gloria Patton, Rhisiart Hopkin and Noel Sanderson and attempted to murder Milos Fogerty in order to salvage your artistic career and from some twisted perverted logic. Do you have anything else you wish to say?'

Ellingham sneered at Drake. 'Nobody understands my art.'

Drake peered into Ellingham's eyes wondering what exactly was going on inside his mind. 'Well, you can explain it to the judge.'

Chapter 44

Drake woke the following morning, tired, grit floating in his eyes, his hand still aching. An image of the various facial expressions Ellingham had employed in his interview had filled his mind making sleep difficult. What chilled Drake was the realisation that Ellingham probably cared little. The deaths had been ghoulish and macabre and there was something evil, truly evil, in Ellingham's mind that justified their deaths. Drake turned up the temperature of the shower until his skin tingled and he let the water pour over him, hoping he'd never have to confront someone like Ellingham ever again.

He skipped breakfast and went straight to the hospital to see Milos Fogerty after texting Sian to confirm when he was collecting Helen and Megan. He found a parking slot easily enough on a Sunday morning and walked over to the main entrance. A brisk walk through the wide, empty corridors took him to the private ward where Milos Fogerty was sitting up in bed. His skin had a sickly grey pallor that matched the misty tint in his eyes.

He gave Drake a blank look. A nurse pulled the door closed behind her as she left. Drake sat awkwardly on the stiff-backed chair next to the bed. Drake wanted to say he regretted they hadn't discovered Ellingham's involvement earlier. Fogerty's ordeal might have been avoided.

'How are you feeling?'

Fogerty nodded. 'Okay, I suppose. What did Ellingham say?'

'He's in custody. He'll be charged with attempting to murder you.'

Drake spent half an hour listening to Fogerty telling him about Ellingham.

A doctor on a ward round came to see Fogerty so Drake left, pleased that Ellingham's final victim had been spared. But his guilt that he hadn't discovered the truth sooner still lingered. He drove to headquarters mulling over exactly what the prosecution lawyers would make of the case. They always liked things neat and clear cut. In this case, the motive was coloured and tainted by a sick mind.

Drake drifted back to the Incident Room. It was empty. He slumped into one of the chairs near the board and stared over at it. They had played musical chairs with the photographs on it since the death of Gloria Patton. He stared at her face. And then at Hopkin and Sanderson. Ellingham's gaze drifted into oblivion. It was one sick performance. Followed by his peroration in the interview. Now he was waiting for the applause. How would he deal with the appearance in court and the life sentence, Drake wondered.

Drake read the time. If he left now he would be on time. He wasn't going to be late.

He left headquarters and drove over to collect Helen and Megan.

Sian opened the door and gestured him inside. She wore a well-pressed pair of jeans and a white blouse. Drake remembered fumbling with the buttons before it was flung to the floor of their bedroom. Now Sian's bedroom.

She stood in the hallway, hands on hips. 'Is the case finished?'

'You look well, healthy.'

She smiled and raised an inquisitive eyebrow. He had seen the same smile a hundred times before and he smiled back. He thought about suggesting they do something as a family, something together but she looked away and shouted upstairs for Helen and Megan. Soon enough they bundled down the stairs, but it was another ten minutes before both girls were ready.

It was a warm spring morning as he made his way through the tunnel under the estuary at Conwy and then through the mountain at Penmaenmawr and Llanfairfechan. Everywhere looked peaceful. Families would be visiting Conwy for the day, children running round the castle, oblivious of what had happened there hours earlier.

He slowed as he neared the lane leading down to his mother's smallholding and he gazed over Caernarfon Bay. Three microlights buzzed around the sky.

'C'mon Dad,' Helen said as he dawdled. He accelerated down to the house where his mother was waiting.

'What's happened to your hand?' Mair Drake said.

'It was nothing.'

'Has it been seen by a doctor?'

'Yes, Mam. Don't fuss.'

Mair Drake liked lunch early, like most farming families, and by half past one they had finished her meal of roast lamb, roast potatoes, roast parsnips and carrots. Helen and Megan managed to demolish enormous portions of trifle at the end.

Drake sat with his mother once the girls had left the table. Unwinding seemed easy in the home he had known as a boy. Even though his flat was home now, it still felt temporary.

'Have you spoken much to Susan?' Mair said.

'I haven't had time.'

'She's still very angry.'

Drake nodded. 'I've suggested she come and stay. She can discuss everything with you and perhaps meet Huw.'

'What did she say to that?'

Drake shrugged. 'She didn't seem too keen.'

Mair had a resigned look on her face. Drake continued. 'Huw invited me to a party at his place last weekend. He was caught up in my recent case through his work and I've spoken to him a couple of times. I met his family and they seemed nice, friendly.'

Drake stared over at his mother, unable to instantly read the emotion in her face. He thought he registered disappointment and regret until she gave a brief smile. 'I'm glad. Your dad would be pleased too. It was something we should have spoken about. Done something about … all those years ago.'

A brief silence drew itself over the table between them. Drake wanted to tell her that keeping secrets was destructive and in families poisonous but his anger was mellowed by the fact she was now confronting his father's past and facing her future.

'Is that big case finished now?'

Drake straightened in his chair, happy to move on from his sister and Huw Jackson as topics of conversation.

'Yes. Luckily. The man responsible is in court tomorrow so the details will be all over the TV news.'

They sat around the table for another half an hour making small talk. Mair Drake talked about her friends, sharing the everyday minutiae of her life and Drake found himself relaxing.

After piling the dishwasher with the dirty dishes, Drake and his mother took Helen and Megan to the beach at Dinas Dinlle. They walked up the beach of pebbles and sand towards the mouth of the Menai Strait and lifted their heads skywards as a light aircraft came into land at the nearby airport. It was clear day and to the west Drake could see Holyhead Mountain and then, after turning back, the Lleyn peninsula stretching out into the Irish sea. Drake knew his daughters would want to visit the café by the car park and they sat at a table in the window as Helen and Megan finished off a large ice cream sundae each.

Back at the farmhouse Drake kissed his mother lightly on the cheek. Then she hugged her granddaughters tightly before kissing them both. They didn't complain and he knew they loved spending time with his mother. He had enjoyed the visit too and he promised himself he would do it more often. Driving back to Colwyn Bay, his thoughts turned to the paperwork that awaited him in the morning. He yawned as they neared Colwyn Bay, his tiredness overwhelming him. He struggled to find the words as he left his daughters at Sian's house. Tonight he would sleep, safe in the knowledge that Ellingham was behind bars.

Epilogue

Drake returned to Mold Crown Court for the last two days of Ellingham's trial. Drake scanned the faces of the jury members; it always fascinated him trying to fathom out what exactly was going on in their minds. Was there a natural leader? Somebody to assume the role of foreman in the retiring room. Spotting that person was difficult as they stared at the judge summing up the evidence, directing them as to how they should be considering the evidence. It cannot have been easy, Drake thought, with Ellingham having not entered a plea to any of the charges he faced. A not guilty plea had been formally entered on his behalf.

At lunchtime the jury retired to consider their verdicts and Drake contemplated returning to headquarters, but it was a journey of at least half an hour back to Mold from Colwyn Bay so he decided to wait. He found an old-fashioned café with net curtains and stiff wooden chairs, ordered some lunch and spent an hour and a half reading the newspaper and finishing the difficult Sudoku puzzle.

Each individual piece of evidence made the case against Jeremy Ellingham overwhelming but the jury would need to be satisfied the case had been proved beyond reasonable doubt. As the afternoon dragged on Drake became increasingly worried and when the jury was sent to a hotel overnight an edge of despair crept into his mind.

He returned the following morning with Superintendent Price and Sara. They killed time making small talk with prosecution lawyers and some of the journalists who had gathered in force with film crews. It was after lunch on the second day when the jury filed back into the air-conditioned courtroom. Even the prosecution lawyers looked tense. Journalists with notebooks pressed against their knees stared over towards the jury. A frown briefly creased the judge's forehead.

A court clerk stood up, adjusting the black gown draped over his shoulder. 'Members of the jury, have you reached a decision on which you are all agreed?'

One of the two people Drake had down as the foreman stood up.

Drake held his breath tightly.

The man had a thin, reedy voice. 'Yes.'

The court clerk started with the murder of Gloria Patton – guilty.

Drake let out a breath, his upper body sagging. It would mean a life sentence. Then the same question about the verdict on the charge of murdering Noel Sanderson – another guilty verdict. Drake looked over at Ellingham sitting in the dock flanked by two security officers. He was fidgeting with the nails of his right hand. Drake looked back at the jury foreman who had just been asked about their verdict on the Hopkin murder charge.

Drake's chest tightened.

'Guilty.'

'And on the count of the attempted murder of Milos Fogerty.'

'Guilty.'

Drake lurched back against the rear of the bench, the wood making a cracking sound. Price nodded contentedly. Drake noticed Sara tapping her clenched right fist discreetly on her thigh. He felt like jumping up and fisting the air.

The judge wasted little time in sentencing Jeremy Ellingham to four life sentences with a minimum term of twenty-eight years. In reality this meant at least thirty, maybe longer, behind bars once the parole system had ground its way through Ellingham's file. Drake watched intently as the security guards led Ellingham down into the bowels of the court. The atmosphere inside changed, faces brightened, conversation was more relaxed.

Drake made his way outside with Superintendent Price and Sara, and they stood on the paved area by the main entrance.

'Good result, Ian,' Price said.

'Thank you, sir.'

'It was certainly a baptism of fire for you, Sergeant Morgan.'

'Yes, sir.'

'Have you heard about Roger Buckland?'

Drake and Sara turned to look at Price.

'I understand he has left North Wales to join a mission in Botswana. One of the charities linked to his evangelical church thought he might be a good fit for their work.'

'Is Norma Buckland joining him?' Drake said.

'Apparently not.'

Price reached for his cap and drew it over his head, adjusting it carefully.

'I'd better go and talk to the press.' Price reached into his inside jacket pocket where he found a printed sheet of paper that he scanned quickly. Then he headed towards the camera crews gathered by the main entrance.

Drake and Sara watched as the various camera crews jostled for the right shot of Superintendent Price explaining that the WPS were pleased with the verdicts and with the sentence handed down. Drake heard the words *teamwork* and *thorough policing* being used.

Then abruptly, the press statement was over, Price declining to take questions. He strode away to his car.

It was late in the afternoon when Drake got back to Colwyn Bay.

Instead of returning to headquarters he parked by the promenade. He walked briskly towards Rhos on Sea, passing the derelict pier, enjoying the fresh air and the momentum from walking after two days spent hanging around a court building waiting for the jury to make up its mind. He reached the entrance of the Porth Eirias visitor centre when his mobile telephone rang. He recognised Huw Jackson's number.

'Hello, Huw.'

'I heard on the radio Ellingham was sentenced to twenty-eight years.'

'The jury took a long time to decide.'

'So that means there's no doubt about Hopkin's death. I know Geraint Wood was still worried he might be under suspicion.'

'Not any longer.'

'He's just won a big commission for an installation in New York.'

'Glad to hear it.'

Behind him Drake could hear a group wondering if they had to book for the celebrity chef restaurant in the visitor centre behind them.

'My daughter is thinking of a career in the police and I was wondering if you could give her some advice.'

'Of course.'

'Perhaps you'd like to come for dinner one evening?'

'Thanks. I'd like that.'

Printed in Great Britain
by Amazon